The Survival
Guide

to Alexander McBryde

Also by Ellie Devine

Cole
Vixen
Snow Struck

The Survival Guide

Guide

to Alexander McBryde

Ellie Devine

For the 12-year old girl who picked up her first romance novel at the grocery store because it had a picture of a sparkly mermaid on the cover and changed our life forever.

We wrote this one together.

P.S. Thanks, mom, for buying me that first romance novel...and not checking to actually see what it was about.

Survival Tip #1

Never approach the beast during mating season (it's always mating season) and if you must approach, come prepared to do battle.

Piranhas.

Great white sharks. A *frenzy* of great white sharks.

The tight, tentacled embrace of a mythical kraken dragging him down into the crushing depths.

All were deaths too kind for Alexander McBryde, scourge of the seven seas, defiler of maidenly achievements, and captain of the S.S. Fuckboy.

Willa didn't care that Alex had an incessant need to dangle his dick like a fisherman casting lures. She really didn't. What she *did* mind was that his latest fishing expedition was keeping her awake. It was three in the morning and his shortsighted decision to seduce one of the few available women on their tiny research vessel made sleeping impossible. Honestly, after a day spent alternately diving and documenting their research, she didn't understand how he even had the energy to engage in sex that thumped and groaned through their shared wall in an auditory display of athleticism better suited to the Olympics.

The woman next door let out a particularly high-pitched gasp followed by a giggle and for a traitorous moment, Willa's mind tried to picture just what exactly Alex could be doing to inspire such feminine enthusiasm.

Stung by a hundred box jellyfish!

Her cheeks warmed and she swiftly stopped her imagination from going any further. Whatever he was doing, it needed to stop. Now.

Sitting up determinedly in her small, hard bed, she walked the three cramped feet to her bedroom door, grabbed her blue robe hanging on its hook, and flung it open. She knotted the belt around her waist with unnecessary violence, imagining she was actually tightening it around Alex's throat, stepped two feet to the door on her left, and raised her fist.

As soon as she knocked, the giggling stopped. There was the gentle murmur of voices, the quiet rustle of sheets, then the door opened and Alex's face appeared in the crack. Her whole body tensed at his appearance. *The Genius of Evil.* He looked like that famously hot statue of Lucifer except he had been painted in glorious, shining shades of gold. Sunkissed skin poured over perfectly sculpted muscles, burnished gold-brown hair that waved gently and fell around a strong, perfectly featured face. Even his eyes were a light, brilliant brown that reminded her of old coins dug out of shipwrecks. He wore only a pair of black athletic shorts and from her quick look, she could see the faintly raised, red scrape of fingernail marks down one hard pectoral.

Bitten in half by a crocodile, still too good for Alexander "Prince of Darkness" McBryde.

"Yeah, dag, what do you want?" Even his stupid voice was somehow golden, all warm and bright even when he was insulting her. It probably had something to do with his accent. Even when they were dropping the c-word, Australians still managed to sound cheerful.

"Don't call me that. And what I *want* is sleep."

"Sorry, love, my bed's already taken." He flashed her a devilish grin and Willa's fingers curled into a fist, the desire to drive it into his face overwhelming.

"That has been obnoxiously apparent for the past three hours. Couldn't you refrain from being a raging manwhore for the few short weeks we're out here?" She asked, careful to keep her voice low so it wouldn't echo down the hall. The walls had already proven unfortunately thin. Alex opened the door a little wider and leaned out.

"Aw, come on, you can't say shit like that anymore. We're supposed to be sex positive now."

"If the condom fits," she snapped.

"That depends on if you've got magnums.

Willa recoiled but struggled to stop herself from glancing down to check if he was bluffing about his size. "I hate you."

"Not very original, Wilhelmina, I think you're losing your touch." He was still grinning, despite Willa hissing at him with all the venom of a sea snake.

"I'm sleep deprived! This is highly unprofessional behavior and I'm going to tell Professor Schwartz." With a huff, she turned and began heading toward the door at the end of the hall. The ship had ten cabins. Five were occupied by crew members and the remaining five belonged to the researchers; Professor Schwartz, his associate from a local university, Professor Ashton, Professor Ashton's research assistant, and Willa and Alex, who had both just finished the fifth year of their PhD program.

Given the extremely limited options on board, Willa would bet the woman currently occupying Alex's room was Veronique, the research assistant, whose happily open marriage made her an ideal candidate for Alex and his allergies to commitment. It was unfortunate however, because Willa liked Veronique and, having met her husband, had assumed she had better taste. Willa knew Alex was, objectively, an aesthetically attractive human specimen. She wasn't blind. But why anyone would willingly put up with his personality long enough to enjoy his appearance was one of life's great mysteries. It was right up there with where eels came from and what lay at the bottom of the Mariana trench.

Professor Schwartz's room was on the opposite end of the corridor. When they first arrived on the boat, he had muttered something about staying out of the line of fire and left them to the terrible fate of neighboring rooms. Unfortunately, their heated rivalry *may* have become the kind of departmental legend told as a cautionary tale. But it wasn't her fault! Willa *lived* for this program. Becoming a marine biologist was all she had ever wanted to do and it *infuriated* her beyond all reason that Alex treated it like some sort of game. Especially since he was always on the verge of winning.

"Wilhelmina!" Alex's voice was a heated whisper behind her but she didn't stop. Now exhausted to the point of violence and lacking any convenient krakens or piranhas, she would go to the only leviathan on board capable of making him suffer. Behind her, she heard a door shut followed by the quick shuffle of bare feet. "Willa, stop!"

She was almost in front of Dr. Schwartz's door when a pair of large hands landed on her shoulders and she was propelled past the professor's door, through one just beyond that led out onto the deck.

"What the hell, McBryde!"

He managed to drag her to the guardrail then swung her around so they were facing each other, the boat bobbing and pitching gently beneath them. He wasn't smiling anymore. Above the rooms and small lab located on the main deck was the bridge, filtering light down onto where they now stood at the back of the boat. It was the only light anywhere, with the sky overhead obscured by clouds. Water churned and splashed against the stern which meant the boat was moving and someone had to be up there, navigating them through the endless dark waves. Whoever it was, Willa fervently hoped they wouldn't look down. She could just imagine what they would think and it was a small boat. Gossip traveled fast.

"You want to pick a fight with me, Jones, that's fine but leave the professor out of it." All traces of teasing were gone. Alex glared at her now, his arms crossed over his broad chest. Willa glared back and propped her hands on her hips, meeting him fury for fury.

"I'm not trying to pick a fight, McBryde. I'm *trying* to sleep."

"Bullshit. All you do is pick fights with me. Ever since the damn sea urchins."

Her eyes rolled so hard it was a wonder she didn't get a concussion. "Oh, get over it! That was an accident, and you know it."

"Like hell it was an accident. I had to get surgery. I'm still paying off the fucking bills!"

"You shouldn't have put hats on them!" Said Willa, equally adamant and angry. No one else made her react this way, like he was the baking soda to her vinegar and every interaction was destined to end in an explosion.

"Strewth, I have never met anyone so uptight—"

"I'm not uptight, I'm *tired*. I've never met anyone so immature and inconsiderate and—and *loose*—"

"Oh, come off it, we weren't that loud."

Willa pitched her voice a little higher, a little breathier and moaned out, "Oh God, oh yes, captain! Make love to me, captain! Your boat is so *big*, captain!"

His cheeks actually turned a rare, faint pink and she felt a rush of triumph. She dropped her voice back to normal and poked him hard in the chest, emphasizing each word. "I could hear every. Single. Thing." He grabbed her hand to stop her assault and her voice went saccharine sweet, "Tell me, was the captain thing your idea or hers?"

He stepped closer, crowding her against the railing and ground out, "Like I'm going to tell you and feed into your pervy little fantasies." His

4

voice went low and mocking. "I bet you had your ear pressed to the wall. You might be an absolute prude but I know just how *insatiably* curious you are."

Somehow, he managed to make the insult sound impossibly lewd and Willa didn't know if the heat rushing throughout her body was fury or embarrassment. "You don't know *anything* about me, McBryde. Because, unlike you, I know how to keep my personal life private."

His crack of laughter was harsh and a little mean and was echoed far off in the distance by the rumble of thunder. "That's because it's easy to keep something that doesn't exist private."

His words landed with more sting than he probably intended but Willa didn't flinch. She never did, not anymore. His eyes dipped, making a slow, pointed perusal of her body wrapped up tight in her robe. "I think you're actually just jealous, Wilhelmina. I've never met anyone who needs a good, hard fuck more than you."

It might have been thunder or anger roaring in her ears as she jerked her hand out of his grip.

"And I've never met a bigger asshole—"

"You didn't let me finish," he said and grinned again, that arrogant, cocky grin that made Willa's blood heat and her vision go hazy with rage. "I would be more than happy to—"

She cut him off again, her voice low and vehement, "I would rather die —"

She didn't get to finish. Out of nowhere, a flash of lightning split the sky and the deck heaved beneath them. She had been leaning away from Alex, out over the rail and she was tall enough that her center of gravity put this just on the far side of dangerous. They both stumbled, Alex's shoulder knocked into her, her arms pin-wheeled but it was too late. She felt the damp surface of the boat drop away from the bottoms of her bare feet, felt herself falling backward. There was the sound of ripping fabric, the feel of fingers scrabbling at her hip, and even a glimpse of Alex's stupid beautiful face as his eyes went wide and he let out an alarmed, "Willa!"

Falling took forever. It only took seconds.

She didn't even manage to scream before she hit the cool water of the Indian Ocean and the world went black.

Part 1

Aposematism is when deadly/terrible things disguise themselves as something beautiful. Ex. poison dart frogs, most male celebrities. Alexander McBryde.

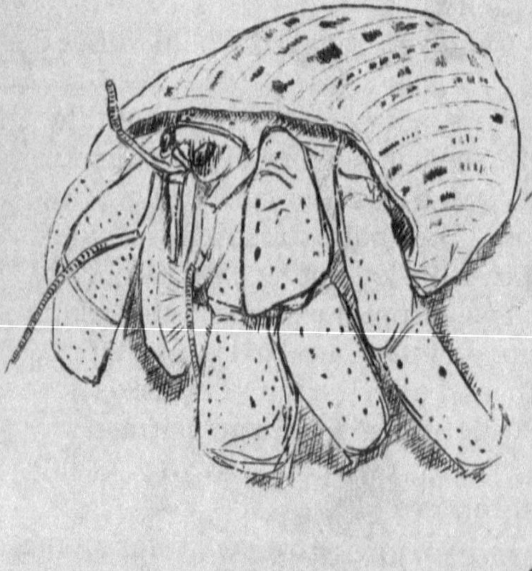

Paguroidea, belongs to superfamily of decapod crustaceans. Adaptable. Can make a home out of anything. ADORABLE. May actually have mystical powers.

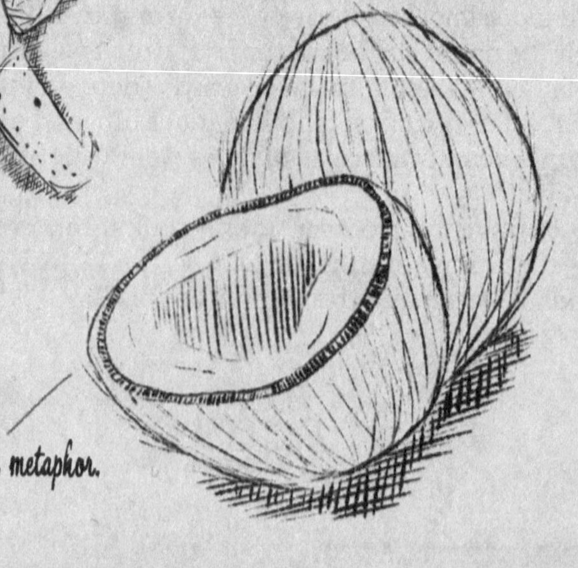

Good for food, weapon, and/or metaphor.

Survival Tip #2

Never look him in the eyes. If you must look him in the eyes, attach them to hooks first. Eyes make excellent fish bait.

Willa woke up coughing. Rolling onto her side, she kept her eyes closed as she heaved up what felt like an entire lung, half her intestines, and at least an ounce of her soul.

"Willa! Willa, are you okay?" The worried male voice battering at her sounded familiar. Like sunshine was familiar. Consistent, warm, but still a little dangerous. Odd. Very odd. Willa didn't usually wake up to male voices. That required going to sleep with a man first.

She cracked her eyes open and slowly sat up. She was wearing her robe but it was wet, the fabric sticking to the tops of her thighs as she peeled it curiously away. Her other hand was sunk into something grainy and soft and she looked down. Sand. Rosy and gold, squishing between her fingers. Extremely odd. Was she on a beach? Had she fallen asleep here? Had she gone drinking last night? She never went drinking but it would explain why her mouth felt like she'd swallowed half the ocean and the headache corkscrewing into her temples.

A hand touched her face, warm fingers curling around her jaw and turning it gently upwards.

"Wilhelmina, look at me."

She looked and shock was a hard slap in the face. The slow, liquid feeling of being caught up in a dream faded and she jerked.

"Alex?" She reached up and grabbed his wrist, trying to pull his hand away. "Why are you here?" She looked past him and caught sight of swaying palm trees and a long stretch of empty beach. It was nothing like the cool, scrubby shorelines near Boston or the well-maintained, tourist-soaked beaches of Mahe. The shock this time was nothing so mild as a slap. It was a one-two punch to the gut followed by a kick to the head.

"Oh my God, where are we?" She rose unsteadily to her feet and Alex followed her movements, catching her shoulders when she swayed.

"Slow down, I think you might have a concussion."

Willa wasn't listening; she was too busy craning her head, trying to take in everything at once. The sun was rising, spilling across frothy, energetic waves and creeping up toward a profusion of spiky green shrubs which tumbled down to meet the sand. There was no sign of the boat.

The boat! She had been on a boat! She refocused on Alex, her heart pounding against her ribs like the waves pounding against the shore a few feet away.

"What the hell did you do?"

Alex's hands dropped away and he looked incredulous. "What do you mean, 'what did I do'?"

"I mean, how did we get here? What did you do?" she said, spitting out each word.

"You think this is my fault?"

"I know it's your fault. It's always your fault."

"Like hell. This one is all you, Jones. And given that I saved your life, you could show a little gratitude."

Denial was swift. Willa did not for a second believe Alex had saved her life. Why would he? They despised each other. She shook her head. "No, that's impossible. You wouldn't."

He crossed his arms and glared. "*You* fell off the boat and I dove in after you." He glanced at the rainforest looming over them and muttered, "Like a fucking idiot."

Willa glared back, her fingers curling into sandy fists at her side. "That's ridiculous. You probably *pushed* me." Her eyes narrowed as a vague memory surfaced, the feeling of his shoulder bumping into her, the two of them struggling for balance. "No, you *did*. You *pushed* me over!"

"I did not *push* you. I stumbled into you. I also tried to grab you and stop you from falling." He pointed at the hem of her robe where a large tear had made a slit near her knee. She remembered the feel of fingers, pressing, grabbing at her, trying to stop her from going over. "If I had intentionally pushed you, why the hell would I jump in after you?"

"Maybe you fell. Maybe it was swift, karmic justice. Maybe you realized what you had done and threw yourself off so you wouldn't have to go to jail for murder!"

"Right, which is why I made sure to grab a life preserver on my way down." He gestured behind him to where a battered ring buoy with a frayed rope sat on the sand practically radiating reproof.

Shit. Maybe she really did have a concussion. Or she *was* dreaming and she would wake up any minute and be back in a world where inflatable tubes didn't give her judgmental looks and Alexander McBryde hadn't saved her life.

"How do my pupils look?" she demanded abruptly. Letting out an annoyed huff, he leaned down and gave her eyes an intensely searching look. At six foot-one, Willa was a tall woman, but Alex still had a good three to four inches on her and it was an unfamiliar sensation, being so close to a man that made her feel almost normal. It was also an oddly vulnerable sensation and she struggled to stand still. It didn't help that their faces had never been so close and they had certainly never maintained such an intimate amount of eye contact. She felt him breathe out, the warm, damp air teasing across her mouth and she licked her lips nervously.

"Well?" she prompted, needing to get away from him.

"They look normal. Are you nauseous? Do you have a headache? Are you dizzy?"

Putting some deliberate space between them, Willa wrapped her arms around herself. Her robe was soaked and while the sun coming up held the promise of heat, the air was still cool and she began to shiver.

"No, yes, and no."

He gave a thoughtful grunt. "It could still be a concussion. I'm worried you were unconscious for so long." He frowned and it was strangely disconcerting. Alex didn't frown. He scowled, glared, looked smugly superior, or grinned cockily. She didn't think she had ever seen him *actually* concerned about anything and she had definitely never seen him concerned about *her*.

"I might not have been unconscious from hitting my head." She hesitated. Revealing even such a small, relatively silly sign of weakness to this man went against every instinct but then his frown deepened and the words tumbled out, stilted and slow. "It's possible I actually just... fainted..."

His eyebrows rose and he gave her a look of disbelief. "Fainted? Like a pissed sheila?"

Willa's neck prickled with embarrassment. "Fainting is a common stress response," she said defensively and felt a twist of relief as the concern on Alex's face slowly bled to mocking amusement. This was familiar ground.

"Are you telling me you've fainted multiple times in your life, Wilhelmina?"

Her teeth clenched and she spoke through them, "I think we have more important things to focus on right now, McBryde."

"I don't know, this seems pretty important considering the alternative is a brain injury."

Fury was a hot, sweet, familiar rush. Willa clung to it like a judgy lifesaver, the only normal thing in this bizarre and terrifying situation.

"If you must know, I fainted the first time I went on a rollercoaster and we got to the top of the first hill, when I watched the crimson wedding scene in Game of Crowns, and the one time I tried to go skiing." The ski incident had been the senior trip in high school. She woke up to a broken arm and frostbitten fingers and spent the rest of the semester enduring jokes that relied heavily on making fun of her height and tree metaphors. Apparently, a tree may not make any sound when it falls in a forest, but if you chuck it down a mountain you hear the limbs break. She shook her head, banishing the painful memory and scowled. "I have a hard time with blood and sudden drops. Lots of people struggle with those things."

"Well, I suppose that's promising news for your brain." He paused and some of the amusement faded. "But let me know if the headache gets worse."

"Around you, that seems inevitable," she said sweetly and he rolled his eyes.

"Next time, I'm letting you drown."

Willa felt a frisson of guilt. Damnit. Him saving her life was going to suck all the fun out of this relationship.

"Why didn't you let me drown this time? Or just call for help? Why did you come in after me?"

"Fuck me dead," he barked, "Just because we don't get on, doesn't mean I'm okay with watching you *die*. And there wasn't time to call for help. The boat was moving too quickly and you hit the water and weren't coming back up." Something harsh and a little scary crossed his face. His mouth went flat and his eyes were a blazing gold that matched the sunrise behind him. "It was the most terrifying few minutes of my life."

Huh, she thought, odd. Unbelievably odd.

Willa was looking at him all wide-eyed and astonished and it was, quite frankly, insulting as hell. Alex knew Willa held a low opinion of him. It was a fact she made clear as often as possible. Which was fine. Really. He had never set out to earn her approval. It had even become something of a game seeing how well he could sink to meet her disdainful expectations. Watching Willa get worked up, seeing the flush that spread across her cheeks as her eyes went bright and shot poison-tipped arrows at him, had been one of the highlights of his graduate career.

Still, that she thought he was the kind of man to just sit back and watch her drown made him feel a little sick to his stomach. Maybe they weren't friends but they had spent the past five years practically living in each other's pockets. She was as certain as the moon, a constant point of reference in his world, waxing and waning in and out of his life. Without her, the world would be somehow...less. Which was maybe why, when she'd fallen into the water, he'd launched himself after her. Like a fucking meteor caught in her gravitational pull.

Groping around for her in the pitch-black water had been the most desperate thing he'd ever done. The ocean at night might as well be the dark, empty vacuum of space. With sharks. He had been terrified the entire time that just like getting sucked into a black hole, she had been swallowed up forever. Even now he kept having to stop himself from reaching out and touching her, wanting the reassurance that she was really here, alive and angry with him as usual. There was also the need to stop himself from reaching out and shaking her. Because even with the relief she was alive, there was no escaping the perpetual low-level hum of frustration that accompanied every interaction he had with this woman.

"You don't have to look so shocked. Despite what you think, I'm not a complete bastard," he snapped. She jumped and actually looked a little guilty which wasn't an expression Alex had seen on her before. It was both fascinating and a little concerning.

"Right. I know. I know." She squeezed her eyes shut, like she was gathering up her willpower and kept them closed as she continued, "I can't believe you did something like that for me." She paused and bit her lip and he wondered if she was stopping herself from including an insult at the end, like how it was *unexpectedly* noble of him. Her eyes blinked open, the look in them so lost he forgot his frustration and felt that same wild, reckless urge he'd had right before swan-diving into the middle of the ocean at night.

"Alex, what are we going to do?" Her voice wavered and it was so different from her normal condescending authority that he again worried she'd sustained a concussion. Her hands tightened on her arms and he realized she was shivering. The Seychelles in July were usually between twenty-five and twenty-nine degrees Celsius during the day but they cooled off at night and the two of them had spent the last few hours in the water. Drying off needed to be a priority, followed by determining if this was one of the few inhabited islands. Knowing Willa was the sort of person who did best with a plan and suspecting she wouldn't take any comfort from him anyway, he kept his voice firm and impassive.

"First, we're going to get out of our wet clothes and dry off. I could also use a bit of a nap, I've been awake for almost twenty-four hours and I'm cactus. When the sun is all the way up, we'll go exploring. It's possible there are people living somewhere on this island and if there's not, then we need to find water and shelter."

She nodded slowly in agreement, which was a novel experience all on its own, but even more novel was the small, amused smile teasing up the corners of her full mouth.

"That sounds like a reasonable plan, I just have one question." The smile expanded. "Cactus?"

He let out a grunt of annoyance, "Surely you're clever enough to figure it out from context. Exhausted. I'm fucking exhausted."

"Right-o, Crocodile Dundee."

His eyes narrowed and he snapped out an order that cleared all the humor from her face, "Strip."

She froze. "Excuse me?"

"You heard me, dag. Strip. You need to get dry and you can't do that in a soaked robe and whatever prudish pajamas you're hiding under there." He raised one, mocking eyebrow, because an angry Willa was preferable to a scared one. "I'm honestly a little surprised you don't sleep in one of those big, billowing nightdresses that button all the way up the neck."

Any nerves or uncertainty vanished, her expression going back to its usual sharp disapproval. "If I'm getting naked, you need to go somewhere else, like, off a cliff."

"Is that any way to speak to the man who saved your life? And we're not splitting up. Trust me, love, you don't have anything I haven't seen before. We've spent the past few weeks diving together. I've seen you in a bathing suit. Suddenly knowing what your nipples look like is not going to drive me into a lustful frenzy."

She didn't say anything but she was still Wilhelmina Jones and Alex had never seen her back down from anything. Glaring at him so hard he could practically feel the prick of tiny arrowheads, she quickly and jerkily unknotted the belt of her robe, peeled it off and dropped it onto the sand behind her. He almost laughed in delighted surprise.

Willa was the sort of person who took the grad student aesthetic a little too seriously. Back on campus, she wore modest sweaters, pencil skirts, and slacks—like some poster child for New England academia. She had relaxed a little while living on a boat, wearing cut-off jean shorts and T-shirts over her suits but Alex still hadn't expected her to sleep in a giant Acca Dacca T-shirt that was obviously ancient and so stretched out it had slipped off a shoulder.

His amusement must have shown on his face because she planted her hands on her hips again and spoke defensively, "What? Everybody likes AC/DC."

"Of course they do. They're Australian, what's not to like?" He shrugged. "It's just not what I expected."

"Right. This may come as a shock to you but not all women sleep in satin negligees."

He gave a genuine yawn but played it up by sending her a bored, sideways look. "You're stalling. I don't give a shit what you wear to sleep. Just take it off. I told you, nothing you've got under that shirt is going to shock me."

"Then why are you watching? You could at least turn around!"

"I said it wouldn't shock me, I didn't say I wasn't curious." He gave her the slow, cocky grin that always managed to get a rise out of her. "Come on, Wilhelmina, you show me yours and I'll show you mine."

"Oh! I hate you, Alexander McBryde," she hissed and then, with a few quick, defiant movements she stripped the shirt off over her head, rolled down her underwear and kicked them away.

The air rushed out of his lungs.

Oh.

Fucking hell.

He had been wrong.

Very, very, *very* wrong.

The first time Alex met Willa had been at a student meet-and-greet their first year of grad school. It had been Professor Schwartz who pulled him across the room to where Willa stood on the fringes of the crowd and when she turned, Alex was struck absolutely dumb.

She was tall, like he wouldn't have to break his neck to kiss her tall, and solid, like the kind of woman a man could lose himself in without worrying about breaking her, solid. As if her body wasn't enough to trigger his fantasies for the next several nights, she had the most unbelievable hair he'd ever seen. Thick, honey blonde curls that framed her like a cloud, floating around her head and cascading all the way down to the small of her back. She was the kind of woman born to be a muse. With her broad, sharp features, she was more likely to be called handsome than beautiful but when all the parts of her were put together, she was nothing short of a work of art. She had looked like a goddess painted in the bold, decadent strokes of some Renaissance painter.

Standing before him now, Alex realized how accurate he'd been. She was *The Birth of Venus* made flesh. Framed by the crystal blue ocean and palm tree studded shoreline, with the curls of her long, blonde hair swirling around her gilded by the sun, one hand held over her breasts while the other tried to shield him from the sweet spot between her thighs, she was a masterpiece. And, just like the first time he met her, he was completely struck dumb.

Her voice was shards of coral sharp as it cut into his sudden paralysis, "Look, I know what I look like and I know you've seen better, but you don't need to rub it in. If you don't stop staring, I'm going to rip your eyeballs out and use them as fish bait."

Christ, she couldn't really think he was standing here comparing her to other women? Even if he wanted to, he couldn't. As far as his brain was concerned, the only woman in existence had just sprung from the waves in front of him. Who knew his kink was classical art?

She didn't give him a chance to respond. Her finger darted out and poked him hard in the chest. "Alright, Dundee, it's your turn. Strip."

He jerked like he'd been stung by a jellyfish. "Right. Sorry." Still staring at her, he absently pulled off his shorts even though the lightweight, athletic material had almost dried. His cock sprang free and he saw the sudden exaggerated rise of her breasts as she drew in a surprised breath.

"Oh my God," she said loudly.

Feeling more than a little dazed, either from lack of sleep, overexertion, or all the blood in his body migrating south, Alex barely registered Willa's shock. Instead, he took her exclamation as the sort of compliment he had received before.

"Thanks."

"That was *not* an appreciative 'oh my God.' That was an 'you just had sex a few hours ago which is what got us into this mess and you're hard again when we're stranded on a potentially desert island' oh my God.'"

Alex pulled his eyes back up to her face. "Love, I'd have to be *dead* not to get a hard-on when presented with all that." He gestured at her nude, masterpiece of a body.

She squirmed uncomfortably and then, for the second time in their entire acquaintance, exhibited something less than her usual aggressive self-confidence. "Alex, can you just—" she hesitated and looked desperately around until her eyes lit on something behind him. She waved toward it. "Can you please just go over to the other side of that boulder and take your nap. I need a few minutes away from all—" she gestured at his face, "this."

He blinked. Willa never said please. He studied her, again trying to detect signs of a concussion, but all he found was her familiar scowl.

"I'm fine. Just go!"

Scooping up his shorts, he tore his eyes away from her, turned, and went.

Survival Tip #3

If you have a choice between a man with a sharp tongue or a beast with sharp claws, always take the beast.

Willa was tired and annoyed. She was also uncomfortably naked. All of which she had decided to blame on Alex since he was the one who had kept her awake last night while noisily diving for Veronique's buried treasure. And now they were here. She had contemplated taking a nap too but Alex made a point of popping his head above the bushes and ordering her not to fall asleep until after they determined whether or not she had a concussion. Of course, Willa didn't think he was *right* but she also wasn't willing to risk it.

Which was why she now stood on the edge of the forest, contemplating entering it on her own. Despite telling herself that for all they knew a resort was right around the corner, terror was a ghost whispering in her attics. If they were truly marooned, they needed to be making plans—needed to find food and water and shelter. Sitting around while Alex napped felt like a waste of time.

Luckily, the rainforest on this island was promisingly verdant and beautiful. Light streamed through gaps in the leaves, picking out flowers and catching the occasional flutter of a wing as birds hopped from branch to branch. It honestly looked like something from another time, wild and untouched in a way the ghosts told her did not bode well for their chances of finding civilization. She paused, poised on the line in the sand where the beach ended and the trees began, unable to take the final step, her stomach suddenly twisting into knots.

She remembered Alex's autocratic tone when he ordered her to stay close. She scowled—he was not the boss of her. She put a defiant foot halfway into the trees and as soon as she touched shade, she felt a shiver race across her skin. For a mirage of a moment, the world seemed to stop, her skin cooled beneath her goosebumps, the sounds of the forest faded, even the sun at her back seemed to dim. Willa jerked her foot back onto the beach and heat and movement returned.

Clearly she had swallowed too much seawater. Or maybe it was a trick of exhaustion. She supposed there was even the slim chance she *hadn't* merely fainted and now her bruised brain was picking up on her guilt and fears and projecting them, turning the benign forest into the setting for a ghost story.

And yet, even with that thought in mind, she took another step back onto the reassuring warmth of the sand. They could explore the forest later. There was plenty to catalog on the beach. Discovering and enjoying the natural world was why she had gone into marine biology in the first place. It was also why she'd been so thrilled to be one of the grad students chosen to attend this research trip to the Seychelles where most of the one hundred and sixty-six islands that made up this tiny country were dedicated as nature preserves.

They were also mostly uninhabited.

As the sun climbed higher, fully bathing the beach in heat, the island's wildlife began to make itself known. Sand crabs scuttled in and out of their hidey-holes, their little claws busily combing through the surf as they scavenged for food. They would be better eating than the hermit crabs she occasionally spotted trundling along the shore in their cumbersome, curved shells but not by much. She watched a particularly large female crab pick at a bloody fish carcass and wrinkled her nose in disgust. Eating scavengers was a good way to pick up a parasite and being naked and trapped with Alex was shitty enough.

Eventually, the sun got hot enough that Willa's thirst and exhaustion caught up with her and she plopped down in the shade of a coconut tree near the boulder where she had laid out her clothes. She looked wistfully at one of the many coconuts littering the beach and licked her dry lips, her brain running the energy expenditure analysis for breaking through a coconut husk compared to the amount of food and water they'd gain. Unless they could find a smart way to do it, it was a grim calculation, they'd be much better off if they could find a stream or even figure out a way to catch rainwater.

She dragged a hand across her forehead, wiping off sweat and adding the loss of moisture into her equation, trying not to let the water literally dripping out of her feed into the anxiety nipping at her heels like a rising tide. This was the problem with sitting. It gave her more energy to think... and panic.

According to the books she had read as a child though, the first rule of being stranded was to *not* panic. Her eyes slid down the beach in Alex's direction, glaring despite the excessively large, oddly shaped boulder blocking him from view. Unfortunately, this felt like it was going to be more *Lord of the Flies* than *The Swiss Family Robinson*. Of all the people to be trapped on a desert island with, it just *had* to be Alexander McBryde, the Devil himself.

She remembered the way he looked at her after she pulled off her shirt. It was the same way he had looked at her when they first met. That same silent, judgmental look of disbelief (and occasionally resentment) most men gave her. Her fingers dug into the sand near her hips and she scowled out at the ocean. At twenty-nine, Willa had mostly reached a point of peaceful indifference with her body. She appreciated that it was strong and capable and got her where she needed to go but beyond her occasional frustration with trying to find pants that fit, she honestly didn't think about it that much. She had better, more important things to do.

When she'd been younger, Willa had constantly dreamed about being one of those short, willowy girls or even just an average-sized curvy girl. As a teenager, she'd wished more than anything to just take up less space. Not anymore. She had learned the hard way that women who tried to fit inside other people's *short*, narrow expectations usually got screwed over. She took up her space now. Physically, academically, conversationally. Which was probably why she and Alex fought so often—they were constantly battling for territory.

And yet...the image of Alex, naked and hard, kept pricking (ha!) uncomfortably at the back of her mind. His face might have been dazed and distracted but his dick had been at attention. She blew out a breath and squeezed handfuls of sand. At least now she knew what had made Veronique gasp and giggle. Big and as golden as the rest of him, Alex's erection promised a *very* good time.

But not for her, she reminded herself sharply. She was a scientist. She understood the concept of a body reacting to certain stimuli. Like the California two-spot octopus. It didn't *think* itself into changing colors, light sensitive proteins in its skin sensed the environment and changed accordingly. Him getting an erection because she was naked didn't change that they disliked each other, it just meant he was a horny octopus and when his body sensed a naked woman, it responded accordingly. Instinct was a powerful thing and at the end of the day, humans were still just animals.

Her stomach growled for what felt like the millionth time in the past hour, reminding her that bodies had other basic demands beyond reproduction. They needed to start worrying about survival more than Alex needed any more beauty sleep. Getting to her feet, she tested her clothes and found them mostly dry. The fabric was stiff with salt as she pulled it on but there was no way she was walking around this island naked.

As she made her way back to where Alex was sleeping, she couldn't help but appreciate the beauty of the island. Blue sky, bluer ocean, shady trees and bushes adorned by fragrant pink flowers. The breeze was gentle and smelled like the sea and wet greenery. It was earthy and fresh and such a dramatic change from the vaguely fishy, metallic smell of living on a boat that Willa found herself sucking in great lungfuls of air until she felt almost drunk with it.

As long as all this beauty didn't kill her, she was prepared to feel downright appreciative they'd washed up somewhere with food (if they could catch it), shade, and, with all the obvious fauna and flora, the likelihood of fresh water. Rounding the large, princess-cut style boulder separating her and Alex, Willa found herself facing another thing that was both beautiful and terrifying.

He looked like Apollo, dumped out of his chariot and left sprawled asleep on the sand. He practically glowed in the sunlight, his long limbs stretched out, his muscles defined even at rest. She deliberately avoided looking below his waist, her earlier exposure to that particular part of him already more than she knew what to do with. Even ignoring that, he was still so beautiful she didn't know whether to curl up next to him like a turtle basking in sunlight or kick him. Remembering his dumbfounded look at her nudity, she landed on kicking him. *Lightly.* In deference to him having saved her life. She nudged at his feet with her toes.

"Wake up, Sleeping Beauty, we've got work to do, survival to attempt."

ELLIE DEVINE

He didn't get up, merely groaned and threw an arm over his eyes. She nudged him again.

"Alex, I mean it. Wake up."

He shifted his feet away from her and muttered something under his arm.

"What was that?"

His arm moved away from his mouth and he spoke louder, his voice rough and gravelly with sleep.

"I said, 'Sleeping Beauty was woken up with a kiss, not a kick.'"

She almost laughed. Biting her lip to stop herself, Willa assumed her sternest tone.

"Kissing people who aren't awake to consent is creepy which I would hope you know. Now, if you do not get up in the next five seconds, my next kick is going to be aimed a lot higher."

That got him up.

"And again, we could do with some gratitude," he grumbled. "You do realize I swam for *hours* right? Tugging your unconscious body behind me like a fucking hero."

Willa rolled her eyes. "That was gratitude. I could have kicked you harder." Trying to ignore the golden gleam of his muscles which were, in fact, annoyingly heroic looking, she turned and gestured out at the beach. "I've been thinking while you've been napping and I think we should start by doing a circuit of the island. We can try and get a sense of how big it is and check for signs of people. You know, boats, footprints, a sign saying 'Stranded People Inquire Within'. If anyone lives here, they're bound to come to shore at some point. We could split up, cover twice as much ground in the same amount of time and hope we meet up somewhere in the middle."

"No, absolutely not."

Willa heard the swish of fabric and assumed he had pulled on his shorts. A quick glance behind her confirmed he was as decent as he ever was. Honestly the man was dangerously attractive even when fully clothed —it was yet another thing to hate him for. "Alex, what exactly do you think is going to happen if we split up? We're in the Seychelles, it's not like we're going to run into lions and tigers and bears. Although if you saw a giant tortoise without me, I might kill you out of sheer jealousy."

"I don't know what could happen and that's why we're not splitting up."

"Alex—"

Gripping her shoulder, he forced her to turn and face him.

"Willa, I did not dive off a fucking boat and swim through the night just so you can be eaten by a crocodile or kidnapped by cannibals."

"Finding cannibals would at least answer our inhabited-or-not question and crocodiles haven't been seen in the Seychelles since the 1800's so..."

"We. Are. Not. Splitting. Up."

She threw up her hands in exasperation. "Fine! I'm only humoring you because you saved my life but be warned, this agreeable, complacent Willa is temporary."

"You couldn't be agreeable if your life depended on it," he muttered and began leading the way down the beach. As they walked, their bodies ebbed and flowed in proximity as they did their best to avoid the various species of crab scuttling obliviously around their feet while flocks of lesser crested terns ran in and out of the surf doing their best to ignore the two humans now occupying their island.

They didn't talk much, both focused on observing as much as they could. This was how it usually was when they actually had to work together, the bickering retreating and the need to prove who was the better scientist stepping in with cool, evenly delivered information. The joint-research paper they had (reluctantly) presented at last year's Marine Life Conservation conference had been picked up and featured at the following International Symposium. Which was probably the only reason Dr. Schwartz willingly brought them on this research trip despite their known enmity.

It turned out the island wasn't very large, likely one of those little drops of land that didn't even show up on a map, and, according to Alex's dive watch, within an hour Willa could see the distinctive wedge shaped, diamond cut boulder where he had slept looming up on the shore. Her heart sped up erratically inside her chest. On their walk they hadn't come across so much as a log in the water that might hint at somewhere a fisherman could tie up his boat. There was no doubting it anymore.

They were alone.

The panic she had been keeping at bay broke free, gathering strength as it rolled up from the soles of her feet, bumped along the ridges of her spine, skipped across the growling, empty pit of her stomach, until finally crashing over and threatening to drown her. She didn't realize how much the hope they would wander across some locals was keeping her afloat until it was yanked away.

She stumbled to a halt. Her eyes fixed out on the miles and miles of empty blue ocean stretching in every direction. She was hungry and thirsty and tired and her and Alex were *alone together*.

"Oh God," she whispered.

Noticing she had stopped, Alex turned and was back to looking concerned and that wasn't right either. He wasn't supposed to be concerned. Not about her, *never* about her!

"Willa? What's wrong?"

"Oh God. Oh no. No, no, no."

"What is it? Are you dizzy? Are you going to faint again?"

"No." She tried to suck in a breath, tried to fight the panic but it was overwhelming. "We're trapped," she choked out, "We're back where we started and there's no one else here."

The concern cleared from Alex's face and he went grim.

"Willa—"

"No, there's no fast-talking us out of this, Alex. We're marooned here, *together*."

"I'm sure they're already looking for us," he tried but she cut him off again.

"So? They may be looking for us but do you know how big the Indian Ocean is? Twenty-seven *thousand* square miles. How long do you think they'll look before we're assumed dead? What if we're stuck out here forever like that guy in that one movie, with nothing but each other and an anthropomorphized life preserver for company?"

There was a hysterical note ringing throughout her tirade and the calm, rational voice in the back of her mind noticed it and told her to calm down. *Remember the Robinsons,* it said, but Willa couldn't hear anything but the gnawing, hungry demands of her stomach and the perpetual, insistent sound of the waves beating against the shore like a taunt, "*you're lost, you're lost, you're lost.*"

Alex's startled look at her outburst was quickly turning to annoyance. She knew the signs, the tightening of his mouth, the hard jut of his jaw. They had spent the past five years annoyed with each other. The familiar, taught curve of his mouth might even have been comforting except now it was compounded by exhaustion. She'd never seen his eyes without their customary glint and his shoulders were rigid with a new tension. He looked like he was struggling to hold himself up and the tiny, barely noticeable flare of concern she felt at seeing this new, beaten down Alex felt like another crack in the foundation of her world.

"Willa, we're not lost in the 1700's. We'll build a signal. There are planes that fly overhead, boats that sail by. They'll be looking for us. We can survive until then." He crossed his arms and blew out a breath, muttering beneath it, "If we can avoid killing each other."

"What if we can't?" She shot back. "What if this is how it ends? This was not part of my plan. There are things I wanted—" she broke off, horrified as the full weight of all the lost potential, all the short-circuited possibilities hit her. She would never graduate. Never get tenure. Never help save even a small corner of the world or unravel any of its mysteries. Anger and fear were a cloud descending over her brain; her grumbling stomach was thunder, her thirst lightning, dry and electric in the back of her throat. The last faint sound of rational thought disappeared beneath the storm bursting out of her mouth, "I don't want to die. Especially not with you!"

"We are not going to die," he said insistently and he looked so sure, so confident and cocky and *calm*. Willa couldn't stand it. He thought he knew everything—about her, their work, and now this—he *always* thought he had the answers but he didn't. Not this time. And she was going to prove it.

"You don't know that! You don't know everything, McBryde!" And then she reached out, grabbed him by the shoulders, and kissed him.

He froze, like one of the species of cichlids that played dead when they thought they might be in danger. It was by no means a sophisticated kiss. It was rough and quick and tasted like sea salt and desperation. Willa's fingers dug into his hard shoulders and she drew greedily at his mouth like a lifeline. This hadn't been part of any of her plans, hadn't been on any of her lists of things to accomplish and check off. But maybe it should have been. The thought, unwelcome and insidious as it was, had barely formed when she felt the hum of a startled groan vibrate against her lips and the brush of Alex's hands at her waist. A different kind of panic skittered through her and in an instant their roles were reversed, he became the predator and Willa retreated.

She dropped her hands hastily from his shoulders and stepped back, flushed and breathing hard.

"What was that for?" He asked, clearly bewildered and for a long, heart-pounding moment, Willa didn't know. All she could think about was the feel of sun-warmed skin against hers and that she now knew how Alex *tasted*. But then he gave her that look again, the same one he'd given her when she'd stripped and her anger snapped back into place. He didn't get to judge her and he didn't get to be right.

"Did you know I was going to kiss you?" she demanded, watching the way his eyes darkened and his tongue darted out, like he was chasing after the taste of her. He shook his head.

"No, of course not."

"See! You *don't* know everything. We *are* going to die and it's *all your fault*." She furiously shoved him back a step then spun around and stormed off down the beach, back the way they had just come.

He let her go, which she would have been grateful for if she wasn't so furious. She was acting ridiculous. More than ridiculous. She had just *kissed* fricken Alexander McBryde and if that wasn't a sign of insanity (or a concussion), she didn't know what was. Apparently as they had paced around the island, she had lost all common sense so maybe if she retraced her steps, she'd be able to collect it, like plucking seashells from the sand.

She was so busy tromping across the beach like Godzilla, she didn't notice the hermit crab until too late. Her foot swung out and connected with something hard. The exquisite pain of a stubbed toe rocketed through her as she watched the creature go flying into the forest.

She swore. Long and loud until her toe felt marginally better. Then, with a determined breath and a straight spine, she went in after the crab. The poor thing didn't deserve to get stuck in the underbrush simply because she was acting like a rampaging monster.

She pushed gingerly into the bushes, brushing aside leaves as big as dinner plates and watching carefully for anything sharp or sticky. She heard Alex shouting down the beach after her but she ignored him. Surely they had determined there were no cannibals and his concern for crocodiles was patently ridiculous. She would be fine.

"Totally fine," she repeated out loud, remembering her earlier premonition and needing the verbal reassurance, even if it only came from herself.

She called out for the crab, crooning for it like one might call a lost puppy. A flash of white moving slowly, jerkily through the loam a few feet to her left caught her eye and she actually laughed, harsh and relieved. She might die on this island but that crab would not! She turned, chasing after the lumbering crustacean. When she was only a foot away, she took a rushed step forward, bending and reaching for the spiraled shell without looking where she was going. She felt her foot catch on something, her body pitched forward through a particularly dense clump of palm fronds and rather than planting face first into the dirt, she saw the ground dropping away.

Her hand closed around the crab and then she was falling with that familiar red alert spike of alarm. As the dark closed in, all Willa could think about was how Alex was *never* going to let her live this down.

He'd been right, something had happened after all.

Survival Tip #4

Being thirsty can severely impair your judgment. Don't drink the tall glass of water until you know it's not poisoned (most water is poisoned).

This time when Willa woke up, Alex was hovering over her, his face clearly caught between fear and fury. As soon as he saw her eyes open, some of the fear receded which only seemed to create room for more anger. There was a vein throbbing in his neck she had never seen before. Huh. Five years later and they were still learning new things about each other.

"I didn't realize when you said you were going to die here that you were actually making a promise," he said through clenched teeth.

"Is the crab okay?" she asked, still feeling a bit dazed. It was clearly the wrong thing to say because the concerned lines reappeared at the corners of his eyes and his hands dug into her hair, gently feeling around her scalp.

"What? Christ, you definitely have a concussion this time. Does any of this hurt? Feel tender?"

It felt quite nice actually. Soothing. So she let him continue even though she was pretty sure she'd just fainted again. Who would have thought her issue with sudden drops would be more of a detriment in a survival situation than her aversion to blood? She just hoped she wouldn't have to skin anything.

"Willa! Answer me."

Whoops. Right. She tried to explain.

"I had a crab..." She trailed off as her eyes focused on something hanging in the tree beyond Alex's shoulder. "Bananas!" she burst out.

"Are these medical diagnoses? Because you definitely seem to have lost your mind at some point in the past twenty minutes."

"What?" She struggled into a sitting position, helped along by Alex's hands slipping down to the back of her neck and shoulder.

"Careful, Wilhelmina. This seems to be turning into a habit." He was searching her eyes again, checking her pupils and the proximity triggered the memory of kissing him. Shit. Maybe she really had broken her brain. She would think about it later. Right now there were more important things. *Edible* things

"Alex, I'm fine. I just tripped."

"Yeah, and slid down a four meter incline head first."

She looked behind her and, sure enough, her body had clearly tumbled through the brush, breaking the stems of plants and causing a small landslide of dead and decaying leaves. Luckily, the incline wasn't break-your-neck steep and the pile up of dirt and leaves appeared to have broken her fall. She was filthy but relatively unharmed. Even her headache from earlier had abated. She felt something wriggle against her palm and raised it up between them.

"My crab! He's okay!"

A muscle in Alex's jaw ticked and joined the throbbing vein in his neck. "Are you trying to tell me you nearly died because you were chasing after a hermit crab?"

"Saving. I was saving him. And no, I'm trying to tell you there are bananas in that tree." Ignoring the irate male looming over her, Willa peeked over his shoulder again and her breath rushed out in amazement.

"Water! Have you tried it? Is it fresh?"

"I have not. I was a little more concerned about whether or not you were alive," he said tightly.

"Well, if it's fresh then we're all saved!"

Clearly her crab was no ordinary crustacean. He had flown into the forest on angel wings. Not only were there banana trees, there was a river being fed by a modest waterfall. The river wasn't large or moving very rapidly, which made sense for an island this size, but the area at the base of the fall flared out and created a decently sized pool before a rocky, mossy shore narrowed it and sent it snaking off into the trees.

The waterfall itself appeared promisingly clear as it poured down over the side of a curved cliff that looked as if someone had taken a giant spoon and scooped out a part of the hill Willa had just tumbled down. Jagged rocks speared up near the base and she realized if she had gone just ten more feet, her carelessness might have resulted in serious injury. She shivered, momentarily distracted from her excitement. Alex must have felt it because his hand gently squeezed her shoulder and her gaze rolled back to his.

"Willa, you need to be more careful. Even if you don't care about giving me a heart attack, surely you've got some sense of self-preservation buried in there." He looked so earnest, so tired and worn out, that her latent sense of guilt developed roots and shot a couple weak, spindly leaves into the air.

"I know. I will. I'm realizing I may not be the best person to get stuck in a survivalist situation. I think being hungry knocks off my body chemistry and my brain loses important functionality."

"That's a very pretentious way of saying you get hangry and reckless," he said dryly and her eyes narrowed. "But I suppose in the interest of your safety we should probably eat some bananas." He didn't let go of her immediately, pausing to scan her critically up and down. "Are you sure you're okay?"

She conducted a quick internal survey. She was starving but beyond that, she really did seem unharmed. She nodded and with Alex's help, managed to get to her feet. Now, in addition to being stiff with salt, her robe and sleep shirt were covered in dirt and the fibrous remains of old leaf skeletons. She didn't even want to think about the state of her hair or underwear.

"I'm a mess," she said, looking down at herself. Gently holding onto the crab's smooth, curved shell, she brought it up closer to her face and admired his waving little claws. "I promise I'm usually a bit more presentable than this."

"Wilhelmina, talking to a hermit crab is not the way to convince me you don't have a brain injury."

"Don't be rude. I'm clearly working my way through the seven stages of getting trapped on a desert island."

After watching to make sure she was steady, he turned and headed over to the banana tree, which was blessedly squat and heavy with fruit.

"Right, the seven stages. So far we've seen anger, melodrama, and bananas. Remind me, what comes next?"

"Well I'm pretty sure fighting to break open a coconut is next." It was the next logical step after going bananas and now that they had food and possibly water, Willa felt capable of anything. Alex reached up, grabbed a few of the ripest fruit on the tree and pulled them down. He peeled one and handed it to her and when she took a bite, it was the best thing she'd ever tasted. She gave a happy little moan.

Alex paused in the act of peeling one for himself, giving her another one of those brief, judgmental looks that made the back of her neck prickle.

"What?" she demanded sharply, or at least as sharply as she could with a mouth full of mush. He gave a slight shake of his head.

"Nothing. What were you saying? Coconuts, right? And then?"

"Mollusks," she said succinctly before shoving the rest of the banana in her mouth and reaching for another. Who cared if Alex thought she was unladylike? The fruit were small and she planned to have at least five.

"These later stages seem to focus heavily on food," he said around his own mouthful.

"They're a metaphor." She savagely bit off the tip of her next banana and chewed, again speaking with her mouth full, "that you can eat."

He winced watching her brutal display. "Right. Any chance the mollusk stage has to do with lust? You know, something about coaxing open a hard outer shell to get to the soft, delicious meat inside..."

Willa ignored him and the way his words sent a strange frission down her spine and spoke to her crab, "You know what the last stage is, Herman?"

"Strewth, she's named the crab," Alex muttered.

She chucked her second peel into the trees and shot him a fierce grin, "Cannibalism."

Wilhelmina Jones was going to be the death of him.

There were other things Alex should have been focusing on: shelter, trying to determine if drinking the water from the waterfall would kill them, hunting and gathering food a bit more substantial than bananas, building some kind of signal to let any passing planes or ships know there were people stranded here. The list went on.

However, all he could think about as they steadily stripped the tree of bananas was Willa. His heart had stopped after watching her tumble out of sight for the second time. It was a miracle he hadn't broken his own neck given how fast he ripped through the trees and clamored down the embankment she'd rolled down.

It was the third time his heart had stopped in the past twenty-four hours. The first was when she fell off the ship. The second was when she kissed him.

Wilhelmina "I hate you" Jones had *kissed* him.

Why? To prove a point? Because she had a concussion? Heatstroke? Or, as he was beginning to suspect, was Willa the kind of woman that needed to be fed? Often. Or all would suffer the consequences. He knew it wasn't because she actually liked him. Willa might currently be experiencing a break with reality, but Alex was not. He knew where they stood. He knew the smart thing would be to forget it, pretend it never happened. But forgetting seemed as likely as an all you can eat buffet suddenly dropping out of the sky.

Unwillingly, his eyes slid back to her mouth, so full and with such a sharply defined cupid's bow her lips looked almost heart shaped. It was a mouth that promised eros and threatened pathos. Which was why it was definitely smarter to forget ever tasting those salty sweet lips—they were dangerous. And yet...if they *did* die here, he was going to spend his entire afterlife regretting not kissing her back.

Her voice brought him back to their present problem and he dragged his attention back up to her eyes.

"Herman thinks we should test the water supply and then work on building a shelter. He said it rains a lot at night." She grinned at him and his breath caught. Four. His heart had stopped four times today. Two. Two smiles she'd given him in the past five years and both had only happened in the past five minutes.

"I think Herman gives sound advice. I also think he would be happier back on the beach," he said, striving to sound like he hadn't just been thinking about kissing her again.

Willa lifted the crab up to eye level and studied him, her dirt-smudged nose wrinkling in a way that was surprisingly adorable. She nodded and sighed, "You're probably right."

"Why don't you give me the crab so you can give your robe a quick scrub in the river and we can put it out to dry before the sun goes down." He checked his watch and frowned. "We've only got four hours of full daylight left." He looked at Willa, in her dirty robe with her mud-smudged face, remembering how it felt to watch her go tumbling out of sight not once, but twice, and had to force himself to say the next words. "We are going to have to split up. I'll go back to the beach to grab the lifebuoy and some coconuts. You stay here and test the water and start trying to pull together something to shield us from any rain."

Still chewing her food, Willa nodded in agreement. "I can do that," she said, without any of the combative energy she'd been vibrating with earlier. He made a mental note to *definitely* ensure this woman never went hungry. Finishing her fifth banana, she handed him Herman and strode briskly over to the river, tugging off her robe as she went. He watched the generous curve of her ass appear below the hem of her shirt as she knelt and began vigorously scrubbing the blue cotton in the water. Needing some kind of distraction, he cleared his throat and gave her an additional warning.

"And when I say stay here, I mean it, Willa. No storming off, no fraternizing with animals from the wrong side of the river, no flinging yourself off anything higher than ten centimeters. If I come back here and find you unconscious again, there will be consequences."

He heard her snort before she slapped her robe violently against one of the large rocks clumped along the riverbed and stood up. She faced him with a raised eyebrow and a quirked mouth.

"And just what might those consequences be?" she asked sweetly. Too sweetly.

"Wilhelmina." He was losing patience.

"I've never seen this serious, bossy side of you, McBryde." She plopped her wet robe into his outstretched hand and tilted her head curiously. "Fascinating."

He clenched his fist around the wet fabric and said tersely, "You'll be really fascinated when I show you my tie-you-to-a-tree-with-your-own-bathrobe side if you don't promise to be here, alive and conscious, when I get back."

Almost as soon as the threat left his mouth, Alex regretted it. The sudden image of Willa tied to a tree, her eyes flaring, her dangerous lips pouting, was more of a threat to his present dignity than it was to Willa. He could just imagine her disgust if he got another erection in front of her today. Luckily, she didn't seem to notice his slip. She merely rolled her eyes and let out an exaggerated huff of annoyance.

"That sounds like it would take a lot of time we don't have." She began pushing him back in the direction of the beach. "Don't worry, Dundee, this sheila will be fine. I promise I'll wait for you to get back before attempting any more death-defying feats."

"I swear to God, if I come back and you're gone or dead..."

"I got it. Go!" She gave him a hard shove and he went, wading back into the dense leaves toward the sound of waves crashing. As he got further away, he even heard her singing in a surprisingly rich, lovely voice. Queen's "Don't Stop Me Now," trailed after him through the trees and just like the AC/DC shirt, it was another surprise. Willa had always seemed more like a classical music type. Even more surprising, however, was her change in mood and Alex wondered if the past five years of animosity could have been avoided if he had just always greeted her with a candy bar. It was a wonder what a little food and water had done to improve her attitude. It was less surprising the negative effect watching someone almost die for the second time had on a positive one. Clearly pessimism and frustration were contagious...and she had kissed him...

He had never met such a confusing, exasperating woman in his entire life.

She was normally so calm and controlled. On campus, she was widely viewed as a ballbuster although Alex knew that was only because she never let any of the over-egoed academics in their university talk over her or boss her around. He had only ever seen her composure slip when they were trading insults. He'd definitely never seen her do anything as silly as talk to a crab. He looked at Herman and shook his head. Was this what she was like off campus with her friends? Playful and weird and a little reckless? He had always imagined her going back to a tidy, boring apartment and essentially popping out a set of batteries to power down.

How could they know so little about each other after all this time? Thinking about all these new unknowns pushed Alex into picking up his pace. Who knew what trouble she was getting into without him. Once he reached the beach, he put Herman down with a solemn farewell, draped Willa's robe over a rock to dry, then jogged down to the abandoned lifebuoy.

It took longer than he liked to gather everything they needed from the beach, fashioning the life buoy into a sort of sled using leaves and bark and piling on coconuts before heading back. As he re-entered the trees, Alex worked to make a more distinct path, pulling down vines and snapping branches. The buoy dragged behind him, helping to further flatten the foliage but as he walked, the rope he'd tied around his chest tightened and the feel of it brought him stumbling to a halt. The sound of the water behind him seemed to swell, filling his ears and all at once, memories of the night before came rushing back. The constriction around his lungs, the weight of Willa's body on that tiny raft tugging at him, making it hard to breathe as he swam, exhausted, directionless, through water blacker than a shark's eyes. The salty, choking taste of fear each time a wave broke over his face. The harsh, desperate sound of his breathing, the only audible noise in an ocean that was silent but, terrifyingly, not at all empty.

This island had been a miracle.

Which was perhaps why his reaction to finding themselves stranded here had not been as intense as Willa's. Anything was better than swimming in what felt like an endless black void determined to swallow them whole. At least here they would be able to see danger coming. They could survive. He resumed walking, even more quickly than before, and when he reached the rockier, less densely forested area around the river and didn't immediately see Willa, he felt that now familiar flash of panic and anger.

"Willa! Where are you?" he shouted, causing a sudden rustling of leaves and startled chirps as birds took off from the trees. For a moment, that was all he could hear but then there was the sound of snapping twigs and the dry clack of rocks shifting and she emerged down by where the river narrowed and bent out of sight. She was flushed from exertion and her T-shirt was clinging damply to her body, the faded gray fabric practically transparent even in the weaker light below the canopy. She looked wild and hot and, most importantly, *alive,* like an Amazon emerging from his fantasies, and the relief that coursed through him was followed by a ridiculous shot of lust and a reasonable chaser of annoyance.

She was safe. She was also on the other side of the river.

Still dragging the buoy behind him, he followed the line of the bank until they were standing across from each other.

"Didn't I say something about staying on this side of the river?" Maybe it was a good thing they were separated because if she had been standing close enough, he might not have been able to resist shaking her.

"Actually, I believe what you said was, no fraternizing with animals from the wrong side of it." She gestured around her, "As you can see, no bad news bears over here." He must have looked annoyed because she hurried on, "The river is only about thigh high here and it's not fast. I was looking for longer, sturdier sticks and it made more sense to look on both sides so I didn't have to go too far in any direction." She scowled. "Quit being such a caveman. I have actually managed to take care of myself, without you, for most of my life."

Alex took a deep, calming breath to stop himself from snapping back an insult. It wasn't what they needed right now and she was right. The past day's incidents notwithstanding, Willa was a smart, capable woman. Even if he apparently knew nothing else about her, he did know that. He exhaled and slowly unclenched the fingers curled into fists at his side.

"I know. I know you don't need me." He inhaled and exhaled again, striving for calm. "But I think," he paused, tried another breath and went on, "I think seeing you almost drown really fucked with my head."

"Oh. Well." She hesitated, her expression softening a little. "I guess I'm...sorry for worrying you." She paused and made a face like she had just tasted something new and strange. Had she ever apologized to him before? If she had, Alex had no memory of it. Apparently today was a day of firsts. Willa's first smile. Her first apology. That first and no-doubt last kiss.

Maybe they were both in shock.

He blew out one more breath and let the rest of his anger go. If Willa could muster up an apology, he could muster up some patience and understanding. "Thank you. Now, please tell me whether or not we can drink the water."

Her expression shifted to what Alex generally thought of as her "Grad Assistant Face," explaining her research like she was presenting a lecture. "I couldn't detect any taste of salt and there's no discernable discolorations. The bottom of the riverbed is mostly shale, which is great because it seems to prevent a lot of dirt or sediment from floating up and clouding the water. No fish that I could see but some frogs and water bugs so it's probably not poisonous. If we could figure out a way to build a solar still that would be better but right now drinking this seems like our best bet." She shrugged. "I already drank a lot so you could always wait to see if I drop dead or get violently ill before risking it."

Alex didn't bother dignifying that last comment with a response. If Willa thought the water was safe to drink, that was good enough for him and he gratefully dropped to his knees and scooped up a couple handfuls.

"Fuck me dead," he groaned. The water was cool and crisp and sang down his throat like a Hallelujah chorus. He'd been determinedly ignoring just how thirsty he was all day. After a night spent spitting out salt water and a day spent sweating in the sun, he would have been willing to trade his left testicle for even a single sip of water. He took another frantic drink and moaned. He was never taking water for granted again. When they got off this island, he was going to be the most well-hydrated motherfucker the world had ever seen.

There was splashing and Willa's tanned calves appeared in front of him. He looked up, water dripping down his chin as his eyes slowly made the very long journey up her legs, past the tempting width of her hips and strong column of her waist. He got to her breasts and the shirt was definitely see-through—her nipples were a deep, dusky rose. Best of all, she was smiling, an amused, slightly patronizing smile but it was enough to make his mouth go dry all over again. His American friends would have called him thirsty.

"Slow down, McBryde. You'll make yourself sick," she said sagely.

Shaking himself, he dropped back on his heels and focused on the tree limb she had propped over one shoulder.

"Is that for our shelter or so you can beat me over the head?"

Her smile widened. "It can always be both. Come see what I've been working on, doing all the heavy lifting, while you've been dawdling around playing with your coconuts."

Matching her grin, Alex rose to his feet and followed her back toward the trees.

"Clearly you've never actually felt my coconuts because if you had, you would know how heavy they are."

"My only interest in your coconuts, McBryde, is cracking them open."

"To eat?" he teased, slapping a particularly large leaf away from his face. She caught the movement and sent him another one of those amused looks.

"Nope, to use as a metaphor." She stepped to the side and threw out her free hand. "Now stop and behold our castle. Be highly complimentary or I will make you sleep in the moat."

Alex looked and was impressed. She had managed to find a couple of trees with low branches close enough to each other that she could run a particularly long, broken-off branch between them. She'd started propping other branches and sticks between the supporting horizontal pole and the ground to form a rudimentary tent.

"This looks great. You were busy while I was off dealing with crabs and coconuts."

"I think you just summarized the past five years of our grad school education," she said in that sugary-sweet voice and the words hit him unexpectedly hard—like a bad stomachache. The insult triggered the memory of her words from last night as well as a hundred other similar insults and for the first time he acknowledged just how much they had begun to bother him. When had that happened?

And why did it suddenly seem to matter?

"I'm going to be the mature one here and ignore that. We have bigger things to worry about than your disgust about me being a manwhore," he said stiffly and started jerking at the knots securing the buoy around his chest, glad there was something else he could focus on. "Just tell me what you want me to do," he said, back to feeling tired and frustrated.

"Alex?"

His fingers slipped off the knots, which were now impossibly tight, and he swore under his breath. "It's fine, Willa, just tell me what to do." He was still glaring down at the rope when her fingers landed gently over his.

"Stop. Trying to force it will just make it worse." She began working her fingernails into the tight joints and her voice was back to being hesitant, "I'm sorry," she said quietly, "I don't know how to do this with you." She was staring at the knots on his chest with the same undue focus Alex had given them. She, however, was having much more luck pulling them apart. He could feel them loosening and see gaps widening between the loops and twists. "If I'm honest, I don't really know how to do this with anyone," she admitted although the words sounded extremely forced.

Stunned by this second apology, he was also now confused, "Do *what*, Willa? Get stranded? Survive on a desert island?"

She shook her head, pulling the end of the rope through the final hole so the knots fell apart and Alex was free. She stepped back but she still didn't look at him.

"No. Get along with people." She shrugged and crossed her arms over her chest like a shield. "Sometimes it feels like...like I don't really know how to be a person. Aside from my parents and Dr. Schwartz, the only even vaguely friend-like relationship I've ever managed to maintain has been entirely online."

"Oh." That wasn't what he had expected. He thought back, trying to remember who her friends were on campus and realized he never saw her with anyone else. Even the night they met, she had been standing on the edge of the party. Watching. Alone. "Willa—" he started but she cut him off.

"No. We don't have the time for a heart-to-heart about my social confusions." She bit her lip and looked up at him, clearly frustrated but, for the first time, Alex didn't think it was him she was frustrated with as she went on. "I'm only telling you this, and believe me, I really *hate* telling you this, so you understand I'm the problem here and you'll wipe that annoying, hurt look off your face." Her eyes slid down to the ground. "I'm sorry for calling you a manwhore last night and for the comment I just made. It was a shitty thing to do."

Alex could hardly believe what he was hearing. "Willa, I didn't realize —"

She shook her head and waved away his words. "Stop. I mean it. It doesn't matter. We have other things to worry about. Like rain."

"But why—" he tried but she continued, speaking over him.

"I think we should finish filling in the sides of the structure with as many sticks as we can find then layer it with moss and leaves. Look for ones with a waxy coating that are more likely to be water repellent. We should also try to make some kind of platform on the bottom so we're not completely covered in mud or bugs when we wake up. There are scorpions and coconut crabs in the Seychelles. I'll keep looking by the river, you can search off the path to the beach." She turned abruptly and began walking into the trees.

"Willa!" he called a little desperately after her but she didn't stop.

She waved a hand in acknowledgement and shouted back, "I won't go far."

Another few steps and she had disappeared into the greenery. He fought the impulse to chase after her. Despite clearly not knowing her as well as he'd thought, he did know just how stubborn she could be. He once witnessed her spend an entire lecture period debating whether or not Bergman's Rule was true for ectotherms with a professor and the next week he had glimpsed her research paper clearly continuing to argue her side. If she didn't want to talk to Alex about the bombshell she had just dropped, there was no way he could make her.

Besides, he supposed he also felt like a bit of a dickhead for not noticing it on his own. While Willa had always seemed to reserve a special animosity for him, he realized now, with the exception of Professor Schwartz, he rarely saw her talk to anyone unless she had to. She wasn't in any of the GA groups, her students frequently cited her as "unapproachable," and after that first grad school meet-and-greet he never saw her at another biology department social event. He remembered the crack he made last night about her not having a personal life and his stomach gave a guilty churn. He really was an asshole.

With a final glance in the direction she had disappeared, Alex turned and headed toward the newly created beach path. He wanted to stay and maybe apologize but knew if Willa found him standing here when she came back, she would probably make good on her earlier threat and beat him over the head. Because she was right. Night was coming and they were running out of time.

For the next few hours, they worked by orbiting around the tent like two satellites, close enough to hear signals but too far to see each other and never in the same place at the same time. The occasional snapping of twigs or bursts of PG-13 swearing told him Willa was okay and every time he went back to the campsite there was progress on their tent. After about an hour and by tacit agreement, they began adding moss and leaves to the structure, doing their best to make it water resistant. At one point, he came back and found that most of the underbrush had been cleared away leaving bare, firmly packed earth inside the tent and the start of a short platform made of more long branches tied together with vines. Eyeing it, Alex let out a resigned sigh. Luckily, his bed on the boat hadn't been much softer so tonight would hardly be a challenge.

By the time the sky started to turn red and orange, their little camp looked about as habitable and homey as something made out of branches could be. The leaves and moss were neatly layered, the lifebuoy hung over the side almost like a cheerful wreath, and Willa's battered robe hung on a nearby branch. They'd built one end of the tent around the base of the closest tree and left the other end open as an entrance. Standing in front of it now, he eyed the inside doubtfully. He hadn't realized just how small and narrow the space was. Neither him nor Will were small or narrow. It was going to be a tight squeeze.

He glanced up and noticed a purple tinge to the clouds and a prickle of unease crept through him. Where was Willa? He hadn't heard a "damn" or "frick" in a while. Turning slowly, he strained his ears, listening for some sign of her.

Nothing.

The forest around him hummed with the sound of insects and frogs, flying foxes barked as they chased mosquitos, but there was no trace of singing, swearing, or a large body moving through the underbrush.

Don't panic. She told you not to panic. She's smart. She's capable.

There was a deafening crack from the direction of the river and his heart did its fifth and potentially final stop of the day. Then Willa's voice cut excitedly through the growing dark and it started back up, hard and fast.

"Alex, come here! I'm by the river!"

"I'm going to kill her," he muttered as he moved down the now heavily trampled trail between their campsite and the river. There was another loud, violent crack and he broke into a run. He burst from the trees and found Willa standing by the water, straddling a pair of rocks big enough to give her a sixty-centimeter boost above the ground. She was holding a large rock over her head and looking triumphant.

"What the fuck—"

His outrage was cut short as she flung down the rock she was holding and another godawful crack sent his hands flying up to his ears. He strode toward her while she scrambled down from the rocks and picked something up from the ground. If she thought she was throwing that rock again, she had another think coming. She spun around when he reached her, her face shining and flushed as she held out something round, fibrous, and...hairy.

"Gravity!" she burst out.

"Excuse me?"

"I had a Newtonian moment," she said, shaking the round, hairy thing at him.

"A what-moment? Wait, is that a coconut?" he asked incredulously. "How did you get it out of the husk?"

"That's what I'm telling you. Gravity! While I was getting leaves I found a starfruit tree and I shook it to get more of the fruit down and one fell near my feet and burst apart and I realized we could use gravity to crack open the coconut husks without wearing ourselves out."

She abruptly crouched down and began to bang the shell against a rock with a particularly sharp edge. One, two, three whacks and the coconut burst into two fuzzy halves and she laughed as she stood back up.

"I did it. I actually did it! Maybe I can do this. Maybe we won't die." She thrust half the coconut at him and, feeling a bit slow, he took it but made no move to bring it to his mouth. He was too busy staring at her in astonishment.

"Try it," she urged and, like an automaton, he did as she said, tilting the coconut back over his mouth and drinking down some of the water. It was warm and a bit salty but it was still good.

"How is it?" she asked, practically bouncing up and down in her excitement. Alex handed the rest of it back to her.

"Amazing," he said but he wasn't talking about the coconut. She nodded, pleased, and took a drink.

"Mmm. Tastes like survival." She laughed again and then she was handing him handfuls of oblong fruit with odd flared edges. "Here, help me carry these. Tonight, we'll have a feast, coconut meat and starfruit."

She stood and began striding back toward the trail, leaving him behind. "Come on, we should get back to camp before it gets completely dark."

Alex nodded dumbly and trailed after her. Earlier he realized he didn't know Willa at all. Now he realized it didn't matter. He knew the most important thing: if he was going to end up stuck on a desert island with someone, he was extremely glad that someone was Wilhelmina Jones.

Survival Tip #5

Men are like weeds. Even the pretty ones have no place in your lady garden.

Alex and Willa sat outside their wooden tent and ate sweet star fruits and flaky coconut meat and each bite was accompanied by the satisfied thrill her idea had worked. Despite being the longest day of her life, it had ended on a good note and that was enough to give Willa hope for tomorrow.

"In the morning, we should go looking for mollusks. The fruit is good but actual protein would be better," she said thoughtfully. Alex hummed in agreement but didn't say anything else. He'd been quiet while they ate and she wondered if he was still angry with her.

She would probably never say it out loud, but while they had worked on their tent, her feelings of guilt had burst into full bloom and she'd finally admitted to herself they were only here because of her. Yes, his wall-banging sexcapades had been inconsiderate but she could have just asked him to quiet down like a normal person. Instead, she had pushed. She *always* pushed. And now they were here.

Last night on the boat he had accused her of being jealous. It was another thing she would never say out loud, but a small part of her suspected he was right. Not about the sex thing, she was *fine* without that, but, one of the things she had always found most irritating about Alex was how quickly and easily he charmed everyone around him.

Willa was an army brat. She had spent most of her life shuttling from one place to another and it didn't matter if it was a new city or a new country, she was never *just* the new kid. By the time she turned ten, she had been five foot eleven and almost immediately labeled a freak amongst each new set of peers.

Blending in and disappearing like a cephalopod had never even been an option and none of the schools of fish, even the offbeat ones, had wanted to swim with her. So she'd grown teeth. At least that way when people saw her alone, they assumed it was because that was how she liked it—not because no one wanted to be around her. The problem was now she felt too much like a shark, always biting first and worrying about the damage later. Which was why even when she tried to play nice with Alex, she hurt him.

Blowing out a sigh, she dropped her head back and looked at the stars, wishing she knew how to be different. If there was any actual power in starlight, surely this was the place to make her wishes come true. Despite being in the forest with its dense canopy, here and there, gaps revealed a night sky that was positively unreal. She had never seen this many stars in her life. Even when they'd been on a boat in the middle of the ocean, she had never *bothered* to look up. She had almost missed this.

"Tomorrow night, if it's clear, I want to stay out on the beach until the stars come out. Have you ever seen anything so incredible?" she asked.

Alex gave another quiet hum. "Once," he murmured.

She didn't ask what it had been. She had seen his girlfriends. She didn't want to know.

"Well I haven't. It almost makes being lost out here worth it."

"Aside from the multiple heart attacks you've given me, it hasn't been too bad, has it? We've got food, water, a tropical beach all to ourselves. People pay a lot of money for vacations like this."

Clearly, they had both reached the next stage of being stranded: delusion.

"Mmm, I'm pretty sure those people still go to sleep on a million thread count sheets and don't have to worry about building a fire." Even though it was nice sitting here in the dark without any light impeding the stars, Willa definitely wanted a fire. The air had cooled off, coconut crabs had been known to attack large prey and Willa liked having all her fingers and toes. She also wasn't relishing the thought of eating raw fish...if they could manage to catch any.

"True," agreed Alex. "That should probably be on the list for tomorrow, along with building a signal."

She sighed. "Some vacation. I think I'll ask for my money back."

He laughed and the sound made her feel warm and sugary inside. It cut through some of her lingering guilt. Smiling, she began crawling toward the tent. She'd eaten enough to quiet the buzz of nerves that had been agitating beneath her skin since she woke up and the overwhelm of the day had caught up with her about three hours ago.

"Well, given the amount of stuff we have to do tomorrow, I think I'm going to try out the thread count on our sheets," she said, reaching the dark opening and peering in at the short, narrow platform piled with layers of moss.

"Same. I'm beat."

She heard him shift and then felt the heat of him crouching beside her. They both stared into the tiny, black interior of the tent and her smile faded. There was a pregnant pause between them.

"Big spoon or little spoon?" he finally asked, his voice falsely casual.

"Everyone knows little spoon is the superior position," she replied, trying to sound equally unconcerned.

"You're right and since you owe me, I'll be the little spoon."

A surprised laugh erupted out of her and as the sound faded into the trees, so did the tension lingering between them. "We'll make it work. You go in first since you're bigger and I'll wiggle into the space around you."

"Like a snake preparing to strangle me," said Alex.

"Just like," she agreed easily. "Maybe we should have a safe word."

She heard him snort as he crawled in and lay down. In the darkness she could just make out his body curling up on his side as he tried to make as much room for her as possible. He was facing the middle of the tent, like he was preparing to be the big spoon.

"Roll over and face the wall," she demanded and heard his exasperated sigh.

"I thought we agreed to spoon, Wilhelmina," his tone was exasperated too but she could tell he wasn't really upset. She began to shimmy in beside him. The wall of the lean-to scraped against her shoulders, so she pressed herself closer, her breasts pushing into the strong, warm muscles of his back. She tucked her legs up underneath his, felt the firm, round press of his ass against the cradle of her hips, and cuddled her face between his shoulder blades.

"What do you call this, McBryde?"

He was silent for a long moment, she could feel the uneven rise and fall of his back against her cheek as he breathed, and then his arm reached back, his hand fumbling around. Confused, she let him grab her arm and pull it tight around his ribs. He kept her hand cradled in his.

"I call it half-assed spooning. If you're going to do it, do it right, dag."

Willa gave an outraged huff and then, without thinking, gave his shoulder a retaliatory nip with her teeth.

"Starfruit!" he said.

"We ate them all."

"No. That's my safeword."

She could *hear* his grin and couldn't stop the answering smile that flitted across her face. She was glad it was dark and that he wasn't turned toward her to see it. Making a soft, mocking sound of disgust she finished their usual script with a sleepy, "Hate you."

He was quiet so long she thought he had fallen asleep but then he gave a rough sigh and said quietly, "Yeah, I know."

Willa woke up more comfortable than she had in weeks. Wanting to enjoy it, she kept her eyes closed and snuggled closer to her pillow. The boat was rocking beneath her, rising and falling gently on the waves and she could smell fresh air and saltwater and something else that was earthy and faintly spicy. She'd been having a delicious sort of dream. Bits of it were still floating through her mind like cotton candy, fluffy and light and too insubstantial to really grasp. Maybe if she fell back asleep she'd fall back into the dream. Ten more minutes couldn't hurt. The professor would understand. She was just so comfortable...

The boat heaved suddenly beneath her, jolting her out of that fuzzy, liminal space between dreams and reality. Her eyes snapped open and she shot into consciousness, her body still caught in the sense-memory feel of falling.

Breathing hard and trembling, it took a few seconds for her brain to catch up with where she was. She wasn't falling. She was safe. She was alive.

"Willa?" A rough, deep voice had the bed beneath her pitching again.

Shit. And she wasn't alone.

The last pastel wisps of sleep dissolved and memories from yesterday came flooding back. Including the knowledge it was Alexander McBryde's chest she was currently drooling on. At some point in the night, he had rolled onto his back and Willa, like an actual boa constrictor, had wrapped herself around him. Her leg was curled around his, her torso draped halfway across his chest and her hand curled loosely around his neck. He was warm and comfortingly solid beneath her, his hair, tangled between her fingers, soft and inviting. All of it felt familiar. Like the taste of cotton candy. Alexander McBryde was *made* to be slept on.

And now Willa was just one of the many women who had.

Mortified, she tried to sit up but the arm wrapped around her waist tightened and she could actually feel the strong, warm flex of his muscles against her back, pulling her hips even closer against his side. It was such a possessive gesture and Willa was horrified to realize she *liked* it, heat and tension coiling in her lower abdomen like a wish. Except this was Alex. He was no girl's fairy godfather and even if he was, Willa wasn't interested in his particular brand of happy endings. She looked up at his face but his eyes were still closed, a slight frown marring his ridiculously handsome features.

"Alex," she hissed, trying to wriggle free.

"Mmm," he sighed, clearly caught in that same hazy dreamspace she had just been catapulted from.

"Alex, come on, I've got to be crushing you." She wiggled harder and was relieved to feel the hand on her waist loosen—only to have it slide down and grab a handful of her ass. Willa craned her neck to look down at her backside in disbelief. Another frisson of warmth worked its way from his palm up her spine before settling in her cheeks. How had she never realized just how big his hands were? If his arm around her waist had been possession, his hand on her butt was straight up ownership. His warm, rough fingers curled, brushing just below the curve of her underwear, along the sensitive skin of her upper thigh and she sucked in a breath.

"So ripe," he rumbled. Then he squeezed.

This time it was no gentle warmth moving up her spine; it was the zing of a lightning bolt. "Oh! You—" Shaking her head to clear it, Willa quit being nice and wrenched herself upward, scrambling her body backward like a crab. She ended up straddling the thigh her leg had been wrapped around, kneeling and glaring down at the prone man who was blinking open his eyes looking bewildered.

"What are you doing?"

"What am *I* doing? What are *you* doing?"

"Well, I was sleeping until you started flailing around."

"You, sir, are a—a scoundrel!"

"A scoundrel?" He yawned and rubbed a hand over his scruffy face. "I didn't think scoundrels were still a thing in this day and age."

"Well you are! You grabbed my butt!"

His hand stilled and he focused on her. "I did?" He looked contemplatively at the offending appendage, flexing his fingers, then he looked back up at her. "Did I enjoy it?"

She made an enraged sound. "I should have strangled you last night when I had the chance."

"I'm not really into choking but I could be persuaded..."

For a moment, all she could do was glare, too flustered to come up with a suitable insult. Eventually, her brain latched on to an old familiar theme and she burst out with, "A gang of textile cone snails!"

"Cone snails?" echoed Alex.

"Are too good a death for you!" She managed to maneuver herself the rest of the way out of the tent and stood with as much dignity as she could manage. "I am going to the river," she snapped.

"Willa, come on, I'm sorry. It's a force of habit!" There was laughter in his voice but she ignored it. She knew she was probably overreacting but that didn't stop her from snatching up her clean(ish) robe from its tree branch, grabbing a coconut, and storming off through the trees.

Once she got to the river, it took her three bananas and half a coconut to acknowledge she had definitely overreacted. The headache throbbing at her temples also forced her to acknowledge she would gladly commit half a dozen morally questionable acts for a cup of coffee. She had always considered herself a reasonable, mature adult. It was demoralizing to realize those qualities relied heavily on the accessibility of modern conveniences. When you stripped her down to basics, she was really just a hangry, caffeine addicted toddler.

Alex emerged from the trees looking wary and she felt another one of those obnoxious pangs of guilt. When he came closer, she held out the other half of her coconut.

"I overreacted."

He took the peace offering and his face relaxed into a smile. "No worries, it happens," there was a beat of silence and then, "So...cone snails?"

Willa blushed and looked very deliberately toward the trees. "Certain varieties are extremely venomous."

"Oh, I'm aware. What I want to know is if there are any other animals in your deadly menagerie I should be watching out for."

"Maybe," she hedged and little amused lines appeared around his eyes.

"Such as..."

"Piranhas," she said through clenched teeth.

"Avoid subtropical rivers, got it. Anything else?"

"Great white sharks."

"Obviously."

"Krakens," she muttered and he leaned toward her.

"I'm sorry, what was that last one?" She shot him an annoyed glare and his smile practically cracked his face in two. "Come on, I'm *dying* to know," and then he apparently couldn't hold it in anymore and dissolved into laughter.

The sound of him laughing felt *good*, just like it had last night, and a small, reluctant smile broke across her face. When he finally stopped, the look he gave her was almost...fond and Willa felt her stomach dip strangely. Maybe she needed another banana.

"You were never supposed to know," she said, shaking her head in resignation.

"Well now that I do, I need to know if I'm safe from the cone snails," he teased.

"Yes." She sighed. "I've called them off."

"Glad to hear it. Maybe we should keep some snacks at the campsite just in case you ever start feeling snail-happy."

She scrubbed her hands over her face and then gestured at him helplessly. "I don't know what's wrong with me."

"We are trapped on a desert island. People cope in different ways. I apparently turn into a caveman and you turn into—"

"A cranky toddler," she interjected. "I think I'd rather be a caveman."

"What I was going to say," he corrected, "Was you turn into an Amazon. A little fierce and wild and man-hatey but strong and smart enough to get things done. After all, we wouldn't be eating a coconut right now without your Newtonian moment."

Pleasure flashed through her. That was perhaps one of the nicest things anyone had ever said to her. It was *definitely* the nicest thing Alex had ever said to her.

"Thanks," she said, pulling one of her curls through her fingers in an old, nervous habit, but then she found herself untangling a stick instead. "Maybe I should work on the wild part. If we ever do get rescued I'll probably have to cut all my hair off just to get the knots out."

"No!"

Willa dropped the stick she was unknotting and looked up at him in surprise. "No?"

His cheeks flushed faintly. "I—I've just always liked your hair." He scratched the back of his neck and squinted past her toward the waterfall. "It would be a shame if you had to cut it," he added. It was the second nicest thing he had ever said to her. Things were getting out of hand. Any more and they would end up becoming friends. He cleared his throat and stood, wiping his hands on his shorts. "Here, come on." He looked back down at her and held out his hand. "I'll help you comb it out in the river."

"You're going to wash my hair for me?" she asked, looking from his hand and back up to his face.

"You don't have to sound so shocked. I'm not proposing anything indecent." He wiggled his fingers at her and grinned. "Just a little hair pulling."

It took a moment for Willa to realize the heat gathering beneath her skin was arousal. Her traitorous body was actually responding to Alex's flirtations. All this time, she thought herself immune to his charms. The realization she wasn't was both shocking and terribly inconvenient. She had kissed him yesterday to prove a point. It hadn't been about attraction, it had been about *being right*. In her defense, she'd almost drowned the night before and been practically delirious with thirst and hunger. But it would *not* be happening again. In the same way Willa only knew how to exist as a shark, Alex only knew how to be a flirt.

She had spent the past five years with a seat in the nosebleed section of Alex's dating life, watching the women who regularly competed for his affections. All of them, every single one, had been Willa's antithesis. Short, *sweet* women. Women with sleek dark hair and a flawless sense of style that managed to be both sexy and sophisticated. They were major league prospects—beautiful, smart, obnoxiously likeable—and despite that, Alex had never been with any of them for longer than a few months. Willa wasn't delusional. If women like that struck out, a woman like her would never even be allowed to play. She had been born to be a spectator and she liked it that way.

Spectators never lost.

Alex might be willing to flirt and cuddle up to her on a desert island but she didn't suffer any illusions his interest would hold up when offered a chance with literally anyone else. Willa, on the other hand, had lived on too little affection in her life to trust she wouldn't get greedy. If she had a small taste of it, she knew she would want more and she could think of nothing worse than leaving here with Alex thinking she had some pathetic, wistful crush on him. Given the choice between a dignified death or awkward survival, she would choose dignity. Which was why any lustful thoughts needed to be shut down before they were allowed to sink any kind of roots in her lady garden.

"Willa?" Alex's smile dimmed and she realized she'd been staring. "I was only joking, I'll be gentle," he said in a tone she could all too easily imagine turning to pity and words snapped out of her before she could bite them back.

"As if I would ever let *you* pull my hair, McBryde." The last traces of his smile disappeared, his hand dropped back to his side, and her guilt returned like a rusty harpoon between the ribs. She fought back a grimace. He hadn't deserved that. They were stuck out here together and he was just trying to be helpful.

Giving herself a mental shake, she tried to offer him a friendly, reassuring, not-at-all-attracted smile. "Sorry, I don't function well without coffee in the morning." Her tone turned self-deprecating. "As I think we've established. Yes. Please. I would appreciate your help." He gave a short nod and Willa stood up. "Great," she said, moving toward the pool, determined to be cool and nonchalant. He had already seen her naked and last night she had practically slept on top of him. Him washing her hair was nothing—everything that happened on this island was about one thing and one thing only: survival. She glanced back at Alex, so golden in the morning sunlight and it felt like she had just walked into a sunbeam, her skin going warm and rosy all over again. Her hands clenched at her sides.

Focus on survival.

That was the only thing that mattered. She turned away from the man behind her, took a deep breath, and jumped.

Survival Tip #6

Sometimes a gentle touch is all it takes to tame the beast. If that doesn't work, grab it by the balls and squeeze.

Alex realized he might have made a mistake offering to help wash Willa's hair when, after getting into the water, she started pulling the Acca Dacca shirt off over her head. Standing in the middle of the pool, the water came up just high enough to cover the tops of her breasts but it was so damn clear he could still see every curve, tan line, and puckered nipple. Evidently it was a bit cold. He hoped it was icy because that was the only way he was going to get through this without getting a stiff cock.

He slowly finished a banana and watched Willa scrub her shirt under the water. Her underwear was next and even from two meters away he could see the shadowed vee between her thighs. She turned and he was treated to the sweet, full curve of the ass he had apparently squeezed this morning. His fingers clenched and squished the rest of his banana.

"Are you going to keep staring like some sort of pervert or are you actually going to help me with my hair?" she called and before he could think of a clever reply he found himself getting smacked in the chest with a wet bundle of cotton. "Be a friend and lay those over a rock for me, would you," she said in that sweet voice she usually used when she was insulting him. Which he probably deserved. It wasn't like she'd signed up to play centerfold in his fantasies.

He draped her clothes over a rock bathed in early morning sunlight then waded in after her, planning to give his shorts the same treatment. Sea salt chaffed and his dick was already suffering enough. Maybe he really was a scoundrel because each step closer he took to the gorgeous temptation of Willa's curves, his body took as an invitation, his muscles going tight with awareness. Even keeping his eyes ruthlessly fixated on her face, there was no reasoning with his body. He'd never been this close to a naked woman without winding up inside her. He swallowed hard, cleared his throat, and prayed she wouldn't look down.

"Given the volume of the problem, I think it would be easiest if you floated on your back so your hair is submerged and the river and I can work together getting it sorted." When she hesitated, he spread his hands, "I am also open to other suggestions." Maybe she would chicken out. Which, now that he was close enough to feel the heat of her, he thought might be best for both their nerves but she shook her head.

"No, I think that will work, I just—" she stopped and let out a short, annoyed huff. "I'm just trying to reconcile myself to this much nudity. Do you know how few men have actually seen me naked? And even if we're not—you're still—" She stopped, sighed, and shook her head. "Never mind. Like you said yesterday, it's nothing you haven't seen before."

Surprise rattled his control and for a split second his eyes slipped, dipping below the water to the stiff, rosy peaks of her nipples. How many other men had seen them? How few had actually tasted them on their tongue? And why, for the love of God, did a small part of him feel jealous of every single one of the bastards? It was startling to realize that even though he had never noticed Willa's apparent lack of friends, the same part of him now feeling jealousy had noticed and been pleased to never see her with a man.

It meant she was untouchable. Not just to Alex but to everyone. Like an actual goddess, beyond the reach of mere mortal men. Clearly, he was a fucking idiot. Of course she had been touched. Just not by him. And now Willa was watching him, obviously self-conscious and as nervous as the virgin goddess he'd been imagining her as, and words, *idiotic* reassurances, tumbled out of his mouth before he could think better of them.

"Does it help to know that whether you're in the water or out of it, I can still see everything?"

She glanced down at her body like she was really noticing it for the first time and he watched her eyes widen. She slapped one arm over her breasts and splashed him with the other. "No, that doesn't help. I knew you were looking but I didn't realize you could see *everything*." She splashed him again. "Pervert!"

A rough laugh forced its way from his throat even though his head was still spinning with his revelations. "I think that's actually pretty normal. A man sees a naked woman, he looks." His voice managed to sound so calm and reasonable he was almost able to convince himself it was the simple truth rather than just a facet of a much larger one—that it was specifically this woman and that's why he was looking.

Something touched his forearm and he jolted but when he glanced down, it was just one of Willa's frazzled curls floating toward him. It swayed and brushed against him like the most tentative of caresses and, unable to stop himself, he grabbed the wayward lock of hair and stroked it through the water. As it went smooth between his fingers, more truthful nonsense spilled out of him as if the words were similarly caught up in the current. "Does it help if I say you're lovely? That you look like a fucking siren, standing here beneath this waterfall, wrapped in all this long, incredible hair." It almost made him wish he was a painter, like this was how Willa was meant to be seen and just like yesterday on the beach, it felt like seeing her for the first time.

"Oh." He heard her breath rush out and looked up from the golden curl in his hand. Her dangerous lips were parted, her cheeks were flushed an even darker pink, and the pretty browns and greens of her hazel eyes had been swallowed up by her pupils. Wilhelmina Jones had never looked at Alex like this.

Like she wanted him.

Desire was an intoxicating rush through his blood. He could kiss her right now, *touch her,* and she might actually let him. For a moment he let himself imagine it, tasting the sharp edges of that maddening Cupid's bow, smoothing it with his tongue before diving into her depths.

But if he kissed her now, as soon as it was over and the lust cleared, she would take it as proof that every horrible thing she had ever said about him was true. That he was just a man who took any opportunity to get laid and didn't even really know the women he slept with. She would be right. Because he didn't really know Willa. And if he kissed her now, he never would. She would never trust him again, not really. If he kissed her now, she would never open up enough for him to discover the pearls he suspected were hidden inside her.

He remembered the way she had looked telling him she didn't know how to be a person. Resigned. Lost...lonely. She may be looking at him like she wanted him now but what she *needed* was a friend. And maybe, if they were actually going to survive here, that's what he needed too, much more than he needed a quick, too-complicated fuck they would likely both regret. So he stepped back.

"On your back, Willa," he ordered and watched goosebumps rise on her arms. Her fingers flexed briefly against her chest and she closed her eyes, like she was pulling herself back from the opposing cliffs they had just balanced on. When she re-opened them, the old Willa was back, cool and remote as she spun her legs up and stretched out, her arms slowly waving at her sides to help keep her body afloat. Her hair caught the current and streamed around his torso, masses of messy blonde curls teasing against his skin like the kiss, the jump, he hadn't taken.

With one hand he reached under the water and gripped the nape of her neck to hold her in place and with the other he started to gently comb through the tangled strands. Willa closed her eyes, as if she couldn't believe this was happening and Alex was glad for the privacy. He couldn't either. As he dragged his fingers through her hair, he felt little pieces of his composure dissolving, just like the knots under his fingers. He'd had fantasies about this, being draped in Willa's cloud of curls. He had told himself they weren't about her, not really, just that he had never seen hair like hers before.

He'd been a damn liar, even if it was only to himself.

He thought about the first time he met her, remembering now the instant attraction. It was a feeling he buried deep after things between them had twisted and gone wrong. Looking down at Willa now, her face slowly relaxing, her lips going soft and inviting, he finally let himself wonder what happened.

Remembering the first dismissive scowl she'd given him made the hand on the back of her neck flex involuntarily. She let out a tiny moan, almost inaudible beneath the sound of the waterfall, but it still sent shockwaves through him. His muscles tensed almost to the point of pain and it was a struggle to keep the hand in her hair from turning into a fist and yanking her up for the kiss he had held back. Blowing out a hard breath, he reminded himself sex would ruin any chances of friendship and being friends with Willa was not only important for their survival, it was important for keeping her as a fixed point in his world.

If Willa was like the moon, Alex knew he was a mere shooting star: pretty enough but not something anyone expected to last. Willa wasn't wrong about him. She was rarely wrong about anything. Which meant Alex would never be good enough for anything more than a hot fuck and bit of fun. Maybe that was the reason she had disliked him at first sight—she had recognized him as a lesser body: unworthy of someone so clearly divine. Which was why he would ignore the heat burning beneath his skin and be happy to be friends, that at least was something he knew he could do.

He gave a final long stroke of his hand around the length of her hair, the seventy-five plus centimeters of it waving through the water like spilled honey, smooth and golden and glinting in the sunlight. So lovely and not for him.

"Willa, I think it's done," he said and her eyes fluttered halfway open.

"Mmm, are you sure? I think I still feel a twig somewhere."

He bit back a groan. If he had the choice and he thought he could survive the ache in his balls, he would gladly spend hours just like this. Unfortunately, they had other things they needed to do. He gave her neck another little squeeze, loving and hating the way she sighed in response, and nudged her upright.

"Come on. Up, ya bludger. Why don't you take your robe to the beach and dry off in private. I'm going to wash my shorts and then I'll join you. We need to get started on the next stage of being lost on a desert island."

She sighed deeply and slowly let her legs drop so she was standing again.

"Right. Mollusks."

"We'll lunch like those snobby assholes with yachts." He gave her another small push. "Go. I'll be right behind you."

"Alright, alright, I'm going. No need to shove." She began wading toward the edge of the river, water sluicing down her back and shoulders and catching the morning light like hundreds of tiny diamonds. His cock got even harder. Strewth, he needed her to leave faster. Or walk slower. He couldn't decide. She stopped when only the tips of her hair were still touching the water, right above where the glorious curve of her ass began, and threw a glare over her shoulder.

"Well, turn around!"

Sighing deeply, he turned and faced the other direction, imagining what he was missing as she splashed onto the bank. He waited, listening to her scuffling on the rocks, and then it went quiet.

"Willa?"

Nothing. He whipped around and just managed to catch a glimpse of her hair disappearing into the trees. "Damnit, Willa." He called after her, "Don't even think about going into the ocean without me!"

Infuriating woman.

It was a good thing that despite her tendency to faint, she was certainly no man's damsel. He smiled a bit, thinking about her "Newtonian Moment" and their "castle" while he drank from the waterfall and pulled off his shorts. As he gave them the same kind of scrub Willa had given her shirt, he couldn't stop his brain from remembering the way she had looked, stretched out on top of the water, the pale triangles of skin from her bikini highlighting all the parts of her body he most wanted to taste. Maybe it was a good thing she was so insistent about being covered or he was likely to lose his goddamn mind before they were rescued.

He was up and out of the water in minutes and then he was faced with a choice. Walk out to the beach naked and still hard, go still hard and wearing his wet shorts, or wank himself off, go naked, and hope his shorts dried before it became a problem again. He really didn't want to walk around in wet shorts and he was comfortable with being naked but he didn't want to make Willa uncomfortable with his rudely horny prick.

Wanking it was.

Leaving his shorts by the clothes Willa had forgotten, Alex stepped into the forest, just off the path they'd made. He braced one hand against a tree and wrapped the other around his cock and squeezed.

"Fuck," the curse ground out of him, every nerve inside his body already fanned to blazing. Just because he wasn't going to act on his attraction to Willa didn't mean he could shut down his body's reaction to being near her, touching her. It was an incredibly good thing she'd actually played along and demanded to be the big spoon or she would have felt his erection pressing against her as they fell asleep.

He spit into his hand and stroked himself and pleasure was a hot ache building at the base of his spine. He groaned, closing his eyes and letting his head fall back. He pictured that pretty ass, round and high like a peach, imagined pressing against it with his fingers, watching the soft, full flesh give as he thrust inside her. He imagined the sounds she would make when he bit her just there, on that curve where the skin changed from the soft creamy white covered by her bathing suit to ripe and gold. His breathing picked up, his hand against the tree fisted and the hand moving up and down his cock squeezed tighter and moved faster.

"Fuck, Willa," he moaned and now she was on her knees, that sharp, full, siren's call of a mouth swallowing his length down deep until he was drowning in her. Her hair was wrapped like rope around his fist, the tug of it bringing her eyes to half-mast, lids heavy with desire as she looked up at him the way she had for that one brief moment in the pool—like she was finally actually seeing *him*, Alex, and he was all she had ever wanted. That was what finally pushed him over the edge and sent all the heat and pressure hurtling through his body. He came hard, with her name on his lips, relieved but far from satisfied.

He stood and waited for the blood to stop rushing in his ears and for his breathing to even out. When he joined her on the beach, he would act normal, they would argue and banter, and maybe get closer to being friends, and Alex would keep himself and his dick under control. She would never know what he had just done and he would focus on the important things, like food and fire, the things necessary for their survival.

Even if it killed him.

When Alex got to the beach, he found Willa facing the waves, her toes teasing the surf. She was wearing her robe, her hands planted on her hips, her shoulders rising rapidly up and down. Fuck, was she crying? Guilt at taking even a few minutes to stroke himself off when she was out here alone nicked at his insides, leaving him feeling wrecked and bloody. It wouldn't happen again. He hurried across the sand toward her.

"Willa, Are you okay?"

She whipped around, obviously surprised, her hand pressing against her chest as she struggled to breathe.

"Are you having a panic attack?" he asked a little frantically. He framed her face with his hands and tilted it up so he could see her expression better which meant he also saw the exact moment she registered he was naked. Her eyes went comically wide before she abruptly jerked out of his hold and turned back around.

"I'm fine," she said breathlessly, "It's not a panic attack. I just, uh, saw something on the water, and ran down the beach to see if it was a boat but it was just some dolphins. I mean it wasn't 'just' dolphins, when are dolphins 'just' anything but spectacular but you know what I mean."

"Right. Dolphins," said Alex, as if that made perfect sense. His racing heart began to slow and he wondered if Willa knew she was a terrible liar. He guessed it wasn't something she did very often. She was always brutally, even aggressively honest with him. "So, you're okay?" he asked, just to be sure.

She nodded vigorously. "Yup, yup. Never been better. Well, I mean I've been better because we're marooned here but you know what I mean. I'm fine, all things considered." She was actually babbling. Either she had been very naughty or the sight of Alex naked was making her nervous.

"Wilhelmina."

She didn't turn around and her reply was syrupy sweet.

"McBryde."

"Are you acting like this because you went in the water after I asked you not to or because I'm naked."

He watched her spine stiffen and her shoulders pitch as she exhaled one final deep breath. Then she slowly turned to face him.

"First of all, you didn't 'ask,' you ordered. Second, you are not in charge here, and third, I am not acting any kind of way. I am being totally normal."

"Willa. Did you go in the water?"

Her face screwed up in what he recognized as her "stubborn look." She crossed her arms, practically vibrating with indignation. "I am not answering that because, I repeat, you are not in charge. I'll remind you I have spent my entire life studying the ocean. I think I'm capable of going into it without dying."

Heat and frustration sank into Alex's bones, lighting up some of the darker, more primitive parts of him. She'd called him a caveman, and that's exactly what this need to protect her felt like. Instinctive. Imperative. And she wasn't the only one who was stubborn. Maintaining eye contact until the last moment, he leaned down, grabbed a handful of her hair and inhaled. She smelled like the fresh, crisp water of the river and the green, earthy leaves they'd slept on last night. She did not smell like the ocean.

"Thank you," he said quietly against her neck. "Thank you for not going in without me." He pulled back and found her staring at him, again with wide, disbelieving eyes, and he admitted this was not what controlling himself looked like. He let go of her hair and took another deliberate step back. "I think we should establish some safety rules for *both of us*. I would really like for neither of us to die here. You're right and I should have asked you not to go in the ocean instead of yelling at you like a dickhead. But can we agree right now, neither of us goes in the water unless the other person is on the beach?"

She bit her lip and it softened her hard expression. "I suppose that's...reasonable."

He pounced on that small capitulation and wasn't beneath offering further bribery.

"Come on, let's go sit on those rocks, I'll braid your hair so it's out of your way and less likely to get tangled and we can talk about other precautions we should take while we're here."

Looking bewildered now, she allowed him to tow her to a crescent-moon scattering of the few boulders on the beach that didn't look as if they had been carved and dropped by giants.

"You're going to braid my hair? How? And I don't have a hair tie."

"Well, I was planning to use my hands and don't worry about the hair tie, I've got it covered."

With his hands on her shoulders, he guided her down and then took up the spot behind her. Her hair was still wet but now that he was really looking, he could see little dried wisps starting to frizz, which meant grabbing handfuls of it and *smelling* her had been even further on the wrong side of necessary. As he carefully started separating it into sections he frowned, wondering what it was about Willa that always pushed him to the extreme edges of emotion. He also wondered if the feeling was mutual as she let out an annoyed huff.

"You know that's not what I meant. Obviously you're going to do it with your hands. Despite the noises Veronique was making back in your room, I don't think even your dick is that talented."

Another pop of frustration went off like a dying light bulb in his brain. Right. That was why. Her tempting mouth full of sharp teeth. He gave her hair a warning tug. "Wilhelmina."

There was a moment of silence and then, "I'm sorry." The apology burst out of her. "You're just so, so naked! It's putting me on edge and when I'm on edge I get mean."

Reigning in his feelings, Alex tried to actually hear what she was saying. Carefully, gently, he began weaving the sections of her hair together, starting at the front above her forehead and following the curve of her head. "Is this the modesty thing or is it something else?" He paused and an actual chill shivered through him, making his hands freeze. "I would never hurt you, Willa, if that's why it's making you nervous."

"Of course you wouldn't." The vehemence of her response brought warmth back to the beach. "I don't think you're a monster, Alex. I just never, for even a second, thought I would be seeing quite so much of you." She tried to turn her head and look at him over her shoulder but he kept a firm hold on her hair and she made a small pained "oof" before fixing her gaze back on the waves and continuing. "Don't you think it's weird? I know you never expected to see me naked, right? There's no coming back from that."

He certainly hadn't *expected* to see her naked but even before they'd been lost out here it would have been a lie to say he never imagined it. So, instead of lying, he focused on the hair in his hands—hair he had imagined but never believed he would touch—and gave an ambiguous grunt.

"Exactly," she said as if they were in agreement, "All we've ever done is fight. It's what we do. And the next time we're arguing, all I'll be able to think about is that you know what my nipples look like. It's a weird feeling and when I don't know how to deal with something I—I bite," she finished, her voice losing steam and ending on a resigned note.

Alex smoothed his hand down the thick braid he was slowly but surely wrapping around her head, his fingertips skimming over the bumps and dips, all the ups and downs. He thought about all the disparaging comments Willa had made over the years about his relationships, all those flashes of teeth. It had been a common theme in her insults and yet he never tried to avoid Willa when he was with a date. It might even have been the opposite. He frowned down at her hair, like spun gold in his hands, and something in his chest tightened.

It had definitely been the opposite.

He had sought her out. He had wanted her to see him with other women because he liked seeing the way her eyes sparked when she looked at him. Maybe his attraction hadn't been as buried as he thought. Maybe he had wanted her to be jealous. Maybe he had succeeded and his accusation about her being jealous had been right. Except now that he knew a little more about her, he didn't think Willa's jealousy had been over Alex, not really, it had been about the simple fact he wasn't alone and he was perpetually rubbing it in her face.

Christ, he was no better than a little boy pulling a girl's pigtails.

Guilt was twisting in his stomach and all he managed to force out was a simple, "Okay."

"Okay?" This time, she weathered the pull on her hair to turn and give him a disbelieving look. "That's it? Just, 'okay'?"

Alex gave himself a mental shake. If he didn't pull himself together, Willa was going to start wondering what was wrong with him. He forced himself to give her one of his old, irreverent smiles and tugged on her hair until she faced forward again. "That's it. The reality is we're here with limited resources. Nudity is bound to happen. As long as you don't feel unsafe, we can work through the social awkwardness. I'll try to be less naked and you can try to be less toothy. Okay?"

She hesitated and then, finally, "Okay."

He reached the beginning of the braid and it was like starting all over, weaving the rest of her hair into another braid that overlapped and wove through the existing loops. As his fingers worked, he thought about sharks, the way their only ability to explore new things was teeth first. It wasn't malicious, it was just how they had adapted to the world. Studying sharks required thick skin and patience. Maybe if that was the way he approached befriending Willa, they would both leave this island with a better understanding of each other.

He tucked the final lock of hair into her braid crown and his eyes focused on the newly exposed, delightfully soft looking curve of her neck. As long as he kept his own hungry impulses under control maybe they could figure out a way to coexist without bloodshed for the *next* five years.

"Alright. I think that should hold," he said, forcing himself to drop his hands from her hair.

"You're done?" She reached up and felt around, then turned and gave him a look of surprise. "How do you know how to do this kind of thing?" A sudden smile broke across her face and she laughed, "I know I can't see it, but it feels perfect."

He shrugged modestly and this time there was nothing forced about his smile. "I have three younger sisters. I was always at the back of the braid train."

"You have *how many* sisters?"

"Three. And each one was more trouble than the last. So, you see, I feel right at home with you." He managed to keep his tone light and some of the guilt and unease storming through his chest calmed when she laughed again.

"Braiding skills aside, after what I've learned about your surprising protective streak in the past twenty-four hours, I pity the little sisters that had to deal with you as their big brother," she teased back and when she smiled, Alex wasn't sure if the flash of white he caught was teeth or pearls.

Survival Tip #7

Channel inconvenient feelings into physical activity. If that doesn't work, just set something on fire.

After Alex finished braiding her hair, they decided the next best thing to do was construct a giant "HELP" sign for any potential passing planes. They managed to work well together...for about ten minutes. It turned out Alex was a bit of a perfectionist when it came to weaving and knotting leaves together so Willa left him to it. It wasn't as if there weren't plenty of other things to do and despite her calling him Dundee, nothing about Alex had ever really hinted at him possessing any wilderness survival skills. She actually suspected he might be a bit of a pampered city-boy—she had once heard him complain about having to go more than a mile to get decent take-out.

Willa on the other hand had grown up with not just one, but two career military parents and camping had been a fixture of their family vacations. Between the childhood campfires and two-minute glimpses of survivalist shows caught while flipping channels, the trick to making a fire without any sort of matches or flint had to be buried in her brain somewhere. At least, that's what she told herself as she wandered up and down the beach gathering tinder, an assortment of sticks and bark, as well as flat, sharp edged rocks and shells that looked like they could be used for cutting. Then she sat down within shouting distance of Alex and got to work.

She understood enough about building a fire to know the whole "rubbing two sticks together" thing was a frictional fallacy, at least the way it was often depicted in cartoons. She still had a vivid memory of being eight and trying to build a fire the way Ampersand the Viking had on one of her favorite cartoons and the sound of her mother's deep, disappointed sigh as she took the sticks away and told Willa it was an inefficient use of her energy. There was nothing General Jones hated more than inefficiency. The rest of the memory, where her mother actually tried to teach her the proper method, was dark and sticky, likely caught up in a s'mores fueled sugar buzz and the all too familiar shadow of shame at failing to meet her mother's same level of daily perfection. But today would be different. It had to be. There was more at risk now than just her mother's disappointment.

She flicked a glance over at Alex, diligently braiding palm fronds together, his fingers strong and sure the same way they had been while moving through her hair. The movements caused the muscles in his forearms to bunch and flex in a way that made her mouth go dry and other parts of her go wet. He was still so very, very naked. He bent over to adjust some leaves and the shell Willa had been clutching in one hand fractured, its sharp, broken points biting into her hand like a reprimand. She sucked in a breath and looked away quickly before he could turn around and treat her to another view that, like everything else on this island, was both beautiful and dangerous.

She forced herself to pick up a stick and, with perhaps more enthusiasm than was warranted, began to saw off the end with a piece of shale to create a flat end. Because that was how you made a fire. Not with two random sticks, but with pieces of wood that had been carved and worked into fitting together just right. They would have a fire today and maybe tomorrow they would be off this island and back in a world where everyone wore pants.

Her face went hot and she told herself it was from cutting the stick as she placed the newly blunt edge on a piece of driftwood, notching it in a hole to keep it steady. She spit on her hands and began to roll it between her palms, trying to generate enough heat to cast a spark. As her hands worked and heat built up against her skin, her mind slipped back to yesterday, to kissing Alex and the similarly warm feel of his shoulders beneath her palms.

She still didn't understand what had possessed her to do it and Alex hadn't brought it up. He probably didn't want to dwell on it any more than she did. It had been a terrible kiss. She rolled the stick faster, working her embarrassment into the wood and trying to force the memory out. She needed to focus on what she actually knew how to handle. Fire? Yes. Alex? Less and less by the minute.

A tendril of smoke appeared and despite having been the entire point, Willa was so surprised she dropped the stick and the smoke dissipated. The memory of the kiss similarly disappeared as she stared down at the wood beneath her hands. A slow, triumphant smile spread across her face. She could do this. The greatest discoveries usually began with something small and unimpressive.

"This time, I'll get it right," she said, determination like kindling burning away all the other confusing, awkward feelings she'd experienced since waking up on the beach yesterday. This was just another type of experiment and that was something she understood. And so, for the next hour she let herself be consumed, sitting on the edge of the forest, shaded by a palm tree, troubleshooting building a fire.

Eventually, Alex came over and gently touched her shoulder.

"I'm going to go look for mollusks but I'm not going to go out of sight of you and this part of the beach."

She didn't even look up. "Okay." The tiny ember she'd managed to create got stuck to the driftwood and went out. "Son of a bitch."

"Make sure you drink some water. Your face is turning red."

"Okay. Don't drink too much water and drown." She frowned down at the smoking bits of wood dust, annoyed with him for breaking her concentration. "And watch out for cone snails and crocodiles," she added sweetly and heard his grunt of amusement. He tweaked a curl that had broken loose at the nape of her neck, his rough fingers brushing across her skin and the gentle tug sent a frisson of awareness down her spine that proved fatal to her focus. It was such a small thing. Insignificant. Thoughtless. But that only made it worse. Willa could count on one hand the number of times Alex had touched her in the past five years and half of those were accidental. Now he touched her like he had a right.

Her stomach tightened with a low, deep ache, and the stick dropped from her fingers. She brought a hand to her neck and looked over her shoulder but he was already striding off down the beach and this time there was no tearing her eyes away. The golden ass was glorious when he moved, all toned back muscles and flexing thighs. Her body tensed as he waded into the water, acutely aware of *every* golden inch below his waist as it was slowly submerged and when he finally dove in the rest of the way, she didn't breathe again until she saw his head pop back up to the surface.

Being trapped in a survival situation was definitely having an effect on her equilibrium. Last night she felt guilty for hurting his feelings and today she was experiencing symptoms of sexual attraction. Toward *Alexander McBryde*. Maybe that terrible, irrational kiss had been some kind of trigger, like spring in the animal world setting off mating season. It wasn't about emotion; it was just pure animal instinct likely heightened by the primitive drive to survive.

Willa was *devolving*. And it was all Alex's fault.

She hadn't been prepared for how good it would feel to have his fingers combing through her hair or just how much the strong, steady pressure of his hand on the back of her neck would make her go warm and soft and *hungry*. She had walked out of the pool feeling languid and relaxed and so turned on her knees were actually weak. She was so discombobulated, she left behind her shirt and underwear. Which was why she had doubled back and how she saw Alex having an explicitly private moment. She should have turned around and left, should have run as far and fast as her legs could carry her. But she hadn't. Maybe she was a scoundrel too.

He had just been too goddamn beautiful. His head had been thrown back, his neck thick and strong—completely bitable—the muscles in his arms had bulged, his abdominals had tightened—completely lickable—as he stroked himself off. Willa had known she should back away quietly and let him come in peace (ha!) but then he *said her name*. He was thinking about her while he touched himself and she found that both odd and intensely flattering. Considering her own thoughts, it wasn't like she could begrudge him his fantasies but, still, that he bothered to have any about her at all was a mystery and Willa hated not knowing all the answers.

Because he wasn't actually interested in her. Data didn't lie and Willa had a lifetime of experiences, some painful, some humiliating, that proved she wasn't the kind of woman to inspire genuine interest. Even for the two men she'd had sex with, she had been a means to an end. Which was perhaps the answer to her present mystery. Maybe Alex was just one of those people who input the last person they saw naked while they gave in to nature. She was just a subject of convenience. There was a momentary tightening of her ribs around her lungs, a sensation that might have been disappointment once upon a time but now merely felt like another data point on a graph—impersonal for all that it was familiar.

She flicked another glance back at the ocean where she could just see Alex's broad shoulders and catch glimpses of gold as the sun caught and lightened strands of his hair. Maybe she would try things his way the next time she managed to find a private moment. Squirming a little, she turned deliberately back to her fire attempts. Private moments long enough to make that happen seemed unlikely given how unwilling Alex was for them to be separated for any real length of time. Which meant she was going to have to channel all this frustrated energy into something else.

She began to furiously roll the stick between her palms again. She would work this wood until it lit up and it would be enough satisfaction to get her through the day. And when, about thirty minutes later, she finally did manage to transfer a little glowing ember of wood dust to a dry bit of coconut husk and blow it into a flame, she yelled so loud in triumph that Alex came running.

"Willa! What—what's wrong?"

She stood up, the last of her awkwardness swallowed by the small fire beginning to blaze at her feet.

"I did it! I made fire!"

"I thought you were dying," he panted.

"Nope, just *killing it*. Suck it, Bear Gryllis! Stick that in your hat and wear it, Dundee!" Another delighted burst of laughter escaped her as she looked down at the steadily growing flames and then back at Alex. Now that he was no longer panting or panicked, a wondrous grin spread across his face.

"Sounds like you need your own show, or at least a movie," he teased.

"Woman vs. Wild." she agreed even if the idea of being on television made her want to vomit.

"I'd watch that show," he said.

"Everyone would. 'Woman vs. Wild' is a much better name for a wilderness survival show." Hope rose in her chest and she turned to face him, so overwhelmed she barely even noticed he was still naked and, because he was wet, actually *glistening* like some sort of well-hung sea God. "Alex, do you realize what this means? We can cook things. We can build a signal. Someone is bound to come close enough to see it at some point, right? This could get us out of here."

"We'll be rescued in no time," he said and despite the words coming out with his usual cocksure arrogance, Willa didn't feel the slightest urge to hit him. She just wanted to believe him because this time he was believing in her.

"We should celebrate," she said. It was something they had never done before. Even when their research paper had been featured at the International Symposium they hadn't exchanged so much as a congratulatory handshake. The hope inside her expanded, loosening the tension caging in her lungs and it felt like taking her first real breath since waking up on the beach yesterday.

"I've got just the thing," he said and flashed her that quick, devilish grin. He took off down the sand and Willa turned back to nursing her fire, relishing the heat on her face even as the sun beat down on her back. A big banana leaf plopped down beside her and she looked at the small collection of tightly closed, lumpy shells and then up at Alex in delight.

"Mollusks," she said happily, then she looked up and gasped, seeing what else he was holding. "And a lobster?"

"Our yacht will be pulling up any moment now," he said, clearly pleased with himself.

"If that actually happens, maybe I'll let you do a guest-spot on my show."

With the prospect of lobster for lunch, they worked together easily, building a makeshift grill over the fire using piled rocks and crisscrossing green branches. Then they sat back and watched it cook while they both worked at prying the oysters open with Willa's sharp rocks.

"It's a good thing neither of us is allergic to shellfish," she said as she slurped down an oyster. It tasted fresh and briny and the buttery smooth texture was a nice change from starfruit and bananas. It was too bad they hadn't found a lemon tree though. Or butter.

"Or a vegetarian," said Alex as he chewed. He swallowed and reached for another. "So, did your dad teach you how to build a fire? Isn't he a general in the military?"

Willa gave an amused half smile and jammed a rock into the hinge of a small oyster. "My dad was in the military but my mom is the general. Thinking it was my dad is a common, sexist assumption." She gave Alex a pointed look and watched him color slightly.

"Right, sorry." He deliberately turned toward the fire and poked the lobster with a stick. "I bet she would be proud of you though, for getting this going."

Willa's amusement went up in smoke and her fingers tightened painfully around the jagged edges of the oyster's shell. "Actually, she would probably be mortified it took me so long. General Jones is very into self-sufficiency." Which was probably why all their family vacations had been camping rather than trips to Disneyworld. Willa looked at the fire, which had taken over two hours to build and felt a little more of her joy evaporate. Fat lot of good that had been. She *still* would have preferred Disney. "Her motto is if you're not struggling, you're not learning," she added, watching flames lick at the lobster's claws and thinking about her parents.

Somehow, she didn't think this was quite the situation the General had imagined. Even in her strictest moments, Willa never doubted how much her mother loved her. Maura Jones was probably sick with worry right now for her only child. Willa couldn't even think about her dad without her throat closing and heat pressing behind her eyes. This wasn't a lesson any of them should have had to learn.

She swallowed hard, the pressure behind her eyes growing but then Alex's tightly muscled bicep passed in front of her and she locked the feelings down, remembering who she was with. Suddenly bursting into tears because she was thinking about her parents was the last thing she wanted. Alex had already seen far too much emotion from her in the past few days.

"Did you like growing up with two parents in the military?" he asked, giving the lobster a harder poke and making Willa wince.

"It was interesting, I guess," she paused, using the cover of trying to open the stubborn oyster in her hand to take a minute and decide what was innocuous enough to share. "I've lived in places all over the world and I suppose I got a fairly good, if sometimes unorthodox, education. I know how to shoot a rifle and speak enough languages to get me around most restaurants or airports." She finally managed to yank the two halves of the shell apart but one of them shattered in the process, scattering broken pieces all over her lap and hands. She scowled at the mess.

"But?" She lifted her head and found him looking at her far too intently. She wished they had never started this conversation.

"Is the lobster ready yet?" she asked instead of answering. He didn't even glance at it.

"It needs a few more minutes. Tell me what the problem was with growing up traveling around the world and learning to shoot guns, which honestly sounds very American."

"What makes you think there was a problem?"

"That you're avoiding answering," he said, and his genuine tone of interest sent her heart racing. It was too much, too *close*. The fire was suddenly overwhelmingly hot, making her feel sweaty and itchy all over. Why was he asking her all of this? Why did it matter? She could feel his eyes on her, the sharp, critical eyes of a man who spent his life observing and dissecting the world around him. Needing him to look away, panic caused some of the truth to spill out of her, as if she could prove once and for all it wasn't really that interesting.

"There's nothing profound here, Alex. It's just like I told you yesterday, it wasn't the best upbringing for fostering social skills. You move all the time, sometimes I would get bounced between my parents if one was deployed and the other wasn't, which meant I was never in one place long enough to get to know anyone past that initial awkward stage. Making friends is already hard but making friends when you're a weird, six-foot-tall teenage girl who spends all her time talking about whales and sea urchins means it's almost impossible." Her mouth twisted into a bitter smile. "Some of the places we lived, it was odd enough to see a foreigner but seeing someone like me? Stretched out, all gangly limbs and bright blonde hair? I spent a lot of my adolescence getting looked at like I was a freak."

"And being a teenager is already rough," said Alex but his tone was dispassionate, like he was simply making another observation and Willa was glad. Any sign of pity and she would have to drag him into the ocean and drown him.

Striving for the same level of nonchalance, she shrugged and picked up another oyster, ignoring the slight tremor in her hands. "I learned to survive in a variety of environments so I guess that's something. Although I clearly missed learning how to build a fire."

"But you figured it out."

"You adapt or die," she said, still struggling to keep her tone light. Alex didn't need to know how real the words felt, how much her childhood had felt like a constant battle to avoid being torn into pieces by her peers. She rose to her knees and peered at the lobster, which was now a bright, *distracting* looking red. "I think it's ready."

To Willa's extreme relief, Alex let the subject drop as they worked together to pull the sticks off the fire and lower the lobster to the banana leaf. Her heartbeat returned to normal and her hands were no longer shaking by the time it cooled and they were able to begin the work-intensive process of smashing open the claws and yanking out the contents of the tail.

"I know we're in survival-mode but there is something primitively satisfying about all of this," said Willa as she used one of the lobster's legs to scrape meat out of the claw. "Like when you dig into a rotisserie chicken with your fingers instead of using a fork and knife."

Alex gave her an amused look. "I haven't had that particular experience, but I agree there is something satisfying about catching and cooking your own food."

"Oh? Does that mean you didn't grow up catching and eating iguanas or snakes or whatever?"

"Is your only point of reference for life in Australia *Crocodile Dundee*?" he asked exasperatedly.

"Not at all." She grinned, glad to be back on safer ground. "I also saw *Finding Nemo*."

"Which, if you ignore the plot, is probably a more accurate portrayal of what my life was like. I grew up in Melbourne. I went to school, helped take care of my sisters, played rugby. There were no iguanas." He paused and popped a bite of lobster in his mouth and for a moment she was completely distracted by the look on his face. His eyes closed, his head dropped back, and he gave a throaty little moan of appreciation. He wore a very similar look when his hand was wrapped around his cock. She watched his throat work as he swallowed and felt her pulse pick up. Then he opened his eyes and looked right at her with a pleased, self-satisfied smirk and she could imagine him looking up at her just like that from between her thighs.

"So good," he said. Flicking a glance at her hands, which were covered in bits of shell, he leaned over and raised a piece to her mouth. "Here, try."

She opened her lips and took it without thinking. His fingers brushed her bottom lip as he pulled away and her body flashed hot. He was right. It was delicious. Feeling a bit dazed, she continued to stare at him as she chewed, a distant part of her mind noting that her symptoms of arousal were getting worse. She hoped it didn't prove fatal.

"Say, 'thank you, Alex,'" he teased and some of her lustful fog cleared. She realized she was leaning toward him and pulled back, shooting him a superior look.

"Excuse you, I built the fire." She gestured between them, flinging fragments of lobster claw into the flames. "This was a team effort."

Laughing, he sat back and the old, playful spark was back in his eyes, "I've just never heard you say it. It was worth a shot."

"I've said thank you," she said defensively.

He shook his head. "Never, not once. 'Please' is also a rare event with you."

"What, are you keeping count? Do you have some kind of manners kink?"

"Manners and classical art, that's me," he murmured and took another piece of lobster. She ignored that last enigmatic comment and focused on his accusation. She had thanked him for saving her life.

Hadn't she?

Wait, *hadn't she?* She thought back through every strange, infuriating, and mortifying experience they had shared yesterday and realized he was right.

Shit.

"I'm not thanking you for the lobster," she said stubbornly. "But I should have thanked you for saving my life." Taking a deep, fortifying breath, she met his eyes. "Thank you for coming after me, Alex," her voice softened, "No one has ever done anything like that for me."

There was a beat of quiet while he held her gaze and for just a single moment, she thought his eyes darkened and flickered toward her mouth but before she could be sure, a smile spread over his radioactively handsome face. "Have you needed a lot of saving in the past?"

Annoyed with herself, Alex's smirk proved an effective match—her temper sparked. Of course he would make a joke out of the first—and last — thank-you she had ever given him. "Jesus, McBryde, do you have to be such a jerk all the time? I was trying to be sincere."

"I know. It's a good look on you." His eyes went warm and he leaned forward again, tweaking another escaped curl. Just like before, she felt the small, intimate gesture all the way down to her toes and goosebumps rose up on her arms. "I couldn't let you drown. The world's just brighter with you in it, Wilhelmina."

This time it wasn't attraction that made her go a little breathless.

Her whole body tensed as the words set off a dangerous swirl of emotions inside her. They were sweet on her tongue and she had been right about the smallest taste of affection leaving her wanting. She tried to pull back, tried to fight her way to safe, familiar ground and ignore the sense of longing suddenly tugging at her.

"Even if you are still a dag," he added with perfect timing, giving her something to latch on to, another small annoyance she could use to bolster herself above the tide of feeling.

"I am not a dag." She chucked an empty oyster shell at him. "Pinched apart by a thousand spider crabs."

"Is too good a death for me?" he finished with a grin. He picked up the jagged edge of the lobster claw and looked at it thoughtfully. "Seems like a slow way to die."

"Entertainment for days," she agreed.

"Still probably better than being taken out by a snail. More manly."

"Unless they go for the sensitive bits first," she said and was amused to see his hand move reflexively to cover his (still naked) groin.

"You're a vicious woman."

"I did warn you. But don't worry, when we get to the final stage of being marooned on a desert island, I'll be kind and make sure your death is quick and manly. It can be a final thank you for saving me."

"Who says I won't be the one eating you, love?" The threat was delivered in a husky purr and despite the way it shivered through her, it was the reminder she needed. She couldn't count the number of times she'd heard Alex call a woman "love." *He only knows how to be a flirt.* Even when he was sweet, it didn't mean anything.

She picked up another bite of lobster and put it in her mouth, determined to overpower any traces of longing or affection. She was *not* falling for any of Alexander McBryde's tricks. She was stronger than that. Stronger than him. She would not be his convenient, desert island stand-in, the woman he screwed because there was no one else around. She may be stranded with the captain of the S.S. Fuckboy but she wasn't going to let him steer her into shallow waters.

She gave him a fierce, vicious little smile and every word dripping in honey,

"In your dreams, McBryde."

Survival Tip #8

If you hear a mysterious sound in the middle of the night...no you didn't.

Willa was tied to a tree. The soft cotton of her robe's belt looped around her wrists and secured to a branch above her head, leaving her stretched out and vulnerable. Her clothes were gone but her hair was free, cascading over her shoulders, teasing the tips of her breasts and tickling the sides of her waist. She struggled and squirmed, trying to get free but she was caught and the thrill of it was a terrifying, electric hum beneath her skin. She heard Alex's voice in her ear, low and deep, sliding through her and settling hotly between her thighs.

"Look at you Willa, like a fucking siren, practically demanding my hands."

She felt them even if she couldn't see them, gliding up from her hips, stroking the sensitive curve of her breasts before landing on the back of her neck. She moaned when he tugged her hair. "Will you take me deep, Willa? Will you let me sink into that hot, wet pussy until we're both drowning in pleasure? Will you let me fuck you until you're singing my name?"

Then he was in front of her, his full mouth bent in one of those devilish grins, his eyes the tempting, forbidden gold of pirate treasure.

He was looking at her like he needed her to live, like his next breath waited just beyond her lips. His erection filled the space between them. Big, God he was big, just like he'd said, and golden and Willa was shocked by how much she wanted it, wanted him. She whimpered and his eyes flared.

"Say yes, Willa. Say 'yes, please, Alex' and I'll show you exactly how talented my cock is. Say it."

She shook her head. He wasn't winning that easily. She wouldn't beg.

"Always so stubborn." His mouth was at her throat, hot words on hot skin, leaving her blazing. He licked down to her breasts. His teeth were a sharp bite against her nipple but then he soothed it with a lick of his tongue. "So sweet." He moved to the other breast and made her gasp. "I know something sweeter."

He was on his knees, looking up at her, pleased and self-satisfied. "I promised I would eat you first." His tongue dragged through her folds, circling her clit. He made a deep, satisfied humming sound and she felt it everywhere.

"Oh my God," she moaned, straining her hips, needing more, so much more.

She felt his mouth move against her, saw the challenge in his eyes as he looked up at her, "Say thank you, Wilhelmina."

"More," she demanded. "Alex I need—" His tongue moved again and the words caught around a moan.

"You didn't say please." He sucked her clit and she could feel her orgasm poised on the tip of his tongue, just out of reach. "Or thank you."

She heard leaves rustling and footsteps approaching. Oh God, there was someone here. They had to hurry—

Willa woke up on the verge of coming.

Gasping and trembling it took a full minute for her to realize it had been a dream. At some point in the night, she and Alex had rolled over so she was again wrapped around him like a particularly horny snake, her pelvis flush against his hip like she had been grinding on him. She bit her lip, fighting back a moan. She was so close. So wet and aroused it was a struggle not to move, not to rub herself against him just a little more, a little harder and release the tension poised between her legs like a rattler about to strike. Maybe oysters and lobster really were an aphrodisiac. Or maybe this was one of the early stages of fatal attraction. Or it was the last. Because no matter what had triggered the dream, if she had woken

Alex up with her unconscious desperation, she would be walking into the sea and never walking out.

"Oh God," she whispered, "Please still be asleep." Too afraid to actually look, she braced herself and said his name quietly, "Alex?"

He didn't respond and his breathing didn't change, his chest still rising deep and even beneath her cheek. She tried one more time, "Alex, are you awake?"

He let out a soft, breathy snore and she relaxed. He was still asleep. Which explained why his hand was back on her butt. Although considering she had been using him as her own personal sexy scratching post, she had probably lost any moral high ground. She let his hand stay where it was and tried to ignore the low, persistent ache still throbbing between her legs.

Outside it was full dark, which meant several more hours of either lying here in sexual frustration or trying to fall back asleep and hoping for chaste dreams. She honestly couldn't believe she'd been so betrayed by her subconscious. She closed her eyes and imagined deliberately cold, unsexy thoughts, like snow down her snow pants and the librarian with notoriously bad breath who worked in the basement of the library. She had almost dropped back off when she heard it again—the sound she now realized had woken her up in the first place. More than the sound of leaves rustling in the breeze, from outside their tent, Willa heard the sound of a large body passing through the woods and a sudden chill shivered down her spine.

It didn't sound like an animal.

It sounded like footsteps.

Soft and distant but they were still definitely footsteps, walking in what sounded like the damp, spongy creak of wet boots. Her eyes shot back open. Straining her ears, she tried to determine if the sound was real or if her mind was playing tricks on her.

Return.

The word whispered like an icy breath against her ear and she turned her head sharply to see if it was Alex who had spoken but his eyes were still closed, his body still loose and relaxed beneath hers. Her skin prickled and a flicker of fear settled low in her belly. She heard the feet take another step followed by the clinking sound of metal and her head whipped back in the direction of the tent's opening. A dash of hope joined the fear. There *was* someone else on the island.

"Alex," she hissed, "Alex, wake up. There's someone outside. There's someone here."

When neither Alex nor the arm wrapped around her waist moved, Willa poked him hard in the chest. "Alex, wake up or I'm going to look without you."

His face was just visible in the dim glow from the dying fire outside their tent and she saw his eyes open into narrow slits as the arm around her waist tightened. "Willa, there is no one outside. Go back to sleep."

She wiggled against him, a spark of pleasure shooting through her as her still sensitized clit brushed over the ridge of his hip, her breath caught but she didn't stop trying to break away until she managed to sit up. "Alex, really. I heard footsteps and something that sounded like metal." She started crawling toward the entrance of the tent but he groaned and reached out, snagging her wrist.

"Willa, we've already established there's no one else on the island and even if there was a rescue boat, they wouldn't come looking for us at night. Now come lay back down, please."

She hesitated. He was right. She knew he was right...but she also knew she had heard something. "But—"

"It was probably just an animal, possum, or a dream," he yawned sleepily and tugged at her, encouraging her to lay back down beside him. She went, slowly, still listening hard for the sound of waterlogged shoes. Her cheek was back on his chest and she felt him sigh contentedly. "We'll check for tracks in the morning, 'kay?" his voice was a rumbly murmur, a clear sign he was already half-asleep. He stroked a soothing hand down her back before settling it in its vacated spot on her butt.

"Alex," she whispered, exasperated.

"Mmm," he sighed and then his breathing deepened again and he was out.

"You really are a scoundrel," she muttered but she let his hand stay. For a long time, she lay there, listening to the sounds of the rainforest and Alex's deep, steady breathing. She waited, her ears perked for the sound of footsteps but after a long time of nothing she eventually fell back asleep.

Willa was alone when she woke up the next morning and she told herself very sternly she wasn't disappointed. After her dreams, she should be relieved. She couldn't bring herself to even think what Alex would have said if he'd woken up to find her panting and rubbing herself all over him. Likely he would never let her live it down and Willa already hated herself enough. She hadn't been able to suppress these new, mortifyingly lustful impulses for a single damn day.

Groaning, she rolled onto her back and stared at the branches and moss over her head. This shouldn't be so difficult. Willa couldn't even remember the last time she had a crush. Not that she had one now. She didn't. This was attraction—instinctual, *animal*. It had nothing to do with higher thought or emotion...but she couldn't remember the last time she felt attracted to someone either. It was another thing that had always made her feel different from her peers. Humans talked about sex constantly and she had very little interest—or the necessary experience— to contribute to the conversation. It was a good thing she had woken up before she made a complete fool of herself. If she had been asleep for even a little longer...Willa bolted upright. The footsteps!

Despite waking up horny and confused, she still didn't believe she had dreamed or imagined the sound of someone walking through the trees. Maybe that was where Alex was now! Down at the beach, leading a bunch of rescuers to their campsite.

Or down at the beach, preparing to shove off without her.

Frowning, she began crawling out of the tent, moving so quickly she didn't see the leaf piled with fruit until she put her hand down and squished a banana. Oh. He had brought her breakfast. She instantly felt guilty for thinking he might try and leave her here. Sitting back on her heels, she stared down at the offering of food and that sweet taste was back on her tongue. This felt too much like caring, like affection.

"God damnit," she whispered. This was not a version of Alex she knew how to handle. Asshole Alex and Flirtatious Alex were easy to defend against, she had spent the last five years battling one and disparaging the other. This though, this new, Caring Alex was dangerous.

"It's about time you woke up, ya bludger."

Willa looked up at the sound of Alex's cheerful voice and felt a moment of complete despair. Day Three in survival mode and he only looked more rugged and delicious. The rough start to a beard was filling in along his jaw and around his mouth, framing it like a spotlight on temptation. Oh God, she had *dreamed* about that mouth. Begged for it. She felt her cheeks heating. Between last night's dreams and the reality of the fruit in front of her, she was questioning whether or not she would have been better off drowning. Her ghost could have spent eternity hanging out with whales and exploring shipwrecks, which was really all she had ever wanted anyway.

"You were restless last night, are you feeling okay this morning?"

She froze, fear like deep-sea pressure compressed her limbs and robbed her brain of thought. Did he know? She checked his smile for any trace of mocking but he merely looked concerned. The pressure eased.

"Yeah, I think I'm just stressed." That was an understatement. "Thank you for bringing me breakfast."

"My second thank you in two days. Are you sure you're feeling okay?"

"I might be better if I wasn't stuck on this island with a morning person," she said grumpily, crawling the rest of the way out of the tent and settling in front of the small fire he'd built up.

"I'm not really a morning person." He sat down next to her and casually snagged a banana. "I'm more of an anytime person. I'm just a fucking delight all the time."

She rolled her eyes and reached for a starfruit. "Right. That's why we've been such good friends all these years."

His smile faded a little. "Willa—"

She cut him off, uninterested in actually exploring that line of conversation. "How long have you been awake? Have you been to the beach? Any signs of our visitor from last night?"

The last traces of his good humor disappeared. "No. Willa, are you sure it wasn't a dream? There was nothing on the beach this morning and I searched the trees around the campsite but there wasn't so much as a leaf out of place."

"Alex, I know what I heard."

"I know but you said yourself you're stressed. Isn't it possible you imagined it? The island is not that big. If someone was here, we would have found some trace of them by now."

Again, Willa knew he was right but another part of her insisted she had heard footsteps and the unmistakable sound of metal clinking against metal. But with no way to prove it, arguing wasn't going to get them anywhere but annoyed with each other, so she sighed and let it go.

"Maybe it is just stress," she said finally. "Or wishful thinking."

"Hey," Alex brushed his fingers gently, reassuringly against her knee. "We've made it three days without killing each other and have done a pretty bang up job of taking care of ourselves. We'll get through this. If we keep the fires lit, someone is bound to notice us."

She nodded, her throat feeling tight which only made things worse. She was used to being in control. She lived her life with a plan, kept things neatly ordered and people classified to strict categories: parent, professor, student, colleague, rival. Here, the taxonomy she'd carefully constructed didn't exist and she'd experienced more emotion in the past three days than she had in the past three years. It was turning her into a wreck.

Beside her, Alex launched himself abruptly to his feet and she looked up at him, surprised and a little lost. He held out a hand to help her up and his cheerful smile was back in place.

"Come on, Wilhelmina, let's go to the river and deal with all that hair of yours, then we'll go out and see what else we can find to eat. I was thinking we might try and make a spear of some kind to help us catch fish, what do you think?"

Looking at Alex with his broad, easy smile, Willa realized fighting to keep her strict classifications in place was only going to make things more confusing. She needed a new category. Maybe, *maybe* if she tried thinking of Alex as a friend, her body would be less likely to try and think of him as anything else. Maybe the way to get her feelings under control was to impose a new order, a new routine. Starting with letting him comb out her hair in the river. Like a friend.

She reached out and took his hand.

"I think it sounds like a plan."

Over the next few days, Alex and Willa fell into a comfortable pattern. In the morning they would wake up, eat a breakfast consisting of whatever fruit they had managed to forage the evening before, and then go bathe in the river. Alex would comb out her hair and then, by unspoken agreement, she would head to the beach to build up the signal fire and dry off alone and Alex would go back to camp to dry off, bank the fire, and make little patches and adjustments to their campsite. The important part was both of them had privacy and Willa tried very hard not to speculate about what Alex was doing with his. Eventually he would join her on the beach and they would both scour the shore and nearby reefs looking for lunch before the sun climbed too high and they had to retreat beneath the trees to avoid getting burned.

Despite it being necessary for survival, Willa actually found herself enjoying their hunt for edible creatures. The sea life around the island was vibrant and beautiful and while she noted the unfortunate effects of coral bleaching even here, she was pleased every time she came across new, healthy outcroppings. If she hadn't been required to participate in actually killing the various crabs, lobster, and occasional fish they managed to catch, she might have been able to pretend this was just another part of their research trip.

In the afternoons they went exploring. They had found some interesting tracks on the beach, clear animal footprints with a heavy almost wavy line running between them that looked like part of the animal's body had been dragged. Willa was convinced it was one of the rare giant tortoises that could still be found in the Seychelles but Alex argued they were only found in the southwest Aldabra group of islands and the tracks were more likely made by a sea turtle. Before they had been stranded, this on-going debate would have been a much more heated source of contention but the friendly truce that had settled between them meant that more often than not, Willa found herself smiling as they both adamantly made their arguments.

Aside from the fact they had yet to see a single plane or boat, the only truly disheartening thing to happen was the rain. For three days it had forced them back to their campsite early in the evening and made it difficult to keep a signal fire going at night. It also meant Willa spent a lot more time curled up against Alex's big, warm body than she would have liked. So far, she had avoided having any more blisteringly sexy dreams but given the deep, nagging tension that still caught her at weird moments, like when he was combing out her hair in the morning or when he smiled at her with that cocky, devilish grin during their debates, she knew it was only a matter of time before the tension had to be released.

Which was perhaps why she was still awake now even though they had technically gone to bed hours ago. Alex's breathing was deep and even in front of her, his back brushing against her breasts with every inhale. Tonight had been another night where she demanded to be the big spoon because she hadn't wanted to risk feeling his dick pressing into her backside when she was already wound so tight. Alex, she had learned, was a very aggressive cuddler.

Whenever he was the big spoon, he made sure there was very little space between their bodies and there was no getting out from under his arm without a show of brute force on Willa's part. Like he really was a caveman. It was a pain in the butt when she needed to get up and pee. It was also, well, nice. She had never been held like that by anyone.

Just as long as she didn't get used to it.

Frowning at the thought, Willa snuggled closer to Alex, her arm tightening around his chest and she heard him mutter something in his sleep. Interested in what a man like Alex dreamed about, she lifted her head, trying to hear better and heard another sound entirely.

Just like the other night, faint but unmistakable, was the soft, steady thump of someone walking through the trees.

Thud. Clink. Thud thud.

There was *definitely* something out there and this time she was going to find out what it was. Then she could prove to Alex she hadn't imagined anything and, more importantly, that she had been right. Carefully withdrawing her arm from around him, she wiggled out of the tent. When she was finally free, she stood up, tilted her head and listened.

Thud. Thud. Clink. A soft groan.

It was coming from the river.

The rain had stopped and Willa crept through the forest as quietly as possible, the moon giving just enough light for her to pick her way carefully toward the waterfall. She stopped at the edge of the trees, just beyond where a thick carpet of moss led down to the river's edge. The sound was louder here and unmistakable. Feet, thumping into mud with a heavy, slightly uneven tread. The clank of metal shifting. The squelch of shoes that had gotten wet. Willa heard it but she couldn't see anything.

An abrupt chill made goosebumps rise on her arms. The hair at the base of her neck prickled. Emotions suddenly ripped through her, sending her heart racing and making her lungs go cold and tight. It wasn't fear. It was something worse. Feelings that didn't belong to her: loss and dread and regret so bitter it made her lips go numb.

This was a mistake. She shouldn't have ventured out at night alone. She should have woken Alex.

Should never have taken what didn't belong to me.

The thought crept through her brain like an icy mist. It didn't make sense and it left her freezing. She wanted to run, to escape. Alex would be warm. He would hold her. She could forget this ever happened. She tensed to run.

She couldn't move.

Frozen in place, barely able to breath, unable to scream, she watched as a figure shimmered into view by the bend in the river. It looked like a reflection, like moonlight on water, breaking apart and coming back together in glimmering pulses. It hovered near the tree line and then began moving closer.

Thud. Clink. Thud thud. Groan.

It moved down the riverbank haltingly, like it was weighed down by something incredibly heavy. With each step it took closer to Willa, the dread, the regret she felt intensified. She was shaking with it, practically sick with it.

Return. Must return.

They weren't her thoughts but they still echoed through her. Cold. Darkest night of winter cold. Bottom of the ocean cold. *A pirate's black heart cold.*

There was a scream trapped in her chest but not enough air in her lungs to set it free. As the figure passed in front of her, she got the impression of a man wearing a big, plumed hat and a billowing coat, dragging a padlocked trunk behind him.

Thud. Clink. Thud thud. Groan.

It moved to the edge of the pool, close to where the water splashed and jumped at the base of the waterfall. Then it stopped. If it had been corporeal, Willa imagined she would have heard the swish of fabric as it turned and looked deliberately at her.

Return.

The thought was an icicle driving through her brain. If she could move move, she would have grabbed her head and sobbed. Their eyes met and she saw a face, bearded and scarred with eyes that glowed like embers drawn straight from hell.

Return!

She whimpered, unable to look away as it stepped back into the waterfall. It watched her until the force of the water sent it scattering, the bright, foggy pieces dissolving into nothing more than strands of moonlight floating down the river. The pressing sense of dread and regret faded, leaving Willa hollowed out and empty.

Collapsing to her knees, she stared at the spot the ghost had disappeared, sucked in a breath and screamed.

Survival Tip #9

For the love of God, don't go chasing waterfalls, stick to the rivers and ponds you know aren't haunted.

Alex woke up to the sound of Willa screaming. He was out of their tent and running before he even had a sense of where he was going. He was being pulled in the direction her voice had come from, the need to find her, protect her, thrumming through him like a drum. He realized when he was already halfway there that he was heading toward the river.

Oh God, what if she was drowning again? Why had she left the tent? Why had she left him behind?

The screaming had stopped but he could hear something else, a dissonance to the normal sounds of the forest he was almost positive was Willa crying.

He swore as he fumbled in the dark, too frantic, too desperate to get to her to let the weak moonlight poking through the clouds help him find his way. His shins banged against something hard and sharp and he stumbled before regaining his feet and making it out of the trees onto the riverbank.

Without the dense canopy, more light illuminated the area around the river and he saw a collapsed Willa halfway between the trees and the water. Her arms were crossed over her stomach, her body curled protectively over her knees as she sobbed, and the sight was enough to make something inside him break. Wilhelmina Jones was not the kind of woman who cried easily and he would have done anything right then if it meant she would stop. He ran and dropped onto the moss beside her, only just managing to stop himself from touching her. He had never seen her like this and he was afraid touching her would only make things worse.

"Willa! What's wrong? What happened? Why did you leave the tent? Are you hurt?"

He heard her breath catch on a short hiccupy sob and then she was throwing herself at him. His arms wrapped automatically around her, his hands moving tentatively up and down her back, caught between wanting to offer comfort and needing to check for injuries. After a minute or two of her crying into his neck he was able to determine that, physically at least, the only thing that appeared to be wrong was that she was ice cold, like she'd been sitting in a snowbank rather than on a tropical riverbank. She was shivering so hard he could hear her teeth chattering.

"Willa, what the hell happened to you?" He chafed his hands against her arms. "Your skin feels like ice."

"I s-saw a g-ghost."

The relief was swift and instantaneous. She wasn't hurt, just scared from a bad dream. "Possum, you had a nightmare. There's no such thing as ghosts," he said soothingly. But rather than being comforted, she leaned away so she could glare at him and Alex was struck by how fierce she looked. Tears had made tracks through the dirt on her face and big chunks of hair had escaped her braids and made snarls around her sharp cheeks. She looked wild but still one hundred percent aware and awake.

"It wasn't a nightmare! It was real! I saw a f-fucking ghost!"

Everything inside him stilled. Never, not once, in five years of knowing her, had Alex ever heard Willa say the word "fuck." Not when an experiment failed or when Alex said something particularly, deliberately obnoxious. It had gotten to the point where some of the other grad assistants had placed bets on how long it would take for her to slip. Sometimes, in his more sleep-deprived moments, Alex wondered if they weren't better off not knowing. Because he was sure whatever forced that word out of someone like Willa would be catastrophic. Which meant either ghosts were real or they had a much bigger problem on their hands.

"Okay, okay, I believe you. Tell me what happened," he said calmly, striving to sound in control for both their sakes. They needed to gather the facts and determine the truth before adding another concern to their list.

"Well, I—I heard the noise again." His face must have communicated his lack of comprehension because the scowl on her face deepened. "The footsteps I heard the other night. You never listen, McBryde." She shoved at his shoulder but didn't actually move off of his lap. He was also relieved to see her tears had stopped and she was no longer taking those gasping, hiccupy breaths.

He nodded slowly, "Right. I remember now. So you heard the footsteps."

"And I went to go find out what it was." When he felt her leave the tent, he had assumed she was going to the bathroom and fallen back asleep. He silently cursed himself for not checking in.

"And why didn't you wake me up?" he asked, working very hard to keep the frustration out of his voice.

"Because you *don't wake up* unless I physically assault you and the last time I woke you up because of the noise, you told me it was a dream and manhandled me until I lay back down. You would have done the same thing this time. You just did! You just called it a nightmare."

She was probably right. It really was too dark to be fumbling around the forest at night. She was incorrect, however, about how difficult it was to wake him up. Alex had always been a light sleeper. But letting Willa believe otherwise had seemed a good idea the night she'd woken him up with her sweet little moans and desperate little sighs. Because she had begged him to still be asleep. Because they were becoming friends. And, most importantly, because the bitter, tight feeling he had felt in his chest as he wondered who she was dreaming about wasn't jealousy. It had been a lie for both their benefit but now he was stuck in it.

"Wilhelmina, if you leave the tent and go wandering around this island at night again, there *will* be consequences. I don't care if you have to jump up and down on my chest to wake me up. We stick together." His hands stopped moving on her arms and his grip tightened. "You promised you would stop doing shit like this."

"How could I possibly predict there would be a ghost?"

"Honestly, that's the best-case scenario in this situation. There have been pirates in the Seychelles. You could have been hurt or kidnapped. Anyone sneaking onto this island at night is probably not the sort of person we can count on for a rescue."

Her eyes went wide and fearful again, "But it *was* a pirate, Alex. I mean, I think it was a pirate. The ghost of one."

"You saw a ghost pirate?" The blatant skepticism in his voice had her shoving roughly at his shoulder again.

"You make it sound ridiculous."

"Then try and make it sound not ridiculous, tell me exactly what you saw."

She closed her eyes, her lips pressing tight like it was painful to remember. "At first it was just kind of a shimmer near the water." Her eyes opened and she looked over his shoulder toward the bend in the river and he felt her whole body tense. "But as it got closer it got more distinct. It was wearing a big, plumed hat and a long coat and it was dragging a trunk. As soon as it appeared I felt—" her voice broke and she sucked in another shaky breath, "Oh, God, Alex, I could *feel* it, despair and regret so deep and heavy it felt like they were dragging me down, pressing in on me so I couldn't breathe. I couldn't call for help."

Her eyes were haunted and the shivering started again, he pulled her closer and she whispered the next words into his chest. "I think it spoke to me. It took something. I think— I think it wants me to return what it took."

He held her until her shaking stopped, stroking his hands up and down her back while he scanned the river, thinking about what she had told him and looking for anything that would give him a clue about what she had actually seen. Because he did not believe in ghosts. Aliens? Yes. Deep-sea monsters? Sure. Those were statistically probable. But a ghost? Ghosts were the stuff of stories and spirituality. It was far more likely Willa had been sleepwalking or heard an animal moving around and let her imagination take over. Escaping volcanic gas causing hallucinations made more sense than a ghost.

"What happened to it? Where did it go?" He asked.

"It looked at me and then it backed into the waterfall and just kind of...dissolved." She looked over at the waterfall, which did appear mistier than usual, the fog around it swallowing up what little light there was so it looked exceptionally eerie. "Maybe whatever it took is hidden behind there. We should check."

"Willa, it is the middle of the night, the only thing we're doing right now is going back to camp."

"But—"

"We can check in the morning." he said, and hopefully in the light of day, she would realize all of this had been a weird dream or even some kind of bad trip. Their diets had been pretty experimental lately. "Come on, it will be warmer near the fire."

He managed to get to his feet, pulling her along with him. There was a twinge near his knee and when he looked, he was just able to make out a bloody scrape.

Following his gaze, Willa inhaled sharply. "Oh! What happened?"

"I panicked," he said dryly, moving to the river to rinse the blood off. He would have to be sure to clean it with salt water tomorrow to prevent infection. "I told you, running around in the dark is dangerous."

"I'm sorry, Alex." He looked up and she was watching him clean himself off, her arms crossed protectively over her chest. She met his eyes and spoke deliberately, "Thank you for coming to help me."

Every hard, frustrated edge inside him smoothed out. He shook the water off his hands and moved back to her side, using a light touch between her shoulder blades to begin guiding her back to their tent.

"Of course, Willa, friends help each other out."

"Are we? Friends?" she asked in a voice that broke his heart. Clearly she was still shaken up because he didn't think even the Willa of yesterday would have asked him such a question. It made him glad he had held himself back in all the lust-soaked moments of the past week because he knew if he had given in, if he had kissed her in the pool or moved his hand between her thighs when she woke up wet and panting, she would never have dropped her guard this much. Getting these little pearls of vulnerability out of Willa was like pulling an oyster apart with your bare hands: practically impossible.

"I don't think we have a choice after all this," he said easily, like it was a foregone conclusion even as his heart beat a little faster in his chest. A few minutes later they were back at their campsite and he was surprised how much it felt like coming home. Across from the opening of their makeshift tent they had layered more sticks and leaves between two branches to create a shield for the fire and it cast a welcoming circle of light around the tent. It hissed and popped as he fed it more rain-speckled wood but its warmth grew enough to put some of the color back in Willa's cheeks.

"I think I'll take big spoon this time," he said, looking her over critically now that he could actually see. For someone who was constantly stumbling into danger, she always managed to come out remarkably unscathed. Which was more than he could say about his rescue attempts.

"You don't have to," she said.

He smiled and tugged on one of her curls. "I don't know, if left uncuddled you have a tendency to wander off."

The color was definitely back in her cheeks now. "I'll stay put this time." She crossed a finger over her heart. "Promise."

"Me and my abused shin appreciate that." He crawled into the tent, facing the center, and gave her an uncompromising look. "I'm still going to be the big spoon though."

"Such a caveman," she sighed but she crawled in anyway and settled in front of him. He slipped his arm around her waist and pulled her close. She was no longer freezing but it felt good, necessary, to remind himself she was safe.

"In the morning, we check behind the waterfall," she said, as if she was worried he would forget.

"Sure," he yawned.

"I'm not crazy, Alex."

"You may not be crazy but you're driving *me* pretty close." He put his hand briefly over her eyes. "Sleep." She was quiet for a few minutes and then—

"You called me 'possum.'"

He flinched and his arm tightened reflexively around her waist. He had been hoping she missed his little slip but rather than explain his unintentional bit of tenderness, he tried to re-direct, "I can't hear you, I'm asleep."

"Come on, I just wanted to know why 'possum'?"

Tired and exasperated and maybe a little embarrassed, he buried his face against her neck and grumbled, "I don't know. My dad calls my mum possum. It's an Australian thing. Stop thinking so much and go to sleep."

"Have you ever seen an American possum?"

He groaned. "Yes."

"So you understand why maybe it comes off as insulting."

"I don't know, I kind of like the American possum. It's just a weird, fluffy, trash demon out trying to live its best marsupial life."

"Are you calling me a trash demon?" She asked, turning her head to look at him over her shoulder, which resulted in some of her hair making its way perilously close to his mouth.

A small chuckle broke out of him and he smoothed her curls down, away from his face. "No, just weird and fluffy. And evidently nocturnal," he added pointedly. She let out an outraged huff. "I won't do it again, if it bothers you." She went still and stiff for a long moment but then, hesitantly, she shook her head.

"No, I—I don't mind, it's better than being called a dag I guess. At least possums serve an important ecological purpose." She yawned widely but then kept talking, "Did you know possums are sometimes called 'living fossils'? Because they've been around for seventy million years? That's older than crocodiles, cow sharks, and even freshwater stingrays." She gave a hum of consideration, "But not turtles or tortoises."

He sighed as she continued to ramble and groped around until he found her hand. He laced their fingers together in a gesture he told himself was absolutely platonic. Just one friend offering comfort to another.

"Willa, my darling living fossil, you wouldn't by chance be afraid to fall asleep now would you?"

There was a long stretch of silence and the sounds of the island seemed to swell between them, insects humming, bats barking, the rustle of critters darting through the underbrush. There were no distant footsteps as far as he could tell but he could picture the grey mist hovering over the waterfall and the way the moonlight might catch at vines and branches to make shadows that shook like something sinister. He might not believe ghosts were real but he knew the fear from a ghost story was, and there was definitely fear in Willa's voice when she finally spoke. "We're trapped on a haunted island, Alex."

He squeezed her fingers and kept his voice low and sure, "We've been okay so far. As long as we stick together and don't go wandering around at night, we'll be fine."

"I don't ever want to feel like that again," she said hoarsely and Alex's chest tightened, remembering her scream.

"It must have been terrifying," he said but she shook her head, her escaped curls brushing softly against his jaw again.

"I'm not talking about the fear, I'm talking about the regret." She shuddered and pressed more firmly into the curve of his body. "I've never felt so...empty and desperate all at once. It was awful. Fear can be managed. You can overcome it. But regret?" Her fingers squeezed his back almost painfully. "Regret like that you have to live with because you can't change the past," she finished, making him wonder what regrets Willa had to make her speak with such vehemence.

Alex himself had more regrets than he cared to think about and at least half of them had to do with the woman in front of him. Where would they be now if they hadn't spent their entire graduate career fighting with each other? What if they had figured out a way to be friends sooner?

Could he have been a man worthy of Wilhelmina Jones then?

"But you can learn from it. Grow, change," he said slowly, wondering if it was really too late. She clearly *wanted* to be friends and wasn't that a start? Could he evolve into the kind of man someone like Willa dreamed about? A man worth keeping? It felt like a dangerous thought.

"Not if you're a ghost," she whispered, bringing Alex's focus back to their present problem. He couldn't become anything if they didn't survive and make it off this island. His dangerous thoughts could wait until they were no longer in actual danger.

"Then we just have to avoid dying," he said firmly but then, lightening his tone, he added, "Although at this point, that may be the only way to get any rest around here."

She snorted a small laugh and Alex breathed out a sigh of relief, glad to feel some of the tension in her body release. "Okay, I get it. I'll go to sleep."

"Thank you."

Quiet settled between them and he felt her body slowly go soft and relaxed beneath his arm. Closing his eyes on another sigh, he held her close and finally began to fall back asleep.

"Alex," this time, her voice was a whisper just barely rising above the nighttime sounds outside their tent. Already half gone, he barely heard her.

"I'm glad we're friends."

His dreams the rest of the night were sweet.

Survival Tip #10

Wilhelmina Jones is always right.

This had to be what a hangover felt like. A headache and the lingering, sour feeling of regret strung between her limbs like old cobwebs. Willa slowly sat up, rubbing her temples and wanting coffee so badly she actually teared up a little. After a full week of being lost in the wilderness, she thought she had started to come to terms with her present, caffeineless existence, but last night's ghost encounter had been too much. She wanted coffee. Coffee, served in a real cup, and she wanted breakfast, a full breakfast, with pancakes and bacon and toast, served on a real plate. She wanted it all so much it took several minutes of pressing her forehead against her bent knees and breathing before she managed to wrestle the feelings back under control.

On this particular morning, she was glad Alex had picked up the habit of leaving the tent before her to go build up the signal fire on the beach and collect firewood. Even if it was *wildly* hypocritical of him to wander off alone and then scold Willa whenever she did the same. When she had pointed that out to him on their fifth day here, he had tried to argue it wasn't Willa being off on her own that was the problem, it was when she made questionable choices in terms of self-preservation. She had found this incredibly insulting at the time, but after last night's misadventure she thought he might, perhaps, *maybe* have a point.

Not that she would ever tell him that.

They might officially be *friends* now, but that didn't mean she was ceding the higher ground. Even if that ground felt shaky underneath her. She winced, remembering what was perhaps the most embarrassing part of last night: her actually *asking* if they were friends. In the light of morning, the question reeked of desperation. Luckily, he hadn't pointed it out. In fact, he had answered like being friends was a given. Like friendship was that easy.

Willa crawled out of the tent, and, just like she had the last few mornings, found the banana leaf of fruit Alex had left for her. Her chest tightened as she traced a finger over the leaf's waxy surface. Was this friendship? Or was it self-preservation? After her mildly incoherent first day here and that mortifying wreck of a kiss, she was inclined to believe the latter. Still, as she scooped up the fruit and walked toward the river, a very small voice in the back of her head pointed out that it was...nice. It was nice to have a friend. Even if that friend was Alexander "Calls You Possum" McBryde and even if it didn't last.

Willa reached the riverbank, putting the fruit down on a flat-topped rock and staring hard at where the pirate had disappeared. As waterfalls went, it wasn't huge, only rising about sixteen feet above the pool, the water falling like ribbons as it snaked through piles of rocks and boulders at the top. The morning light caught the mist, casting rainbows against the spray and whereas the night before it had looked eerie, it now looked like something out of a fairytale. It should have been reassuring but the feeling of regret was still clinging to her bones and suddenly all this pretty paradise felt like aposematism. Just like the bright, beautiful colors of a poison dart frog, the beauty seemed more like a threat. A threat they had no choice but to face until they were rescued.

If they were rescued.

Frowning at the rainbows, Willa grabbed a starfruit and dropped down on a rock, plucking at a new hole in her sadly decrepit shirt. They had *better be rescued*. The little clothing she had was not going to last much longer. She was still toying with the hole when Alex came strolling out of the trees. She dropped her shirt and watched as his eyes quickly looked her over, like he was checking to make sure she hadn't gone even further off the deep end after last night. His gaze lingered on her hair for a moment too long and she self-consciously lifted a hand to feel all the curls that had broken free of her braid crown. She bit back a frown thinking she probably looked more like a mad scientist than a credible witness.

"Good morning," she said primly, hoping the subdued tone would counter the previous night's histrionics. She watched his mouth twitch into a smile.

"Good morning," he replied in that same stiff, formal tone. "And how are we feeling today?" he asked, reaching her side and sitting down on a boulder opposite her. He took a banana from the leaf tray, and she resisted the proprietary urge to snatch it back. Honestly, people who managed to live kind, decent lives without the aid of coffee were absolute saints. Taking a bite of her own fruit to forestall snapping at him, she glanced down and, seeing the small scrape on his shin from the night before, found a little more grace.

She swallowed and met his eyes. "I feel like I wish last night was a dream but I also know I really did see a ghost." She looked toward the bend in the river and shuddered. "I can still taste the regret."

"It could have been something you ate, like a chemical reaction, like being on shrooms," he offered and Willa, losing a little of her new-found patience, scowled and crossed her arms.

"You know, pirates were some of the first people to visit the Seychelles."

"Yeah, but a history of pirates is not the same as a history of ghosts."

"Didn't you do any research before this trip? They have that too, actually, so my story is entirely plausible which means we are checking behind the waterfall."

"Willa—" he started but she wasn't listening. She was doing this whether he came with her or not. Without giving herself time to overthink it, she stripped off her shirt so it wouldn't sustain any more damage and began wading into the water. The sound of Alex's voice abruptly cut off but she didn't look back. She had seen a ghost and she was going to prove it. There was the splash of water behind her and she relaxed a little knowing he was coming with her after all.

"It could be dangerous," he said. "We shouldn't be taking risks out here."

"It's not like we're going cliff-jumping. We're literally just checking out some rocks but if you're that concerned, you can stay here and if you're right and I die, feel free to tell *my* ghost 'I told you so.'" She thought he might have made some kind of grumbled, smart-ass remark in response but they had reached the waterfall and the words were drowned beneath its dull roar. Pushing through, Willa made her way to the rock wall set about two feet back from the falls. Light filtered in between the watery ribbons and from the sides where the wall curved in and created a gap between the rock and the arc of the water. Not quite knowing what she was looking for, she began running her fingers over the stone, clawing and tugging at the moss and algae that had grown over the damp surface.

"You know, I don't think this is an Ali Baba, Cave of Wonders situation, dag, it's just a wall of rock," said Alex conversationally and Willa might have been annoyed at the nickname and amused at his choice of reference if she hadn't had her fingers knuckle deep in a sizeable gap in the stone. She peered into the hole and when she didn't respond he tried again, "Willa?"

"There's something odd about these gaps," she muttered, pulling her fingers out. She rubbed at the stone below it, trying to wipe away some more of the algae. There were marks there, something that cut in deeper than the plant roots around it, almost like a design or an engraving. She squinted and leaned closer, trying to make it out. "Look at this and tell me what you see," she said and ignored Alex's sigh as he shifted in the water, his body pressing up against her back to avoid the falls in a way that temporarily broke her concentration and sent heat fizzing beneath her cool, damp skin.

His fingers brushed hers, nudging them out of the way as he traced over the lines and she was temporarily transfixed by the sight of their hands next to each other. Nothing about Willa was dainty, including her hands, but Alex's were still larger and stupidly attractive in a way that made no goddamn sense. Veins shouldn't be sexy but, as usual, Alexander McBryde defied all expectations. Inexplicably annoyed, she curled her fingers into a fist and dropped her hand to her side, safely out of his reach.

"Strange. I guess it does kind of look like some sort of cuneiform," he paused, a small humming sound of contemplation vibrating out of his chest and into her back but then he shook his head, like he was resisting being drawn into her midnight fictions. "Or it could be nothing," he said firmly, grabbing a vine clinging to the wall and pulling it away to reveal the shallow indentations it had managed to dig into the stone. "Nature is messy. It could be anything."

Feeling another spike of annoyance, Willa elbowed him away from her and moved to the far side where the waterfall ended and the curve of the rock jutted out. "This rock is completely solid, there's no gaps." Her hands traced illustratively over the stone. It was smooth here, a solid wall of granite but as she moved back inward cracks and holes appeared. She pulled down more vines and moss so he could see that this part of the wall was made up of smaller rocks and boulders. "But this section is different. This looks like someone *put* this rock here." She looked at him expectantly. "Like they were filling in an opening."

He pushed experimentally at the rock and when it didn't budge, he reached over and waved at the wall in front of Willa's face. "Open sesame," he said, deliberately meeting her eyes and she was amused despite herself.

"Honestly, Alex, where is your sense of scientific inquiry?"

"I left it on the boat along with soap, my cell phone, and the first aid kit."

"We wouldn't have service out here anyway," she said, going back to running her hands over the wall. She was so sure there was a secret here, she could *feel* it, and she knew if they just looked hard enough, they would unlock it. She sank down further in the water, her hands dipping below the surface. "You know, if I was a pirate who had hidden my treasure in a cave behind a waterfall and then filled in the entrance, I would make sure to leave some kind of opening."

"Willa, just one question, *do you hear yourself?*"

She did and maybe if their roles were reversed she would be standing and looking down the way Alex was now—arms crossed, full of sarcasm and scientific skepticism. But she knew what she had seen.

"Of course I do but—" she broke off as her hands found a smoothed over edge and when she reached further, she found the definite feel and shape of a hole. Excitement was a heady rush. She flashed Alex a triumphant smile and, without another word, dove beneath the water. Keeping her eyes open, she was able to make out the blurry outline of a hole. A *big* hole. Big enough for even a broad-shouldered man to swim through. Another rush of excitement, of confidence that she was *right,* had her pushing inside the dark opening without a second thought.

The world around her went pitch black but she continued to feel her way along, running her fingers along the top of the hole until the feel of rock came to an abrupt end. The water lightened back up, not a lot, but enough for her to see light overhead and it was all the reassurance she needed. Where there was light there was bound to be air. She pulled herself the rest of the way out of the short tunnel and pushed herself off the bottom of the pool, breaking through to the surface with a gasp. It took a minute or two of treading water for her eyes to adjust to the gloom but once they did she couldn't stop the grin that broke over her face.

Take that, McBryde! She wasn't delusional after all. Because looking around her now, there was no denying this was *something*—it was the kind of cave every little kid imagined a pirate having. The air around her hung damp and heavy, stalactites dripped from the ceiling, and in some of the few fragile beams of light managing to snake through the waterfall and cracked rock, she thought she even caught glimpses of a bat or two swaying upside down overhead. It was quieter in here, the sound of the waterfall on the other side muffled and distant. She swam further in and the appearance of a ledge felt abrupt in the half-light, but it wasn't a surprise.

There was a humming, expectant tension beneath her skin and the word the ghost had whispered into her mind the night before was building inside her, echoing as if she had actually released it to bounce against the cave walls until the thought felt deafening.

Return.

Return what? And why go to the effort of filling in a cave entrance unless you had something to hide? Willa put her hands on the edge of the ledge and with a great heave, pulled herself out of the water. Faintly, she heard Alex calling her name and in some far, far corner of her mind she knew he was probably worried and angry. Swimming through dark, mysterious holes was probably one of those questionable choices of self-preservation he kept yelling at her about. But it didn't matter because as she looked up, as her breath rushed out and her hands covered her mouth to hold back a shocked, disbelieving laugh, she had one of those singularly blunt existential moments—the kind that made you explicitly aware of yourself and your place in the universe. And in that glittering, golden, profound moment, she knew all the mistakes she had been making lately had been to lead her here. This wasn't a mistake; it was destiny.

She couldn't wait to see Alex's face.

She had been *right*.

⁂

Willa had disappeared into the rock.

The ridiculous, infuriating woman had swum into places unknown without even stopping to consult him. She had to have a death-wish. The only question was who she was trying to kill because Alex felt on the verge of a stroke. He shouted her name, knowing it was likely useless, especially if she was trapped or drowning, but she had surprised him before, sometimes even pleasantly. Except after another ten seconds where she failed to reappear, another bolt of panic struck him. He swore and dove in the same place she had vanished. Keeping his eyes open despite the discomfort, he was able to determine she had been right about one thing, there was some kind of opening in the rock wall. A large, dark, terrifying hole that had anxiety and fear bursting through him in equal measure. He surfaced and sucked in a ragged breath.

If she didn't come out in the next thirty seconds he was going to have to go in there.

And he really, really didn't want to.

Why did Willa always seem to have a direct line to his worst fears?

He tried calling her name again, his heart pounding so hard it made the blood roaring in his ears even louder than the crashing water behind him. The seconds ticked by and each one was a unique torture: imagining Willa trapped, struggling, praying for him to save her; him, trapped, crushed to death in a small, confined hole, the pressure pushing him down down, down until he was swallowed up by the earth. He squeezed his hands into fists and forced himself to breathe.

"Willa, God damnit!" he shouted, banging against the rock. She wasn't giving him a choice. He had to go in after her. He closed his eyes, taking a few short, quick breaths to gather his courage and then he sucked in a huge one, preparing to dive but just before he took that terrifying plunge, he heard her.

"Alex! You're never going to believe this!" Faint and muffled but unmistakable, Willa's voice cut through his fear and froze him in place. Relief had his knees going weak but then anger was a hot, hard chaser, making him feel like he might actually have the strength to kick through the wall.

"Willa! What the fuck were you thinking?" he shouted back.

There was a long pause and then, "I can't hear you. You have to come in."

"Like hell I do," he said, outraged all over again. "No!" he yelled, as loud as he possibly could.

"I'm not coming out until you come in!"

Alex stared at the wall, seriously considering leaving her in there. She would come out when she was hungry. She couldn't make him go in that hole. Nothing she had found on the other side of it could possibly be worth it.

But it could be dangerous.

And Willa was stubborn. So goddamn stubborn. Even if she came out eventually there was no telling what kind of risky situation she might get herself into in the meantime. And he wouldn't be there to help simply because he had a touch of claustrophobia. After all, she had managed to get through the hole and come out the other side. If she could do it, so could he. And once she was within arm's reach, he could drag her out, by the hair if necessary, and make sure she never did something like this again.

"Alex, come on! Don't be such a baby!"

Oh, yeah, she definitely had a death wish.

"Fine! I'm coming in," he hollered back and then, without giving himself any more time to get worked up about it, he sucked in a breath and dove. Finding the hole was easy but as he swam inside and the watered darkened panic began to stream in. Rough edges brushed his shoulders and it felt like the hole was getting narrower and narrower.

Just get to Willa.

He repeated the thought over and over like a mantra in his head, imagining her as the moon—the light at the end of the tunnel. The temperature of the water changed, cooling, reminding him of swimming through the ocean at night, Willa's unconscious body dragging behind him, darkness everywhere he looked. The panic built and he lost control of his lungs, losing more oxygen than he had intended. His chest started to burn and he knew, he just *knew* this was going to be how he died. Crushed to death inside a hole on some speck of sand island in the middle of the ocean. He wondered if Willa would even miss him when he was gone.

But then, suddenly, there was light overhead and Alex's entire body shot toward it. He broke the surface, floundering until he realized his feet could just barely touch the ground. He sputtered, coughing and choking and spitting out water while simultaneously trying to catch his breath. The entire trip had taken less than a minute according to his dive watch but it felt like he had lost a lifetime.

"Jesus, Alex, did you forget how to swim down there?" Willa's voice rose up out of the darkness, too-sweet and warm, and easily distinguishable now that they were together again. He blinked a few times, trying to clear the blurry aftermath of swimming with his eyes open and adjust to the dark.

"I panicked," he rasped, finally finding her in the shadows. She was treading water about 35 centimeters away from him and from what he could see, looked completely unscathed. As usual. "I thought I was going to drown in that fucking tunnel," he said harshly but Willa didn't seem to notice his anger.

"What are you talking about? It can't be more than two or three feet long. Drowning would take some serious effort." She came closer, reaching out to grab his arm, and he could see her excitement even in the dimness. "Now quit being dramatic and come see—"

"Fuck me dead, Willa, don't you ever think about anyone but yourself?" The words exploded out of him, loud and furious and shaped by the rough, dull blade of fear still digging around in his burning lungs. He saw her expression stiffen and she stopped pulling his arm. Her fingers dropped away and even as angry as he was, he wanted to pull them back, needing something to anchor him back into the reality where they weren't both stuck drowning in darkness.

"Excuse me?" she asked, her voice cold and sharp in contrast.

"You disappeared into a potentially dangerous hole without saying a goddamn word," he ground out and watched the frown deepen on her face.

"It wasn't dangerous," she snapped and Alex felt his anger ratchet up another notch. How could someone who regularly planned out meticulous and rigorous experiments be so short-sighted about real, everyday life?

"But it could have been. What if it collapsed? What if you got stuck? What if it kept going and there was no way for you to back out?" He shot back, his voice rising with each terrible scenario.

"But none of that actually happened," she shouted, "You're yelling at me about possibilities!"

"Yeah, terrifying, incredibly real possibilities!" He reached out and gripped her shoulders, needing her to hear him, to understand. "Maybe you're fine taking stupid risks with your life but I'm not."

"What?" she asked, and there was a different note to her voice this time. She sounded almost disconcerted, like she was again surprised he might actually care. It was their first morning on the beach all over again. She still didn't believe Alex might give a shit about whether she lived or died. This time, however, he let himself shake her, just a little, in the hopes that maybe it would actually get through all that lovely, thick hair and penetrate her even thicker skull.

"At what point are you going to realize we're stuck in this situation *together*? I hate small, enclosed spaces but I swam through that fucking hole because I was worried about you, because I would rather face that than the possibility of being lost on this island without you."

"I never asked you to save me," she said defensively

"But that's the thing, you don't have to ask. Are you saying you wouldn't try to help me if I was in danger?"

"No, of course I would—"

"And that's the point I'm trying to make," he cut in, "We're in this mess together, so start fucking acting like it."

There was a long stretch of silence as they stared at each other and then, finally, Willa dipped her head in the tiniest nod of acknowledgement. "Okay."

"Okay?" he echoed, as if the repetition would make it true. Willa scowled and pushed at his chest, forcing him to release her shoulders.

"Yes. Okay! I really am going to try and be better and more considerate of your feelings." She turned in the water. "Now will you come —"

Alex reached out and grabbed her wrist, spinning her back to face him.

"Hold on." He dragged her back through the water until their faces were close and their legs brushed as she continued to tread water. "I want to be very clear about this, Wilhelmina. You're going to do better than try. Because the next time you do something deliberately dangerous, I'm going to do exactly what I promised our first day here. I will tie you to the closest tree and keep you there until you can convince me you're going to follow the rules. Do you understand?"

Their faces were close enough that even in the dim light he could see her eyes widen and her lips part and even though he couldn't remember the last time he had been so angry, he also couldn't remember the last time he had cared or wanted anyone so much. He hoped she listened because if he ever actually tied Willa up, he suspected they would both be in very big trouble. And then she surprised him. Pleasantly. And made it that much worse. Rather than fighting or snapping back she gave another one of those tiny nods.

"I understand."

"Good," he said roughly, squeezing her wrist gently once more for emphasis and then letting her go. "Now show me why it was so goddamn important I join you in this hellhole."

"What?" she asked blankly, then she blinked and seemed to shake herself. "Oh, Right." The excitement filtered back into her voice even if it seemed a tiny bit more subdued. "You're not the only one who deserves an apology," she said as she swam past him.

"Does that mean you're actually going to *give* one?" he asked, trying to follow her movements and realizing the cave or grotto or whatever the hell this place was, had a ledge that stuck out into the water. In a sudden whoosh, Willa planted her hands on the rock and lifted herself up, the graceful column of her spine and the round, tempting curve of her ass passing just half a meter away from his face and just like when she had suddenly stripped off her shirt earlier, Alex forgot what he was doing. Someday he might get used to the way the sight of a naked Willa hit him low and hard in the gut but it wouldn't be today. Maybe swimming through that nightmare hole had been worth it after all.

"Do you need help getting up?" she asked but there was sugar in her voice and Alex shook off his lustful paralysis. He looked up, past the very, very long adventure of her legs and thought Wilhelmina Jones might benefit from more than just being tied up. She could use a spanking too.

"You're really pushing it today, Jones," he snapped and then, without her assistance, he boosted himself up out of the water and onto the dry ledge. He clambered to his feet and before he had even managed to get his bearings, Willa was shoving something into his hand. The object was round and flat, with raised patterned ridges on each side. It was also cool against his palm and not like a rock plucked from the bottom of the river. It had the distinctly smooth, cool feel of metal. He brought it up to his face and tried to peer at it in the half-light. "Is this some kind of coin?" he asked in astonishment.

"Yes! Look at it in the light."

"What light?" he said, exasperated, but nevertheless raised it higher, trying to catch it in one of the few strands of sunlight managing to filter into the cave. The coin winked brightly back and he sucked in a breath.

"Is this gold?"

"*Yes,*" Willa said. "And there's so much more. Alex, look at all this."

Clutching the gold coin, he slowly turned, and disbelief ripped through him like a tsunami, pulling the earth out from under him and rearranging the natural order of everything.

Willa had been right. Impossibly, fantastically right. She had found more than just something, she had found treasure, the kind of treasure you only saw in books or movies or childhood dreams. There were three wooden chests that had split apart like overripe melons, hundreds of years of sitting in a damp cave rotting and collapsing the wood and causing a mess of gold and silver to spill across the floor. Alex crouched down, reaching out to trail his fingers over strings of pearls, heaps of gold and silver coins, ornate golden goblets, and loose jewels that flashed even in near darkness. It was unbelievable.

"Strewth," he whispered.

"I know," exclaimed Willa, "I told you I wasn't crazy."

"I never thought you were crazy," he said faintly. "I just thought you were dreaming. Or tripping." He moved over to one of the broken chests and picked up a sword sticking out of the corner, a sword that had once belonged to an actual pirate, and held it up so a ruby the size of a quail egg caught the light. "Fuck me, this has to be worth millions of dollars."

"That sword alone," said Willa, her voice excited and as bright as the diamonds currently scattered around his feet. "All of this? Hundreds of millions." She spread her hands to encompass all the loot. "How are we going to get this out of here?"

"I don't know." Alex walked around her and peered into the dark. The treasure was pushed a couple meters back from the edge of the ledge but beyond it, blackness stretched. "Maybe this connects to a tunnel that lets out somewhere a little more accessible." He took another step, feeling his foot crunch down on something. There was a snap, a crack, then several things happened at once.

Willa shouted his name and he felt her body slamming into his from behind, knocking them both to the ground. A second later something whistled through the air above their heads followed by a deafening crash. A sudden wash of light filtered into the cavern.

Dazed and winded, Alex looked to the side and he could clearly see Willa's golden hair tangled against his arm. She was breathing harshly in his ear and he could feel her entire nearly naked body pressed against his back. Her skin was cold. Too cold. But her breath was warm and that was what he focused on, fighting to get air back into his lungs until the two of them were breathing together. After a couple moments of them both catching their breath, Willa broke the silence. "Are you okay?"

"Yeah, I think so," he said but his voice came out rough and wheezy. She rolled off him and he was able to draw a deeper breath. Shifting beside him, she rolled onto her knees and he glanced over to find her looking down at him, her eyes huge and afraid.

"Oh God, Alex, that was so close." She took a deep breath and it came out shaky. "Are you sure you're okay?"

Rolling over and sitting up, he gave himself a quick once-over to confirm and nodded. "I'm fine but what just happened?"

She shook her head. "I don't know but I think it might have been a—a booby trap." She bit her lip, still looking utterly terrified and he followed the source of light now filling the cavern. Three long metal pikes had crashed into the stone wall. Two still quivered, embedded in the rock, but the third had crashed through a weak point creating a sizable hole. For a long moment he just stared at the deadly metal rods, then he looked back at Willa and raised his eyebrows.

"For someone who keeps falling off boats and hills, you have incredibly fast reflexes."

She gave something between a sob and a laugh and then launched herself at him, throwing her arms around his neck and knocking all the breath he'd just managed to regain back out of his body.

"You asshole, you almost died," she said, hugging him tight. Alex patted her back and tried to subtly gulp down air.

"I guess this makes us even."

She laugh-cried again. "No, it doesn't. You were right. I never think about anyone but myself." Another sob ripped out of her. "If you died it would have been my fault."

"Shhh, possum, it's alright. We're both okay." Just like the night before, the reality of Willa crying made something inside Alex come apart. The anger he felt earlier when his life hadn't really been in danger was nowhere to be found. In fact, as he moved to stroking her hair, he felt remarkably calm. Or maybe he was in shock. Either way, he continued trying to soothe Willa who was busy castigating herself.

"...You were right, we should never have come in here. I don't know what's wrong with me. You should have let me drown, you stupid, noble idiot."

"If you really feel that bad about it you can give me your share of the treasure. How's that sound?" He teased, hoping to bring back some of her earlier defiance.

She sniffed and said with a hiccupy little breath, "You can have all of it."

"Beauty. Now I really can be one of those monied dickheads who float around on their yachts surrounded by gorgeous women in bikinis." She pulled back and shoved at his shoulder.

"Asshole. You know, it's probably cursed. Pirate treasure is always cursed," she said, her eyes shooting poisoned arrows at him and making him grin. There was his Willa.

"You have a point. I guess we'll have to figure out who it belongs to and return it, the way your ghost wanted."

Willa's glare shifted toward the wall with its lethal adornments. "I'm going to exorcize him straight to hell. He sent us in here knowing it was booby-trapped."

"He is a pirate."

"It would serve him right if we dumped all of this into the ocean. Let him spend eternity hanging out here with his unfinished business." She rose to her feet and glared into the darkness over Alex's shoulder.

Shifting nervously, Alex glanced behind them at the still unpenetrated darkness. "Willa, maybe we don't provoke the ghost until after we're sure there's no more booby traps."

Still clearly shaking with anger, she slowly nodded and looked down at him. "Right. Well at least this makes getting this stuff out of here easier. Just hold on, I'll be right back." She dove into the water and disappeared and Alex didn't breathe again until he heard her call from the other side of the wall.

"I'm going to try and knock out more of these rocks." The sound of metal hitting stone echoed through the cave and he realized she must have found the third pike. As he watched the opening grow, the knot that had been tied around his lungs eased as he realized he wouldn't have to swim through that fucking underwater tunnel again.

While Willa worked on that, Alex used the additional light to cautiously explore more of the cave, his ear cocked for danger. The walls were rough, with deep shadowed grooves that had the hair on the back of his neck rising, imagining them the perfect place for more booby traps. He peered into the darkness beyond the treasure chests. It was clear the cave continued, the walls coming together to form a narrow passageway but despite the additional light, the darkness stared back, black and impenetrable and, now that he knew ghosts were real, with an air of malevolence he didn't think was entirely imagined. He looked back at the pikes in the wall and for a visceral moment imagined what would have happened if Willa hadn't moved so quickly. He shuddered.

No, there was not a single goddamn thing that could get him down that tunnel.

He turned back to the treasure and crouched near one of the water-swollen chests, pushing back the damp, crumbly lid. The rotted wood disintegrated toward the floor but the treasure inside looked pristine, and Alex's breath rushed out in disbelief. On the top of a pile of gold doubloons, uncut diamonds and ropes of pearls, was was an elaborately detailed crown. It was the kind of thing you saw in a museum—and it was sitting in a cave in the middle of nowhere. Shaking his head, still riddled with disbelief, he picked it up, his fingers tracing over flower petals made of gold and silver leaves dewed by diamonds and sapphires and amber. It was unbelievable. Another clang from Willa hitting the rock wall reverberated around him and he looked toward her. She had gone right to it, to all of this, which meant she really had seen a ghost—and they really were trapped on a haunted goddamn island.

"Wilhelmina Jones is never wrong," he muttered, carefully putting the crown aside and resuming his search for things that might actually help them survive. He managed to find four gold goblets, a pewter cauldron, and a jeweled dagger by the time he heard a large splash followed by the sounds of Willa climbing up onto the ledge.

"I think I managed to make the hole big enough for—ooh," she broke off and Alex looked up from the chest to see her reaching for the flower crown he had put aside. "God, the craftsmanship it took to make this," she said, running her fingers reverently over the veined detail impressed on the silver leaves, then, with a look of pure glee, she placed the crown on her head and turned to Alex. "What do you think?" she asked and he lost his breath for a second time.

She was a goddess again. Gleaming gold crown on wet golden hair, tendrils and curls making filigree swirls on the skin of her shoulders and the curves of her ruby-tipped breasts. Sunlight poured in from behind her, turning her into a gilded masterpiece. She was the Venus Botticelli would have kept private—too beautiful and explicit and enchanting to share with anyone but the lover who inspired him. All he wanted to do was bow at her feet and worship.

But he couldn't say or do any of that. She had a weapon now.

So, he bit his tongue and swallowed hard. "Now is not the time to play dress-up," he said, forcing himself to turn away. "We should be focusing on getting the things we can use out of here and then get a move on with trying to hunt down lunch. The rest of this can wait."

He heard her sigh. "Fine," she agreed, albeit begrudgingly. He glanced back to see her putting the crown down with a regretful look of longing but then she straightened and moved toward him, surveying his little pile of useful items. "I can't touch the bottom in here so it will be easiest if you pass stuff through the hole to me. I'll help pull you through after so you don't have to swim through the tunnel again." She looked at the yawning black opening that led deeper into the cave. "Unless you want to risk seeing where that goes."

"Absolutely not. I think I'm done with risk for the day," he stood up, explicitly aware of how close they were to each other and the heat coming off Willa's body. She was still only wearing underwear and it would be too easy to reach up and trace the swirls her hair made on her skin with his fingers. Perhaps he wasn't as done with risk as he thought. He took a deliberate step toward the ledge and the cool plunge he clearly needed. Willa followed behind.

"Me too, actually," she said but then her voice went sweet, "Watching you nearly get impaled was not at all as satisfying as I always imagined it would be."

Alex felt a flash of exasperation but wasn't sure if it was directed at Willa or himself. They were back on safer ground, perhaps not exactly where they had started but at least somewhere familiar, somewhere they could stand comfortably together and fight off whatever new dangers this island had in store for them.

"Glad to hear it," he said dryly, playing into their usual script and when Willa grinned back at him, it was worth it.

"Although maybe it was because *I* wasn't the one doing the impaling. In my daydreams I'm always the one wielding the spear or harpoon gun or —"

There was a satisfying splash and subsequent spluttering as Alex shoved her back into the water.

Survival Tip #11

Never underestimate the statement power of pearls.

They had found treasure.

Willa was still experiencing the sweet, satisfying rush of having been right chased by the acidic taste of almost-regret.

If she hadn't been looking up.

If she didn't have exceptional eyesight.

If she had hesitated for even a second.

Alex would be dead.

She still wasn't entirely convinced she had really seen or heard the danger coming. Right before she lunged for him, she had gone blisteringly cold and her skin had felt too tight. As if she wasn't alone inside of it. Of course, the idea she had been even momentarily possessed was not a happy thought but it was still better than the alternative.

Swinging one of the metal pikes through the air like a walking stick, Willa walked back toward the river. Overhead, the sky was orange and pink and she watched the wispy clouds begin to go purple and navy through the gaps in the forest canopy. Maybe tonight would be clear and they could spend some time on the beach with the stars and a roaring bonfire. The sooner they got off this cursed island the better.

She yawned, losing track of the sky. It had been a long day. After pulling out the more useful treasure, she and Alex had hurried to get through the other parts of their daily routine. He had re-braided her hair and then they had gone down to the beach searching for food. Watching Alex try and spear fish with one of their newly acquired weapons had been amusing but a small, nagging part of her wondered just how much longer they were going to have to live like this.

After eating yet another meal of oysters and a particularly large crab (no fish), they had returned to the pirate cave and started hauling out treasure. They tumbled a couple of large rocks into the water so it was easier to crawl in and out of the hole she had created and then they spent the afternoon making trips back and forth from the cave to their campsite with armfuls of loot.

Seeing the treasure in actual sunlight only made it seem more unreal. There were bars of gold and silver, heaps upon heaps of golden guineas, cups and bowls made of precious metals, several cracked porcelain figurines, a small, elaborate reliquary containing a pile of dust, three more jeweled swords, fistfuls of loose jewels, and jewelry so decadent and beautiful Willa hadn't been able to stop herself from playing a *little* bit of dress-up.

There really was something very soothing about wearing a crown.

Reaching the river, she paused on the bank and watched as Alex waded out. He was pulling the lifebuoy-turned-sled behind him and he was naked, having stripped off his shorts so they would dry before the sun set.

He was also draped in pearls.

Ropes of creamy white and luminescent black pearls on a gold chain were looped around his neck. The first few ropes were tight against his throat and then the loops widened, falling to sway against his chest and down even further. One particularly long strand almost touched his cock and the sight made her feel a little lightheaded. There was just something about seeing a man wrapped in pearls that was unexpectedly appealing. Holding onto his spear, with the warm light of the setting sun gilding parts of him and casting other parts in shadow, he looked very much like a godly statue sprung to life.

"Are you going to keep standing there or were you planning to help?" the god asked.

Jumping a little, she had to straighten her crown while she shook her head guiltily. "I wasn't staring,"

"I said standing. And what I meant was move your ass and help me with this."

She didn't move, she was too busy fixating on the way some of the pearls pressed against his throat as he talked. "You're wearing a lot of pearls, McBryde."

"I thought they really set off my tan," he shot back.

"They definitely set off something." Her gaze flicked back down to his dick and her face heated.

"Wilhelmina." There was a warning note in his voice and she blinked and reminded herself that friends weren't supposed to ogle each other. Her movements were slightly jerky as she moved to help him. They had used one of the swords to cut the rope on the buoy and then tied it so they could each help drag their cargo over the uneven ground. She bent to pick up her pull-rope and resolutely looked anywhere besides Alex's personal bit of gold as it flashed by at eye-level. Together they pulled the gold bars and bowl of small, loose treasure through the trees.

"You know, we could have just left this shit back in the cave. We're not going anywhere, it's not going anywhere..." Alex said with a particularly hard tug on his rope as the buoy dragged over a clump of leaves

"We *are* going somewhere. We're getting off this island. You said it yourself, there are planes, there are boats. People are looking for us. And leaving all this in there makes it more likely some of it will get left behind. Besides, that cave gives me the creeps and I want to examine the treasure."

"You mean you want to wear it," he said, giving her crown, emerald necklace, and fingers full of rings a pointed look.

"Says the gentleman draped in pearls."

"They kept sliding out of the fucking bowl!"

She smirked. "Hey, you don't have to justify it to me. There's room for two queens on this island."

He knocked his shoulder into hers as they drew up to the campsite. "You're a brat." The lifebuoy slid to a halt beside the rest of the treasure they had managed to bring out of the cave and Alex dropped his rope with a grateful huff. "And on that note, I think I'll put my shorts back on and de-jewel." He pointed imperiously at the treasure. "You can unload."

Willa gave him a short bow and snuck one last, fascinated look. "Whatever you say, your majesty."

She thought she heard him mutter something about her asking for a royal punishment as he unlooped the pearls and, embarrassingly, it set off a burst of heat inside her. Trying to avoid getting caught staring (again), she set about the task of unloading. She stacked the gold bricks into a neat little pyramid, putting her crown on top, then began tugging at the large pot of gold coins. She managed to pull it off the sled but then noticed something odd peeking out the top. Digging into the treasure, her hand closed around the cool, glass neck of a bottle.

"What is this?" she asked, pulling it loose. She moved closer to the fire, examining the contents sloshing inside. Alex's voice was smooth when he answered and far too close to her ear.

"That, Willa love, is a good time."

Her head whipped toward him as a shiver worked its way down her spine. He was wearing his old, devilish grin. "Is this alcohol?" she asked incredulously and his grin widened.

"The best rum a pirate can steal I expect."

"Where did you find it?" She turned the bottle and ran her fingers over the thickly detailed maker's mark impressed on the foggy green glass. The whole thing was heavy in her hands. Like a bad idea.

"It was tucked close to the wall of the cave." He plucked the bottle from her, clearly unphased by its weight and picked up the jeweled sword leaning against a tree.

"Grab us a torch, would you? The stars are coming out and I think we've earned a bit of a vacation."

"This doesn't seem like what you're supposed to do when you're stuck out in the wilderness."

"Neither is chasing after crabs or diving into mysterious holes and yet." Giving her a pointed look, he began walking in the direction of the beach. "Come along, Wilhelmina."

Frowning, she nevertheless grabbed one of the thicker sticks with its end in the fire and hustled after him through the dark.

Sometime later, after re-building the fire on the beach to an impressive size, Willa flopped back on the sand and gave a tired groan. Overhead, the stars were spilling across the sky, reminding her of bioluminescent plankton and making her think dreamily that this was what it looked like when the universe moved. Below her bare legs, the sand was still warm from the day's sunshine and a balmy breeze fluttered through her poor, ragged AC/DC shirt. Birds called sleepily to each other, the waves beat against the shore while trees rustled and breathed against her neck—the universe could move all it liked, she decided, she was staying put.

"Maybe we do deserve a vacation. All this heavy lifting and constant need to gather food is exhausting." She stretched her toes toward the fire and wished for s'mores. Or a hamburger. She would kill for a hamburger.

"Sounds like you need a drink," Alex said, turning away from the fire to face her.

She smiled hesitantly and lifted a finger. "One pina colada, please, bartender."

"Coming right up." He picked up the bottle of rum and the sword and with one smooth stroke, popped off the top of the bottle.

She actually yelped in surprise. "What the hell?"

"It's a party trick." He took a shot of the rum and Willa watched his eyes close in a familiar look of pleasure. "Ah, beauty, that is what I needed. Here, try it." He pushed the bottle toward her. "Careful of the broken glass."

She took a tentative sip and fire exploded in the back of her throat. "Oh God," she gasped.

Laughing, he plopped down next to her and pounded her on the back. "Careful there, dag, this is vintage. You're meant to savor."

"It's not vintage, it's vile," she said, thrusting the bottle back at him. He took it but he was still laughing.

"You take that back," he said, "This is quality."

"If that's quality, I never want to find out what crappy rum tastes like."

"You don't know? Haven't you ever gone out for cheap drinks? Had a weak, over-sweetened pina colada on a beach somewhere?"

She shook her head and watched dubiously as he took another sip, that same lip-bitingly appealing look crossing his face as he hummed in pleasure. "So good." He passed the bottle back. "Try again. Ease it in slow. Give yourself time to adjust to the feel of it in your mouth before you swallow."

And just like that, the heat she'd felt earlier was back, bursts of it coloring her cheeks, lighting up her chest, and making other parts of her warm and liquid. For a moment, her traitorous brain imagined him back in his pearls, imagined the longest strand brushing across her lips as he stood over her and said the exact same thing.

She grabbed the rum bottle and took a deliberate sip, determined to make the alcohol the only source of heat in her body. This time she was able to swallow without coughing and she took an additional sip just to prove to herself she could. The rush of heat down her throat was dizzying.

"Phew." She swayed a little and Alex put a steadying hand on her shoulder.

"Easy there. You don't drink very often, do you?"

She shook her head and took another tiny taste. It got less vile each time she tried it.

"Bars aren't really my scene and it's sad to drink alone," she said with a shrug. "You know, if this is poisoned we would never be able to tell."

Alex's smile faded and the thumb still resting on her shoulder began to stroke lightly at the base of her neck. She wondered if he was even aware of it or if it was just a reflex. Meanwhile all the nerve endings in her body seemed to have migrated to that exact spot. She took a much longer sip of rum this time and focused on that burst of heat instead.

"No self-respecting pirate would poison his rum. It would be blasphemy," he said as Willa swallowed and let out another sharp gasp. His eyes narrowed and he reached over and took the bottle. "Are you telling me you never go out?"

Dropping her head back, she gestured expansively at the sky. "I'm out right now."

"That's not what I mean and you know it."

She shrugged again and spoke to the stars swirling above her. "I don't understand the point of it."

"To meet people, have fun, maybe get in a bit of trouble."

She gave a mock gasp of outrage. "I would never!"

"What? Get in trouble?"

She laughed and if there was a slightly bitter note to the sound, she ignored it. "No. Have fun. Meet people."

"Willa—"

"Oh, come on, don't get sentimental on me now, McBryde, it was a *joke.*"

He clearly didn't think it was. "We could have gone out together."

She snorted and sent him some serious side-eye as she jerked the rum bottle out of his grip. "Are you sure *you* don't have a concussion? We weren't friends." She took a swig, ignoring Alex's wince and feeling downright piratanical. "We wouldn't be friends now if present circumstances hadn't forced us to work together and who knows what will happen when we leave here." She sighed and took another drink. "*If* we leave here."

He took the bottle away again and set it out of reach then he turned and gave her a look that was far too serious for someone drinking three-hundred-year-old booze. "Why weren't we friends? You seemed to hate me from the moment we met."

He asked like it mattered to him, like he had actually been hurt.

Like it was somehow her fault.

Willa felt more heat flood her body but this time it was for a completely different reason.

"Are you kidding me?" she asked, outraged. How could he not know? As if it was something she had just decided on a whim. Sharks didn't have whims. They had instincts and he had proved hers right from the very beginning.

Clearly bewildered, he shook his head. "No, really. I feel like we met, you hated me, and then suddenly we were enemies."

Drawing away from him, she crossed her arms over her chest and tried to glare, any intensity however was undermined by a hiccup. "Don't you remember—hic—the night we met?"

"Of course I do. It was at the graduate student meet-and-greet. You were wearing a dark green dress." He reached out, as if unable to stop himself, and twined one of her escaped curls around his finger. "Your hair looked like a halo."

Her nerve endings had become sponges, soaking up the rum and making her explicitly aware of even the lightest touch. That small, affectionate brush of his fingers should barely have registered but instead a shiver raced across her skin. Only the memory of what came next kept her addled brain from doing anything stupid. Like kissing him. Again. Which was also perhaps why her next words had more snap than intended.

"I'm impressed you remember what I was wearing because you seemed to make a point of ignoring me for the rest of the night." She jerked her head, tugging her hair out from between his fingers and a line appeared between his eyebrows.

"What are you talking about? I didn't ignore you."

She snorted again and it was like the rum had stripped her tongue of the ability to lie. "Oh please. Professor Schwartz introduced us, you gave me the look all men give me, barely managed to say hello, and then you were gone. You spent the rest of the night talking and making friends with everyone else in the room but you barely said one word to me. The only other times you even looked at me were when you were surrounded by other people and laughing." She flopped onto her back and glared at the sky. She remembered exactly how it had felt, that sharp sting of immediate rejection, it was something she had felt a thousand other times in her life but no matter how familiar it was, she never got used to it. "I've been on the wrong side of the playground often enough to know what it means when people look over at you and suddenly burst out laughing. You made it really clear that night you were the new popular kid and I was the weirdo outcast. So, I just thought, 'to hell with him,' and that was it."

"You thought I was making fun of you the whole night?" His voice rose but when she flinched, he made a visible effort to get himself under control. "And what the fuck is this look?"

"You know," she waved her hand around searchingly, struggling to pick out the right words from the undulating sea of her brain. Clearly this was a sign she needed more rum. For, like, sea legs or something. Mental sea legs. "It's that blank, uncomprehending look men give you when you're not beautiful and therefore not worth their time." She tried to peer around his shoulder. "What have you done with the rum?"

Laying down on his side so he was facing her (and blocking her view of the alcohol), Alex propped his head on his hand and met her eyes.

"You're right, Willa, you're not beautiful."

She sucked in a sharp, hurt breath then told herself she didn't care. "I don't need you to state the obvious, McBryde. Isn't that what I *just said?*"

"Will you let me finish?" He didn't raise his voice this time but the words were still low and harsh. "You're not beautiful." He paused and his eyes were intent on hers, as if daring her to interrupt and she bit her tongue, wanting to know what he was going to say even if it hurt. "You are, however, something rare and unique and completely striking and most men don't know what to do when confronted with a true work of art. Most probably don't even recognize it and even fewer know how to actually appreciate it. Whatever this look is, it's not a sign that you're unworthy. It's a sign they are. Most people spend their whole lives as stick figures, but you?" He blew out a breath and shook his head. "Willa, you're a fucking masterpiece."

Her lips pursed and rather than feeling better, what he said only made her feel worse. Nothing he was saying aligned with the data she had spent a lifetime gathering. Which meant either she was wrong or Alexander "Master of the Line" McBryde was full of shit. She knew which conclusion was more probable. "That is the most nonsense thing I've ever heard you say and considering some of the conversations we've had in the last five years, that's saying something."

He scowled back. "It's not nonsense, it's the truth. I was looking at you for the rest of the night because I was trying to figure out how to talk to you. You didn't even smile when we met."

"Why would I smile at someone who looked like he couldn't wait to get away?" She rolled onto her side so she was facing him and poked him in the chest. "You talk to women all the time, what was there to figure out?"

"Yeah, *women*. Not fierce Baroque Amazons."

"So, what? You're telling me all this time I've just been too intimidating?" She laughed but it was harsh and bitter. "Come on, Alex, I may be socially inept but I'm not oblivious."

"Considering some of the things you've done in the last five days, that's debatable. And if you truly think there's never been a single man who's looked at you and *wanted*—" He broke off abruptly his eyes dark and intense and a quiver looped around her stomach. The way he was looking at her was almost, *almost* enough to make her believe he was telling the truth but then he pressed his lips together and shook his head, breaking eye contact. "Look, few men, few *people*, are willing to take on a challenge without some encouragement. A smile, a little flirting. You know, a little reassurance you're not going to shoot an arrow through their heart."

"So you're saying if I had smiled at you that first night you would have stayed and talked to me?" The skepticism in her voice should have flayed him, stripped him down to the truth. But he didn't give up.

"No, Wilhelmina love, I'm saying I would have fallen at your feet and worshiped." Each word was low and rough and for a single moment she enjoyed the way they shuddered through her, the way they arrowed straight between her thighs and sent heat rippling out through the rest of her limbs along hyper-sensitive, drunken nerves. There was so much heat in his gaze but she didn't know if it was genuine or just the reflection of the fire burning away behind her.

The Genius of Evil she reminded herself. Alexander McBryde was the devil. Maybe they were friends now, here on this island, maybe he even meant what he said, calling her love with that silver tongue. That didn't mean it wasn't still forked or that he wasn't still a flirt. Under different circumstances, Lucifer had been an angel too.

Willa had no intention of falling, not for him and not for the pretty, pyrite nonsense he was spilling into her ears. She had no intention of entering into the hellfire but she had drunk enough rum that she thought maybe she could play just close enough to feel the heat on her skin. Just enough that she could prove him a liar. She reached out, her palm brushing over his shoulder as she leaned toward him. His breath stuttered out, his eyes darted to her mouth but then he shook his head.

"Willa, I don't know if we should—"

She cut him off. "You started this, McBryde."

Her fingers closed around the neck of the bottle behind him and she pulled back abruptly, dropping it down between them. "I'm definitely ahead," she said sweetly. "Catch up."

Survival Tip #12

If you don't want to make decisions like a pirate, DO NOT DRINK LIKE ONE.

They were playing a dangerous game.

Perhaps the rum hadn't been the best idea in the world but when he'd found it, all Alex had been able to think was "Yes, thank God, a break." For the past week his brain felt like it had been neatly divided into two camps: survival and Wilhelmina Jones. It turned out survival was the easy camp. It was Willa that made everything, *everything,* hard.

He shifted uncomfortably on the sand, stiff at the vision she made with her back to the fire, the light making her body a shadowed outline through her threadbare shirt. It would have been better if she was naked—then there was no mystery. But there was something about the way the firelight made the curve of her waist a flickering tease through the fabric that put his imagination into hyperdrive, like he was reverting to being a hormone-fueled teenager who spent all his time wondering about girls and their pretty curves hidden just out of reach. It made a man want to explore. It could have also been the rum, infused with the wandering, roving spirit of a pirate. Or it was just Willa.

She was laughing, her earlier anger swallowed up with each additional sip of rum. It was another surprising thing about her. Uninhibited, her laugh was loud and bright and hearing it felt like taking a shot of champagne, the joy of it fizzing through him. It felt like a loss having gone five years without it and a precious gift to be hearing it now. It was brilliant. And torturous. It made him want things he had already decided he couldn't have, and it had been a long time since Alex needed to deny himself. He was out of practice.

Strewth, had he really told her a smile was all it would have taken to turn him into a supplicant the night they met? He should be relieved she hadn't believed him because nothing had changed. She still didn't trust they would be friends after they made it off this island and he wondered if the reason was because of what she believed about herself or because of what she believed about him. He didn't know which answer was worse. Either way, he needed to find a way to make Willa trust him...which meant any more honesty between them could prove disastrous.

Which was why the game they were playing was so dangerous.

Sitting cross-legged, facing each other, he held out both of his hands, palms face down, and waited, watching Willa closely. Moving more rapidly than a woman who'd had at least three shots of rum should be capable of, her hands darted out, seeking his. He pulled back but he was too slow. She managed to slap the tips of his fingers and let out a whoop of triumph.

"You know, it's a wonder you managed to save me at all with reflexes like that. My grandmother is better at this game than you are." She shoved the rum into his hands, her cheeks flushed, her mouth stretched wide in a grin. "Drink up, Dundee."

Alex took a sip of the rum, savoring it in his mouth before swallowing. It had the faintest hints of coconut and lime and he felt the warmth as it set little fires all the way down to his gut. Smoke tinged the edges of his brain but where the liquor had touched his lips felt cool.

He might have been losing a little bit on purpose.

"Okay, what truth do you want?" he asked, putting the bottle back down next to them.

Willa tapped her chin contemplatively and then tilted her head curiously. "Why did you become a marine biologist?"

"Because I saw *Jaws* at a formative age and instead of being scared I was mad on the shark's behalf," he answered instantly. It was the rote answer Alex gave whenever anyone asked this question—which they always did. He was willing to bet no one ever asked an accountant why they wanted to become one but even people who were afraid of the ocean found it fascinating. Being forced to give free lectures was an occupational hazard.

Unfortunately, Willa was a marine biologist too. She grinned but her eyes narrowed in calculation. "No, the real answer. Those are the rules of the game."

He looked away from her out over the ocean, so dark and restless, dangerous—it had almost swallowed them whole—and yet still so beautiful and grand and unknown it made him ache with the same kind of wonder he imagined others had toward God. "Because I love it. The ocean was part of all my best moments. Going to the beach with my family when I was a kid, campfires with my best friends, my first beer with my dad on my sixteenth birthday, just the two of us on a boat, fishing, my first kiss—" he broke off, veering away from those deeper waters and shrugged. "I love it so I wanted to take care of it."

He looked back and Willa had lost her smile. She was looking at him like he was some new specimen under a microscope.

"Wow, that's actually really...sweet," she said curiously and Alex felt the back of his neck get hot. Somehow Willa was the only woman in the world capable of so neatly scalpelling him open and getting to the truth of his insides.

He tried to change the subject, "What's the real reason you became a marine biologist then?" He watched as Willa immediately withdrew, even with the rum making her cheeks pink and her eyes bright, he saw the moment the distance in them grew.

"It's not my turn," she said quickly, wiggling her fingers at him. "Hands up, McBryde."

Alex put his hands up, determined this time to—

Smack!

Jesus Christ, how was she so fast.

"How old were you when you had your first kiss?" she asked, and despite the easy demand in her voice, Alex noticed she was fidgeting with one of her curls. It was something he had noticed she did when she was nervous, like an Amazon plucking at her bow string. That small display of nerves was the only reason he was able to say the words.

"I was eighteen the first time I kissed a girl." Ten years later and it was still one of his most vivid memories. "Her name was Fay Taylor and she worked at the pub me and my mates went to every weekend." He watched her for weeks, working up the courage to ask her out and when she said yes, he spent days agonizing over planning the perfect first date.

He had been so goddamn determined she was The One. He'd been so young. And clueless.

Willa's mouth fell open and she shook her head. "I don't believe you."

He raised an eyebrow at her. "Why would I lie about this?"

"I don't know but it has to be a lie. Eighteen is so old."

His friends had thought so too. Anytime a pretty girl walked by, they had teased him mercilessly. But, back then, he had big plans for his first kiss and he told her what he told them. "I didn't have time to go out flirting and chatting up girls when I was younger. I was too busy going to school and working or taking care of my sisters." It wasn't the whole truth and Willa seemed to know it. She was a lot more critical than even his best friend had been. Every day up until the day Alex kissed Fay, the dickhead had offered to kiss him just so Alex would stop being a bloody embarrassment to the rugby team.

"Those are terrible excuses. You said you played rugby. You never kissed a cheerleader under the bleachers after a game? Or cut class to make-out with a lab partner in a broom closet?"

He shrugged. "Nope. Whether you believe me or not, I made it all the way through high school without kissing a single person." And before she could pry further, he forced his most provoking grin and asked, "When was your first kiss?" Just like before, she let the subject drop.

"It's not my turn to tell the truth," she said primly and then she smiled, a pretty display of lips and teeth and smug and Alex's heart did a strange flip in his chest.

He cleared his throat. "Bring it on, dag." He'd barely finished speaking before her hands were shooting out but this time they swished through nothing but air. He met her astonishment with a slow, superior smile.

"I win, Wilhelmina."

Her eyes narrowed again at his tone but there was the slightest tremble in her hands as she took the bottle of rum and tipped it back. Alex waited until she was done, watching with shameful anticipation as she swallowed and then dragged her thumb across her lip to catch an errant drop of rum. She licked it off and his body responded with a hot, hard rush. "How old were you when you had your first kiss?" He asked, his eyes still fixed on her mouth. He watched it purse and then, after several silent moments, finally mutter,

"I was eighteen."

His eyes shot back up to hers. "Are you kidding me? You said that was old."

She glared, her cheeks flushing a deeper shade of red he suspected was caused more by embarrassment than rum. "It's different!"

"How?" he insisted.

"Because unless you underwent a serious ugly duckling transformation in college, I'm sure the girls were all over you in high school. I can't believe you didn't kiss a single one. Or snog? Is that an Australian thing?"

"No, we pash, and whether you believe it or not, I didn't pash a single girl in secondary school. I wanted the first one to mean something." The truth slipped out of him before he could stop it and it was his first time ever saying it out loud.

"That doesn't sound like the typical attitude of a teenage boy." Willa's voice was skeptical but her eyes were bright and interested and the rest of it came spilling out, like a part of him had been waiting to tell someone this secret his entire life.

"My dad has only ever kissed my mum. I grew up hearing him talk about how she was going to be his first and last kiss." He looked up at the stars, remembering the soothing, tired sound of his father's voice as he told Alex and his sisters the story of the first time he saw their mum. It was the first bedtime story he remembered. "I guess I thought it was romantic," he muttered even though there was no guessing about it.

He had been so determined to follow in his father's footsteps, so convinced he would see a woman and just know she was The One the way his dad always claimed to know about his mum. His parents had met when they were sixteen and had been together for twenty-nine years. Alex was born before they graduated secondary school and despite the challenges, their home had always been a warm, loving place with his parents' love story making every day feel like they were all part of some happy ending. Some kids grew up believing in magic and fairytales but Alex had grown up believing in True Love.

"And that was one of your best moments?"

He nodded slowly. "It was," he said, remembering the moment so sharply it hurt. It had seemed like the perfect first kiss: a pretty girl, sunset on St. Kilda beach, their future stretching out in front of him like the endless, painted waves—it had felt like a destiny being realized. He shook his head at his own past foolishness. "I thought it was true love."

"I'm guessing it wasn't?" Oddly, there was none of Willa's usual bite to the question, it was soft, gentle even.

Alex had dated Fay all through Uni. She was the first woman he ever kissed and asking her out was of the first things he ever did that was just for himself. Maybe he had been too greedy or too selfish or maybe he had just been unworthy but whatever the reason, Fay had taught him a lesson he needed to learn.

He shook his head. "No," he said simply, "It wasn't."

"So it didn't mean anything after all," said Willa, her voice surprisingly sad.

"I wouldn't say that. I think all kisses mean something," he said slowly. Even that first and last kiss with Fay. It had meant growing up. He thought about the day he went to surprise her with a ring in his pocket and found her flat empty. No phone call, no note—nothing. She was just gone. He found out later she had moved abroad with someone else and it had felt like his whole life, the foundation of his family and dreams, had cracked open and swallowed him whole. That was the day all his silly, fairytale delusions about love died. His gaze fell from the stars to Willa's face. "They just never mean true love," he said finally.

There was a moment of silence, Willa was still looking at him like a woman who wasn't half drunk on three-hundred-year-old booze and he shifted again on the sand, still uncomfortable but for different reasons. He shrugged and shot her a half-smile. "Didn't yours mean something?"

She made a face. "The boy I kissed *was* a typical teenage boy." Pausing, she took another fortifying sip of rum and rushed on, "Ryan Hoffmaster. Senior prom. We didn't go together but he saw me sitting alone and—" she cut herself off abruptly, her rum soaked cheeks paling a little as she looked down at the sand.

"And what?"

She shook her head, or rather she shook the entire upper half of her body, as if the alcohol had tied all her joints together. "It's honestly too humiliating."

Of course that only made him more desperate to hear it, like it would somehow restore balance to whose guts were spilled across the beach.

"What if I promise to share something embarrassing as well?" He offered and that caught her attention. She looked up at him with an expression that was too calculating for someone without full control of the rest of her body.

"How embarrassing?"

"The most," he promised. She stared at him for a few moments longer and then finally gave another full body shake.

"Okay." She took another sip from the bottle then poured out the words in a rush, "I found out afterwards he had a bet with his friends."

Alex froze. "What?" The lingering taste of rum on his lips went sour. "He made a bet about whether or not he could kiss you?"

Willa shook, the rum sloshed. "No. About whether or not I was a virgin. He won fifty bucks." She took another sip of rum and gestured dramatically out at the ocean with the bottle. "Although I've always felt I should have gotten half. It was my hymen after all." She said it so casually, almost flippantly, as if this bastard didn't deserve to be beaten to a pulp and keelhauled.

"Are you saying you had sex with this bastard?" He willed her to say no, to tell him he had misunderstood but she hiccuped and nodded.

"See? I told you it was embarrassing. He is one of the two men who have seen me naked." She giggled tipsily and gestured at Alex. "Well, three now, but you don't count because we haven't had sex."

"Why? Why would you sleep with someone like that?"

She shrugged again. "It was prom. He was popular. It's what you're supposed to do. I guess I was also curious but I didn't really get what all the fuss was about after." She frowned and looked contemplatively down at the rum. "I still don't get it. The second time wasn't great either and that guy stole my Bio notes right before the final." Her frown deepened. "I got an A minus."

Rage went splitting through him, like a thermal vent, dark, boiling, and on the verge of cracking his surface open. Alex was going to hunt both these men down and murder them. Oblivious to his fury, Willa went on, her voice taking on the educational tone she used while lecturing.

"Did you know the average amount of time people engage in vaginal penetration is three to seven minutes? I looked it up after the first time because it was over so fast I thought we had done it wrong. Maybe his friends should have only given him twenty-five bucks." She laughed, she actually fucking *laughed* when Alex was ready to crush this guy's dick between a couple of coconuts. "It took longer to get my dress back on than it did for him to orgasm." She took another shot of rum and looked up at the stars. "I wonder what happened to him."

Alex swiped the bottle out of Willa's hand. She had definitely had enough. "If there's any justice in the world he's dead or living some lonely, miserable life," he said and meant it, looking at Willa with her face highlighted by cool, silver starlight and her hair glowing from the flames. It was easy to forget that a star in all its distant brilliance was a fire burning a million times hotter, a million times brighter than any bonfire. That Ryan kid was worse than a bastard. He was a fool. A second glance, a closer look, it was so obvious Wilhelmina Jones was a star and instead of recognizing her for what she was, the foolish bastard had treated her like a match, something small and insignificant and disposable.

Alex hoped the other man was burning in some awful, personal hell because he was now starting to see Willa's own singed edges. He leaned toward her, knowing he should keep his mouth shut, knowing that later, once she sobered up, she would hate that she had shared this much with him, but anger was even more intoxicating than rum.

"Listen to me, that is not what sex should be like."

"What? Fast?" She tilted her head at him, clearly bemused.

"No, it can be fast but it should never leave you wondering if you did it wrong." He reached out and grabbed her hands, building a bridge between their bodies.

"Alex, this isn't how you play the game," she said playfully but he only squeezed her hands tighter, needing her to listen and really hear him.

"That bastard didn't deserve to touch you. Neither of them did."

"Alex—"

"No." He pulled her hands so she was forced to lean closer. "This isn't a game. He didn't deserve to touch you and you deserved something better your first time than a quick fuck with some ungrateful prick who didn't even bother to make you come." She was no longer smiling but he didn't stop. She needed to hear this. "Sex is like kissing, it should always mean *something* because a *person* always matters. It may not be profound and it may not be true love but at the very least it should still mean everyone has a good time."

"Is that what you meant when you said you would have worshiped me? It would have been a good time?" she asked, her voice breathless and fluid, the ends of each word running into the next, and Alex knew without a doubt she was drunk. Drunk enough to forget. Which meant he could be honest—just one more time.

She probably wouldn't believe him anyway.

"No, Wilhelmina, worshipping you could only be profound. I would have spent hours, *days,* exploring every last inch of you, would have made it my goddamn reason for being to find the soft, hidden parts that make you tremble and beg. Then I would have fucked you, long and hard until my name was the only thing you remembered."

"Oh," she breathed and their faces were so close now that Alex felt that small exhalation against his mouth. His insides twisted again but this time it wasn't his heart, it was much, much lower. Desire made his whole body tighten painfully. His eyes dropped to her lips so he saw the exact moment they softened into a frown. "I'm sorry," she whispered.

Confused by this sudden apology and carried away by just how much he wanted her, his voice was almost as quiet, "For what?"

"For giving you a—a meaningless kiss. The other beach. On the—the day. You deserve better too." Her words were halting and she blinked slowly, as if it was a struggle to keep her eyes open but then they met his and held. "Could we try again?"

Alex felt the world around him stop.

"Try again?" She couldn't really be asking what he thought she was asking. Had he fallen asleep? Was this a dream? But then she nodded slowly, her hand slipping out of his to rise and press against his chest, right over his pounding heart, and he knew that even his subconscious wouldn't be so bold.

"It can just be a good time. It won't mean anything else. I just want to understand." Her eyes drifted shut and a throaty little hum escaped her. "I want to forget everything but your name. Alex. Please," she said and she was so close now, he felt the words vibrate through the air and brush against his lips. He was completely lost, wanting her so much he could barely breathe. He had to say no. She was drunk. But God, all he wanted to give her was anything and everything she asked for. He braced himself, gathering the willpower he would need to push her back but then she saved them both by pitching forward. He barely managed to keep her from face-planting into the sand.

His heart was still racing, his cock throbbing as he stared down at the now unconscious woman in his arms. She had asked him to kiss her.

No.

This strange, infuriating, brilliant, absolutely magnificent woman had asked him to do more than kiss her. She had even said please.

The rum had been a terrible idea.

Because she would forget this but Alex wouldn't. Never, for as long as he lived. Willa whispering the word please was going to be the beginning and end of his every erotic dream from now on—and that was all it would ever be—a dream. Because they had been trapped here together long enough for him to finally admit another truth even if this time it was only to himself: having sex with Willa could never just be a good time. Not for him. He already liked her too much.

For months after Fay disappeared, Alex had barely been able to function. He had given her his first kiss and the only real dream he ever had. He never wanted to feel that empty or that broken again. That was part of the reason none of the relationships in the past few years had lasted beyond a few months. Maybe Willa was right about him—but a scoundrel never got his heart broken and a fuckboy was never around long enough to be left.

He lowered Willa gently back onto the sand and she curled toward him, her breath fanning against his wrist, her fingers coming to rest a few centimeters from his. Even unconscious she looked fierce, the only softness in the broad, sharp angles of her face the Amazon-bow curve of her mouth. His heart beat with a slow, dull ache. She could break him. Would break him. If he gave her the chance. Because even after everything, she was still Wilhelmina Jones and he was still Alexander McBryde and just like the night they met, looking at her now, she was still a masterpiece and the certainty he was unworthy sat deep like a blade, heavy and painful inside his chest.

Survival Tip #13

Don't ask a dead man to tell tales unless you want to hear a ghost story.

Ten months since he had seen his love. Ten long months of sailing and stealing from right beneath her rich, powerful husband's nose. She was alone when he slipped into her bedroom, her husband no doubt off rutting with his mistress. It made things easier. Need was a savage thing inside him and Rigobert would have killed anyone who dared get between him and Joséphine.

She was still asleep as he strode to the bed, her mass of dark hair plaited, her round cheeks flushed pink with dreams. She looked fuller than when he last left her, her breasts spilling out of the low neck of her fine cotton chemise. He noted with pleasure that she still wore his token, the thin gold chain disappearing into that pretty valley.

He kissed her palm. "Wake up, my treasure, your heart has returned."

She came awake with a start and for a brief moment he saw the joy on her face before it was swiftly swallowed by fear. "Rig, you cannot be here!"

"Here is the only place I can be. I need you. I've missed you."

"You don't understand—" she was cut off by the sound of feet marching toward the door. He rose, his hand going to his sword as her voice trembled, "Last time you came, you left more than just me behind." The footsteps drew closer, accompanied by the telltale clink of swords. "There was a child."

Rigobert looked sharply down at her. "A child?"

She nodded. "François has sworn to see you hanged. You must go. Out the window, quick!"

There was no time. The doors burst open and half a dozen guards streamed into the room, led by the governor of this small island, Joséphine's husband. He was smiling, a cruel, self-satisfied smile while he pointed a pistol at Rigobert's heart.

"At last, the vulture returns to feed on the refuse," he said coldly, his eyes flicking to his wife and back. "I had almost begun to think you forgot about my whore wife."

Rigobert's hand tightened on his sword. "Call her a whore again and I will cut the tongue from your mouth." He took a step toward the governor and the man cocked his pistol. There was the rustle of fabric and then Joséphine was at Rigobert's side.

"François, please, let him go. I will do anything."

"I want nothing from you, wife. At least the whores on the docks are honest. They never aspire to live anywhere but on their knees." He sneered, "Perhaps that is where I'll leave you. You and that bastard child."

"You lichieres pautonnier!" Rigobert launched himself toward the other man. A shot rang out. Hands on his back shoved him aside. There was a sharp, pained intake of breath. Spinning he found blood blossoming against the white of Joséphine's chemise. In the room next door, a baby began to cry and that was where she looked as she collapsed. He caught her as she fell. Cold like the freezing black water at the bottom of the ocean filled Rigobert's veins. He shook his head in denial.

"No. Joséphine! Why—"

"Our son needs—" she stopped, the words catching on a choked cough. Tears trailed from the corners of her eyes and despair was a dagger in his back. "Save him," she whispered. Her hand reached for his cheek and her beautiful blue eyes, dark and more lovely even than the sea sucked him in, her last demand a storm that threatened to sink him. "Kiss me."

"It should have been me." He pressed a kiss to her lips and she sighed her last breath into his mouth. It settled inside him like an anchor.

"Such a touching scene," said the Governor, "But don't worry, you'll be joining her soon enough." He turned and spoke to the soldiers who had followed him into the room. "Take him to the jail and fetch someone to silence the whelp."

Rigobert stood, breaking the chain around Joséphine's neck, the gold token he'd given her ten years ago pressing into his palm. The reminder of his devotion written in the encrypted alphabet they had created as children burned him like a brand. He said nothing as he picked up his sword and faced the charging soldiers. Nothing as he killed the first two. Nothing as he plunged his sword into the governor's gut. He twisted the hilt and blood flowed like water onto his hand. He killed every single man who had born witness to Joséphine's murder and done nothing. He didn't look back at her body as he left. He couldn't, just like he couldn't speak past the regret wrapped like two hands around his throat.

Cold and determined, he collected his crying son, wiped off his bloody blade and returned to his ship. Any mercy, any last shred of decency or honor he had maintained so he could return to Joséphine feeling like a man even marginally worthy had died with her. Tonight, the world had taken the only thing he ever really loved, swiftly, brutally, and without a second thought. He hoped the world was ready, because he planned to do the same.

Waking up in a standing position was odd, waking up freezing cold in pitch darkness was terrifying. For a moment, while her brain struggled to understand what was happening, Willa was convinced she had been buried alive and bit back a scream. There was a bitter taste in her mouth, so strong she could barely breathe around it. Gasping, almost hyperventilating, she pressed a hand to her chest where her heart beat in agony. She had never experienced a broken heart before but the pain, the sense of loss was so crushing it almost sent her to her knees. She was so distracted by what she was feeling she almost didn't realize what she was seeing.

Again, it was like moonlight on water or sunshine glimpsed through a heavy fog. The pirate's ghost cast just enough light for Willa to see she was in an unfamiliar cave. In front of her, just visible, was a raised stone altar and sitting on top of it was the most decadent, opulent cross Willa had ever seen. About a foot and a half tall it was pure gold and encrusted in gems and she knew without any sort of professional treasure qualifications that this was the most valuable thing the pirate had stolen.

Return. The order reverberated through her and she felt the first faint traces of warmth as anger sparked through her.

"Are you kidding me? You *possessed* me, you bastard!" It was the only explanation for how she had wound up here. The last thing she remembered was falling asleep on the beach with Alex.

Oh God, Alex. How long had she been gone? He was going to be furious.

RETURN!

Feeling like her hand had just been plunged into a bucket of ice water, Willa struggled for control as it was raised toward the cross. However, rather than grabbing the cross itself, her hand closed around a small, gold pendant hanging on it from a delicate gold chain.

As soon as her fingers closed around the pendant, the dream came rushing back.

The pirate. His murdered love. His son. And just like that, she knew. The ghost didn't care about the rest of the treasure, it was this, this small, relatively worthless love token that he wanted returned.

"Return where?" She cried furiously and an image of the woman, Joséphine, floated up in her mind like a water lily, her beautiful face blossoming bright and clear despite being anchored in the dark, sucking emotions still weighing Willa down. "She died! It's been, like, three hundred years." This was absurd. She was arguing with a ghost but she was too angry, too full of these awful second-hand emotions to be afraid.

Return.

Willa dropped the necklace around her neck to keep it safe and then propped her hands on her hips and glared...at the air. "If you want me to return this, you're going to have to show me the way out." Worried he might take her out the same way he'd brought her in, she added hastily, "And if you even think about possessing me again, I will chuck this necklace straight into the ocean."

Unlike the first time she'd seen the ghost and been able to make out its features, now he was nothing more than weak glimmers scattered across the cave floor. He led her down one of the dark tunnels and as she followed her hand rose to touch the charm hanging between her breasts. As soon as she touched the strangely warm metal, she was hit with another wave of borrowed emotion so strong she stumbled. This time, however, it wasn't regret or despair she felt. It was longing.

She jerked her hand away and the feeling dissipated just as she burst out through a wall of hanging vines into the jungle. She stopped and looked behind her at the tunnel she'd just emerged from. Set into the side of a hill, surrounded by huge leaves and the twisted roots of trees erupting out of the earth, the entrance of the cave was completely obscured by vines and hanging moss. Willa marked the spot with some stones before jogging toward the sound of the ocean, hoping she wasn't too far from last night's fire.

When she finally tumbled out onto sand, the sun was just finishing its rise over the horizon, painting the ocean in glorious reds and pinks and turning the billowing white clouds lounging around it gold. There were dolphins playing in the surf and birds diving into the water to catch their breakfast. For a moment, Willa just stopped and stared at it all. Every horror movie she had ever watched was a damn lie. This haunted island was the most beautiful place she had ever seen.

Smiling bitterly, she built another pile of stones to mark the spot, then took off down the beach. It wasn't long until she could smell their fire and as she followed the curve of the island, she had a glimmering spot of hope that she would get back to Alex before he woke up. After yesterday's close call with the booby trap, the words he had shouted at her felt like a scab, an itchy reminder of past mistakes urging her to move faster, to find him and explain.

He wasn't on the beach when she finally reached the smoking cinders and her hope turned similarly to ash. Grimacing, she imagined his face when she found him and fought back a shudder. Calling his name, she headed back into the forest on the slim chance he thought she'd merely woken up before him and gone to the river.

She stopped at their campsite first but Alex wasn't there either and the fire had almost completely gone out. She added a small piece of wood so he would know she had been there and then headed for the river. If she didn't find him there, she would wait. Going out to look for him just increased the chances they would keep missing each other. Emerging from the trees onto the riverbank, she fully expected to see him standing grumpily in the water ready to tell her off for disappearing again but there was no sign of him.

She called his name again, just in case he was in the cave but after a few moments of nothing but the babble of the river, Willa huffed out a breath. Damnit. He was definitely out looking for her and if his past reactions were anything to go by, when he found her this time, he was going to be more angry than Willa thought was reasonable. After all, it's not like she had *wanted* to be possessed.

Her skin crawled just thinking about it. The pirate, *Le Vautour*, may have loved the beautiful Joséphine but he clearly had no sensitive feelings for anyone else. In life he'd taken what he wanted and in death he was the same. He had taken Willa's body without her consent and a part of her now felt...tainted.

Suddenly filled with a desperate need for a bath, she stripped off her clothes and began wading into the river. The day was promising to be hotter than usual, the sun already blazing despite having just risen and a low mist hung over the cool water as the two elements clashed. Against her heated skin, the river felt like a balm, soothing and familiar. Irrationally she wished Alex was here now, yelling at her while he combed his fingers through her hair. It was another thing she would never admit, but those moments had become her favorite part of each day. Already feeling better, she began scrubbing her skin, scooping up water and thinking about how she would give her left arm for a loofah and some soap. Which was how Alex found her.

Crashing out of the underbrush, he came to an abrupt halt at the edge of the water and there was silence as they stared at each other. He looked rough. There were scratches on his torso, shadows under his eyes, and his hair looked wild, with leaves and twigs stuck in it at odd angles. He looked every inch a caveman. And he was staring at Willa with an expression she didn't recognize. Crossing a self-conscious arm over her breasts, she tried to smile.

"Oh, there you are."

He didn't say a word, just continued to stare at her with a tight, flat mouth and hard eyes. It was a look that made her insides twist uncomfortably. She began wading toward him, deciding she would rather not be naked for this conversation. "Alex, let me explain." She was almost to him. "I didn't mean to be gone—" her words were cut short as he lunged for her. Before she could even inhale to scream, he had her over his shoulder, his arm clamped tightly around her thighs as he spun and began heading toward camp. It took a moment for Willa to catch her breath but once she had, she let it out with an undignified screech.

"What the hell. Put me down!" She slapped at his (tanned, beautifully muscled) back and when that didn't work she took a deep breath and actually smacked his (firm, glorious) ass. His retribution was swift. He still hadn't said a word but he turned his head and bit the soft flesh of her hip. "Ow! Goddamnit, McBryde, you have no right to do this. Put me down right now or I swear to God—" she slapped him again and this time he returned it in kind. The warm, rough flat of his palm falling hard and quick against her ass, her *bare-naked ass*. The sting reverberated through her and despite knowing it was wrong in this particular situation, something deep and low inside Willa thrilled at that rough contact. Closing her eyes, she sucked in a calming breath even as her cheeks went hot.

She wouldn't even be able to look him in the eyes when she killed him for this.

Before she could compose herself enough to issue any more threats, he was hauling her into the circle of their campsite. She felt him bend as he grabbed something from near their tent but she couldn't see what it was through the aggressive tangle of her hair. In another dizzying whoosh, she was suddenly back on her feet but she wasn't given any time to orient herself. Alex's chest was pressing against hers, the tickle of his chest hair on her naked breasts sending another one of those humiliating thrills through her. She tried to blow the hair out of her mouth so she could yell at him as he pushed her back, his arms coming up along her sides and caging her in. Her back met the rough trunk of a tree and she tried to look up at him through her hair.

"Alex, what the hell do you think you're doing?" she was finally able to demand. He still hadn't said anything and Willa was starting to worry. She thought she heard him mutter, "what I promised," but it was too low to be sure. He pulled back, his hand brushed against her stomach, and then something tightened around her waist, pinning her arms to her sides. When she looked down, she saw his hands finishing off a knot in some rope they had cut from the lifebuoy and her mouth dropped open in outrage. She shook her head furiously to get her hair completely out of her face and glared up at him.

"You actually tied me to a tree?" Despite yesterday's threat, she hadn't, for even one second, ever considered Alex would have the audacity to tie her up. He made a show of checking the knot by tugging on it and then stepped back, surveying her. He gave a brief nod of satisfaction, crossed his arms and just continued to look at her with flinty eyes and a hard pressed mouth.

Swallowed by a blue whale and slowly dissolved in stomach acid, she thought viciously as she struggled against the rope and it rubbed against her skin, silky little abrasions on her arms and ribs. "Untie me," she demanded before abruptly remembering her dream, the one she'd had their second night in the tent. She had been naked and tied to a tree then too and just the memory was enough to make her go slick between her thighs. Any lingering ice from her possession was gone—she felt like she was on fire. "This isn't funny, McBryde," her voice shook but it wasn't from fear. Overhead, there was the distant rumble of thunder. A storm was coming.

He kept his eyes on hers, as if her body didn't even exist below the neck which was...comforting? Disappointing? There was tension in his shoulders but unlike in her dream, it wasn't from lust. He was angrier than she had ever seen him. Finally, after several more tense moments he spoke.

"Three and a half hours."

That confused her enough that she stopped struggling. "What?"

He tapped his dive watch. "You have been missing for almost four fucking hours," the words dropped between them, heavy and strained from his clenched jaw.

Had it really been that long? No wonder he was mad. She tried to explain.

"Alex—"

"How many times have you promised to stop doing this?" Some heat broke through all that cold anger and blasted against her skin. Unfortunately, Willa's own temper had always been made of matches. She lit up, her struggles renewed, and she knew in that moment if the pirate hadn't died hundreds of years ago, she wouldn't have hesitated to kill him.

Sometimes violence *was* the answer.

"I didn't do anything wrong. If you would just—" Alex cut her off again.

"But you did. I've been looking for you since before dawn. I don't know what you were thinking or if you were even thinking at all—"

"Excuse me?" she said, outraged. Another, louder crash of thunder pressed in around them and her skin felt tight and hot. She strained against the rope, the violence in her body turning back toward Alex. "You're walking on dangerous ground, McBryde. You don't know anything —"

He stepped closer, his hands coming up and pressing into the trunk on either side of her head, his face stark and haunted as he leaned down enough for their eyes to be level. "I know I woke up on the beach alone. I know I couldn't find you. I know I thought you were dead."

The first raindrop fell, hitting his cheek and sliding down his neck. Willa watched it and imagined curling her hand there. Imagined him pinned below her. Imagined squeezing. Warm rain began to fall on her shoulders, sliding over her breasts, down her sides. She imagined it was Alex's fingers, touching her everywhere.

She felt the heat rolling off his body, felt the tension coming off him. This was the edge of the lightning storm—the air between them charged and crackling. A shiver ran down her spine but she still wasn't afraid. How many times had he come after her when she needed him? She trusted he would keep her safe. She trusted *him*.

Even when he was a caveman.

"Alex—"

"No." His voice broke around the word and she felt his thumb skim lightly down the side of her throat, following the line of her pulse, so much hotter and more electric than any rain drop. There were darker brown rings around his pupils and he was so close now she thought they might swallow her up. "There's no fast-talking your way out of this, Willa. This time, you're the one who doesn't know anything."

There was another long roll of thunder, and she heard the echo of her words from their first day on the beach. Right before she had kissed him. And maybe it was the after-effects of being possessed by a reckless, lovelorn pirate or maybe Alex was right, and she just never thought things through. Whatever it was, her next words were no thought and all feeling.

"Prove it."

He froze. She saw surprise go streaking through his eyes but it was almost immediately swallowed up by the darkness of his expanding pupils. The tension in his body was practically audible and Willa swore she heard it release, like another roll of thunder, right before his mouth came crashing down on hers.

The first press of his lips was rough and deep, like he had been holding this back for so long, he couldn't stop from needing a little bit of everything at once. There was the brief, hot touch of his tongue against hers, the light scrape of his teeth against her lip, the pull of his lungs as he breathed just a bit of her in. It really was a good thing Willa was still tied to the tree because being kissed like this by Alex was the physical equivalent of a bat to the knees. And the head. The rope around her waist was the only thing keeping her upright.

His hands dropped down, one threading into her hair, cradling her head as he took the kiss deeper, while the other slid over slick, hot skin to settle at the base of her neck, fingers tightening around her shoulder, his thumb still pressed against her racing pulse. Willa had never understood love songs or poetry that expounded on the soft, sweet power of a kiss.

She still didn't.

But with the way Alex was kissing her, she didn't want to. *This* was what she wanted. It wasn't rosebuds at dawn or soft music and moonlit dinners. It was clinging deadly ivy wrapped around the trunk of a tree and the hot, gasping desperation that came after the dinner candles were blown out. It was all-consuming—base—a point of no return.

The skies cracked open and the world narrowed to just the two of them, alone together again in the middle of a storm. Alex closed the rest of the distance between their bodies, pressing her back, and for the first time in her life, she couldn't think. She could only feel.

Him.

Everywhere.

She wanted more.

Everything.

She kissed him back.

Survival Tip #14

If you meet a man with the ability to tie you up in knots...enjoy it.

More.

It was the only thing Alex could focus on. Willa's body was hot and vibrant and whole against his. *Alive.* He could feel her breasts pressing into his chest with every breath she took, could feel proof of her heart beating as her pulse sped beneath his hand. All his reasons from last night for not doing this had been lost in the jungle as he tore through dark trees calling her name. He needed more. Needed her close, needed her safe. Whatever it took. Whatever it cost. Maybe he couldn't make her love him but he could make her want him. Crave him. He could make her desperate for his hands, his mouth, his cock. This was something he was good at. As long as they were on this fucking island, Willa was going to be his. He was going to fall asleep inside her every night so he never had to wake up to another morning like this. He *couldn't* wake up to another morning like this. He wouldn't survive it.

She moaned and he wanted more of that too. More of her dangerous mouth going soft and hungry. He wanted to hear her sigh and beg and say his name so many times it became a habit. His calls would never go unanswered again. He slid his tongue along hers, chasing the sound of her pleasure and tasting the dare still sitting on the tip, sweet and bold and so undeniably Willa.

Prove it.

Sharp, dangerous, *impossible* woman. He was going to prove to her exactly how little she knew and make sure she enjoyed every second of her ignorance.

He dropped one of his hands to her butt and squeezed, a reminder and a rebuke that this was how she should have woken up, with his hand full of her. Rain was falling steadily now, and Willa's magnificent hair was clinging to her neck, her breasts, the soft curve of her ribs, everywhere Alex wanted to cling too. She was the siren he had feared. Lightning split the sky overhead and he pressed closer to her, grinding his hips against hers and even through the barrier of his shorts the feel of her almost overwhelmed him. But, then, she always had. It was why he had walked away from her the night they met. He hadn't been ready for her. Maybe he still wasn't but it didn't matter. Walking away was no longer an option. He kissed her harder, feeling the tentative touch of her tongue against his, the rush of her breath carried by a moan and decided there were much worse ways to die than drowning in the sweetness of Wilhelmina Jones.

More.

She was so lovely and hot and vital moving beneath his hands, he wanted the feel of her skin branded into his fingertips. His hand slid lower, between the lush vee where her thighs met and then pressed up, between her soft folds, finding the kind of heat that seared him down to his bones. Their mouths broke apart and they both gasped.

"Dangerous girl," he groaned. "This pussy is so wet for me already."

"Alex, I'm still tied up," her voice was breathless, her lips kiss-swollen, but, best of all, her body was straining toward him, against the rope around her waist and he felt a deep, primitive satisfaction seeing the marks desperation made on her skin. Even knowing they would fade, the memory of her wanting him wouldn't.

He circled her clit once then slid back down to her opening and circled her there, feeling the way her body pulled at his finger. Thunder shook the trees around them. "I think you like it." He dragged his mouth up her neck, nipping at her earlobe. "If I had known, I would have tied you up years ago." He found her breast with his other hand, stroking along the sensitive curve and then pinching lightly at her nipple so she moaned. "Maybe this is how all our fighting could have ended."

Her head dropped to the side, giving him more room to kiss his way along her jaw, down her neck and back up, back and forth just like the fingers still moving between her legs. He licked the rain off her skin and felt the way her thighs started to tremble, heard the slight quiver in her voice. "Th-that's right," she stuttered. "We were fighting. I'm still m-mad at you, McBryde." Then she inhaled sharply as he slipped a finger inside her. It took everything Alex had not to come in his shorts like a fucking teenager at the feel of her body closing around that single digit.

"I'm still mad at you too." He bit the base of her neck and felt an answering clench around his finger. This woman was going to ruin him. "Furious even." He soothed the same spot with his tongue then began kissing his way down her chest. "Do you want me to stop?"

"No." His mouth finally closed around her nipple, and the next words burst forcefully out of her. "Don't stop." If his hands hadn't been busy, he might have been tempted to beat his chest with his fists. Sweet. She was so secretly, perfectly sweet. It made her so much more dangerous than she already was. He slid another finger inside her and felt her whole body quake. "Alex, Please."

He lost what little remained of his mind.

More.

He pulled his mouth from her breasts and her body arched, trying to follow as he moved back toward her lips. The kiss he gave her was obscene and they were both breathless by the time he pulled away. "Let me show you how a woman should be worshiped, Willa." He withdrew his fingers from her body and the sound of protest she made might as well have been a hand stroking his cock. "Let me show you how *you* deserve to be worshiped." He dropped to his knees in front of her and raised the fingers that had been inside her to his mouth.

The taste of her hit his tongue, salty sweet and better than a million fantasies. His eyes closed and he let out a deep, satisfied hum and when he opened them again, Willa was looking down at him dazed and wide-eyed. He ran his hand up the side of her thigh and then traced the damp seam of her sex. "Looks like I am eating you first, Wilhelmina." He nipped and kissed at the crease where her leg met her hip and felt the shiver that went through her. "Let me hear what it sounds like when you come. Let me taste it."

"Is this a dream?" she asked hoarsely.

"Have you dreamed of this before?" He thought of the night she first heard the ghost, how she had woken him with the hot grind of her pussy against his hip. Even just the possibility she had been dreaming of him made it feel like he was coming apart at the seams. Even with her hands tied, she knew how to undo him. Unable to resist anymore, he reached down and pulled his cock out of his shorts, giving himself a rough stroke while she watched. He heard her breath hitch, saw the way her eyes dropped and darkened as they followed the movement of his hand. "Have you dreamed of this too, Willa? Did you see how fucking hard you make me and wonder what I would feel like inside you?" He pushed his thumb through her slick folds and circled her clit. "All you ever needed to say was please."

"Alex." The strain in her voice was evident and it was there in her body too, pulling toward him against the rope, but she didn't answer. It was foolish to think she would. Alex would care about it later. Instead, he focused on what he could have now.

"Let me make you forget everything but my name, Willa. Say yes." He felt the sudden tension in her body and held his breath as he waited for her to change the world as he knew it. He saw the moment she decided, her eyes moving from the hand still wrapped around his erection up to his face and settling on his mouth like a tangible caress.

The thigh beneath his hand relaxed and, finally, she gave a firm, husky, "Yes."

The word had barely left her lips before he was slipping one of her legs over his shoulder, leaning forward, and dragging his tongue up her center. They both groaned. This was what he needed.

More.

He felt the last of the nervous tension slowly drain out of her and be replaced by demand. Her heel pressed into his back, dragging him closer as he worked her with his mouth and with every moan and sigh, his own body became tenser, his cock so hard it was a wonder he didn't faint. Part of him still couldn't believe this was happening, that it was Willa here beneath him, her body slick and eager, and another part of him couldn't believe it had taken so long. Even if this didn't last beyond the island, even if he never touched her again, part of him was going to be stuck in this moment forever.

He looked up at her and her eyes were closed, her head back against the tree but Alex wanted there to be no question in her mind about who was making her feel this way. He stopped sucking on her clit and his fingers tightened on her thigh. "Look at me," he demanded and waited until her head dropped back toward him, her face wild and needy and so beautiful it made his whole chest ache. "I want you to see what you deserve," he said roughly, stroking his hand up and down her leg before finally settling it on her perfectly ripe ass with a squeeze that made her squirm. "And I want you to know exactly who you're begging for—" he let go of his dick to slip two fingers back into her tight, hot opening and it forestalled the protest he could see poised on the tip of her tongue, "Because you will beg." He curled his fingers and stroked her deep.

Her body sagged against the rope and she let out a single succinct, "Fuck me."

There was no higher praise.

There was also nothing she could have said to make him more desperate to see her stripped completely down to sharp, uninhibited teeth. His mouth was back on her perfect pussy but somehow she was the one pulling him under, the taste of her on his tongue, the pulse of her around his fingers, the steadily growing song of her moans and gasps. The storm was right overhead. Rain slid over her body and fell on his tongue, sweet and salty as he tried desperately to get closer, to get deeper and deeper under her skin. Finally, she let out another desperate, "Alex, please" and then she was coming and he was drowning in her. She was all he could hear, taste, smell—all he could want and he wasn't sure if it was thunder or his heart drowning beneath this woman who was a force of nature. He waited, lapping at her until her body calmed to a dull pulse and then he was shooting to his feet and crushing his mouth against hers.

Her kiss was languid despite his urgency as he wrapped his fist back around his cock. There was no thought, no finesse as he stroked himself and, embarrassingly, all it finally took was the slow slide of Willa's tongue across his lip and the faintest scrape of her teeth to send him over. The tension that had been holding him together gave out with a bang and he flew apart, groaning deeply as he emptied out across her stomach.

His head dropped into the curve of her neck and for the next few minutes all he could hear was the sound of them both trying to catch their breath as the storm moved on. Eventually, the rain slowed to a light patter and as other sounds filtered in, birds calling, the breeze sifting through the trees, the perpetual crash of waves, so did reality. He felt the rope still tied around her waist pressing into his abdomen and the release he had left all over her stomach sticky on his own skin.

His entire body tensed as the full weight of what he had just done came down on his head like half a dozen coconuts falling at once. He had tied a woman to a tree and...ravished her. Like a goddamn caveman. He straightened abruptly and found Willa with her eyes closed and her head pressed back but she stirred when he pulled away.

"Are you okay?" he asked.

Her eyes blinked open, still dazed and a little abstracted and then she looked down between their bodies. "I'm still tied to a tree."

Alex swore, hastily moving to unknot the rope. As it fell away, he rubbed her arms where the friction had turned them pink. "Sorry. I mean how do you feel?"

She looked from his hands massaging her arms up to his face and he saw some of the old sharpness come back into her eyes. "Are you looking for a performance evaluation, McBryde?"

"No, of course not—"

"I give it a B plus—" she said almost at the same time.

"I meant—wait, what do you mean a fucking B plus?"

"One should always leave room for improvement," she said primly and Alex was so caught off guard, he actually laughed. "Also I was mad at you," she added and he stopped. All at once he remembered how this had started and just how angry he had been. He fought the urge to push her right back against the tree and tie her up all over again.

"Right. You still haven't explained where you were."

"You never gave me a chance."

"You practically dared me to kiss you."

"Yeah, well, you tied me to a tree."

"Irrelevant but I think you actually liked it."

"Also irrelevant. Liking it doesn't change the fact that you had no right to do it in the first place."

"I gave you fair warning yesterday. I wouldn't have done it if you hadn't run away."

"I didn't run away, I was *possessed* by a ghost. Which I would have told you if you had given me a chance."

That pulled Alex up short. "What?"

She crossed her arms and looked almost as satisfied as she had right after orgasming all over his face. Was there anything Wilhelmina Jones liked more than coming out on top? "I woke up in a cave with that goddamn ghost hissing in my ear about returning this."

She gestured to a small, gold pendant hanging between her breasts Alex had originally dismissed without a second thought. Willa had tried on so much jewelry yesterday, his mind hadn't registered this necklace as something different. He had also been far more focused on the fact she had been missing and his relief that she was safe...among other things, prettier things, things that were also round and golden and even more tempting than some long-dead pirate's treasure.

She was right. He really was a scoundrel...and a bastard.

This time when he looked her up and down, he was just checking for injuries. Feeling too late and a little frantic, his hands skated up her arms and he gently tilted her face from side to side, searching for cuts or bruises.

"Jesus, Willa, are you okay? Are you hurt?" He traced a gentle thumb along her jaw while he checked her pupils, searching for signs of a concussion. He saw them expand as she reached up and grabbed his wrist, pulling his hand away from her chin. "Alex, I'm fine."

"I'm sorry. You're right, I'm a fucking dickhead. Instead of listening to you I—" he broke off with a rough curse. "Fuck—I tied you to a tree."

"And I enjoyed it," said Willa with a sigh. "Alex, it's okay. Being possessed wasn't great but the worst part was knowing you would be worried. At least now I know what the ghost wants." Her expression soured and she muttered, "No matter how unlikely."

"Yeah, but Willa everything we just did...if I hadn't—I mean if I had just listened...I attacked you."

Her head drew back and she gave him an incredulous look. "Excuse me?"

"I literally *tied you up*."

"Alex, you would have stopped if I had told you to stop." She looked so sure, he felt a small twist of relief he didn't deserve.

"But Willa—"

She held up a hand and cut him off. "No. Maybe you shouldn't have tied me up but everything else we did," she paused and he watched her cheeks color, "I asked for it. I—I wanted it." An entirely inappropriate hum of satisfaction went through him. Hearing Willa say she wanted him was even better than her saying he was right but then she went on. "I think as long as we were trapped here together some sort of biological crisis was inevitable. At the end of the day, humans are still animals and instinct is a powerful thing."

Her gaze dropped down to the remains of his orgasm drying on her skin and she dragged a finger through it, the look on her face similar to the one she had when dissecting an urchin—pure scientific interest. She made it sound like what they had just done was nothing more than an experiment and Alex once again had the thought that no other woman possessed the ability to mix him up quite so badly. He already wanted her again even as she gave him a small, careful smile and gutted him gently with his own words. "I know this isn't love, Alex. It's just our lizard brains looking for a good time."

His chest felt strangely tight and tender even before she stepped closer and poked him in it. "Maybe next time, I'll tie you to the tree," her voice was sharply sweet but Alex still heard an underlying quiver and remembered that for all Willa seemed like a shark, these were waters she didn't have much experience swimming in.

And he had tied her to a fucking tree.

She was right. Humans really were just animals and he was a goddamn beast.

"You can tie me up anywhere, anytime, Wilhelmina," he said, maybe a little too fervently because she cocked an eyebrow and took another step forward, forcing him back.

"That's a lot of latitude. What if you're just being an ass?"

"Get the rope."

"What if I want the last banana?" Another step, another retreat.

"Get the rope."

"What if I want to finally prove to you the animal making those tracks on the beach is really some kind of undiscovered aquatic pig?" Her finger was still on his chest and she pushed him back a few more steps.

"Get several ropes and maybe a gag." His back came up against another tree and the scratch of the bark on his skin was too little penance.

"What if—" she hesitated and bit her lip, her eyes fixated on the point where her finger pressed into his chest. She gave a small shake of her head, then her whole hand flattened, her palm warm and familiar as it settled above his heart. "What if I want to keep being animals in the woods? Just while we're here?" She looked back up and there was indeed something a little animalistic in her eyes—a combination of hunger and wariness that had his heart twisting. "What if I want to fuck you, Alexander McBryde?" Her voice was low and husky. Dangerous.

She was definitely going to kill him.

Any vague, foolish hope he might be able to evolve into a man worthy of Wilhelmina Jones died in that moment. She had just made it very clear, here was the only place she could be an animal with Alex. It wasn't love. It never would be. She had never even admitted to *liking* him. The smart thing to do would be to stop all of this now—avoid becoming the typical male of a species who wound up trading something vital—like his heart—for the chance to mate. But he didn't want to. Crude and unevolved as he was. It was too late to go back to the way things had been and the truth was he wanted this too much. Her. For as long as possible.

More.

Maybe he would get lucky and they would never be rescued.

He leaned down and kissed her, his tongue finding hers as she rose up to meet him. He kissed her until it was breathe or die and then for a few seconds beyond that point. He finally pulled back and his voice was a low growl against her mouth, "Get the rope."

Survival Tip #15

A controlled experiment is a safe experiment.

This was happening.

Willa's stomach quivered nervously but something else, something rooted deep inside her felt like it had woken up after a thousand-year sleep. The aforementioned lizard brain probably. She knew he was still just a horny octopus—parts of last night might have been a shadowy blur but she still remembered what he had said about a kiss never meaning true love—but at some point, she had become a horny octopus too. She wanted to touch him, everywhere and all at once.

A voice in the back of her mind was shouting a warning about getting too close or feeling too much. Alexander McBryde was still a certain type of dangerous but this morning she had woken up in a dark cave with the taste of regret on her tongue and kissing him had made it disappear. And it was just sex. If Alex could have casual, meaningless sex, then so could she. Maybe it was evolution, maybe it was devolution but they were stranded out here together and at least he was the kind of danger she could control.

Alex had backed into a tree opposite the one he had tied her to but Willa decided she wanted a different setting for this new experiment.

"Take these off," she said, running her finger beneath the waistband of his shorts and watching his breath hitch, "And go lay down."

"So bossy, Wilhelmina," he murmured but he did as she ordered and this time when he stripped off his shorts and bent over, Willa let herself enjoy it, the way the muscles in his thighs and ass flexed, the long, strong line of his back and the brief glimpse of gold hanging between his legs. He really was an exemplary specimen of a man and the quivers in her stomach were no longer nerves, they were anticipation.

She followed him over to the opening of their tent and when she knelt, she found him lying on his back, his hands propped behind his head as he watched her with dark, challenging eyes. Willa had never been the type to back down from a challenge. She crawled in and settled on top of him, pressing herself against his half hard cock. She gave an experimental little roll of her hips and he reached out to stop her, his head falling back with a groan.

"Willa—"

"Keep your hands behind your head," she ordered, grabbing his wrists and moving them back. His eyes opened and narrowed on her face which was now much closer to his.

"I can't touch you?"

"No. Consider this a metaphorical rope." She leaned back again, trailing her hands down over his chorded forearms. "It's my turn to examine you."

He let out a short, disbelieving laugh. "You make me sound like a cadaver."

"A very warm, very well-toned cadaver," she said soothingly tracing the line delineating his bicep. He let out another huff of laughter and his arm jerked involuntarily away from her fingertips. Apparently, he was ticklish. "Fascinating," she murmured.

"Only you would turn sex into an experiment," he said, sounding resigned but when Willa looked at his face, he was watching her with something that looked oddly like affection. "This is why you'll always be a dag."

Her hand paused near his collarbone. "You know, I looked dag up the first time you called me one." It was six months into their first year of grad school. He came across Willa in the library and asked if she wanted to join his study group with that cocky, too-charming smile. She had actually paused to consider it but then she noticed the smudge of lipstick on his neck and a moment later, a tiny woman with bird bones, a sleek dark bob, and smudged red lipstick had come around the corner. Presumably, Alex's "study group." Willa had realized he wasn't really asking her to join him, he was making fun of her. She didn't even bother replying, simply turned and walked away and he had laughed, calling her a dag and jokingly trying to coax her back.

She watched him more closely after that, always ready—eager even—for a chance to show him her teeth. She bared them a little now, scowling down at him. "I never understood why you called me the Australian equivalent of a nerd. Even with your extracurricular activities in the stacks, I saw you study just as much. You might look like you do—" she gestured dismissively at his face, "But you're just as much of a dag as I am."

"And how do I look, Wilhelmina?" His voice was practically a purr. "Devilishly attractive? Horribly handsome? So sexy you can't stand it?" She felt her cheeks warm, the heat sliding through her to meet the heat of Alex's body where he was pressed against her and making her a little worried about the fire-starting properties of friction—because Alex was more than just attractive or handsome or sexy. He was hot. So very, infuriatingly, *hot*.

"As usual, you're focusing on the wrong point," she said while her hips, this time involuntarily, rubbed and slid over him. He groaned, his face going so goddamn beautiful in bliss and for a moment, Willa was focused on the wrong point too. Unable to resist, she resumed running her hands over his chest.

"What was the point?" He asked, looking a little dazed as he watched her touch him.

She could feel him getting harder beneath her and her body softened in response. It took her a second to remember. "Why did you call me a dag?" She finally managed.

He stretched his arms further back and allowed his head to fall so he was no longer watching as she traced the lines of his abdominals. He looked like he had their first morning on the island stretched out across the sand. A sun god at rest.

"Maybe it was meant to be an olive branch," he said hoarsely and when she ground down a little harder, pleasure shooting like sparks through her, he groaned out her name. "Willa, this is torture." But he said it like he wanted more and the power of that was almost as good as the way his hardening cock dragged against her clit.

"What do you mean?" she asked, trying to focus on finding other ways to put that desperate look on his face. She leaned down and sucked his nipple into her mouth, biting it lightly the way he had done to her earlier.

His breath this time was accompanied by a startled moan. She sat up, grinning and pleased with herself. "I think we both should have known I would enjoy torturing you, McBryde."

"'Dag' is usually a term of endearment," he said with a strained laugh. "Willa, let me touch you." She also, she realized, enjoyed hearing him beg.

"No. Your hands are tied." She skipped her fingers over his ribs, finding another ticklish spot and when he laughed again, she leaned back down and pressed a kiss near his throat, feeling the sound against her lips. His laughter trailed off and became a low moan as she pressed kisses up his neck.

"And you're a liar," she said into his ear before biting and tugging at the lobe. "It literally means an unfashionable geek." He was definitely hard now. She sat back up and there was no hiding how wet she was as she dragged herself backward on his cock, pulling her hips back far enough to stroke the head of him. She looked down at the precum smeared across her fingers in fascination, then, just like Alex had done to her, she brought it up to her mouth, met his eyes, and licked it off.

"You're going to kill me," he whispered and she smiled, dropping her hands back to his chest and sliding them upward until both were wrapped lightly around his throat.

"I have imagined killing you multiple times over the past few years," she said sweetly. Beneath her hands, his throat was strong and warm, she felt his pulse beating quickly against her palm, felt him swallow. "Every time you called me a dag, I pictured just wrapping my hands around your throat and squeezing." She flexed her fingers for emphasis, careful not to actually choke him. Beneath her, his erection twitched and his pupils blazed with an unholy light as he looked up at her. This time it was her swallowing hard as she processed his physiological response. "I didn't realize you would like it," she said.

"I normally don't." He shook his head and her fingers tightened reflexively. She felt him twitch again beneath her and when he spoke, his voice was deep and graveled. "A dag is someone who doesn't care what people think. You've always gone your own way, even if it was a little weird or abrasive. I always liked that about you," he paused and lifted a hand as if to stroke her cheek but he stopped before actually touching her and it dropped back to his side. "I always liked you, Willa. Even when I hated you." For a moment, the heat in his eyes cooled and he looked almost regretful but then she blinked and he was once again all wickedness and warmth. "I also like the way you look at me when I call you a dag. It's the same way you're looking at me now, all hot and bothered."

"This must be my 'Choking Alexander McBryde' look," she said, stunned and almost dizzy from his admission.

He had liked her?

"Remember my safeword is starfruit," he said, his tone teasing despite the obvious strain. Because that was who he was. Aside from when they were bickering, and sometimes even then, Alex was always a source of teasing, good-natured cheerfulness. Everyone in the department liked him. Maybe that's why Willa had always found him so insufferable. Because she had liked him too. Even when she hated him.

Her heart started to race, the words poised on the tip of her tongue but it was too big, too much control to give away all at once. She still had no idea what would happen when they left here. There were too many variables in this experiment. So she focused on what was in front of—and beneath—her.

Pulling her hands away from his throat, she leaned down and kissed him instead. He kissed her back—instantly and without hesitation, making her feel momentarily weak. It was like he already knew exactly how to kiss her to throw open every internal door she kept locked, like he knew exactly where to find the most wanting, needy version of herself.

But it was his turn to fall apart.

She pulled away and began kissing her way down his body, taking her time to see what spots made his breath hitch and which ones made him moan. His erection dragged against her abdomen and then between her breasts as she made her way lower and when her tongue traced along the seam where his thigh met his abs, his head jerked up.

"Wilhelmina, what do you think you're doing?"

"How many times do we have to go over this? I'm conducting an experiment." She began to stroke her fingers up his inner thigh and felt him tense beneath her.

"I thought you were just going to touch me."

"I am touching you," she pointed out right before curling her hand around the base of his cock and squeezing. His whole body jerked. "Interesting," she said, pumping her hand slowly up and down and watching more precum emerge from the tip. She remembered how he had touched himself that morning in the woods. She hadn't been able to look away, her eyes following the swift, clearly familiar rhythm of his hand.

"Our second day here, I saw you touch yourself," she admitted, her eyes now fixed on her own hand attempting that same rhythm.

"What?" he gasped and she felt him looking at her but she didn't look back. His skin was so soft here. Soft but hard. She wondered what he would feel like inside her. They couldn't. Not here. It was too big of a risk. But now it was all she could think about. Alexander McBryde inside her. Filling her, stretching her. Hot. So very, very hot.

"What were you imagining?" she asked, wanting to know if she was alone or if he had thought about it too. "You said my name," she said faintly, her eyes now fixed on the crown of him. She stroked her thumb over it, dragging the beads of moisture there down. He moaned again and the sound made her feel almost drunk. God, he was so fucking pretty in pearls. This was a different kind of treasure, finding him, touching him, listening to him come apart. It made her greedy. She wanted to ruin him the same way he had ruined her. She wanted to make him forget everything but *her* name.

She leaned over and sucked him into her mouth.

"Fuck, Willa," Alex cursed, his hips rose, trying to push deeper inside her even as he broke the rules of the game and reached down to grab a fistful of her hair. He pulled her head back so she was looking up at him. "It was this," he said, his eyes wild and intense as they met hers, "I imagined your pretty, perfect mouth sucking my cock." His hand tightened in her hair, sending pinpricks of pain and excitement down her spine. She liked this. Just like she had liked it when he spanked her. Perhaps she liked Alex *especially* when he was a caveman.

"Show me."

He groaned and briefly closed his eyes, like he was gathering himself together, but then he was guiding her head back and rubbing his hard tip against her lips.

"So tempting, so dangerous," he said, watching intently as her tongue came out and tasted him again. "I can't believe—Willa, are you sure you want—"

Ignoring the tug of his hand in her hair, she licked him from where her hand was still curled around the base all the way up to the crown and the way he broke off and sighed out her name sounded just the same as it had that morning in the woods. She wanted to hear it again, wanted to be the one who made Alexander fucking McBryde into the most wanting, needy version of himself because anything he could do, she could do better.

She licked the head again, then looked up to find him watching her with an expression caught somewhere between disbelief and desire. "How do I do this right?" she asked, trying to ignore the thrill of nerves and need humming beneath her skin.

His eyes darkened even as his mouth went soft and tender, she felt his thumb stroking gently against the back of her neck. "Willa, love, there's no way you could do it wrong," he said, "Humans are designed for pleasure. Find yours and I'll find mine too."

The sweet taste was back on her tongue and there was no escaping what had put it there. This was affection. He was just so *good*. Beneath the cocky smile and kill-me looks, he was the type of man who dove into the ocean at night to save someone, the type of man who combed a woman's hair and brought her fruit and called her a masterpiece. Alex was the kind of dangerous man it would be so easy to fall in love with.

How infuriating.

Part of her wanted to pull back, wanted to slam every door shut and go where he could never touch her. But this was a different sort of possession. Like when she had touched the pendant and been filled with that wild, burning, endless *longing*. Like she had spent her whole life lost at sea and Alex was land and fresh water and a fruit-ripened breeze. There was no resisting, no turning back.

She retraced her tongue's path up his erection, kissing him as she went, then she closed her mouth around the tip. His hand tightened in her hair, sending pleasure sparking through her and she moaned around him.

"Fuck," he said harshly. She began pumping her hand again as she took down more of him, enjoying the feel of him against her tongue and the way she could feel his legs begin to tremble. "God, yes, that's it, Willa. That's so good. You're so good. Such a good fucking girl." The words came out in a fervent rush and Willa's body gave a low, hard pull. She wanted more, more evidence of Alex falling apart for *her*.

His hand began to help guide her head, the gentle tug of her hair somehow familiar and relaxing just as much as it was new and exciting. "Sweet Christ, Wilhelmina, you look so pretty with your lips stretched around me." She glanced up and Alex was propped on his arm so he could see her. He looked so beautifully hopeless. "I should have known you would suck cock like a siren trying to steal my soul."

Sweet.

Everything was so goddamn sweet. Willa wanted more. She sucked him down as deep as she could, moaning at the way his fingers twisting in her hair made other parts of her throb. He tried to pull her head away, "Willa, I'm going to—" She squeezed the base and sucked, hard. She wanted all of it. He swore and then he was pulsing against her hand and filling her mouth. He said her name like a prayer as she swallowed every last bit of him down.

When he was finished, Willa slowly drew back and raised her head, looking down the long line of Alex's body to his face. He looked wrecked—delightfully so—and *she* had done that. She smiled and their eyes caught as he opened his again. She saw the focus and the intent come back to his face, his eyes narrowing.

"Come here, Wilhelmina," he said, his voice rough and full of promise, he tugged the hand he still had buried in her hair, encouraging her to crawl up his body and the slide of his skin against hers was another new but still familiar thrill. He rolled them so he was on his side, Willa's head pillowed on one of his arms. He pressed his hand against the side of her face and dragged his thumb over her lips, "Dangerous girl," he said softly. Affectionately.

Willa's heart started to race, sweetness flooded her senses and it was terrifying—more terrifying than a ghost could ever be—but then Alex kissed her and it didn't matter.

All she felt was him.

Survival Tip #16

If you ever hear the call of the wild, let that bitch go to voicemail.

Alex was afraid to close his eyes. Lying behind Willa in the tent, his body curled protectively around hers, every time he tried, his brain brought him back to that moment of waking up on the beach with his arms empty and they snapped back open. It was making him want to tie her up all over again...but she needed rest.

She had fallen asleep after coming again two more times on his fingers. Even then, it had been hard to stop. Watching Willa open up and let go, seeing her go soft and pink while she said his name all breathless and sweet could easily become an addiction.

She sighed in her sleep and rolled over, cuddling more closely into his chest, her hand sliding into its normal spot near the base of his neck. Her fingers stretched and flexed like a feral kitten and Alex thought his heart might pound right out of his chest.

He couldn't lose her.

The want in him mixed with the anxious energy thrumming through his body and he caught himself reaching for her, stopping before he could wake her up again. Knowing he wouldn't be able to resist temptation very long, Alex forced himself to carefully pull his arm out from beneath her and crawl out of the tent.

He picked up one of the long metal pikes from the booby trap thinking he would go down to the beach and fish. Willa hadn't eaten since last night and she would be hungry when she woke up but as soon as he stepped to the edge of their campsite, panic came rushing up to choke him. He looked back at the tent, at the glimpse of Willa curled up on her side, her face pillowed on her hands pillowed on top of her outrageous hair looking so fucking vulnerable that his heart stopped. What if he came back and she was gone?

He knew what she would say if she was awake—that he was being ridiculous or that she didn't need him looking after her and maybe both of those things were true but it didn't change that just the idea of letting her out of his sight made his hands go cold and his heart start to stutter. He wanted to be here when she woke up, wanted the reassurance of her body within reach even if that meant her hangrily threatening him with cone snails or urchins or carnivorous deep-sea shrimp for being an overprotective caveman. He wanted to hear her moan his name again. Wanted to hear her say please. Wanted to see her reach for him without any hesitation or wariness.

He just wanted her to want him.

He was so fucked.

Blowing out a hard, frustrated breath, he dropped his head back and glared up at the glimpses of sky visible through the canopy. Blue and cloudless. It was another day lost in paradise and for the first time since washing up here, he was grateful. He looked back at the tent and felt that hungry, primitive beat of urgency pounding in his blood. Thirty more minutes. He would give Willa half an hour more to sleep and then he was waking her up with his tongue between her thighs. He would eat and then they would go hunt down lunch together.

He was pacing and checking his dive watch for the third time when he heard it. Distant at first and barely noticeable, a constant, rushing sound similar to the sound of waves crashing on the beach, but as it came closer, Alex realized it was coming from above the trees. His head jerked backward, again searching the sky and when he spotted it through the leaves, his heart sank.

A plane.

A fucking plane.

It was flying lower than a commercial airline and looked small, like some person's private puddle jumper, but it was still the only sign they had seen of the world beyond this island. It was a chance to be rescued.

Alex didn't move. They hadn't rebuilt the signal fire on the beach and he doubted the one crackling nearby was giving off enough smoke to make it through the trees. If he did nothing, it would pass by and no one would know they were here. He wasn't ready to be rescued. Not now. Maybe not ever.

The plane was no longer in view but he could still hear it, heading in the direction of the beach and the guilt was crushing and instantaneous.

He deserved every absurd, painful death Willa could dream up.

He took off running, his heart pounding and his stomach churning, hope that he wouldn't make it like a knife in his back as he sprinted faster than he ever had in his life. He burst onto the shore, frantically waving his arms over his head, knowing there wasn't time to throw wood on the fire, chasing the plane down the beach even as it drew further and further away. He kept running until it disappeared over the horizon and then he dropped to his knees in the sand and panted, trying to catch his breath and hating himself for hesitating. If Willa found out, she would never forgive him. Even if she didn't, he might never forgive himself.

"Fuck!" he yelled, furious with himself and with the universe for choosing this as the moment to show a little mercy. He stared in the direction the plane had gone as if he could will it to turn around. He knelt there until his knees started to tingle in protest and then slowly climbed to his feet.

There would be others, he told himself as he began the walk back to their section of the beach. There had to be. If there was one, there would be more. They wouldn't be here forever.

"Alex!"

His head whipped up and Willa was there in the distance calling his name. She must have woken up hungry because she had put her Acca Dacca shirt back on and was holding the metal pike he had abandoned back at camp. She truly looked like an Amazon, her silhouette tall and lush and strong against the backdrop of the jungle, weapon in hand, her golden hair wild and exuberant around her shoulders. She turned toward him and the bow of her lips drew back and sent an arrow straight toward his chest—she smiled—one of her rare, broad, full-hearted smiles.

His breath caught, his heart flatlined and the certainty he was a selfish bastard fell into step beside the bone-deep sense of relief the plane had gone on without them. If here was the only place he could have her, then here was the only place he wanted to be. He realized he was smiling too as she began walking toward him, sure he had never seen anything lovelier. As he watched her long legs eat up the distance, he wondered what she would say if he insisted she lay down on the warm sand and let him between them. He was suddenly starving and she looked like a fucking feast.

He opened his mouth but before he could say anything, something exploded out of the ocean. Salt water stung his eyes and his hands flew up instinctively to cover his face. There was a low, growling hiss and then Willa was screaming and pain like he had never felt in his life was ripping through his leg and raging up through his body like fire. Blinded by salt and sand, he hit the ground hard, his breath knocked out of him, the pain itself suffocating. His body was being dragged, the grit of sand making it feel like he was being skinned alive as he struggled to grab hold of something, anything, to keep from being pulled beneath the waves.

He could barely think beyond the pain and desperation but one ridiculous thought found its way above the agony and fear: they finally knew what had been making the strange tracks on the beach.

Willa woke up shivering. She had been dreaming about...something... she frowned, realizing the memories were already slipping away. She sat up, trying to remember and rubbing her palms against her arms to try and warm herself up. She looked around, wondering where Alex was and ignoring the twinge of disappointment she felt over waking up alone. She would never tell Alex she liked waking up next to him, some secrets were meant to be taken to the grave, but given everything they had done before falling asleep, it felt like a not-so-subtle reminder—don't get attached. Whatever they did here didn't mean anything, they were just two animals alone in the woods. Really, she should be grateful that after last night she hadn't woken up with him hovering over her. Still, frowning, she crawled out of the tent and looked around their campsite, expecting to see Alex or food or something to indicate where he had gone but there was nothing. Her stomach growled and she pressed a hand against it, her annoyance growing as she pulled on her T-shirt and grabbed one of the metal pikes they had been using to try and fish. It swung by her side as she headed toward the beach, sourly wondering how many otters it took to smother a man.

She called his name when she reached shore, looking around for his tall, familiar frame and spotted him striding toward her, gilded by sunlight and so ungodly attractive it made certain unmentionable parts of her body beat a little faster. Her breath caught and her response to finding him was completely involuntary—she smiled and when he smiled back, that cocky, devilish, too-knowing grin, she was embarrassingly, undeniably glad he was here and looking at her like that. For a moment, it was almost like this really was a vacation. Like they were two people, two friends, who had just decided to get away from the rest of the world. It was a feeling she had never had before and for the first time in days, Willa felt hopeful that everything would be okay, that they were actually going to get through this.

She was only a few yards away from him when fate decided to punish her for having such a horribly optimistic thought. There was a splash as something huge erupted out of the water. Droplets of sea spray landed on her cheeks as something dark green launched itself out of the surf.

Directly at Alex.

She heard his startled shout go sharp with pain as his leg was grabbed, watched his body hit the sand and his hands scrabble for a grip as he was dragged back toward the ocean.

Willa was running before even really comprehending what she was seeing, before she could even really acknowledge that Alex was being pulled across the beach by a large, hissing, saltwater crocodile.

A *motherfucking crocodile.*

She took the metal pike still gripped in her hand and brought it swinging down, screaming as she plunged the tip through the crocodile's head. The feel of flesh and bone resisting reverberated up the metal and Willa fought to hold on as 2,000 pounds of mean muscle whipping beneath her. She threw her entire weight down onto the sharp point, twisting it so the old metal screeched. There was blood everywhere, streaked across the sand, running down Alex's leg, splashed across her hands and a loud buzzing filled her ears. When the crocodile finally stopped moving, she fell back in horror, her ears still ringing as she struggled to breathe.

She looked around blearily and saw Alex. He was collapsed on his back, panting and grimacing in pain. He had managed to pull himself free of the croc's mouth and she could see a jagged row of punctures lining his calf. She crawled toward him, her fingers sinking into sand dyed red. Blood. There was just so much blood. The back of her tongue tasted sour and darkness was a fuzzy threat at the edges of her vision. She knew she was on the verge of fainting.

"Alex," she said his name, repeating it over and over to keep the darkness back until she reached his side. "Alex."

"Wilhelmina," her name was a harsh rasp, "Are you okay?"

A bubble of hysteria rose inside her. Even after being bit by a crocodile, this infuriating man was worried about her. She held onto the feeling, using it to rise above the static trying to overwhelm her brain.

This time, she would take care of him.

Looking determinedly away from his leg, she focused on his face instead and breathed hard through her mouth, so the coppery smell of the blood wasn't as strong.

"We need to get you back to camp," she said tightly.

"Willa, you don't look so good," the words were strained, he was too pale, and Willa felt pressure behind her eyes.

"Shut up. Just shut up." She forced herself to look down at his leg and it was bad. Torn flesh and blood seeping onto the sand. Her body went cold and she felt a strange, determined calm settle over her. Alex was not going to die. She knew what to do, General Jones had made sure of that.

She moved down to his leg and stripped off her shirt, using it to make a pressure bandage around the wound. Alex swore as she tightened it and Willa bit her lip hard, using the pain to keep herself focused and conscious. Once the bandage was secure, she reached down and looped one of his arms around her shoulders and then heaved to get him off the ground. Despite moving him as carefully as possible, when his leg shifted on the sand, his hand tightened painfully on her shoulder and his face went sheet white.

"Alex?" she asked, feeling momentarily more desperate than she ever had in her life. "I could try and make a sled to pull you back."

His jaw clenched and he gave a sharp jerk of his head. "No. Take too long. I can do this."

"Okay. Give me as much of your weight as you can. I can handle it," she ordered.

He let out a ragged breath and groaned as he put the toes of his injured leg on the ground. "Going to be a long walk," he said darkly. Willa didn't reply, she was too focused on breathing and trying not to pass out.

They made their way slowly toward their tent, a walk that normally took a few minutes stretching into what felt like hours. When they did finally make it to camp, Willa lowered Alex onto the end of their short sleeping platform.

"Keep applying pressure. I'm going to boil water so we can clean it."

"Okay," said Alex faintly.

Willa hurried to build up the fire then left him to watch it as she grabbed their pewter bowl and ran for the river. However, once she was out of sight, all the fear and anxiety came rushing up to choke her and she doubled over and threw up.

Willa gave herself exactly one minute to shake and cry, tears slipping hot and fast down her face while she gasped for breath. Alex almost died. He almost *died*. He would have if she hadn't been there and if they hadn't stumbled across the pirate treasure. She just managed to stop herself from pressing a bloody hand to her mouth and swallowed down the urge to throw-up a second time. Sucking in a breath, she pinched herself, again using the pain to focus.

She had to keep it together. He could still die if the wound got infected. Which meant Willa didn't have any more time for falling apart. She finished running to the river, scrubbed the blood violently from her hands, swished out her mouth, and wiped away any trace of tears, then she filled the bowl with water and walked back to camp as fast as she could without spilling it.

Alex looked up when he heard her. The rum bottle was in his hand and the contents sloshed as he used it to gesture down at his leg. "I don't think it's broken," he said, wincing as he peeled up a corner of the shirt with two fingers. Willa was relieved to see the wound had mostly stopped bleeding. "I think it miscalculated. I don't think it got as good a grip on me as it would have liked."

She nodded stiffly as she placed the pot over the fire and then went to tear off some strips of fabric from her robe, wetting them in one of the small goblets of water they had boiled the day before.

"Right, lucky," she agreed woodenly, dropping to the ground near his feet. She carefully pulled the rest of the shirt fabric away, her chest tightening and her hands trembled as Alex let out a pained hiss. She reached for that same cold calm she had felt earlier as she carefully began to clean the bite and it was almost like she stepped back, out of her body, watching from a distance as Alex took a long swig of rum and her fingers moved the soft blue cotton between punctures, cleaning away sand and grit and blood.

"This seems like a great time to say, 'I told you so,'" Alex choked out, his breathing growing labored as Willa swept the cloth around the ragged edge of what looked like the deepest puncture. "There were fucking crocodiles after all," he added and took another rapid shot of rum, his knuckles white around the neck of the bottle.

Willa's shoulders stiffened, the ice cracked, and suddenly the tears were back, welling up in her eyes. She struggled to blink them away but didn't quite manage it. One slipped free and then Alex's hand was on her face, his thumb brushing it away.

"Oh, no, possum, don't do that. You were meant to snap at me about crocs having been extinct here for the past two hundred years."

She shook her head mutely and went back to determinedly getting out the last of the sand.

"Wilhelmina, look at me," it was a command and she wasn't in the frame of mind to deny him so she bit her lip, swallowed back the rest of the tears, and looked up. His face was drawn with pain but his eyes were warm. "I'm alive, okay? Because you saved me. That's what we're going to focus on."

Willa knew he was right. She needed to focus on this moment so she didn't pass out or vomit again. He was alive.

But for how long?

They were stuck out here without any sort of medical care beyond rags, rum, and boiled water. And he had been bitten by a fucking crocodile. Which was why she needed to focus. She needed to pretend everything was going to be okay, so Alex could pretend too. So, shoving down every last weak, panicked emotion, Willa forced herself to scowl at him.

"How do you know I'm not crying because the crocodile didn't succeed? I could have had this whole island to myself."

"There you go, that's my Willa," he said weakly, his thumb brushing affectionately along her jaw and making her entire body ache. "Now, if you're okay, I think I might just pass out for a little bit."

"Good," she said, pulling the rum out of his hand and frowning down at the bite. "This next part is going to hurt." She tipped the bottle and was glad when Alex really did pass out because she could no longer see the agony on his face and he could no longer see the tears on hers.

Survival Tip #17

Dead men tell no tales. They tell jokes (don't laugh, it only encourages them).

The first thing Alex felt when he regained consciousness was panic. He woke with his hands reaching for Willa and when they came up empty, it was a nightmare come true. His chest constricted making his pounding heart feel too big, too much inside him. She had been taken again and it was his fault. He had failed to keep her safe. He jolted upright, needing to find her, but the pain that went rocketing through him stole his breath and had him falling right back down. Memories came rushing up like a riptide. The ghost. Willa tied to a tree. Willa coming, sweetly desperately for him. The plane. Hesitating.

The fucking crocodile.

His whole body ached and his leg felt like someone had doused it in gasoline and lit a match. "Jesus motherfucking Christ," he swore, and like some shadowed apparition, his savior appeared in the opening of the tent, her hair backlit by the fire and glowing golden like the halo in some goddamned stained-glass window. For just a second, he forgot about the pain in his leg, his hand dropping to his chest. His heart was still beating too fast but seeing her, alive and safe, it was no longer panic making it feel like too much inside him.

"Alex?" Her face was shrouded in shadows but her voice was hoarse and worried. "What is it? What do you need?"

His hand flexed over his heart, like he was still reaching for her, and his answer was out before he could think about it.

"You."

There was a pause and then, "What?"

He didn't like that she sounded more worried, didn't like that he couldn't see her face with the fire at her back, didn't like that he didn't have the warm reassurance of her body next to his. Everything hurt and it was all he could think about. "Why are you out there?"

He could *hear* her frown. "Because you're injured."

"So?" He didn't know what that had to do with anything. She should be next to him. He needed her next to him.

"You need to rest."

"So do you."

"I'm keeping the fires lit. We should have worked harder to keep them going at night."

"Are they both lit right now?"

"Yes, but—"

"Then come lay down. Rest with me for a few minutes." He thought of every selfish decision he had made in the past twelve hours. Tying her up. Waiting too long to chase down the plane. Kissing her.

"Alex—"

"Come on, Willa, lie down with me." He lightened his tone, hoping to dispel some of the awful worry in her voice, hoping she wouldn't notice the desperation in his. He was still being selfish but he couldn't stop. "Would you really deny a dying man his last request?"

He could see the way her body tensed and knew instantly it was the wrong thing to say. "Don't," she said harshly. "Don't joke about it."

Impossible woman. She was still all teeth and it shouldn't have made him like her more or want her suddenly, fiercely, but it did. "Willa. Please."

There was another pause, then her shoulders dropped and she leaned forward onto her hands and knees, crawling carefully into the tent. With Alex on his back, his injured leg elevated on a log softened by layers of moss, she had no choice but to settle on her side, half draped over him the way she usually was in the morning—something both of them had so far avoided pointing out. Her hand was hot resting on his chest and he had the slightly delirious thought that if she pressed a little harder, she would be able to reach inside him and brand her fingerprints on his heart.

"Are you happy now?" she asked tightly.

He slid his hand down her back, settling it in its usual spot on her ass. "Now I am."

She laughed but there was a small watery hitch in it. "Godamnit, McBryde. Sometimes you make it really hard to hate you."

She pounded her fist lightly on his chest and he tried to ignore the way his heart pounded back, hoping she couldn't feel it. "Good," he said but it was entirely too fervent. He gave a light squeeze of her bottom to distract her...and because she felt good. Round and full and comfortingly familiar in his hand.

There was a burst of warmth against his chest as she let out a huff of exasperation. "Even if you are still a scoundrel."

"A scoundrel and a masochist," he murmured, "I can't believe how much I like hearing you insult me." His gaze dropped to her face, to the broad, fierce angles of it now visible and highlighted by the flickering fire. He loved this, seeing her in all these new and different lights. Sunrise, sunset, moonlight, firelight, changing her from a Baroque goddess to an Impressionist dream—different but still a fucking masterpiece. "Fighting with you was always so much fucking fun, Wilhelmina." He didn't mean to say it out loud but his mind was hazy with the possibility he wouldn't get another chance. He might not have been a country boy but he had still been raised in Australia. He had heard enough stories about croc bites to know how they usually ended.

She was quiet for several long moments and then her hand flattened on his chest and stroked up, threading into the curls at the base of his neck—another painfully good and familiar gesture. "You were the only one who wasn't afraid of me," she finally said quietly.

Alex had to choke down a wave of sudden grief. His lonely shark. He didn't want to die. He didn't want to leave her here alone. His arm tightened around her but he couldn't speak past the noose that already felt tied around his neck and for the next several minutes they were both quiet. Finally, Willa cleared her throat.

"Why did you choose the grad program in Boston?"

It was such an abrupt and odd question given the circumstances that it pushed Alex a few inches beyond his despair. School felt like a different reality.

"Why? Are you thinking we wouldn't be in this situation if we had never met?" It was probably true but, even now and despite everything, he didn't regret it. He really was a selfish bastard.

She glanced up at him with a glare. "No, actually, I was thinking you're too smart to be so dumb. Australia has some of the best marine biology programs in the world. Why leave behind everything you know to do a program in Boston?"

"Are you saying the program in Boston isn't great?"

"It is. It's just—" she hesitated and looked back down at his chest, her voice dropping again. "I just never understood why you chose Boston when someone like you could have the best."

He frowned and shifted uncomfortably, wincing as the movement caused pain to go swimming through him. Maybe it was that his reasons for leaving Australia now seemed silly and trivial or maybe it was the odd note in her voice, making what might have been almost a compliment feel somehow sharp and pointed, but rather than reply, he turned the question back on her. "I could say the same about you. You grew up traveling and I've never seen you accept anything but the best, why didn't you do one of the programs in Australia?"

Her body tensed against his but finally he heard her blow out a sigh. "Because I grew up traveling and in Boston I could have a home. I thought...I thought things might be different—that I might be different—if every time I met someone, I knew it wouldn't ultimately end with a good-bye." The words were soft, slow, like each one was a pearl being painstakingly threaded onto the most delicate of chains...and then looped around Alex's throat. The choking grief was back.

He closed his eyes and swallowed hard. If she could be honest, then so could he and really, at this point, what did he have to lose? "I wanted to be different too. That's why I left."

After Fay disappeared and his sisters grew up enough they didn't need him anymore, Alex had been completely lost. Lost and purposeless. Leaving home had seemed like the only way to move past everything—to finally grow up. Or maybe it was just easier to run away.

"Did it work?" Willa asked, her fingers tracing slowly, soothingly, up and down the back of his neck.

He opened his eyes, looking down at the bridge of her nose, the curve of her cheek, small glimpses of her face that were still enough to make his heart race and his body ache in ways that had nothing to do with his injury—this woman he had told himself he wanted to keep safe but had failed at the most critical moment because he was holding on to her too tight.

"Unfortunately, I think I'm the same person I've always been." Too dumb for someone so smart, wanting something so much he lost sight of everything else. "Did it work for you?"

She didn't respond and for so long he thought she might have fallen asleep. He tugged lightly on her hair. "Willa?"

Finally, she looked up at him, a small, humorless smile on her face as her eyes met his.

"Unfortunately, I think, maybe, it did." The words fell on Alex's chest like stones. Guilt. Grief. Something big and sharp that landed like another arrow in his heart. Her hand left his neck and moved back to his chest, another weight as she pressed herself upright. She was no longer looking at him. "I should go check the fire on the beach."

He put his hand over hers. "Don't leave." He left the most important word unsaid—*me*. Even knowing it was inevitable, the thought of her leaving the tent, of going out of sight, going where he couldn't reach her, made him feel like he was drowning—panicked and short of breath.

"Alex—"

"Everything hurts, Willa, please. Stay." His hand slid up to her wrist and tugged, trying to convince her to lay back down, wanting her to look at him. "Distract me."

She was frowning but her eyes moved back to his face. "Distract you?"

"Yes, I don't care how, talk about whales, threaten me with urchins, call me a scoundrel, just stay—"

She cut him off with a kiss.

It was surprisingly sweet and almost tentative, her lips just a light brush over his, even as her body, naked and warm and perfect, pressed more deliberately into his side. It was like cool, comforting rain on a blisteringly hot day or dawn after a nightmare—something that made the pain of living worth dying for. Everything else faded into the background, his hand found the back of her neck and he pulled her closer, deepening the kiss and soaking her in like the desperate man he was.

She made a sound, a honeyed little moan as he slipped his tongue into her mouth searching for more of that sweetness. His other hand explored all the pretty lush curves of her, her waist, her hip, the sensitive stretch of skin where her breast molded to the harder planes of his chest. Her hands stayed chaste, one still pressing down above his heart and the other tucked against her own, but as the kiss went on, as her tongue found his and their breathing deepened, her hips became needy and restless against his side. He could feel how hot she was, could feel her growing slick and sweet and it was a victory because it meant everything else had faded away for her too.

Following the divine curve of her ass, he slipped his fingers up between her plump folds and stroked and she gasped and broke away from his mouth. Panting lightly, she looked down at him with wide eyes, flushed cheeks and kiss-swollen lips, her face full of innocent shock. It was such a delightful contrast to her usual bold sharpness.

"Alex! What are you doing?"

"Your pussy is too far away from my mouth," he said because it was true but also because her reactions when he said things like that was something to savor. "And I like hearing the way you say please when you come."

Her eyes got impossibly wider but her pussy pulsed against his fingertips. "Oh my God," she hissed and he was reminded of the first time she saw his cock. "You're injured!"

"I am very aware of that. If I could move, I would already be inside you." He circled her opening and then moved up to circle her clit, watching her eyes flutter closed and her teeth press into the fullness of her bottom lip. He decided that if these were his final days on earth, he wanted to spend it putting this look on Wilhelmina Jones' face, wanted to distract her from what was coming. "I want this pussy to be my last meal."

Her eyes flashed open and she glared down at him. "What did I tell you about joking like that?"

"I'm not joking. I mean it." His other hand rose to her face, his thumb brushing along her cheek. "Even if I die here, I would choose all this again." God, he really didn't want to die, but he hoped that someday, when she was rescued, she would remember this moment and believe him. "I wish I had kissed you sooner." He traced the curve of her lips. "I wish I had kissed you first."

"Goddamnit, McBryde." She was still scowling but her eyes had gone shiny and her voice trembled. "If you die, I swear to God, I'll kill you."

He actually smiled. "Now who's joking?"

She shook her head. "It's not a joke. It's a promise."

Dangerous girl. Impossible woman. How had he missed what was right in front of him for so long? How could he have missed *her* when he would rather fight with Willa than fuck anyone else? He really was too dumb for someone so smart. "And what will you do if I live?"

Her eyes searched his face and then she lowered her head, bringing her mouth a breath away from his. "If you live, I'll give you anything you want." She pressed one more light, sweet kiss against his mouth and breathed out the last few words, "I might even say thank you."

Hope made the sting of despair sharper. Desire and that big, sharp feeling he feared might be love expanded inside his chest. "That's definitely something worth living for."

There were several long quiet moments where it seemed like they were simply breathing each other in, their mouths a whisper apart, their eyes locked but there were still too many shadows flickering between them to see clearly. Finally, Willa gave a small shake of her head and the spell broke.

"Good," she said, drawing away abruptly and Alex was too caught up in a haze of lust and regret to keep a firm grip on her. All at once, she was out of reach. "I'm going to check the fire on the beach," she said, each word short and clipped and this time there was no coaxing her back. Alex was forced to watch her disappear into the dark, leaving him behind.

He must have fallen asleep because he remembered waking up. Then he remembered wondering if he had died and Willa was burning his body or if she had sent him out to sea. The line between fire and ice had disappeared and he was somewhere between the two. Eventually he determined he wasn't dead because Willa would occasionally appear, her voice sharp and worried as she helped him drink water or encouraged him to take another bite of a banana. There was also the pain. Periodically his entire body was set aflame or flash frozen as Willa changed the dressing on his wound. Sometimes he thought he heard her crying and he would be filled with a different sort of pain, a kind that forced him out of his feverish haze long enough to plead with her to come lie down beside him. Time passed. Hours, maybe days.

The world seemed to be getting darker. Farther.

The next time Alex opened his eyes it was because Willa was saying something and she sounded urgent. She was shouting at him. She sounded angry. He heard his name, like a curse.

Alexander McBryde.

Maybe she was threatening him with cone snails. Maybe he smiled. He wanted to smile.

And then he could no longer keep his eyes open. He heard Willa say his name again, felt her hand on his face and the brief press of her lips against his. A last kiss.

It was the only one that mattered.

Then, he was fairly certain, he died.

Part 2

Historic landmark and historic euphemism—the city of Paris is happy to see _everyone_.

Pirate treasure isn't the stuff of dreams, it's the stuff of nightmares.

Nectar of the gods/the REASON for survival.

Survival Tip #18

Feelings are like giant squid: too big to handle and more prevalent than you think. Avoid both.

Alex was dead. His skin cool and clammy beneath her hands. She looked at his face, ashen now beneath his tan. She had spent so many years despising him but even before they had been trapped here together, his was the face she knew best. His smiling, pirate treasure eyes, his broad, wicked grin, the small scar that nicked his left eyebrow and occasionally made him look more rakish than anyone had a right to. No matter how she felt about him over the years, she had always looked for his face in every room she entered because she knew he was one of the few people who would look back. He saw her—so clearly it was frightening.

And now he was gone.

She didn't know what this feeling was inside her. It was too big to comprehend, too raw and painful to examine closely. All she knew was it was devastating, like a hurricane sweeping through and leaving behind everything familiar broken.

"This is your fault," said a voice over her shoulder, so cold and accusatory that her next breath felt like needles of ice in her lungs. She looked up and the pirate was there, older than he had been with Joséphine, but younger than the spectre he had become. His dark hair was brushed back above his collar, his eyes like flat, dark coal, his mouth sharp as a cutting blade as he looked down at her. "This is your fault," he said again and Willa couldn't stop the sob his pointed words cut out of her chest.

He was right.

They would never have come here if she hadn't gone looking for Alex that night on the boat. If she had been less judgmental, if she had just ignored him and the way he made her feel. If she hadn't wanted him to look at her the way he looked at everyone else.

Sharks were meant to be alone.

"This is our fault," said the pirate, dropping to his knees beside Willa and when she looked back down, it was no longer Alex lying cold and unmoving on the forest floor, it was Joséphine. Beautiful even in death, her black hair spread amongst the flowers, her white chemise stained red with blood. "This is what happens when we long for something never meant for us."

He looked up from the pretty corpse in front of them, his eyes met Willa's and she recognized the stark, awful loneliness, the guilt and shame still living alongside that longing which was as inescapable as a sickness. "This is what happens," he said grimly and then, with only a flash of sunlight on silver as a warning, he reached up and plunged a jeweled dagger directly into Willa's heart.

"Alex!"

She came awake with a shout, her hand gripping her chest, pain radiating outward and settling into her bones. It was all she had become the past week, pain and guilt and desperation moving her from one moment to the next. She pulled in a deep, shuddery breath and pressed her face into the mattress, trying to block out the images and memories that accompanied every nightmare she had any time she managed to fall asleep. The pirate might have loved his Joséphine but he had also been a cold and ruthless killer. All Willa dreamed about now was death.

Maybe it was all she deserved to dream about.

There was a small tug on her hair and she jolted upright, her heart suddenly racing as she turned to look at the man lying in the hospital bed she had been resting her head on. Alex was looking back, his gaze heavy-lidded but alert with one of her curls wrapped around a finger.

"G'day, Wilhelmina," he said slowly, his voice low and raspy after almost a week of disuse.

For a moment, Willa couldn't say or do anything as she was caught beneath a landside of half a dozen emotions: relief, worry, guilt, longing, anger, fear. Finally, she managed to force out an accusatory, "You're awake!" He had passed out during their miraculous rescue from the island and it had been four days since then, with every single one of them filled with the fear he would never wake up again.

"Miss me?" A weak smile stretched his dry, chapped lips and it cracked her right down the middle, simultaneously making her want to cry and begin shouting. She crossed her arms and gripped her shoulders, as if that might stop her from finally falling apart.

"You bastard," she hissed because it was easier to be angry than it was to admit how terrified she had been. "You almost died."

He coughed and cleared his throat and she immediately stood, reaching to pour a glass of water from the pitcher on the nightstand. After he finished the glass, he looked back up at her, more alert and with that teasing, familiar golden glint she had missed so much. Her heart kicked painfully against her ribs.

"Are you upset it was only 'almost?'" His voice was stronger now and it moved through her like an earthquake, making her even more desperate to keep him from seeing all the ways she had fractured since watching him slowly fade away in front of her.

"I'm going to kill you," she bit out and the damn man grinned.

"So that's a yes."

Tears rushed up behind her eyes. She had missed this. Missed him. "You're insufferable," she said, the words catching as she dragged an arm roughly over her eyes, trying desperately to keep them from falling.

"I know." He put the water glass back on the side table then snagged her wrist and pulled. "Suffer a little more and lie down with me."

The shadow of her nightmare kept her feet momentarily stuck to the floor but Alex was awake and he was *looking* at her, his expression teasing but hopeful and it would have been a lie to say she hadn't missed this too. So she ignored the ghost whispering recriminations in her attics and gave in to the pressure pulling her forward. She settled next to Alex on the bed, exactly the way she had inside their small tent on the island, her head resting on his shoulder, one of her hands on his chest where she watched it rise and fall with his breath. There was comfort in that, in the proof that he was really alive and, when his hand slid down to settle in its usual place on her ass, there was comfort in that too because it meant he was still himself.

His fingers squeezed lightly. "Missed you," he sighed and even though Willa wasn't sure if he was talking to her or her butt, another knot tied itself inside her throat.

She swallowed hard and managed to force out a terse, "Still a scoundrel."

There was a rumble beneath her fingers as he let out a low, hoarse laugh. "Fuck, I really missed you."

He said it so simply. Like it was easy. Like Willa was someone actually worth missing. Like it wasn't her fault he was lying here in a hospital because she had dragged him overboard. Because she was too much. Too tall, too judgmental, too abrasive, too demanding. Too cold. Too afraid. Her hand curled into a fist on his chest and the tension stringing her together became almost unbearable. She couldn't say anything, it felt like her vocal cords had been tied into a sailor's knot.

His hand covered hers and she jerked her head back, looking at him in surprise and he was looking back, his grin replaced with concern. "I'm sorry, Willa. I'm sorry you faced all of that alone." His hand left hers to reach up and touch her face, this thumb brushing beneath the dark circles under her eyes. His frown deepened. "You haven't been taking care of yourself, possum."

The fucking bastard.

She was too much and no longer able to contain it.

She fragmented, falling to pieces with great, chest-wracking sobs that burst suddenly out of her as the pain and exhaustion and fear finally broke free. She tried to stop, tried to pull all the feelings back but they were another force of nature and at the end of the day, Willa was only human. But then Alex's arms were wrapping around her, pulling her practically on top of him as he stroked her hair. He let her cry without letting a single one of her jagged edges push him away and it was the first time in her life Willa wondered if there might actually be someone who had hands big enough and tough enough to hold all of her.

"...the urchin went flying! Luckily it wasn't harmed but I was worried..."

Willa tried to open her eyes but they felt wet and sticky and the throbbing in her head made it hard to focus. She felt like a sea sponge that had been kidnapped from the ocean, used to scrub a thousand pots and pans, rung out and then chucked in a landfill. Just absolutely, body and soul destroyed.

"...Honestly, that they didn't kill each other on that island is the most astonishing part of the whole thing..."

It finally registered that the voice talking animatedly nearby was Professor Schwartz. It also registered that Willa was still lying on top of Alex after *crying herself to sleep like a pathetic loser,* and the professor was on the verge of discovering them *cuddling.* She forced her eyes open and jolted upright in alarm. Her elbow hit Alex hard in the sternum and he came awake with a loud grunt.

"Dammit woman, why are you always flailing around in bed?" he asked grumpily, even as he tried to pull her back down. This caused another burst of panic and in her haste to get away she wound up rolling off the bed and onto the floor. Luckily her ass was well padded and somewhat broke her fall but she was still left gasping as the air was knocked out of her.

Alex's face appeared over the side of the bedrail, obviously divided between concern and amusement. "I don't want to say you deserved that for elbowing me but I'm not *not* saying it."

Willa flushed as she jumped to her feet and grabbed his shoulders. She shoved him roughly back onto the bed, explicitly aware she had cried all over his hospital gown earlier as she whispered menacingly, "It's not too late for me to murder you, McBryde." Beneath her, his eyes darkened and his grin sharpened into a smirk as his amusement shifted.

"So rough, Wilhelmina," he murmured and the tone of his voice pierced through her panic. For just a moment he sounded like the old, cocky, flirty Alex and rather than being annoyed by it, it made her body go warm. She froze, their eyes catching and in his she found the same, hungry expression he had given her when he dropped to his knees and begged to taste her. Her face got even hotter and her eyes dropped to his mouth. She remembered what it felt like to kiss him, what it felt like when he kissed *her* everywhere *except* her mouth and for the first time in the past week she felt something other than raging, reckless despair.

She still wanted him. With the kind of fierce, awful longing that made her fingers curl and her heart ache. All she wanted to do in that moment was strip down, climb back into the bed and feel Alex's warm, golden skin against hers. She didn't understand how someone could make her feel so fundamentally human and explicitly animal, didn't understand how he had become something that felt essential, like eating or breathing.

But animals adapted to survive in their specific environments and they were no longer on the island, no longer just two animals alone in the woods. There were new, different dangers to be considered here and she had already endangered him enough.

Alex's hand had found her wrist, his thumb stroking over her suddenly rabbiting pulse. She froze.

"Willa—"

The sound of the doorknob turning ricocheted around them, hitting the moment so that it broke. Panic returned and she frantically shook her head at him and straightened, "Quiet! Don't tell the Professor we were sleeping together. It will make him think we're *actually* sleeping together." And that would be disastrous.

She admired Professor Schwartz immensely but the man was a terrible gossip, as evidenced by the conversation he was currently having with whatever unfortunate stranger he had trapped outside the door. If he thought Willa and Alex were sleeping together, the entire biology department would know by Monday and the only thing worse than facing her peers and professors' disbelief would be their faux-pity when Alex inevitably started dating someone for real.

Ignoring the weird tightness in her chest and Alex's frown as she pulled her hand away, she turned and forced a smile just as the Professor came striding into the room. He was alone, confirming Willa's suspicions he had simply been gossiping to whomever was closest, but she was still glad to see him.

Shorter than her by a good five inches, Dr. Schwartz still had a way of filling up a space with the kind of warm, exuberant energy that drew people in and made them willing to follow him into adventure—like a teddy bear crossed with Indiana Jones. Which was probably how he had managed to talk his way onto the coast guard boat that rescued them from the island. Willa had almost collapsed in relief when she saw him running up the beach toward her, although it was unfortunate that he (along with several members of the Seychelles coast guard) now numbered amongst the men who had seen her naked.

"I hear our patient is finally awake!" He said cheerfully, adjusting his glasses as he looked speculatively between the two of them. His gaze settled critically on Willa. "Don't tell me you stayed here last night, Willa?"

The truth was she had stayed here every night since they arrived back on Mahe but neither the professor nor Alex needed to know that.

"Of course not, Professor."

His expression was still skeptical but he didn't question any further. Dr. Schwartz might be a gossip but he wasn't *rude*. "Well, it's good you're here. I spoke to one of the nurses on my way in and she said Mr. McBryde can be released in the next few days. In which case, I thought we should discuss your flights."

"Our flights?" echoed Willa.

"Yes, your flights home," said Dr. Schwartz as if this was something already established rather than complete news.

"Home?" and this time it was Alex providing the echo in the room, his deep, Australian-tinged voice abruptly reminding Willa that *his* home was on the other side of the planet. Her hand reached up and grabbed one of her curls, tugging on it hard enough to hurt as the professor continued.

"You've been through something traumatic. You didn't think I would put you back to work did you?" Dr. Schwartz's expression managed to communicate both consternation and deep offense. Honestly, his eyebrows alone could have starred in a one-man show. "Of course, I think you should go home. You need time to rest and recuperate and I know your families are worried. I'm sure they want to see you." He gave Willa a meaningful look and she knew instantly she was not the only one receiving daily calls from her parents. She had spent at least an hour every day for the past four days convincing them not to hop on the next plane to Mahe.

Still, she shook her head. "Professor, we can't leave you to clean up our mess. We're still waiting on the expert from UNESCO to come verify the treasure and I'm sure there will be miles of red tape to hack through as we figure out what to do with it. The authorities are still asking questions about how we found it." The authorities had asked a lot of questions after they were rescued and clearly only believed half the answers Willa had given. They had been incredibly, although perhaps reasonably, suspicious about the fact Willa and Alex had wound up on an island that didn't appear on any maps. Willa suspected this was somehow the ghost's doing but telling that to the overly-stern, overly-uniformed authorities had seemed like a good way to wind up in a psych ward.

"Willa, you should know by now that I thrive in chaos." The professor gave her a Cheshire Cat smile. "Besides, I suspect that, very soon, my two favorite students are going to come into a great deal of money. I hope when they do, they consider supporting the conservation and research efforts we're conducting here in the Seychelles."

"Funding and a bigger boat maybe?" asked Willa with a small smile as Alex let out a bark of laughter.

"With higher guardrails," he added with a smirk in her direction.

"And thicker walls," she said so sweetly it made her own teeth hurt.

"I don't think I even want to know," muttered the professor, again looking back and forth between them. "But now that we've confirmed my lack of altruism, I can book your flights tonight." His smile went kind and paternal, reminding Willa of her dad and why she had taken to the professor so quickly in the first place. "Soon all of this will feel like a bad dream," he said and her stomach twisted.

Her hand rose to the pirate's love token still hidden beneath her shirt, the professor's words bringing back images from her nightmares. They were one of the reasons she had taken up residence in Alex's hospital room, because every time she woke up from one, she needed the reassurance that he was not actually dead. She had tried taking the necklace off once they reached Mahe but as soon as the gold left her skin, it felt like being possessed all over again. Clearly the ghost was determined to make sure the necklace was returned.

She glanced over at Alex and their eyes met. Even after sleeping for several days in a hospital, he still looked rough around the edges, like the pain of his injury had settled into the lines around his eyes and had yet to soften. She saw his smile fade as it flicked to where her hand rested on her chest and she dropped it to her side. Alex had suffered enough. He deserved to go home.

Willa would just have to do what she had always done: face the ghosts alone.

Survival Tip #19

A near-death experience will always show you who someone truly is. This is why you must ensure your enemies are near death at least once. Twice if they're really obnoxious.

It was going to be a long journey home. As the crystal blue water and verdant green of the Seychelles fell away, Alex watched clouds coming up to meet the plane and realized he was actually sad to be leaving. It was dusk and already the sky was changing from blue to pink to gold. A few stars poked through wispy grey fog and the moon was a thin, almost transparent looking sliver. He remembered sitting beneath that sky, drenched in starlight and drinking rum on a lonely beach and not feeling lonely at all. He had found so much more than lost pirate gold here, he had found something rare and lovely and absolutely maddening.

Maddening and also, currently, just mad. With him. As usual.

He looked over at Willa, she was sitting with her arms and legs crossed, her body positioned as far away from him as possible as she glared out the window. Every inch of her was communicating a clear "fuck off" and yet, just like when he had woken up and found her sitting beside his hospital bed, the wave of relief he felt was so intense that for a moment he wondered if he had actually died and this was heaven. Even angry, she was just so fucking magnificent.

He poked her side. "Willa, you haven't talked to me since we left for the airport. It will be very boring if you keep this up all the way back to Boston." He wasn't afraid of her sharp edges but still, when she turned those arrow-sharp eyes on him, he wondered if sitting in silence was the safer option.

"You shouldn't be coming back to Boston at all. You should be going home," she hissed, clearly cognizant of the people sitting uncomfortably close. Alex adjusted his cramped legs for what felt like the hundredth time in the past thirty minutes and thought wistful thoughts about first class leg room. Next time. Once they were millionaires.

"Technically, I am going home. All my stuff is in Boston. I know you did your best to ignore me all these years, but that is where I live." He kept his voice low and reasonable even knowing it wouldn't do any good. He had said the same thing when she confronted him after overhearing his phone call to his mom saying he wouldn't be coming home until Christmas.

"Your mother was *crying,* Alex. I heard her. We only have a month until the semester starts again and you almost died. Your family deserves to see you." Alex looked away to hide his wince. She was right. His mom had cried while his dad had looked stoically heartbroken. All three of his sisters had tried to convince him to change his plans and the guilt at disappointing them was a slow, painful parasite gnawing away at his insides. But of all the people who could understand his decision to stay, he knew his parents would.

Maybe it was just another juvenile fantasy but Willa hadn't just saved his life, she had given him a reason to live. When she promised him anything he wanted, the answer had been easy—he wanted her last kiss. Maybe that made him a scoundrel but he no longer cared. He had been given another chance to coax Wilhelmina Jones apart and find the heart inside her—he wasn't going to waste it.

"I know they do," he said quietly and her expression became determined.

"It's not too late. Our first layover is in Abu Dhabi. You can change your flight there."

"I'm not going to do that."

"Why?" and there was something harsh and desperate in her tone. "You can't be doing this because of me." She said it so decisively, as if it couldn't really be because he cared about her. He wondered what scared

Willa more, the idea that he did care about her or the idea that he didn't. It was part of the reason he hadn't told her how he felt over the past few days. He was still afraid if he tried to hold on to her too tightly now, if he was honest about how much he wanted her, how much he liked her, that she would disappear, this time for good. They were no longer trapped together and between his injury and the painkillers, if Willa ran, Alex was in no condition to chase after her.

"Willa, I am coming back to Boston because this adventure isn't over. We still haven't decided what we're going to do with the treasure and we have to figure out what we're going to do about this." He reached up and tapped the gold medallion he could see outlined through the front of her shirt, working hard to ignore the way it brought his hand in close proximity to her breasts and that she wasn't wearing a bra. The same way she hadn't worn a bra since their rescue because clearly she believed in torture as well as marine animal-assisted murder.

She batted his hand away. "You may find this shocking, McBryde, but we have these things called phones. We don't actually have to be next to each other to make decisions." Her voice dropped to a harsh whisper. "And I knew I shouldn't have told you about the freaking ghost and his ridiculous demands." After Dr. Schwartz left the hospital, Alex had bullied her into telling him everything that had happened on the island, starting with her possession by the ghost through their rescue. The plane had seen them after all (and Willa had promised to kill him at a later date for not telling her he had seen one...if Alex's guilt for not immediately chasing after it didn't kill him first).

"It's not like I don't know where to start looking," she continued, "I've out-studied and out-researched you for the last five years. I don't need you hovering over me while I start looking for Joséphine's grave."

Alex felt his jaw clench. Talking to Willa when she was being stubborn was like pulling a hook out of a fish's mouth—slippery and sometimes more complicated than it needed to be, especially since she was no guppy and had considerably more teeth. His fierce, defensive little shark. She would never admit there was something she couldn't handle but the fact she was fighting him so hard made him suspect there was more she wasn't telling him. Something was going on with the fucking ghost, he just knew it.

She hadn't left his side the entire time he was in the hospital despite having a much more comfortable bed at a nearby hotel. And, as much as he liked to imagine it was just concern for him, he had watched her sleep and hadn't missed the way she winced and moaned like she was in pain.

He also hadn't missed the anxious turn of her mouth whenever she toyed with the necklace through her shirt and every time he suggested she take it off, she became cagey and changed the subject. Willa might be keeping secrets, but Alex still wasn't letting her face everything alone. Not again.

"Willa, I know you could do all of this without me but you don't have to. We started this together and that's how we're going to finish it," he said firmly even as she continued to glare at him. He leaned over, bringing their faces close and dropped his voice, "We're friends now, Willa, whether you like it or not, and friends don't abandon each other. Now you can be angry until we reach Abu Dhabi since I plan to sleep most of the way but I want you all smiles by the time we hit Europe, do you understand me?"

"You know, telling a woman to smile is not a good look these days," she said with a scowl but he didn't miss the way her eyes briefly dropped to his mouth, sending a hot, electric bolt of awareness down his spine. It had been too many days since he kissed her. If he was a braver man, he might have done it then but all he could think about were all the small, subtle ways she had withdrawn in the past few days since crying in front of him. He needed to be patient and prove to her he wasn't going anywhere regardless of whether she was tender and soft or fierce and sharp. They had time now. He would be a better man than he had been on the island. If he didn't try to hold on too tight, then maybe, just maybe, he could keep her even after this was all over.

"Well if you smiled more, I wouldn't have to say it," he murmured. Her eyes flashed back to his and even though they were absolutely lethal, he could have sworn her lips twitched.

"Oh", she breathed out, "I hate you, Alexander McBryde." It was something she had said hundreds of times over the years but there was no longer any bite or venom to it. It was no longer a weapon but a sign she was laying down her bow and ceding the battle. It wasn't quite as good as hearing her say he was right, but there was a strange sort of pleasure in it anyway because they both knew the truth.

Even if she had yet to admit it.

"No you don't," he said easily, dropping his head on her shoulder with a yawn. The pain pills he'd taken shortly after take-off were starting to kick in. "Have I ever mentioned that I love how tall you are?" He rubbed his cheek on her shoulder, the smell of her hair pillowed beneath him tropical and familiar. No one else had ever fit next to him the way she did.

She was quiet while he settled himself but when he let out a soft, contented sigh, she huffed out an exasperated, "You're ridiculous," but she didn't push him away and that was another small victory.

He smiled and by the time the overhead lights went out, she was breathing deeply, her head resting against his.

Alex woke with a jolt as his seat shuddered beneath him. The plane cabin was dim, Willa was sleeping with her face against the side of the plane, her lips pressed into a frown. He wasn't surprised she hadn't woken up. She had stayed awake all through their six-hour layover in Abu Dhabi and been restless the first few hours after boarding this flight to London. He checked the flight path navigator on the small screen in front of him and was glad to see they had just flown over the border into France. They were almost there and he would finally be able to properly stretch his legs. Being over six-feet and forced to sit in coach was definitely one of the circles in Dante's Hell.

Another shudder worked its way through the plane and suddenly the overhead lights flickered on. There was a brief crackle of static and then—

"Ladies and gentlemen, this is your captain speaking. You might have noticed we just experienced a little turbulence. It seems we've just lost one of our engines but I want to assure you the other three are in good working order and are enough to get us to London safely within the next two hours. However, as an added precaution, I do ask that folks make sure their seat belts are securely fastened and that you refrain from moving around the cabin for the remainder of the flight. Thank you for your patience and understanding."

Alex sat up straighter and he wasn't the only one. All around him, people were slowly waking up and he tried to decide if he should wake Willa or let her stay blissfully unaware of this new development. He looked at the flight attendants but they were still up, quietly chatting with each other and preparing the last meal service. That more than anything calmed his nerves and he decided to let Willa sleep. There was no reason they should both be worried.

Twenty minutes later however, another shudder went through the plane, this one bigger and more dramatic. Willa sat up abruptly beside him.

"What was that?" she demanded groggily as a sense of dread settled over Alex like a cold, damp fog. Before he could respond, however, the captain's voice again came through the speakers.

"This is your captain again. We've just lost a second engine. I apologize for the inconvenience but just to be safe, we are re-routing to Charles de Gaulle airport in Paris. Once we've landed, there will be a brief layover while we secure another plane to take us the rest of the way to Heathrow. Again, we apologize for the inconvenience. Please remain in your seats and keep your seatbelts fastened. Flight crew, please prepare for landing. We will be starting our descent in ten minutes."

Willa looked at him, her eyes big. She was definitely awake now. "Oh God," she said, clearly afraid. She wasn't the only one. Fear was a sharp, chilling buzz beneath his skin. He reached over the armrest and grabbed her hand. It was ice cold.

"It will be fine, possum. We'll be fine." It was all going to be fucking fine. They just had to get through the next twenty minutes.

"Or maybe we're cursed," she whispered, her other hand rising to press against the pendant trapped beneath her shirt.

For a moment, Alex was distracted from his rising anxiety. He shook his head at her. "What?"

"Cursed!" she snapped. "Maybe we touched an evil pirate's treasure and now we're doomed!"

"I'm sure that's not—" he broke off as the plane suddenly dropped what had to be several hundred feet like a stone. Around them, people screamed and the captain came back over the speakers. She was no longer calm.

"We just lost a third engine. I am landing this fucking plane. Everyone hold on to something."

The front of the plane dipped down and people slammed forward. Alex was forced to let go of Willa's hand and grab the seat in front of him to keep from breaking his nose. The cabin became chaos. Plastic cups and napkins floated through the air, a book went sailing by, there was a pained yelp as an old man in front of Alex was hit in the head with a tablet. The plane was roaring as it ripped down through the atmosphere, some people were screaming, others crying, and a few were laughing hysterically.

He looked over at Willa but she was silent, her eyes closed, her lips pressed tightly together as tears streamed down her face. Alex felt like he was having an out of body experience. Maybe he was screaming or swearing, he didn't know. All he could think about was that he was the world's biggest, dumbest bastard for wasting a single second with the woman beside him.

Fuck patience.

He should have kissed her the day they met.

Should have stayed and smiled. Called her beautiful until she believed him. Been the friend she needed. Loved her until she believed she deserved it. He wanted to take her out for weak, overpriced pina coladas. Wanted to hear her laugh at a thousand more jokes. Wanted to fuck her, hard and fast until she screamed and then make love to her, slow and worshipful until she begged. He wanted to be the one she reached for, the one she told her secrets to through sharp, pretty teeth. He wanted to be the one holding her every time she cried. Even if things ended, even if he wound up with a broken heart, he wanted Willa's hands holding the pieces.

They couldn't die yet. Not now. Not like this.

The horrible scream of the last working engine echoed through the cabin as the entire plane abruptly leveled out. Alex's body was slammed back into his seat and then with a tremendous jolt, they bounced hard, one, two, three times onto the tarmac. Wind was rushing past the windows and the entire cabin shook and swayed. There was no way they were getting through this. The entire plane felt like it would roll over at any moment. He found Willa's hand again and squeezed it tight. No one was screaming anymore; it was like every single person was holding their breath. Finally, after a small eternity, the plane slowed and eventually ground to a halt but Alex was pretty sure no one exhaled until the captain's voice crackled through the plane.

"Welcome to Paris," she said hoarsely and it was like a spell breaking. People laughed, perhaps harder than they should have, but adrenaline and relief were heady things. A couple people whooped and even more started clapping. Alex looked over at Willa whose head was pressed back against the headrest, her eyes still closed as she took deep, shaky breaths.

"Willa, you alive?" he asked and her eyes opened, her pupils still big and dark with fear.

"Yes. You?" Her voice was shaky too and he reached up and brushed the wetness from her cheeks.

"Yup." Then he knocked the armrest out of the way, grabbed the front of her shirt to pull her close, and kissed her. He felt her surprised intake of breath, felt her hand, still holding his, squeeze around his fingers but then she was leaning in and kissing him back. Lust and desperation and relief they were both alive had his hand slipping from her shirt to the back of her neck, pulling her closer, taking the kiss deeper.

More.

Nothing else mattered but this. Nothing else *existed* but this. Fuck, he had never wanted anything more than this. He traced her lip with his tongue and dove into her mouth and she was there, sweet and eager to meet him. One of her hands fisted in his shirt near his ribs, the other found its way into his hair, the scrape of her short, practical nails up the back of his neck making him groan. She was so soft and so *much,* her body was an entire world to explore as he stroked down her side, tracing and mapping her curves—the gentle rise of her breast, the lush flesh of her hip. He squeezed her there, imagining what it would be like to sink into all that softness, remembering what it tasted like on his tongue. This was what made life worth living. He wanted her naked.

More.

Her hand moved to the hem of his shirt, a few fingers slipping beneath, touching his bare skin and that was enough to make his heart race and his cock ache. She moaned when he gripped the back of her neck tighter and tasted the sound on his tongue as he went deeper. He wanted her spread out, open and wet and hungry for him. He wanted to hear what sounds she made in those first few breath-stealing moments when he entered her for the first time. Wanted to know how many times he needed to make her come before she was begging and saying she hated him with her voice needy and desperate. He wanted inside her, every part of her.

She was already inside him.

More.

He loved her. So fucking desperately. The fear that had made him deny it for so long felt small and petty now. Life was too short and fragile. He loved her and he needed to tell her, now, before anything else could go wrong.

Stopping was the hardest thing he had ever done but this was more important. The lust and need raging through him were nothing compared to the panic, the urgency to tell her the truth, to admit what he should have told her a thousand times already.

"Willa, I need to tell you something," he said, still working to catch his breath. She was breathing hard too, her cheeks flushed, and he watched as her eyes fluttered back open, dazed now and no longer afraid. Her fingers rose to touch her lips and made him desperate to kiss her all over again.

"Alex, why–"

"Because we almost just died. I'm sorry, I should have done this sooner. I'm an idiot but I need you to understand—I don't expect anything from you—" She started to frown and his stomach dropped. Shit. He was fucking this up, he just needed to say it. He took a deep calming breath. "Willa, I—"

"Excuse me, sir? Ma'am?" Like a fucking apocalypse, a flight attendant broke into Alex's confession and it was like a black hole opening up but in reverse—the world abruptly filled back in around them. Overhead, the captain's voice was crackling through the speakers, sharing what was undoubtedly important information and all around them, people had started standing and shifting. Someone who looked like a passenger but spoke like a nurse or doctor was talking to the man in front of Alex who had been hit with the tablet, checking his vision and asking questions. Somehow, Alex had momentarily forgotten that the reason for this new urgency was that they had almost been in a plane crash.

"Sir, Ma'am, if you could please collect your carry-ons and move into the aisle, we are trying to get everyone off the plane as quickly as possible," said the attendant in a falsely bright voice.

Alex was still gripping the back of Willa's neck, unable to force himself to let go. He was terrified that if he did, he would lose this moment, lose his chance to tell her how he felt before some other absurd catastrophe actually managed to kill him. Even if she didn't love him back, even if she ran, she deserved to know he loved her. She wasn't alone.

A throat cleared and Willa's eyes shifted to look over his shoulder, reminding him how very not-alone they were. He followed her gaze to the flight attendant whose mascara was smudged down her cheeks and her smile forced. "Sir? Please?"

He nodded slowly. "Right, of course." He slowly uncurled his fingers and stood up, Willa watching him with a frown on her face. People around them were staring, one woman with short hair and a spiked earring grinned and gave Alex a thumbs up while a disapproving middle-aged man finally removed his hand from his teenage son's eyes. That urgency was still racing through him, making his insides feel jittery and feverish, but when he held out his hand, Willa took it and his body calmed. Squeezing her fingers, he hoped she understood it was a promise to resume this later. He was done waiting, done being a coward.

Before they left this city, he would tell Willa he loved her. They had survived so much already; it was time to start living.

Survival Tip #20

Forget the day, carpe deum

Looking out the window of their taxi at the bustling Parisian streets, Willa couldn't help but think she was extremely tired of finding herself in places most people dreamed of visiting their whole lives *against her will.* She might never go on vacation again.

After they exited the broken plane onto the tarmac, it was announced another would be along shortly to take people the rest of the way to Heathrow. She and Alex had looked at each other and in wordless agreement elected to instead take a shuttle to the main terminal. Willa wasn't getting on another plane for the foreseeable future. Boats were also on her shit list. She would rather *swim* back to Boston at this point.

She glanced over at Alex who was looking out his own window, a frown on his ridiculously handsome face, and felt a quiver work its way around her stomach. Whether it was a good or a bad quiver had yet to be determined.

He had kissed her.

And it had felt different from the way he had kissed her on the island. It had still been hard and hungry and desperate but it also had been sweet. Tender. It had consumed her. There had been nothing beyond the feel of Alex's mouth on hers, the squeeze of his hands on her hip and back of her neck. It was astonishing how easily fear could transform into need. He could have stripped her naked right there in the middle of the plane and Willa was not at all certain she would have stopped him. Clearly you could take the human out of the wild but you couldn't take the wild out of the human.

Except he hadn't touched her since. He had barely looked at her. Maybe he was regretting it already. What had he said on the plane? *I'm sorry. I'm an idiot. I don't expect anything from you.* Those were the kinds of things someone said before letting another person down gently, weren't they?

Another quiver looped around her belly and she looked back out the window at the cheerfully lit cafes and restaurants streaming by, all crowded with people despite the late hour and clouds gathering overhead. It was a reminder that the real world was waiting for them. Soon this adventure would be over, they would be back in Boston, back to the way things had been before. Her and Alex would go back to running on parallel tracks, same direction but never intersecting, never touching or entwined the way they had been the past few weeks.

A kiss never means true love.

She snuck one more glance at him as their taxi pulled up in front of a modest, five-story building with a pizzeria on the ground floor and a sign that simply said "Hotel" attached to the first. Heat gathered low in her belly as she looked at the strong curve of Alex's forearms, the way they flexed as his hand tightened around the handle of the cane given to him at the hospital. The cane he needed because he almost lost his leg, almost *died*. Because of her. The heat was extinguished in a wave of guilt.

This is what happens when we long for something never meant for us.

"I think we're here," she said, ignoring another, much stronger quiver as it moved all the way through her, making her feel shaky and unbalanced.

Maybe she was still in shock. Maybe that explained the strange ache in her chest.

"Already?" He straightened and looked around and Willa felt another line of tension wind around her spine. Maybe Alex was in shock too. That or he had popped another pain pill when she wasn't looking. They had been in this taxi for at least 45 minutes. At the airport, she asked the driver if he knew a decently-priced place to stay close to the center of the city and he had given a very gallic shrug, a short, "Oui" and took off. He was now looking impatiently at them in the rearview mirror.

"Uh, merci," she said, "Garder la monnaie," she added in her rusty French as she passed cash over the seat. He perked up upon seeing the tip and gave Willa a crooked smile.

"Dites au concierge que Luc vous a envoyé," he said gruffly and made a shooing motion.

Alex was already out of the car, grabbing their carry-ons from the trunk and as soon as Willa closed the cab door behind her, it sped off, merging seamlessly back into the wild Paris traffic.

She moved next to Alex on the sidewalk, grabbing the handle of her roller-bag as they both paused, looking up at the hotel sign and breathing in the heavenly smell of cheese and carbs emanating from the pizzeria. They had only really been inside the hospital and airports since being rescued and neither had expected to find themselves in Paris. This wasn't where they had planned to be and there were no obvious answers for what would happen next. It felt like a new jungle, with more unknowns to be faced. Overhead, thunder rumbled and Willa told herself not to take it as a bad omen.

"I think the entrance is around the corner," said Alex, who still appeared distracted. Willa wanted to ask if something was wrong (aside from the obvious "everything") but then, seemingly without thinking, he reached out and grabbed her hand. "Come along, Wilhelmina."

His palm was warm against hers, his fingertips calloused and familiar. She looked down at their joined hands and her mind went blank. The heat still burning like lusty coals deep inside her found oxygen and sent fire licking up her back, burning away some of the awful tension. She followed wordlessly behind him as they walked into the hotel lobby, knowing she should let go of Alex but unable to force her fingers to uncurl from his.

The lobby was small and dominated by a red concierge desk and several oversized vases filled with plants. The man behind the desk wore a matching red tie and was similarly shaped to the vases, wide on top and narrow on the bottom. "Bonjour," he said politely as they came to a stop in front of the desk. "Welcome to Boucanier d'Amour. Do you have a reservation?"

"Uh, no. Our flight was...canceled," said Alex and Willa snorted beside him.

"Our taxi driver, Luc, said this was the best hotel in town," she added.

The concierge nodded as if he believed her. "We are always happy to hear our hotel is appreciated. How many rooms?"

Willa felt Alex tense beside her and realized this was their first night somewhere there was no plausible reason for them to share a room, let alone a bed. He was still limping but could clearly manage on his own and Willa had deliberately avoided telling him about the nightmares. She looked up at him, their eyes met, and it felt like the popping of a match one inch from a line of gunpowder.

He was wearing a very similar expression to the one he'd had right before tying her to a tree—wild and *intent. This* was why he had barely looked at her since deboarding the plane. She let out a quiet but audible "oh," as a line of heat blazed throughout her entire body, starting at where his thumb stroked along the side of her hand. That one little touch triggered the memories of a hundred others, of his hands tangled in her hair or wrapped around the back of her neck, the sting of his palm as he spanked her ass and the slide of his fingers pushing inside her. The feel of his hands on her body had become so familiar, she would know his touch even with her eyes closed.

Her heart raced, her body ached, she should let go but she couldn't. Not yet. They had unfinished business—she had promised to give him anything he wanted if he lived. She wouldn't go back on her word. If he wanted her, he could have her, even if what he tried to tell her earlier was that all of this was only temporary. Willa was used to disappointment. Just once, she wanted to experience the high before the low.

"Un, je pense," said the concierge wryly and Willa managed to tear her gaze away from Alex and back to the other man who was looking at them with a knowing expression. The back of her neck prickled in embarrassment but she nodded and pulled a credit card out of her purse.

"Oui, merci."

Alex's thumb was still making lazy circles on her skin and while the concierge was busy entering her information into the computer, he lowered his head and murmured in her ear. "You're blushing."

"No I'm not," she whispered back even though she could feel the heat in her face.

"You are and you should be." His hand slid out of hers to curl low and possessive around her waist. "I'm done waiting. I want all of you, Willa." His voice was low and quiet but with that same urgency she had heard on the plane, "Every last dangerous, soft, hidden sweet inch of you." He pressed a kiss below her ear, she felt the briefest flick of his tongue and had to bite her lip to keep from exploding.

"Room 4F, you can take the elevator to the right," cut in the concierge pointedly and if Willa hadn't been blushing before, she was now. With the same polite smile, he slid her credit card and a hotel key over the counter and then beside them put three condoms and a tourist map of Paris. "There is much to enjoy in the city of love, no?" He asked and Willa had no idea if he was referring to the Eiffel Tower or the tower waiting to be erected in Alex's pants.

Her life had become a joke.

Alex "Completely Shameless" McBryde however just grinned, handed Willa the map and cards, swiped up the condoms, and said a chummy, "Thanks, mate" as he slipped the hand on her waist into the back pocket of her jeans. He began propelling her toward the elevator and Willa was so caught up in the horny mortification of it all, that all she managed to choke out as they waited for it to arrive was a vaguely threatening "Pugilistic porpoises" in Alex's direction. He laughed, a low, dangerous rumble that, embarrassingly, made Willa's knees go weak.

The elevator pinged open, they stepped inside, and there was a moment of quiet as the doors closed and they started moving.

"Tell me you want this." The words were a quiet demand beside her and Willa looked over at Alex in surprise. He was looking back, his eyes searching her face, the laughter fading from the curve of his mouth as he went serious and intent again. "Tell me you want me."

Her whole chest tightened. This felt different than being two animals fucking in the woods. Telling him she wanted him felt like an admission. Wanting something she knew had never been meant for her was how all her recent nightmares started. She hadn't been able to admit it on the island, she had been too afraid of how much of herself she would lose in the process. She was still afraid. But she liked him too much to lie. She had hurt him in so many ways over the years, she didn't want to do it again. That would be the bigger regret, one she was no longer sure she would be able to live with when all of this was finally over.

"I want you, Alexander McBryde," she said just as the elevator doors opened. Neither of them moved. Willa could feel her heart pounding, keeping time until Alex finally blew out a deep breath, his hand coming up to stroke gently along her jaw.

"Thank fucking God." He pressed a hard, fast kiss against her mouth, his arm reaching out to catch the elevator doors from closing. "I don't think three condoms will be enough," he muttered, setting off more quivers in Willa's stomach and at last making her realize what this feeling was: anticipation.

Luckily their room wasn't far and once they were inside, Alex was tossing his backpack down and turning to Willa with an expression that hit her right in the chest and sent heat spinning out.

"Strip."

That one, guttural word felt like a hook dropping deep inside her and she knew even if she tried, there would be no getting away from this moment or this man. She let go of her bag and it rolled away, hitting the wall with a soft thump as she planted her hands on her hips and tried to at least appear like there was some fight left in her.

"Excuse me?" she demanded, but there was no disguising the way her voice shook as she took a step toward him. He smiled. Not his usual cocky grin or the charming, boyish smile that made everyone want to be his friend, but a smile that said he knew exactly what Willa dreamed of in her most fevered, secret fantasies...and he was going to make them all come true.

"You heard me, dag, strip." The old nickname was practically a purr, setting off a spark she once might have labeled annoyance or exasperation but which now lit her up and revealed something entirely different inside. She had never wanted anyone like this. It felt like her next breath, her next heartbeat, hinged on this man touching her.

She stripped off her shirt and Alex let out a groan.

"Fuck me dead." He sounded hungry and reverent all at once. "I've missed those." He didn't come closer, didn't touch her, but Willa could feel his eyes on her like a tangible caress. "You haven't worn a fucking bra in weeks. It's been torture."

Surprised and without thinking, her hands rose to cup her chest. "Bras feel too constricting now." She looked down, noting how her breasts barely managed to fill her hands. "I thought they were small enough no one would notice." Alex's short, abrupt laugh had her looking back up.

"Dangerous girl," his voice was strained. "I noticed. Every goddamn day. All I could think about was sucking you through your shirt until I could see you, pretty and pink and needy through that white fucking cotton." His eyes moved back to hers. "You're a terrible tease, Wilhelmina."

He really was the devil. It was the only explanation how, with just a few words, he had her body humming, her nipples going tight and warm, like he had already had them in his mouth. Unable to stop herself, she ran her thumbs over them, pressing them into her fingers with a light pinch that sent a small bolt of pleasure between her legs.

"See," Alex snapped and he almost sounded angry, "An absolutely shameless tease. This is why I had to tie you up." The reminder was another flash of heat. She remembered the feel of the rope, the freedom in finally letting go, the decadence of Alex's tongue between her legs. The power she felt making him fall apart afterwards. It had happened less than two weeks ago but she felt like a different person now. Or maybe it was the world that was different. Now she felt every second like it was sand slipping through an hourglass whereas on the island, time has felt like a sandy beach with no end in sight. The only way to survive now was to focus on each moment and make the most of it so she had no more regrets later.

"Of course we don't have any rope when it's my turn to tie you up," she kept her voice low and sweet, her thumbs still stroking back and forth because she couldn't stop and because if he was going to accuse her of being a tease, she might as well be one. "When are you going to touch me, Alex?"

He swore under his breath, his eyes back on her hands, but he still didn't move. "When you're naked." He crossed his arms and the look on his face made her feel extremely flammable. "Keep going, Wilhelmina. You show me yours and I'll show you mine." And just like their first morning on the beach, those words were fuel to fire. This time however, it was more than a dare and Willa wanted more than to simply show him up.

She slipped out of her shoes and unbuttoned her jeans, not sure if either of them was breathing as he watched her slide them over her hips and down her legs, leaving them puddled with her underwear on the floor. When she straightened, he looked like he was barely holding himself in place. His voice was rough as he glanced at the fluffy, messy bun on top of her head and simply said, "Hair."

He was such an odd man.

She pulled out her hair tie and shook her curls out, knowing she probably looked messy and wild and nothing like the beautiful, sleek women Alex had dated in the past but telling herself it didn't matter tonight. She heard him take a harsh breath, watched his shoulders drop and his hands relax while he looked at her the way he always did, like he was seeing all her dark, strange hidden corners but wanted her anyway. Like he cared.

"There you are, there's my Willa." He said it softly, like it wasn't meant for her at all but she felt the words anyway, tasted sugar on the back of her tongue. Maybe it was good he wasn't touching her yet because it gave her a chance to savor, gave her a few more moments alone inside her skin before all she could think about, all she could feel, was him.

Rain began to fall outside, pattering against the large French windows while thunder rumbled in the distance. The room was softly lit, dim, warm light from a small lamp in the corner mixing with the blue gray shadows cast by storm clouds and streetlamps. Willa had never felt brighter. Everywhere Alex's hot, hungry gaze touched her set off a flare of heat, like a star placed on her skin until she felt like a sky full of constellations. This is what it must feel like when the universe moved and you were at the center.

"Your turn, Dundee."

The corner of his mouth curled up as he pulled his own shirt over his head and dropped it to the side. Later, she might be embarrassed that her breath actually caught at the sight of him but he was a God. How did she keep forgetting that Alex was blinding? Both demons and angels must weep.

"Jesus, McBryde, what is up with your genetics?"

He let out a short, startled laugh. "What?"

Willa just shook her head, knowing she probably looked hopeless because this was another admission but it was true and he deserved to know. "You're just so fucking beautiful. I don't understand how you're real."

His hands paused on the button of his jeans and his eyes narrowed on her. He took a step forward.

"What did you say?"

Heat was flooding her cheeks, tingling down her throat as she blushed. "You heard me."

He took another step forward and her heart skipped. "Fucking beautiful, Wilhelmina?" Another step and he was crowding her up against the door. "I think that's the first real compliment you've ever given me."

"I've complimented you before." She couldn't remember actually doing it but she was sure she had. Alex brought his hands up on either side of her head and leaned close. He still hadn't touched her yet but all she could feel now was the heat of his body so close to hers.

"Yeah, but you only say fuck when you really mean it."

Something shifted beneath her ribcage and goosebumps raced across her skin. She didn't know if it was fear or lust or something bigger pulling her apart and putting her back together with the knowledge that Alex *saw* her. He knew her in ways even she didn't understand.

If he didn't touch her now, she was going to fucking die.

She slipped her fingers into his loosened waistband and erased the space between them, the feel of him against her somehow strange and new and sweet and familiar. Thunder crashed overhead and she felt it vibrate through her chest. It felt like bricks falling. She pressed upward, closer, her breasts moving deliciously against him, knowing she was going to sound desperate but not caring. She wanted him too much.

"Alex, fuck me, please."

Survival Tip #21

The third time really is the charm. The fourth and fifth are even better.

Alex was going to die if he wasn't inside her soon.

Later he would find candles and roses and tell her he loved her; it would be romantic and perfect—perfect enough that she would believe him when he said it. Now however, he was going to give her exactly what she wanted—what they both wanted. So much it felt like drowning—breathless and desperate and all-consuming.

This time, she kissed him.

She closed the distance between their mouths and he could breathe again, her lips warm, her tongue sweet as it found his. He had thought he would be able to take this slow but he forgot that the sight of her nipples did in fact whip him into a lustful frenzy and for the first time in five years they were alone, safe, and she wanted him.

She *fucking* wanted him.

His hands found her hips and he pushed her more firmly back into the door, in love with her and the way she fit against him. Her hands tightened briefly in the waistband of his jeans and then they were climbing up his sides, her nails pressing into his back and neck like she was trying to get even closer. He ground his hips against hers but it wasn't enough, he needed more, needed friction and heat and her body, hot and wet around his. He slipped his hands under her thighs and, clever girl that she was, when he lifted, she wrapped her legs around his waist without ever breaking the kiss. Admitting he loved her was hard but loving her was so goddamn easy.

He drew away from her mouth, pressing kisses along her jaw, down her neck. He sucked below her ear and she moaned, her hips arching away from the door, rubbing along his aching cock through his jeans.

"Alex, please."

Strewth, but he loved it when she begged.

"Please, what?" He gave her throat a sharp, demanding nip with his teeth and her fingers tightened in his hair.

"Please fuck me."

God, she really was going to kill him. He would never get over hearing those words on Wilhelmina Jones' lips. He kissed her, wanting to taste them, diving deep, their tongues meeting, their breath mingling as he stepped away from the door and moved toward the bed. He followed her down to the mattress, obsessed with the way her softer body gave beneath his, reverent of the fact that she was tall and strong enough for him to let go and sink in. This woman could handle him—she could handle anything.

Her hands were sliding down his back and pleasure was the press of her fingers, sinking into his ass through his jeans, dragging him closer while she rolled her hips beneath him and moaned.

"Alex, please," she gasped, "Show me yours, I want—"

"I know what you want, dangerous girl," he said, dragging his mouth down her throat, kissing and breathing in whatever subtle perfume she wore, a scent he hadn't even realized he missed while they were lost at sea. She smelled warm and decadent—her perfume had always made him think of golden hues, like her hair or glittering, sun-baked deserts. Before, when they were constantly dancing around each other, he always knew when she had just entered or left a room on campus, the smell of her perfume giving him a jolt of anticipation. It did the same thing now, making his groin tighten and his heart pound.

He had wasted so much time.

He wanted to spend the rest of his life making up for it.

Willa writhed and arched beneath Alex, desperate to get her hips even closer, to feel the press of him against her clit—a little more, a little harder and she was sure she could come. But he kept holding himself just out of reach. It wasn't fair. The way he knew exactly where and how to touch her to make her feel like this. It wasn't fair to make her beg and then make her wait. God, it felt like she had been waiting for this for forever.

"Alex, more," she demanded and she felt him laugh, the sound ending with a ragged moan as he thrust against her one more time before lifting his hips away completely. "Wait, no, I need—"

"I know what you need," he said roughly, cutting her off. "And I'm going to give it to you." His tongue traced downward, toward her breasts. "But the first time you come for me tonight, I'm going to taste it." The words slid through her like a shot of rum—overwhelming and a little harsh and setting off a burst of heat low in her belly.

"But—"

"I'm not rushing the first time with you, Wilhelmina," his voice was deep and sure, like he already knew there would be more between them in the future. Willa's heart seemed to trip in her chest but then his mouth closed around her nipple and she didn't know if it was because of his words or because of what he was doing to her. A delicious wave of pleasure slid through her body, the beat of it settling between her thighs. She felt his tongue, the light scrape of his teeth, while his other hand stroked and pinched and found other little spots that made her feel too wild and impatient.

He toyed with one breast and then the other until Willa was no longer thinking of anything but Alex and the way his mouth felt as he kissed his way down her body. He slid off the bed and settled between her thighs, his hands hot and firm on her skin as he pressed her wide. "Fuck, look how perfect, how wet and ready you are for me." He let out one those deep, hungry groans and Willa was too lost to be embarrassed, it just made her want him more. She felt his finger trace from her clit down to her opening and bit her lip on a moan. His head moved closer, she felt his breath as he said just one word, "Mine."

Then his mouth was on her, his tongue dragging from her opening up to that most sensitive spot and that one word was a constant echo in her head as he worked her body like the silver-tongued devil he had always been. He slipped two fingers inside her, stroking deep and the tension that had been building inside her exploded. Willa came hard and fast and with a curse, her hips rising to press against his face so that she felt his deep, pleased laugh rumble through her entire body.

Pleasure was still swimming through her limbs as Alex surged to his feet and kissed her, a deep, delicious kiss that tasted like both of their satisfaction. But it wasn't enough. God, what if it was never enough? What if she felt like this forever? What if she wanted that one word to be true? She threaded her fingers through Alex's hair and kissed him harder, deeper, like she could somehow draw out all the promises she was still too afraid to want from inside him. Even after feeling all the pirate's regrets, even knowing inevitably what would come when the sand in the hourglass marking her time with Alex ran out, Willa kissed him honestly now, putting all the feeling she had for him into it. Even if it wasn't forever, she wanted him to know: right now, in this moment, he was hers too.

Willa was kissing him like she wanted to steal the breath out of his lungs. Hungry. Desperate. He wanted to give it to her. He wanted to give her everything. He felt like he might die anyway if he didn't. He broke the kiss and the sound of protest she made, her needy little sounds as he pulled back to finally strip off his jeans and grab a condom went straight to his painfully hard cock but this was something he knew how to do well and do quickly.

In only a few seconds, he was back, recapturing her mouth while he stroked himself through the pretty, pink folds of her pussy. It was bliss. It was torture. He needed more.

"Say it again," he demanded against her mouth, "Say you want me."

She groaned, her hips moving restless and impatient beneath his. "Yes," she said breathlessly, "Want you. Need you. Alex, please—"

He didn't make either of them wait any more. He thrust inside her and nothing had ever been more perfect than the feel of Wilhelmina Jones around his cock.

Nothing had ever been more perfect than the feel of Alexander McBryde stretching, filling, pushing his way inside her. The hard drag of his body over her sensitized one lit her up where he was touching her and made her acutely aware of the dark places where he wasn't. Willa understood now why people risked everything for the chance to feel like this. Alive. Perfectly and completely connected. For a moment, he held himself still over her, his eyes closed, his expression tense but Willa needed movement, friction. Heat. She rolled her hips and he groaned, his eyes opening to glare down at her.

❧

She was so impatient, his Willa.

"Fuck me," she demanded, her hands stroking up his back and adding to the pressure already building at the base of his spine. "Please," she added with that perfect hungry desperation that made him helpless and determined to make her come again and again until even begging was too much for her. He pulled back and thrust, a slow, deep, hard slide that made her body quake around him. He did it again, faster, harder and she rose to meet him and then their bodies were moving together and he lost track of where he left off and she began.

He was so deep inside her. Everywhere their bodies touched, heat crackled and sent pleasure sparking through her. Friction, fire. God, this man made her burn.

Her mouth was a miracle, her pussy heaven. He didn't care what it took, he wanted to stay here forever.

The heat was building, pressure and delight where their bodies were joined. He fucked her hard but his mouth was so fucking sweet, his tongue tangling with hers. His skin beneath her palms was warm, like gold left out in the sun. She couldn't get enough. She was too greedy. She wanted all of him.

She was making the most perfect, needy little sounds as he moved inside her and he remembered the way they built, the way they became moans and pleas, the way she said his name when she came. Almost the same way she said his name when she was angry—like he was the best and worst thing to ever happen to her. It didn't make sense, the way it made him want her so badly except that maybe he felt the same. She was all his worst fears and all his best dreams, no one else made him feel so much, so intensely, all at once. Even now, pleasure was a raging demand inside him but he held back, equally desperate to stay inside her and in this moment.

More. Everything. God, she was so close. Tension was gathering inside her again, but it felt like it was waiting, throbbing just out of reach. Why did everything always feel just out of reach? She couldn't stand it, not anymore.

"Alex, more. Please."

Whatever she wanted, he would give it to her.

He kissed her, a long, explicit tangle of tongues and teeth and then he was pulling back, his arms were looping under her legs and pressing her knees back, her hips rose off the mattress and the next time his cock slid home, Willa thought she might actually pass out. This was what she needed. Her whole body felt electric.

Alex fucked her then, hard and fast and so deep she could feel him everywhere. Her eyes opened, she didn't know when she had closed them, and he was in front of her, wicked as the devil and golden as a God. Their eyes met and she couldn't look away. He was so deep inside her, finding and filling up all her most secret, tender places. There was no escaping the truth anymore: she did not hate Alexander McBryde. Not anymore. Not even a little bit. Maybe she never had. Maybe hate had simply been the only word that felt big enough for the way he made her feel. Wild. Out of control. Full of this wonderful, terrible wanting. She still felt like she was reaching, afraid to take that final step toward the ending they had been building together. Alex's hands found hers, pressing them into the mattress and, somehow, he pulled her forward and over the edge.

"Come for me, Wilhelmina. Be a good girl and come all over my cock," he ordered because he knew she liked it when he talked that way, could feel it in the way her body tightened around him and the way she got wetter when he whispered filthy things in her ear while his fingers were deep in her pussy. He shouldn't have been surprised how easily this woman gave herself over to passion. She never backed down from a challenge.

Maybe she wouldn't back down from him. Maybe she would love him just as much as he so desperately loved her. He watched her eyes close, her head fall back, watched as her whole body arched and felt her moan as she came around him. She was a fucking masterpiece. Venus. Ruler and owner of the heart going wild in his chest and finally, at last, Alex let himself follow after her.

Survival Tip #22

Fake it 'till you either make it...or break it.

Alex woke up to the sound of rain on the windows. It was still storming and lighting flashed through the room as he looked at the clock on the nightstand. It was 3:00 a.m. Which meant it had been two hours since they had fallen asleep and two hours too many since he heard the sweet, desperate moans Willa made when she came. He rolled over, his tired cock already stirring as he thought about introducing Willa to the idea of slow, sleepy sex in the middle of the night. His hand slid across the bed, seeking her familiar warmth but he found nothing but cold, empty sheets.

The fear and panic was instantaneous. He bolted upright.

"Willa?"

A low, anguished moan came from the direction of the bathroom. He stumbled out of bed, his heart racing and his legs shaky. Now that he was fully awake, he could hear water running and the awful, unmistakable sound of Willa crying. For a moment he wondered if she was crying because of what they had done together, if she had woken up and regretted it, and he had to put a steadying hand on the wall as he flung open the door and flipped the light switch. Willa was there on the floor, her back pressed against the large square tub steadily filling with water and wrapped in a dark red towel that for one awful, heart-stopping moment he mistook for blood. Her legs were pulled in, her forehead pressed against her knees. Hot steam swirled around the room and words had been scrawled through the condensation on the mirror above the sink.

Find Her. Return.

"Fuck!" Alex rushed forward, shutting off the taps before the tub could overflow and then crouching down in front of Willa. He ran his hands up her arms and she was cold again. Even colder than the night in the forest or the morning after she had been possessed. Colder than when their plane had begun falling from the sky. "Willa, possum, look at me. It's okay, you're okay."

Her head tilted back and there were tears on her pale face, her lips were practically blue. "I'm not okay. He's *inside* me. I want him out. It hurts." Her eyes were glassy and blank, like she was still caught up in some nightmare.

Anger slammed through Alex. He had never felt more powerless and furious in his life. "Take the necklace off, love, give it to me. I'll wear it until we figure this out." He was already reaching for the chain around her neck. He wanted it off her, wanted that harsh, broken look gone from her face. But, clearly panicked, some awareness came back to her eyes and she shook her head and grabbed him, trapping his hands against her skin.

"No, you can't! I can't take it off. When I try it feels the same, like–like it's not my body anymore." She was shivering again, so hard that her teeth clacked together. "I—I'm so c-cold."

He swore and looked around, needing to do *something* and his eyes fell on the steam rising from the water in the tub. Perfect. Alex stood. "Come on, Wilhelmina, let's warm you up."

He stepped into the tub and, still looking lost and terrified, she allowed him to tug her in after him. She was still wearing the towel as he turned her around and sat, pulling her down so she was caged between his thighs in the hot water. It was a large tub but Willa and Alex were not small people. Water spilled onto the floor and there was no space between their bodies. It was like having an ice sculpture pressed against him. Alex leaned forward and wrapped his arms around her, they would be cold and warm up together.

"Better?" he asked into her ear.

"I'm wearing a towel," she pointed out hoarsely but he merely tightened his arms.

"Yes, but are you warmer?"

She nodded slowly, "Yes."

"Good. Now just breathe and tell me five things you can see."

Normally, he was sure Willa would have resisted or called him bossy but her body was still trembling against his and instead she answered without question.

"I see—I see the towel getting wet," she said haltingly, her hand floating through the water to touch a corner of the towel that had drifted up, still looking too unsettlingly like blood.

It was his turn to shiver. "Okay, good. What else?"

"I see my hair," she found a curl and stroked it between her fingers and Alex felt her trembling slowly stop.

"Yes, it's everywhere, as usual. What else?"

"I see the gold veins in the wall tiles." And she reached out and touched that too.

"That's three."

"I see...the veins in the back of your hands," she murmured, her hand finding his and tracing the back. Tension zipped up Alex's spine and Willa was right to call him a scoundrel because now was really not the time for lustful thoughts.

"One more, possum," he said roughly and her head came up, her hair brushing against his cheek, and he felt her whole body suddenly stiffen.

"I see the message from that fucking ghost on the mirror," she choked out.

Godamnit. He should have wiped it off. He found Willa's hands again, covering them and threading his fingers through hers. "Look back at my hands, Willa. You're not alone. Focus on that." Her breathing sped up again and his fingers tightened, "Breathe with me, Wilhelmina."

And for the next few minutes they were quiet, the two of them simply breathing together until the rise and fall of her chest was no longer panicked and the message on the mirror fogged up and became only a faint outline.

"Better?" he asked eventually and she nodded.

"Yes," she said but then her voice hardened. "I hate this."

He did too. "Tell me everything. I know you've been holding back."

He felt her stiffen again. "I don't know what you're talking about."

"You cry in your sleep," he said quietly, hoping she wouldn't hear just how worried, how frustrated he was at being so powerless. He was also mad at himself for being so easily put off. He should have pushed her to confide in him sooner. Instead, his own foolish fear of driving her away had kept him from standing by her side. Once again, he had fallen short of what she deserved. "Tell me."

Her body was still tense but then, like she was truly caving inward, all at once she let go, sinking back into his chest, her head falling onto his shoulder, her eyes closed and her mouth pinched. "It's hard to explain." He felt another shiver run through her and her next words were quiet and halting. "Ever since we were rescued, I've been having dreams of the pirate's life. They're like...like nightmares but worse. I wake up and I can still feel every emotion, every memory or the reality of his awful, violent life in my body—the warm, wet feel of blood on my hands, the sound of a baby crying, smoke from cannons stinging my eyes and nose, the burn of a bullet in my shoulder." Her voice dropped and shook, "The regret and despair rotting me from the inside out. I'm starting to lose track of what's me and what's him." Her next words were a whisper, "I think he's stronger than me."

"Impossible." The word was out before he could think about it but Alex knew it was true.

"What?" She turned her head to look at him and he met her eyes.

"It is impossible for him to be stronger than you. You're fucking Wilhelmina Jones. I've never met anyone stronger or smarter or braver than you."

Her eyes widened, her cheeks went pink and she tried to turn her face away, "You're ridiculous," she muttered but he caught her chin and forced her to keep looking at him.

"I've also never met anyone more stubborn," he said, frowning and trying not to wonder if this was how she would react when he told her he loved her. "I mean it, Willa. Dead or alive, no man stands a chance against you." He certainly hadn't, no matter what lies he told himself the past five years.

Her face was unreadable as she looked up at him and then, finally, she gave a slight shake of her head and reached up, sliding her fingers into his hair and pulling his face down to hers. She pressed a soft kiss against his mouth. A smarter man might have questioned it, but Alex felt only relief and longing and that constant, low-level hum of desire. He stroked his thumb along her jaw and kissed her back until the last traces of cold left her lips. She pulled away and her eyes searched his face for a few moments longer. Then she gave another shake of her head and let out what sounded like a resigned sigh. "So fucking sweet."

Those three words were arrows that landed square in the middle of Alex's chest, hitting the three words still waiting there.

I love you.

He wanted to say them. His heart was racing, toward her probably, so eager to throw itself in her hands, he opened his mouth, feeling that new, rising sense of urgency paired with old, familiar feelings of fear and doubt but then she continued.

"Thank you, Alex." Her voice was soft and heartbreakingly unsure, "I'm...glad you're here. I think..." She hesitated and looked back toward the mirror. He felt her shiver against him. "I think, maybe, I needed a friend."

His heart stopped and he swallowed the words down. It would be selfish to tell her now when she was still shaky and overwhelmed. She was already possessed by one extremely selfish man; Alex didn't want to be another. He was going to be what she needed for now. He was going to prove he was worthy of someone like Wilhelmina Jones.

"We're going to figure this out, Willa, I promise," he said, tightening his arms around her to remind her he was here, that he had her back. He was going to help her get rid of the fucking ghost inside her and then, hopefully, she would have room for him.

"We'll figure it out," she echoed and some of her old confidence found its way back into her voice.

Alex nodded, filled with grim determination. "Together."

Survival Tip #23

When sailing through storms, make sure to tie down anything important. To the bed if necessary.

In a rare turn of events, Willa woke up before Alex the next morning. After they had dried off and crawled back into bed, she managed to fall asleep with Alex's arm wrapped tightly around her waist. Thankfully, she had not dreamed of death, however, the dreams she'd had instead had been a different sort of unsettling. A heated mix of sex and longing with shifting images that moved between Rigobert and his Joséphine and Willa and Alex and various combinations of the four of them that had Willa coming awake flushed and on the edge of another orgasm. Sex or violence —she really was possessed by the soul of a pirate.

She was wrapped around Alex in her customary morning chokehold. His hand was on her butt, as usual, and it would be so easy to wake him by sliding her hand down, below the sheet, and curling it around his cock. Memories of last night, of the way he touched and teased and made her come apart again and again added to the restless beat still throbbing between her legs. But she held back. Because more than sex had happened last night.

She tilted her head back so she could see Alex's profile. Beams of morning sunlight broke through the breezy linen curtains and he looked gilded and godlike again. He had the kind of profile that belonged on coins. High cheekbones, square jaw, a straight nose that might have been a little too long if it wasn't situated in the center of the other perfectly proportioned features of his face. He had shaved at some point in the hospital but had left a close-cut beard that framed his mouth and jaw and made it impossible for her to forget what he looked like as a delightfully wild caveman on their island...which made it too easy to pretend he could be hers and they might go on together just as they had the past few weeks.

But then the rest of last night came flooding in. Waking up under the harsh fluorescent bathroom lights, the word 'Return" standing out so starkly on the mirror while the pirate's heartbreak and regret made each breath so painful she thought she would die. It felt like a threat and a warning all at once. Return the necklace, return back to normal, return back to the real world and to who Alex and Willa had always been. Return before it was too late and Willa found herself just as brokenhearted as the ghost.

She slipped out of the bed.

She needed a chance to think without Alex crowding her mind and her senses and her *everything* the way he always did. He pulled thoughts and feelings out of her she didn't recognize, made her do things that felt strange and exciting and terrifying. He was somehow both so much better and so much worse than the ghost. She needed a cold shower and a chance to clear her head.

She had only taken a few steps toward the bathroom when her foot came down on something sharp and she bit back a curse. Glancing back at Alex to make sure he was still asleep, she looked down at the floor to see what she had stepped on. It was a pen cap. The pen itself was a few inches away and beneath it was the map of Paris the concierge had given them yesterday. Willa stilled, a deep sense of trepidation filling her as she looked at the wrinkled brochure. A cold shiver worked its way down her spine as she reached out to pick it up.

It felt like the moment she had stumbled across the pirate's treasure—surprising but still with that deep sense of knowing, like what was happening was all part of some unavoidable destiny. She looked down at the map and there it was, predictable but somehow still awful: her farcical fate.

Willa knew where to find Joséphine because the pirate had left her directions. Scrawled over Sorbonne University was a big, red X.

For the second time in less than twelve hours, Alex came awake with a jolt and inner buzz of panic.

"Willa?"

She wasn't in his arms. His leg ached and there was an awful sense of something being wrong clouding his brain. When she didn't respond, the feeling of wrongness intensified. He sat up and swung his legs over the side of the bed, reaching for his phone and straining to hear if there were any sounds coming from the bathroom. No crying, no running water, just an awful nothing. The only sounds he could hear were the muted blare of car horns and mid-morning traffic outside the window.

How long ago did she get up? This was the second time she had been able to slip away from him in his sleep and he wondered if it was the pain pills. He wondered if he should stop taking them as he looked down at his phone and felt his stomach do an unsettling elevator drop and rise as he saw a text from Willa on the screen.

Out hunting and gathering. Be back soon.

It was okay. Willa was a grown woman. There were no crocodiles in Paris. She spoke the language. The sky was gray and overcast but if she got a little wet, she wouldn't melt. She was clever and strong and fierce. She would be fine.

He still wanted to tie her to the bed when she came back.

That was until he noticed the text had been sent an hour ago. What was taking her so long? He told himself to take deep breaths, to hold back the panic as he raised the phone to call her. She had probably stopped for a café serré. Not even several weeks in the wilderness had managed to break Willa of her caffeine addiction. Just yesterday, Alex had watched her consume two espressos with an almost viscous, slightly concerning glee.

Before he could pull up her number however, her name appeared on the screen. The relief was instantaneous. His lungs expanded and so did his heart. Safe. She was safe.

"Wilhelmina, you had better be on your way back to this bed," he said as soon as he accepted the call, knowing he sounded like the worst sort of caveman and not caring.

"Uh, 'allo?" The person on the other end of the call sounded too French to be Willa. "Is this Alexander McBryde?" asked the voice with too much phlegm and not enough consonants. His chest immediately tightened back up.

"Yes. Who is this? Where's Willa?"

"My name is Professor Levasseur. Uh, I believe your woman, Willa? She has fainted here. You were the last person she messaged."

Ice and fire, fear and fury were a rush through Alex's blood. "Is she okay?" he demanded. She had better be or he would kill her.

"Ah, oui. I believe so, yes. Perhaps it was just the heat of the day? She is awake now and in my office but, uh," the woman hesitated and seemed to choose her words carefully, "She does not seem quite well."

"Like she's sick?"

"Uh, non, not sick. Confus." She hesitated again and then said quickly, "Before she fainted, she kissed me."

Survival Tip #24

Those who don't learn from history are doomed to become possessed by a ghost and forced to experience it first-hand. So study hard.

If she was thinking more clearly, Willa might wonder if what was happening to her was some sort of *Possession Lite*. She was aware of pulling on her clothes and slipping on her shoes, she was aware of walking out into the early morning sunshine and she was aware of lifting her arm to call over a taxi. She could feel the sun beating down through the window making her feel almost unbearably hot and remembered to send Alex a text so he wouldn't worry. She knew exactly what was happening but it felt like she was watching it all happen from a distance.

The taxi dropped her off at the university's campus and then she was standing in front of an office in a hallway lined with half a dozen other offices like she had known exactly where to go the entire time. There was a name plaque beside the door.

Simone Levasseur

Willa knocked and when a soft, feminine voice called, "Une minute," her heart started to pound, there was thunder in her ears, the pendant resting against her chest was so hot it felt like it would sear right through her flesh to her heart. She couldn't think, her soul was on fire, she couldn't move, her body was ice. Then the door opened and she was consumed.

He had found her at last. The only treasure he ever lost, the only person that ever really mattered. Black hair falling in thick waves around a heart-shaped face, eyes the deep, dark blue of the sea at dawn—the same face that had haunted him for centuries, the face he had missed too much to move on without. She was so lovely, had always been so breathtakingly lovely. He had loved her forever. Would love her forever. He knew that now after spending a small eternity without her.

He stepped closer, brought his hand up to cradle the side of her face. Warm. She was so warm beneath his fingers. Warm and soft and alive. He would have waited a thousand more eternities for this.

"My treasure. Your heart has returned."

Her eyes widened in surprise, her pretty cheeks flushed. He watched her mouth let out a small, breathless, "Oh."

He had taken her last breath, now, finally, he gave it back.

Rigobert dropped his head and kissed his Joséphine.

Survival Tip #25

Even in a controlled experiment, be careful what you hypothesize—it might just turn out to be true.

Willa didn't know where she was or how she got there. She didn't know anything until she suddenly became aware of Alex crouching on the ground in front of her. She heard him say her name, sharp, so sharp it managed to cut through some of the thick fog clouding her brain. She shivered.

"Alex?" she asked, or thought she did. She didn't feel quite connected to her body. She wondered if this might be another dream. He *was* too attractive to be real. Maybe he had always been a dream. She reached out and touched her fingers to his cheek. *Warm*. Warm gold beneath her fingers. No, more precious than gold.

"Treasure," she murmured. She had found treasure.

Both his hands came up to cradle her face, his fingers familiar and sure against her neck as he turned her toward him. Must be a dream. This was how they started. His hands on her. Filling her senses. Possessing her.

"Wilhelmina, look at me," his voice was warm too, so warm, like sunshine. So bossy. Such a caveman. She *liked* when he was a caveman.

More of the fog cleared. *How embarrassing.* "Focus, possum," he ordered and she watched his mouth move. Pretty, tempting, aggravating mouth. She liked that too. He brushed some of her hair away from her face and she felt the calluses on his fingertips, saw his concern. For her. She liked *everything* about him. He was a blue sky in a clouded mind. *Oh no.* Sweet. He was so sweet. *Too sweet.* She *more* than liked everything about him. "Willa, I need you to say something, love."

Love.

Oh, God.

She *fucking* loved him.

Willa came completely back to herself all at once and in such a rush of mortification that for a moment she thought she might faint again. She felt herself sway in the chair but Alex was there, his hands on her arms, steadying her, his eyes looking at her intently, *seeing* her, and somehow being the light she needed to find her way back to herself.

Oh God, she loved him.

What was she going to do?

"'Would you like some water?" asked that too familiar, melodic voice. Willa looked from the water bottle being held out to her, up to the face of the woman who was an identical copy of the woman she had been dreaming about for the past few weeks. Rigobert's Joséphine. Right down to the small beauty mark high on her left cheek. This was the woman *Le Vautour* loved so deeply, so fiercely that her soul had called to him over the 28.3 million square miles of the Indian ocean hundreds of years later. It was her, or the reincarnation or angel or zombie or *something*, version of her. The semantics, the details didn't matter, it was her. Willa remembered kissing her and even now had to resist the urge to do it again because even now she could feel the pirate demanding control of her body.

It was all too much. Alex and ghosts and the fact that even though he was part of the problem, all she wanted to do was throw herself at him and beg him to handle it. But that wasn't who she was. She never wanted to be the type of woman who needed a man to save her and hadn't he already saved her too many times? What if she started to rely on it? *Depend* on it? She dug her hands into her hair in frustration, knowing her curls had to be a large tangled cloud around her head. She probably looked wild. She felt wild. Wild and lost in a jungle of unfamiliar feelings.

She buried her face in her hands, "Oh God."

Distantly she heard the slight crinkle of Alex grabbing the water bottle and his quiet voice, "I'm sorry, Professor, could you give us a few minutes alone?"

"Oui, bien sur, take all the time you need." Willa could hear the kind concern in the professor's voice. Truly, she was a paragon of hospitality considering an Amazon had appeared outside her place of work, kissed her, and then passed out cold. She had probably been terrified. Willa glanced up as she heard the door close, as if unable to stop herself from watching the woman disappear.

Return.

The word was an icy demand that made Willa shudder and drop her face back in her hands. Maybe she should just drown herself in the Seine.

"Willa, look at me," Alex's voice was gentle but firm and Willa looked up. She could see the worry on his face, the tension in his shoulders. He was still kneeling in front of her like a man on the verge of a proposal. A bubble of laughter rose inside her from origins not quite sane.

"Tell me what's going on," he said and the bubble broke free. Willa laughed. It was laugh or cry. Alex's frown deepened.

"I think I've lost my mind." *I love you. I'm possessed.* "It's her, Alex," is what she said out loud.

"Who?" He looked searchingly into her eyes and Willa wondered if he was looking for signs of a concussion. They were at the end of this story but they were right back where they started. This time, however, Willa knew why her heart had started pounding and her body hummed. It wasn't anger. It was everything—fear and love and hopelessness and longing.

"The person he loved. It's her. Joséphine," she said, unable to look away from him. Willa had felt these same feelings when she kissed the other woman even though they hadn't belonged to her. This was how Rigobert felt about Joséphine and when he lost her, he had tried to burn down the whole world and himself alongside it.

Love was terrifying.

"Who? The professor?" Alex's face shifted to worry with traces of confusion and despite the fear beating inside her, Willa still hated that she was worrying him. She needed to focus. She needed to explain. She was a shark and sharks never stopped moving forward. That was the only way to survive. She would hack through all these other feelings later.

"Yes. Professor Levasseur is an exact copy of the woman the pirate loved. She looks like her, she sounds like her, she—she even...tastes like her." *Oh God, Willa had kissed her.*

Alex took a deep breath, and then gave a short nod, like he was making a conscious decision to believe her. "Okay. So what do we do? Give her the necklace?"

"We can't just give her a three-hundred-year-old gold necklace without some kind of explanation, Alex," snapped Willa, feeling a comfortingly familiar spark of simple exasperation.

Some of the worry eased from around his eyes. "There you are," he murmured and Willa flushed hearing the affection in his voice. *Oh no.*

"What if I just tell her the truth?" she said, trying to keep her voice from shaking despite the effort it took to suppress all the other feelings roiling inside her like a hurricane.

Alex's gaze slid to the side and he stood up at last. "Please don't take this the wrong way but I don't think telling someone you're possessed by a ghost in your current state will be very convincing." He reached under her chin and tugged on something near her collar. "Your shirt's inside out and backward, Wilhelmina."

Her blush deepened. The Seine was becoming more and more appealing.

"What if we tell her it's an inheritance from a long-lost relative?" he suggested and she felt another one of those exasperated sparks.

"McBryde, do you, by chance, read romance novels?"

"What? No, of course not," he said but his eyes moved deliberately to the bookshelves over her head. She could swear his cheeks even went pink.

"Right. Well, if we're looking for something she'll actually believe, I don't think that's much better than ghost possession."

He blew out an annoyed breath but he still wasn't looking at her. "I'll have you know I inherited some money from a distant great uncle. It's how I—" He broke off abruptly and Willa watched him frown.

"What?" She asked, craning her neck to see what he was suddenly fixated on over her head. He reached out and pulled a book off the shelf, reading the cover with an expression of blatant disbelief. "Alex, what? What is that?"

Wordlessly, he handed Willa the book and she read the title.

L'amour et les pivots: Comment l'histoire d'amour du Vautour a changé l'histoire or, translated, *Love and Linchpins: How the Vulture's love story changed history.* That someone had written a book about *Le Vautour* was unsurprising. Academics loved even the most obscure of subjects. The punch to the gut was the author.

Simone Levasseur, PhD

Willa turned the book over to the back cover and there she was in the author photo, looking beautiful and very French in a bold red lip and large fashionable scarf.

"It's her," she breathed out, stating the extremely obvious.

Maybe, *maybe* Joséphine had not quite forgotten Rigobert either.

Survival Tip #26

If you're being haunted by your own mistakes, get a new perspective. Try being haunted by someone else's instead.

"You found *Le Vautour's* treasure," repeated Professor Levasseur, looking between Alex and Willa who now sat in two chairs on the other side of her paper and book-strewn desk. Her expression was one of polite disbelief and Willa shot Alex an annoyed sideways glance. They had debated which explanation seemed more plausible—being possessed by a ghost or finding the long-lost treasure of the pirate on whom the professor was apparently an expert. The treasure argument had won...barely.

"Yes. It's a long story but we had a bit of a mishap in the Seychelles and we just...happened to come across it," said Willa, regretting every moment in her life that had led to her sounding this ridiculous.

She was pretty sure Professor Levasseur felt the same, she looked like she was regretting ever letting Willa into her office despite their hasty attempts to make her look a little less unhinged. Alex had done a hasty braid in Willa's hair and she had made sure all her clothes were on her body the way the manufacturers intended before they went looking for Dr. Levasseur.

"I'm sorry, but this a joke, yes?"

"I understand why you might think so, but I promise she's telling the truth," said Alex, smiling at the other woman with the kind of innocent, 'you can trust me' smile that only a consummate seducer could pull off. And apparently not even clones or doppelgangers or mysterious changelings (Willa still hadn't decided what this woman was) were immune to Alex's godlike charms. The professor's expression went far too sultry and she eyed him with renewed interest.

"Monsieur McBryde, I would love for this to be true but such a discovery is unimaginable. That treasure is as lost to history as the man who stole it." Maybe it was just that she was French, but the casual, frustrated way the professor spoke about *Le Vautour* sounded like she had known him. Her disappointment in his choices wasn't academic, it was *personal*.

"*Le Vautour*, you mean?" asked Willa quickly, chasing after that hint of connection. Just as she hoped, the professor's eyes lit with the zeal of an academic getting to talk about their favorite subject. She looked away from Alex and focused back on Willa, giving her the kind of look that only existed between two women when they were about to talk shit about a man.

"Oui. Rigobert Olivier, he was an excellent pirate but an extremely foolish man."

Something inside Willa shifted and a chill shivered across her skin.

"What do you mean he was a foolish man?" she heard herself ask.

"Mizz Jones, do you know why Olivier spent three decades haunting the oceans, plaguing ships, and doing his best to collapse the economies of entire countries?"

"Because they took the thing he loved most," said Willa slowly, fighting to stay afloat above the feelings of loss and regret flooding her.

"*Non*." The professor shook her head and waved her hand dismissively. "*Le Vautour* spent his life trying to take everything because he did not take the one thing that truly mattered."

"I don't understand."

The professor let out a small sound, like someone anticipating a challenge, then began shuffling through the papers on her desk. Alex and Willa watched wordlessly as she shifted books and flipped through piles before she finally pulled out an extremely crumpled piece of photocopied paper and handed it to Willa.

"*Voila*, this is the biggest mistake Olivier ever made."

Willa took the paper and Alex leaned over, his face hovering near her shoulder so he could read what looked like a photocopy of a very old letter, the handwriting sharp and dramatic and somehow familiar. Her hands shook as she started to read it aloud, doing her best to translate for Alex as she went, Rigobert's emotions slid through her as if she were penning the words herself.

June 10, 1710

> *My dearest Joséphine,*
> *You must marry him.*

Saying it makes my hands tremble and my breath painful but it is the only thing my wretched heart has to offer. He can give you the life you were destined to live, the life you deserve to live. You are a lady and I will never be more than the boy you found mucking out your family's stables. Forgive me, my love, for not having been born anything but a bastard. You say you will give everything up, but I will not let you.

You have been the only light, the only soft, kind, beautiful thing in a life otherwise mired in filth and darkness. You deserve to spend every day surrounded by beauty. I would burn the world for you but I cannot make it blossom. I would protect you from ever knowing such an existence, even if it means I spend the rest of my life in shadows.

I have enlisted in his majesty's navy and will be leaving at dawn. Do not wait for me. Shamelessly, I must beg you to live well and happily so that I may face death with peace in my heart.

> *Yours forever,*
> *Rig*

Willa's entire body was shaking now, her knuckles white as they gripped the paper. She could feel the devastation, the way telling Joséphine to marry another man had torn Rigobert's heart and soul in two. He had longed to run away with the woman he loved but his own life had been hard and cruel since the moment he was born. It was better to let her go than drag her down.

"Wilhelmina." Sounding concerned, she heard Alex say her name as if from very far away and she wanted to respond but she was still stuck in the memories the letter had brought rising to the surface, snapshots of the pirate's life that made the sorrow and bitterness he felt writing that letter even more sharp and profound. A lifetime of disappointments and heartbreak. He had learned a long time ago it was better to abandon hope and choose the heartbreaks you could live with rather than risk the ones you couldn't. He could live with Joséphine belonging to another man if it meant she could be happy but he could not survive her choosing him and watching her love turn to bitterness and regret the same way it had for his mother after she had chosen Rigobert's bastard of a father.

"Do you see now how he was a fool?" asked the professor and Willa lifted her head to see the consternation on the other woman's face.

Her *face. The face of the woman he loved. How he had missed the easily mobile lines of that face, so bright and expressive. She was so full of passion and life. How could he have taken that from her?*

"No," Willa or Rigobert shook her head, feeling lost and broken and desperate as she looked back down at the letter. "He made the best choice he could for the woman he loved," she said hoarsely, not quite sure if it was her or the pirate himself speaking.

"*Exactement!*" exclaimed the professor, bringing her hand down hard on the desk for emphasis and then swinging it back up to point at Willa. "He made the choice *for* her." The professor shook her head in disgust. "Joséphine was a lady in a time where women had little options and like your typical foolish man, he thought he knew better what was in her heart. If he had trusted her to choose her own destiny, perhaps she would not have died the way she did. Perhaps they would have grown old together in a cottage by the sea, poor and happy, or perhaps, he would still have become a pirate and she would have joined him in his plundering. Instead, he made a cowardly choice. He chose fear over love and there is no greater mistake, no bigger regret anyone can have in this life."

The professor's words settled in Willa's chest like stones skipped across a lake, the weight and impact of them growing larger and larger until she thought she might burst apart. Rain started to patter against the windows and the Parisian sky framing Joséphine/the professor was filled with swirling gray clouds broken up by bits of blue sky.

Return...please. This time, the feel of the words sliding through Willa's brain was softer. It wasn't warm necessarily or even pleasant but it didn't hurt because this time it wasn't a command, it was a request.

She traced her fingers over the markings at the very bottom of the letter, words printed in the lovers' secret alphabet. The same ones pressed into the gold pendant still resting above her heart.

"*My soul will wait for you,*" she said quietly.

"*Excuse-moi?*"

Willa looked up and found the Professor watching her closely, her dark blue eyes narrowed, *eyes the same color as the heart of the sea, eyes that had stolen his own heart the first moment he saw them.*

Please.

Willa placed the photocopy on the desk and met those eyes, letting the feeling of a summer rain wash over her, not fighting it as her skin went cool and her body a little distant.

"*My soul will wait for you,*" she repeated, tracing lightly across the odd symbols. "This was the last promise Rigobert made to Joséphine and perhaps the only one he kept."

The Professor's lips parted and she looked as if she had just been struck by lightning. "How—?"

Willa pulled the necklace up over her head and this time, taking it off didn't feel like being plunged into an ice bath or swallowed by crushing darkness, it felt like a release, like the moment your head broke above water after a long dive and you took your first breath. She placed it on top of the letter and heard Professor Levasseur's sharp intake of breath.

"You're right. Rigobert Olivier was a foolish man. You were also correct however, when you said he was an excellent pirate. He stole many things over the course of his life but I think, by the end, he realized what was most important."

"Is that—?"

"Part of the treasure we found. It was separate from everything else except a cross. I'm sure it belonged to Joséphine. I don't think he ever stopped searching for her."

For you.

"*Oui,*" said the professor faintly. "It is painted in a portrait of her." Her hand rose to press against her chest, exactly where the pendant would sit if she had been wearing it. "May I?"

"*Please,*" said Willa although it wasn't really her saying it.

A cloud shifted in front of the scattered sunlight, stretching the shadows in the office and turning the windows temporarily into a washed-out mirror. The rain outside fell harder and then he was there, no more than a reflection in the darkened glass, standing beside Joséphine at last. Rigobert's ghost appeared younger than it had on the island, his face less scarred and weathered, his eyes no longer blazing with despair. There was still regret but, for the first time, Willa also felt hope, coursing through her like a warm ocean current.

The Professor's fingers closed around the necklace and she sucked in another sharp breath, her eyes fell closed and her head tilted backward. Willa watched the pirate brush a loving hand over his Joséphine's face and press a kiss against her mouth. Maybe it lasted a second, maybe it was an eternity, but Willa could do nothing but sit there and bear witness to the sad ending of this love story, wondering how it might have been different if Rigobert had chosen love instead of fear. She wondered when it became too late to choose differently.

A hand closed around Willa's and the moment broke. The clouds outside shifted and the pirate's reflection disappeared as sunlight hit raindrops. Willa saw a flash of a rainbow before that too disappeared like it was simply a figment of her imagination. The hand holding hers squeezed and she looked over at Alex.

She had almost forgotten he was here. Almost. Alexander McBryde was impossible to forget completely. He had been quiet throughout this exchange, giving Willa the space to lead but he hadn't left her alone. He had been beside her the entire time, watching and waiting in case she needed him and pulling her back, grounding her, when she did.

She loved him.

Her heart was back to racing.

"Pardon," said the professor, pulling Willa's attention from the man sitting beside her and the confusing emotions that welled up inside her when she looked at him. The other woman fanned a hand in front of her face, looking mildly disoriented, "I think for a moment, I too felt the heat of the day. How very strange."

Willa stood up abruptly, clearly surprising the other two people in the room. "If you're not feeling well, we should go."

"Oh, no, I didn't mean—"

Suddenly, Willa wanted to be anywhere else. She needed to be alone inside her skin for the first time in weeks. Alex was still holding her hand and she slipped hers free, taking a step back toward the door. "Really, we've imposed on you long enough."

"Willa?" Alex was wearing a confused expression similar to the professor's. It was endearingly attractive and Willa felt a rush of longing so deep and overwhelming it stole her breath and this time, there was nothing she could blame the feeling on except her own heart.

She needed to get out of here.

"We should go," she insisted.

"But I have questions about the treasure," started the professor but Willa cut her off.

"I'm happy to give you my phone number and email address. We don't know too much about the treasure yet honestly, but once we do, you'll be the first person we call."

"Oh, but—"

"I'm actually still feeling a little faint," said Willa and watched as the professor's face fell.

"Oh, *bien sur*, you should see a doctor if you don't feel well." The professor held the necklace out toward Willa, clearly reluctant to let it go. Willa took another step back toward the door.

"You can keep that," she said, holding out her hands as if to ward the necklace off.

A mixture of delight and denial filled Professor Levasseur's eyes. "Oh, *non*, I could not possibly—"

"You have more use for it than we do. You can use it for your research. Consider it a gift, from one academic to another."

"*Vraiment*? Truly?"

"*Oui*," said Willa fervently, hoping she never had to touch the thing again. She glanced at Alex. He was still standing by his chair, arms crossed, looking at her with that focused way of his, like he was trying to see into all her dark corners and learn exactly what was going on inside her. A bolt of panic had her moving back the last step to the door. She put her hand on the knob and gave the professor one final, weak smile, "*Je suis désolé de t'avoir embrassé plus tôt.*"

I'm sorry about kissing you earlier.

An apology was really the least she owed the woman. If Willa kissed any more people without permission, she was liable to end up in jail...or in love. She flashed another glance at Alex and felt her heart give a nervous kick in her chest. She might prefer jail—she was good with predictable routines.

A smile broke across Professor Levasseur's mouth, broad but somehow still a little flirtatious. "*Il y a pire que d'être embrassé par une belle femme. Je suis content que nous nous soyons rencontrés.*" *There are worse things than being kissed by a beautiful woman. I'm glad we met.*

Willa felt herself blush and for a moment, understood why Rigobert had fallen so deeply in love with his Joséphine. There was something bright and charismatic about this woman's soul...and Willa had already proven herself to be tragically susceptible to such persons.

God, it was hot in here. Had it always been this hot? She needed air and space and maybe a coffee. Definitely a coffee. She couldn't think. And so, feeling a little frantic, she nodded a good-bye in the other woman's direction, pulled the door open, and strode quickly from the room, leaving Alex behind.

Alex watched Willa practically sprint out of the professor's office with about as much of an idea of what was going through her head as when he first got the phone call saying she had kissed a stranger.

"Your girlfriend is a little odd, yes?" said Professor Levasseur, also looking at the doorway where Willa had disappeared. She looked down at the necklace still dangling from her fingers. "She is also a little... *magnifique*." A coy smile slid over her lips and she looked back up at him. "And a good kisser, *non?*"

Alex was struck by the sudden image of Willa and this stunning woman kissing and felt a shameful hum of excitement. It was a very pretty thought although not currently appropriate. Willa would have called him a scoundrel.

He needed to go after her.

He cleared his throat. "Yes, uh, she's all of that. Well, except my girlfriend. She's not my girlfriend," he said as he began heading toward the door. She was just the maddening woman he was desperately in love with and who had once again slipped out of sight. He was cursing his injury and again contemplating the merits of rope when it came to chasing after Wilhelmina Jones. "I promise we'll follow-up about the treasure. I'm sure we can use your expertise."

"Monsieur McBryde," said the professor, quickly coming around the side of her desk and moving toward him. "Before you go, could you please tell me the true reason you came here?"

He paused as she moved close to his side. Their eyes met and he noticed hers were a rather lovely blue and curiously intent. Clearly, she suspected their excuse of looking for an expert on *Le Vautour* was a lie. Clever woman. But Alex was out of his depth. He barely understood how or why they had come here. Which was yet another reason he needed to go after Willa. Despite feeling impatient, he shrugged and gave the professor his most charming, chagrined smile. They might actually need her expertise at some point, he didn't want to be an asshole. "Would you believe me if I said it was just a coincidence? We found the treasure and happened to be in Paris?"

"How did you know it was *Le Vautour's* treasure?"

Damn. It was a good question and the answer was again that Willa was possessed by *Le Vautour's* ghost. He tried to look innocent and unaware. "Lucky guess?"

Her eyes narrowed. "Monsieur McBryde, do you believe in destiny?"

He had, once. He was no longer so sure, despite the way his heart beat like it had a purpose whenever Willa walked in the room. He loved her.

He needed to tell her. But it didn't stop the fear he felt, imagining that telling her might mean losing her. "I don't know, maybe, but I don't see what—I mean, I really need to go—"

He tried to take another step back but she put a staying hand on his arm. "I do. I began believing in destiny the first time I heard the story of Rigobert and Joséphine. That letter was not the end of it, it was simply a pivotal moment. Their destiny was always each other."

Their destiny was always each other. Alex's gut twisted and he wasn't sure if it was relief or fear. He felt compelled to point out the obvious. "But Joséphine died." Willa had told him the story. Joséphine had chosen love and it had cost her everything.

Professor Levausser gave a very gallic shrug. "*C'est la vie.* Everyone dies. It is one of those inescapable things. Everyone's path there is different but along that path are immovable markers guiding you toward it. No matter what other choices you make, some things are just destined to appear along the way. Rigobert and Joséphine made many mistakes, said good-bye many times, but destiny always brought them back to each other."

"Professor, I'm sorry but I really—" started Alex, feeling oddly warm. He suddenly understood why Willa had sprinted out of here, the air felt too dense.

"This feels like one of those moments, no?" she said, cutting him off. She squeezed his arm lightly, "I do not believe it was a coincidence that brought you here and I would like, very much, to hear the whole story someday."

"I'm not sure you'll believe it," he said without thinking, there were still moments where he didn't believe it. But the professor just shrugged again.

"There is only one way to find out." She let go of his arm and stepped back. "It was very nice to meet you."

"You too." Feeling overheated and strangely flustered, Alex turned and began moving quickly toward the door.

"Oh, and Monsieur McBryde?" He felt another flash of impatience but she went on before he could respond. "It is very clear when you look at Mizz Jones how you feel about her. If she is not your girlfriend now, perhaps you should tell her."

Alex froze and turned slowly back toward the professor. She was watching him with a smug, too-knowing, somehow very French smile.

"Sorry?"

She tapped the photocopy of the letter sitting on her desk. "Rigobert's mistake was choosing fear over love but Joséphine's mistake was choosing to let her love go without a fight." The professor's face went steely with conviction but her eyes had an unfocused, distant look to them. "Joséphine should have followed Rigobert, to the ends of the Earth if necessary, to prove to him there was no reason to be afraid." She looked down at the necklace cradled in her hand and her voice softened, "When destiny gives you a gift, you must hold on."

Willa didn't stop moving until she had passed through the university's front doors. It was no longer raining and the air was crisp and cool. The comforting smell of wet pavement, proof of roads and sidewalks and civilization, helped stem some of the panic that had driven her out of the professor's office. She curled her fingers into fists and forced herself to take a few deep breaths, watching as people walked by, tourists with cameras and backpacks and sunburned cheeks, families pushing strollers, even a tiny, ancient looking man with a well-coiffed poodle. There were people driving scooters amidst the terrifying rush of cars and the clink of cups on saucers from a nearby cafe as people sat and sipped their afternoon coffee—a perfectly normal afternoon in the city of lights and love. Willa might feel radically altered but the world carried on.

"Willa."

She heard the doors open behind her, and closed her eyes briefly, trying desperately to hold on to some semblance of calm. She could feel Alex, even from a distance. He appeared and her whole body felt like she had just stepped into the sun after spending forever in the shade. Then she felt him tug the end of her hastily-done braid and her heart took off. How could she ever have thought she could control any of this? Him, her feelings, any of the thousand moments that had led her to this one.

She was more foolish than the pirate had ever been.

"Hey, are you okay?" he asked and she opened her eyes, turning slowly to face him.

It was like getting punched in the heart.

He looked so sweetly concerned. He also looked sexily disheveled, with his hair combed back from his face and yesterday's wrinkled jeans and T-shirt. Clearly he had thrown on whatever was closest and raced to come save her. Again. Because that was the kind of man he was—good and kind and caring.

Oh God. She really, really loved him.

"I'm fine," she lied. Because she couldn't tell him the truth. A kiss never meant true love. That was the agreement they had made. They were friends.

"What happened up there? Why did you rush out?"

"You couldn't see any of it?" It was all so clear for her but what if everything had only happened in her head? What if all those little things, those small signs that Alex cared about her only existed in her head too? It wouldn't be the first time she had imagined a man's interest was genuine but this time the stakes were so much higher. Having sex with someone who didn't care about you was one thing, falling in love with someone who didn't love you back was a much more terrifying prospect.

Alex shook his head. "The professor looked a little odd after you gave her the necklace but that was it. Are you sure that's what you were supposed to do? Do you still feel possessed?"

She did but it wasn't because of the ghost.

Rigobert was returned to Joséphine," she said and then repeated her lie, "I feel fine now."

"So it's over?" Alex pressed, his golden, buried treasure eyes making her feel too warm as he looked her over. She slid her gaze over his shoulder, watching the people walking up the steps to enter the university behind him. Just like at their university back in Boston, Alex attracted attention. Willa watched a group of young women poke each other and giggle, their eyes eating him up as they passed. She could feel the past few weeks already slipping through her fingers, could feel the weight of reality pressing down on her chest and making everything inside it go tight.

"Yes," she said, nodding slowly, "I think it's over," this adventure, this temporary break from reality and everything it meant was over. There would be nothing keeping Alex by her side any more.

"Then we should celebrate," he said, catching her off guard, Willa looked back at him in surprise.

"What?"

"Celebrate," he repeated, looking oddly determined. "We made it off the island, you got rid of the ghost, we should celebrate. Let's go out tonight."

"Out?"

"Yes, Wilhelmina, out. Proper out." He gave her his most devilish grin. "We'll meet people, have fun, maybe get in a bit of trouble."

Longing hit Willa hard. She wanted this. Wanted one more night in this weird fever dream she had fallen into.

"Okay," she said and Alex's face lit up.

"Okay?"

"Yes, okay. I'm sure I can manage to be fun for at least one night," she said testily even though her heart was once again pounding and the quivers were back, racing around her stomach.

Alex slipped his fingers into the front pockets of her jeans, using them to tug her toward him. "Don't sell yourself short. You were fun last night too."

Her breath caught, her heart stuttered. He was still a flirt. A terrible, terrible flirt. But it worked. She wanted him—this—too much to let go before she had to. She pressed her hands against his chest but she didn't push him away, she only just managed to stop herself from pulling him closer. "Still a scoundrel," she said with a scowl but there was no bite to it —it was the best she could do.

His smile widened. "You sound hungry. Should we go eat?"

The truth was she was starving, it felt like she hadn't eaten in years. She was afraid that even if Alex brought her something she knew would kill her, even if she knew how the meal would end, she would eat it anyway.

She was doomed.

"Yes," she said, nodding, "Please."

Survival Tip #27

Never avoid the beast. Face it head on. It's the only way to survive...and win.

Willa looked around the bar where Alex had instructed her to meet him, wondering what was taking him so long and tugging nervously at the too-short hem of her new dress.

After eating lunch, they had gone back to the hotel but then Alex had made some excuse about needing to run a few errands and had insisted Willa stay back and rest. Which was obviously impossible. How was she supposed to rest when her brain kept circling back to the fact that she was in love with Alexander McBryde...and that it couldn't end well.

So instead of resting she had showered and paced and finally ventured out to a nearby shop because if they were going out, she needed the necessary armor to pretend she was someone else. For just tonight, she was going to pretend to be the type of woman who went out with a man like him—the kind who wore a dress that looked like a silk negligee with delusions of grandeur. Of course, then he had texted to say he was running late and she should meet him at the bar.

He was ridiculous. Of all the bars in Paris, Alex had chosen a Tiki bar called The Cocos & Bananas. The whole place was dark and full of plants, there was a waterfall rushing behind the bar and a river that snaked under clear glass floor tiles before emerging to circle around a stage where people danced and performed a tropical island-themed burlesque. With the moon overhead shining down through the vaulted glass ceiling and all the nudity and foliage, it was almost like being lost back in the Seychelles. Except this time Willa was alone despite being surrounded by people.

Where the hell was he?

Before she could once again turn and scan the room, a hand slid over her butt and even before he spoke, she knew it was Alex as heat went flaring up her spine.

"You are a cruel, cruel woman, Wilhelmina Jones," said Alex into her ear, his voice like a shot of three-hundred-year-old rum, smooth and intoxicating and full of promise. His hand settled on her waist and she felt the rest of him pressing against her back, setting off a dizzying rush of feelings inside her, desire and longing and the now bittersweet taste of love and affection.

"You're the one who was late," she pointed out, feeling embarrassingly breathless.

"I know, I'm sorry." The hand on her waist stroked back and forth, rubbing the satin against Willa's skin and making her shiver. She felt him press closer and then his face was next to hers and she heard him give a pained groan. "Christ, you don't know how sorry."

She turned her head and caught him looking down the front of her dress which draped strategically over her breasts. She felt herself blush. "Alex," she hissed even though there was something thrilling about the way he was looking at her. "You're being indecent."

He squeezed her waist. "This dress is indecent." His other hand swept her hair away from the side of her neck and he pressed a kiss to her shoulder, near one of the dress's thin straps. "You look absolutely stunning," he murmured and Willa's heart did a somersault inside her chest. He was the cruel one. It was like he was determined to make her miss this—him—for the rest of her life.

She turned in his arms, needing to face him, needing just a little space so she wouldn't make an absolute fool of herself before all of this was over. Of course then she caught a glimpse of the rest of him and thought making a fool of herself might be inevitable. He was wearing a dark green suit with a white button-up and he was so attractive it almost hurt to look at him. She had seen him *naked* but somehow the three un-done buttons exposing the gold skin of his throat felt pornographic.

She needed to pull herself together.

"Is this usually how you approach women in bars, McBryde?" she asked sweetly, desperate for some measure of control.

His eyes narrowed. "It depends on the woman." He took a step closer, bringing his hands up so he was caging her against the bar. He dropped his head, bringing their faces close, and said, "It also depends on what I want from her."

Oh no. Why had her knees gone weak?

This was a game Willa didn't know how to play.

"And what do you want from me?" she asked, feeling shaky from the effort of not leaning into him again. He didn't answer for a moment, his eyes searching her face, and then, at last, he smiled, not his usual cocky smirk but something softer and sweeter that made her whole chest ache.

"You'll find out later." He took a step back and Willa slowly let out the breath she had been holding. "What I want right now is a drink." He checked his watch and then looked back at her with a raised eyebrow. "How does a pina colada sound?"

Feeling whiplashed, Willa just nodded and he raised his hand to get the bartender's attention. As he placed an order for two pina coladas, memories from their drunken night on the beach rose up inside her. Most were vague and fuzzy, clouded by rum and smoke, but she remembered laughing and feeling like she wanted to cry, other feelings, embarrassment and comfort and longing were mixed in there too. Alex had always been able to make her feel too much, even the first night they met, his apparent rejection had stung so much more than other ones she'd endured. She had wanted to like him. But that was something she did remember from their night on the beach—his confession that he simply hadn't known how to talk to her.

She wondered what would have happened if she had simply smiled at him that night. She didn't know what would happen between them after they left here but she didn't want to go back to the way they had been before.

"Alex, let's start over," she said the words quickly, before she could overthink it and it clearly caught him by surprise.

"What?"

Feeling foolish but determined, Willa tried to explain. "Our entire relationship started off on the wrong foot. The night we met, you said you didn't know what to say to me."

He looked slightly pained. "Yes, but—"

She cut him off, "How do you usually decide what to say to a woman?"

"It depends. But I don't see—"

"On what?"

He let out a frustrated huff. "On what she is," he said bluntly before she could cut him off again.

Willa's hackles immediately rose. "What is that supposed to mean?"

"Nothing as terrible as you're obviously imagining, Wilhelmina. It just means I observe her and the surroundings and adjust my approach based on what I see."

Her eyes narrowed. "Elaborate."

He blew out another exasperated breath but he was biting back a smile. "Okay, look, take here for example, try to think of this bar like a coral reef. Everyone is here looking for something and everyone has a different role in the ecosystem. If you block out all the noise and distractions, you'll start to see who goes where. It's not that different."

Willa looked around the bar but all she could see was people, people talking, people touching, people being loud and social and overwhelming. She shook her head and looked back at Alex. "Show me."

His smile softened and he moved around to her side so they could take in the scene together while he spoke close to her ear. "Okay, see that group of women at the end of the bar?"

Willa turned slightly, acutely aware of his breath on her skin and the way her body brushed against him as she shifted. "The group of six?" she asked, incredibly proud of herself for keeping her voice calm and steady.

"Yes. See how they're moving together? How they're angled in with their drinks pulled in close to the center of their body? They're not looking around, not scoping out possible partners or signaling that they're open to being bought a drink. Their attention is entirely focused on each other. Imagine that's a school of snapper fish using a shoaling strategy to avoid predators. They're not here looking for a mate, they're here to drink, enjoy the show, and get home safe at the end of the night." His arm moved back around her waist, his palm hot against her hip as he continued, "Trying to break one off from the group would be a challenge and even if you managed it, your chances of success are low because she's going to do whatever she can to get back to her group and away from you."

"I can't decide if this is awful or fascinating," said Willa, her whole body going somehow tense and relaxed as his fingers began to stroke lightly back and forth over her thigh. She reminded herself to breathe as she watched the women and saw exactly the sort of protective ebb and flow she had witnessed in schools of fish. "Do another," she demanded.

He grinned and scanned the bar, using the movement as an obvious excuse to press in closer behind her. His other hand settled at the base of her neck and squeezed, directing her toward the stage. Willa had to bite back a small moan. If he kept touching her like this, making her feel like this, she might have to find a cone snail.

"Alright, there's another easy one. See that group of guys?"

Willa looked and shuddered. It was a group of four men, all were staring and hooting up at the dancers. They looked young, American, and almost all of them were wearing t-shirts emblazoned with the name of a college or sports team, two were wearing baseball caps.

"Underclassmen," she said darkly.

Alex chuckled and nodded. "Or a group of male, juvenile bottlenose dolphins. They're here looking for excitement. They'll be rowdy and loud, maybe play a game of pass the puffer fish to get a little high, and will happily stick their dicks into anything, even potentially each other, at the end of the night. If you're looking for easy, likely unsatisfying sex, they're your best bet."

"You could write your dissertation on this. Okay, so we've got snappers and dolphins. What am I?"

His response was immediate. "You're a shark."

Willa's stomach dropped. If Alex already knew, there was no possible hope of denying it. Maybe there was no point in starting over. Animals adapted to fit their environment and once they returned to Boston, wasn't it likely they would revert to their previous behaviors? Willa would always be the same awkward, sharp woman he had first encountered. She would always be a shark.

Before she could respond, she felt Alex stiffen and mutter, "Fucking finally," as he pulled his phone out of his pocket. Willa caught a glimpse of the name Charlotte scrolling across the screen before he shoved the phone back in his pocket and took a step away from her. "I'll be right back."

"What?" she asked, her stomach sinking even further. He had just arrived and already he was being pulled away by another woman.

He seemed nervous as he held up two fingers. "I just need a few minutes, don't go anywhere."

Willa watched him disappear back into the crowd and was torn between the desire to chase after him and the desire to run as fast as she could in the opposite direction. It was already happening. He was right next to her but he was already drifting away. She didn't know if she could survive watching him disappear completely.

She already had too many regrets.

She should have been nicer to him, should have smiled the night they met, should have learned so much sooner how to be a different kind of animal—one that understood better how to be part of the world rather than one that always went in teeth first. Even now, even without trying, the people jostling their way up to the bar gave her a wide berth, casting glances up at her and then scooting a little further down.

She wasn't cut out to be in love.

Their drinks arrived and Willa picked hers up and took a long sip, relishing the feel of rum burning down her throat. It was harsh and overwhelming but it was quickly followed by the sweetness of coconut and pineapple and tropical island tinged memories. It was perfect because of course it was, because Alex was apparently always right when it came to her. Because she was a shark and he was truly an excellent marine biologist.

He was going to break her heart.

Willa saw him re-enter the bar and her foolish, masochistic heart turned over in her chest, wanting him so much she felt almost sick with it. She watched how the tides shifted in his direction. Two women sitting together in orange and white striped dresses waited for him to walk by before turning to whisper and giggle with each other. Another person, large and curvy and gorgeous with a glittery blue beard and stunning grey-blue dress actually winked at him and blew him a kiss making Alex grin that sinful, devilish grin even as he shook his head and kept moving.

This was how it had been all day. Alex moved and people looked. He smiled and they drew closer and Willa knew it was more than just his appearance. He pulled people toward him in the same effortless way Willa repelled them. He was just...attractive, on every possible level and Willa was just as susceptible as every other creature here. She couldn't look away, couldn't escape—she didn't even want to, even though every instinct she had told her he was a danger to her safe, predictable existence.

He was halfway across the bar when a woman with blood red lips and barracuda eyes stepped into his path. Alex stopped and Willa's heart stopped too. She saw the woman slide a hand up Alex's chest and the rest of the bar faded out of existence, disappearing into a red haze.

Without any sort of conscious thought, she was moving, cutting her way through the crowd and, given that she was a head or more taller than most, especially in heels, people automatically shifted out of her way. Alex and the other woman were clearly visible. He had grabbed her wrist, like he was trying to remove her hand from his chest but barracuda eyes brought up the other one and ran it down the lapel of his suit jacket. Willa's eyes narrowed and she barred her teeth, imagined ripping that hand right off. When she reached the couple, she wasn't gentle as she neatly cut between them, elbowing the other woman back as she reached up to grab the edges of Alex's jacket.

She caught his look of surprise but then she was kissing him and it took less than half a breath before his hands were slipping around her waist and he was kissing her back.

It was by no means a sophisticated kiss. It was hard and hungry and tasted like sugar and rum. Willa slipped her hands up, burying her fingers in his hair and digging into his shoulder, drawing him closer, nipping at his lip with her teeth and feeling him groan against her tongue. She felt the smooth satin of her dress tighten around her as his hands fisted in the fabric, gripping her tighter and pulling her closer. This hadn't been her plan but it should have been. This was what made the universe move, what made it bright and magical. This was what made it all matter. Love or instinct or possession, everything inside Willa was inevitably drawn toward him.

Kissing Alex felt like destiny.

Just as quickly as she had pulled him in, she pushed him back. She met his shipwreck eyes, saw the gold in them glinting like a treasure just out of reach and she shook her head hopelessly.

"I hate you, Alexander McBryde," she said hoarsely and then, hating herself even more, she turned and fled.

Alex was once again chasing after Wilhelmina Jones.

She had kissed him in front of everyone and just like the first time she kissed him, he had no idea what it meant. Why had she kissed him and run? The foolish hope she was actually jealous and staking a claim on him made his heart beat even faster as he moved quickly through the crowd, catching glimpses of her torturously seductive pink dress and halo of golden curls ahead of him.

People parted for her, like they recognized a goddess was passing through their midst. He saw a few men appreciatively eye her ass and considered stopping to pluck out their eyes but he didn't have time. He'd made *plans* for this evening damnit. He was going to tell Willa he loved her and nothing, not even the woman herself, was going to get in the way of that.

He tried calling after her, but it was swallowed up in the music and hum of the crowd. Perhaps he should have chosen somewhere more refined for his declaration but when he found this place, it had felt familiar and perfect, a chance to go back to that night on the beach and tell her what he should have told her then.

Finally, he managed to push through the club's front door and saw Willa crossing the street toward one of the bridges arched over the Seine. How did she always move so fast? Ignoring the pain in his injured calf, Alex took off at a run, just managing to cross the street before the light changed. He finally caught up to her on the bridge, grabbing her hand and forcing her to turn around and face him.

"Willa, stop," he said, trying to catch his breath, "Where the hell do you think you're going and what the hell was that?"

"Alex, let me go," she said, trying to tug her hand out of his as she stepped back, closer to the railing.

"No," he said because it was that simple. He wasn't letting her go without a fight. Not again. "Tell me why you keep running away from me. I know you don't really hate me." The words didn't even bother him anymore. He knew her, knew what she was, and he wasn't afraid of her teeth.

She glared at him but he could feel her hand trembling and there was a quiver in her voice, "Why do you always think you know everything? It's infuriating. You're so infuriating."

"I don't know everything, but I know you and I know that you don't really hate me." He reached up and tugged coaxingly on one of her curls. She was so pretty, even—especially—when she was like this—wild and fierce. "Tell me what the problem is and we'll fix it together."

Together.

He was always so insistent they were in this together.

Oh, God. Why did being around him make it feel like her chest was expanding, like he was pulling her open, reaching inside, and wrapping his hand around all the things she tried so hard to keep hidden. He really was infuriating.

"It's you!" she said desperately, "You're the problem."

"Me?" he asked and she watched hurt flicker across his face. She wanted to bite her tongue. She didn't want to hurt him but what if that was all she was capable of? She tried to pull away but he still refused to let her go.

She shook her head. "Alex, please, I just don't think I can do this."

She was too much and also never enough. Alex deserved someone like him, someone kind and generous and beautiful.

"Do what, Willa? What did I do wrong?"

He was frowning. She hated it when he frowned. He deserved to be happy. She wanted him to be happy. "Nothing! You didn't do anything wrong. That's the problem."

She wasn't making sense. She knew she wasn't making sense. But she couldn't think anymore because her mind was full of nothing but him: the feel of his hands combing through her hair, the sweet taste of him on her tongue, the sound of his laugh and the way he smiled at her—so bright and playful, even when she was threatening him with cone snails or crabs or electric eels.

His frown deepened, "I don't understand what—"

"That's why I can't do this. Tonight was a mistake." She shook her head and tried again to pull back, but it was too late, the truth slipped out and carried her forward. "I can't be here and feel like this and know that at some point I'm going to have to live without you."

The burst of hope inside Alex was staggering. His heart started to beat too fast, and suddenly he felt like that teen boy again, the one who believed in fairytale happy endings and love at first sight. He reached into his pocket, closing his fingers around the jewelry box that had been delivered while they were back at the bar. This was it. This was the moment to finally tell her. "Willa—"

The roar of a motor cut Alex off and Willa watched in horror as a moped jumped the curb to go around a car. It was too close and without thinking, she reached out to grab Alex's jacket, yanking him out of the way. The moped sped by and Alex lost his balance. He pitched forward, knocking into her and Willa felt a sickening jolt of deja vu as the world around her slowed down and her body began to fall backward over the railing of the bridge toward the Seine below.

This time, when her life flashed before her eyes, it wasn't all the moments she had spent alone, it was all the moments she had spent with Alex, from the night they met, when she had glimpsed the gold in his eyes for the first time and wished for something impossible, to the thousands of his small, sweet shows of affection, to tonight when he held her close and explained the world in a way that made her feel like she could understand and be part of it.

She wished she had kissed him longer, harder, more.

She wished she had chosen love over fear.

Alex's hands closed tightly around her and just as quickly as the world had gone sideways, he pulled her into his arms and set it right again.

"Jesus, Willa, are you okay?" His tempting golden eyes were frantically searching her face and Willa at last gave in. Maybe Alex wasn't a treasure meant for her but she was going to do her best to steal him anyway. It didn't matter what other people would say or if it ended with her in an emotional gallows. She would rather be a fool than a coward.

"I love you."

Alex froze. Willa's chest was rising and falling too rapidly, her eyes were still big and a little wild and for a moment, he didn't know if he had actually heard her say 'I love you' or if it was his own imagination, pulling at all his hopes and fears after yet another moment where it felt like he might lose her.

"What?"

"I love you," she repeated a bit more forcefully and Alex, who hadn't thought he had any more heart left to lose, fell in love all over again with this brilliant, magnificent, *impossible* woman.

"Unbelievable," he muttered, slowly shaking his head and feeling Willa stiffen against him.

"I didn't say it because I expect anything from you," she said, her eyes dropping between them. Her hands came up to his chest as she tried to push him away and all he could think about was how his heart was in her hands. "I know you said a kiss never means true love, I just didn't want to regret—"

Alex kissed her. He couldn't stop himself. She loved him. And she had said it first. Because Wilhelmina Jones always, *always* had to be first, be the best, be one step ahead of him. He was going to spend the rest of his life chasing after her and he Couldn't. Fucking. Wait.

Willa didn't know what was happening but Alex was kissing her like he had no intention of stopping. His hands were warm and familiar against her neck and cradling her face. This kiss was softer, gentler than the one she had given him back at the club. It was sweet, so fucking sweet. Willa would dream about this kiss, this moment, for the rest of her life.

When Alex finally managed to force himself to pull back, he didn't wait another second to admit the truth.

"I love you," he said and watched Willa's mouth drop open. He pressed another brief kiss against her shocked lips and said it again. "I love you. Every single time I kissed you, I was madly, truly, deeply in love with you."

Finally saying it out loud felt like the lifting of a curse. He stroked one of Willa's soft, golden curls, marveling that she loved him, that he would get to love her the way she deserved to be loved. She was his fairytale and this time he knew it would be a happy ending.

"You love me?" Echoed Willa, still looking adorably stunned and also, heartbreakingly, a little lost. "Why?"

"Because you're a shark," he said gently, tracing his fingers along the sharp sweep of her cheek. This would be a regret he lived with, knowing he had done things to make her doubt not just him but herself. "Because you're smart and fascinating and so perfectly, stunningly formed. Because I lose my breath whenever I see how fearlessly you face every challenge. Because you feel essential." He shook his head, at a loss to explain all the reasons and ways he loved her. "I told you, you're a masterpiece. The world feels most beautiful when I'm with you."

He was so ridiculous. Willa could feel tears pressing at the corners of her eyes, felt herself blushing. He was just so ridiculously lovely. "Godamnit, McBryde," she said, shaking her head. "You weren't supposed to be this perfect."

He frowned even as he continued to stroke and pet her, those little, unconscious touches that made Willa feel so seen and cared for that one of the tears she had been holding back slipped free. He brushed it tenderly away and shook his head. "Not perfect. I should have told you sooner. If I was brave like you, I would have said it first. I was so worried about doing it perfectly, so afraid of losing you, that I hurt you instead."

"I don't feel brave," she said, curling her fingers more securely around the edges of his jacket, still in disbelief that he loved her, that she wouldn't have to let him go. "That's why I ran. It's terrifying how much I love you." Alexander McBryde, noble scoundrel, protector against maidenly insensibilities, and captain of her lost, foolish heart. She flattened her hand, feeling his heartbeat against her palm. Hers. He was hers. "I think if you had died on the island, I would have become another ghost haunting it. I don't think I can survive without you."

"Good because I can't survive without you either. You're the only reason I made it off that island. You made me a promise, remember?" He gave her his old, devilish smile, the one that made her heart flutter and made other parts of her go warm and liquid. "You said you would give me anything I wanted if I lived."

"That doesn't sound like me," she said and his smile widened.

"There's my girl," he said, and he sounded so fond Willa thought she might actually swoon. "But you did and I know what I want." He pulled out the jewelry box and pushed it into her hands.

"Alex, this had better not be a ring," said Willa, her voice shaking slightly as she held the blue velvet box a little like someone might hold a blue sea dragon.

Alex bit back a laugh and shook his head. "Don't worry, Wilhelmina. When you're ready, someday I'll get you a ring and do a better job than I did tonight planning something wildly romantic to ask you to let me spend the rest of my life worshiping you." He was already imagining it as he watched her cheeks flush prettily and her eyes go bright and shiny, like they were filled with all the stars he had ever wished on. "But I realized on that island that it wasn't a man's first kiss that mattered." He reached up and opened the box, revealing the engraved circular gold pendant sitting there on a long, delicate chain.

Your last kiss.

Willa read the words engraved on the necklace and couldn't stop herself from reaching up to gently touch the gold. *Treasure.* This man was the most perfect, beautiful treasure.

"This is what I want, Willa," he said, his voice gentle and earnest as he cupped her face and tilted her head up to look at him. "I want you to be my last kiss." Then he smiled and Willa was completely lost.

Another tear slipped down her cheek and once again he wiped it away. She glared up at him, slipping her arms around his waist and holding on tight. "Goddamnit, Alex."

"Is that a yes?"

Willa took a deep breath and took the last, final step overboard, knowing she was falling into an entirely new adventure. Then she smiled, one of her rare, broad, full-hearted smiles that made Alex feel like his own heart was being struck by a dozen love-tipped arrows. She nodded.

"Yes. I fucking love you, Alexander McBryde."

And Alex knew, without a doubt, that she meant it.

THE END

Part 3: Epilogue

A year later

The fire in front of them snapped and crackled, sending smoke up into a star strewn sky. Around them the wind whistled through trees, sending branches creaking and bringing with it the scent of pine and loam. Alex had never been much of a camper and after his and Willa's stint on the island, he thought he could go the rest of his life without sleeping outside again. But, he admitted, there was something comforting and familiar about being back in the wilderness with Willa, even if West Virginia was drastically different from the Seychelles and even if he would never admit such a thing out loud. Willa would be entirely too smug to hear she had been right about him enjoying it. Although she probably knew. She was clever that way.

He looked over at where she was sitting huddled next to her formerly exclusively online friend, Sunny, watching interestedly over the petite redhead's shoulder as she sketched out her theories about Mothman anatomy. Sunny Baleen was a bit of an odd duck, which Alex supposed was inevitable for someone who spent her life driving around in a van hunting cryptids but Sunny and Willa got on like a house on fire and Alex was happy to enjoy the show. He was even happier to see her making friends. He didn't care if Willa decided she wanted to buy a van and take up monster hunting too, as long as he got to ride shotgun. Although he supposed a boat was probably more her style and he would happily wear a bikini if that was what she wanted.

Willa looked up from Sunny's drawings and caught him staring. She made a face at him and he grinned. His touchy little shark. He crooked a finger at her and she raised an eyebrow back. He could practically hear her thoughts, *you're not the boss of me, McBryde* and that was all it took for him to want her, need her, with the kind of gnawing, hungry desperation that honestly should have been a little embarrassing.

He stood up from his camp chair and made a show of stretching, enjoying the way Willa watched him with obvious appreciation—two could play at being a tease—but when he strolled leisurely around the fire toward her, her eyes narrowed.

"Where do you think you're going?" she asked, her voice sweet, her smile full of teeth. Fuck but he loved this woman. He held out his hand.

"I thought we might go for a little walk. The moon is full, the stars are out, and I thought we could find a nice tree to—"

"Alex!" Willa cut him off, her cheeks burning in a way that had nothing to do with the bonfire blazing only a few feet away. Beside her, Sunny giggled and shot Alex a conspiratorial look. "You're insufferable sometimes," Willa huffed even as she climbed to her feet and slipped her hand in his.

"You didn't let me finish. I was going to say, find a tree I could use to teach you how to lure and weaponize fruit bats. You know, real Crocodile Dundee shit."

Willa rolled her eyes. "You are never going to let that second movie go."

"I just think it's worth pointing out that you're not the only one suffering for this relationship," he said easily and earned another giggle from Sunny.

"You two are *adorable,*" she said, a wide, amused smile on her freckled face and Alex smiled back. He really had always been fond of ducks.

"Pass the potato, possum, and let's go." Willa gave another long-suffering sigh but dutifully unzipped the front of her jumper and took out the pigeon that had been dozing against her chest. She passed the bird to Sunny who took it, much like they really were passing a potato, and then Alex was pulling Willa away from the circle of firelight.

They didn't speak as they walked, both content to let the sounds of the forest fill the space between them. Bugs hummed, frogs croaked, somewhere an owl called out a single lonely question and below all of it was the constant, steady rush of the nearby waterfall. That was where Alex led them until they were standing at the edge of the river looking out at the moonlight being fractured over wet rocks.

"Feeling nostalgic, McBryde?" asked Willa, her voice a quiet, teasing murmur in the dark. "Or were you hoping for more treasure? Maybe Mothman has a secret goldmine tucked away somewhere."

Alex turned toward her with a smile, slipping his hands around her waist and into the back pockets of her jeans just because he could and because he liked the way she looked at him when he did, her eyes full of lust and her mouth pursed in exasperation. "You know this ass is all the treasure I need Wilhelmina," he said and he gave it an affectionate squeeze to show he meant it.

She shook her head but she was smiling too as she slid her hands up his arms and curled them around the back of his neck, tugging at the hair near his nape. "I knew it. You really did bring me out here just so you could feel me up." She pressed her hips more firmly against his but gave a sigh of mock disapproval. "Once a scoundrel, always a scoundrel."

Alex guided her back a few steps until she was pressed against a tree and then, again, because he could, he pressed a soft kiss against her mouth. He traced the sharp curve of her cupid's bow and fell in love all over again.

"I love you," he murmured after finally pulling away. "Do you remember the first time you kissed me?" he asked and even though the light of the moon washed most of the color from Willa's face, he could tell she was blushing by the way her cheeks darkened. She suddenly became very interested in the branches over their heads.

"I try not to," she muttered and shook her head slightly. "I should probably apologize for it."

He dropped kisses on her burning cheeks. "Don't you dare."

"Alex, it was not a good kiss."

"You're right, it was not a good kiss. It was the best kiss." His lips brushed over the tip of her nose, which was wrinkled adorably in disbelief, then he pulled back. "Wilhelmina, look at me." He waited as she huffed out a breath and reluctantly met his eyes. He pressed his thumb to the corner of her mouth, remembering the moment she kissed him for the first time. It had been wild and salty, sweet and awkward. It had been hot, so fucking hot. Like the woman in front of him. It was the perfect last first kiss. "Marry me."

Willa's fingers in his hair pulled painfully and her lovely mouth fell open beneath his touch. "Excuse me, what?"

"Marry me," he said again, his voice calm and sure.

"Is that a question?" she asked and Alex imagined a flash of sharp teeth in the dark. He grinned, the cocky grin he knew she hated to love.

"Absolutely not. Come on, Willa, don't be stubborn. Marry me."

"Are you sure?" she demanded.

"I've never been more sure of anything in my life. The truth is I was chum in the water the first time you kissed me."

"Not a flattering analogy for either of us."

"But fitting anyway. I love you and all I want for the rest of my life is to be inside you."

Her nose crinkled again but he could tell she was biting back a smile. "That's just gross. I believe I was promised romance."

"Says the woman who turned the first time we had sex into an experiment. You can try to deny it but I know you're too much of a biology nerd not to appreciate the analogy. So, what do you say, dag, marry me?"

"Was it actually a question that time?" she asked sweetly and Alex laughed.

"Of all the times to be stubborn, Wilhelmina."

"Of all the times to be bossy, McBryde."

"Did I mention I'm a millionaire?" he added and her lips pursed as she tried to hold back a laugh.

"Oh yeah? Prove it. Where's the ring?"

"I'll draw you a treasure map later," he murmured and then he pinched her butt and made her squeal. "Willa, answer now, please," he said sternly and finally a broad, incandescent smile broke across her face.

"Fine. Yes, Alexander McBryde, I love you and I will marry you." She pressed a gentle kiss to his mouth and then drew back, "We can be each other's last kiss," she said and he knew it was a promise even more precious than the gold necklace she hadn't taken off since that starry night in Paris.

"Thank you." He kissed her hard and long, with the sound of the river like a memory behind them, all the little moments that had brought them here, to this moment, to together, rushing past. They were both breathing hard when he finally pulled back, giving her lip a final sharp nip with his teeth before giving her his morningstar smile, meeting her eyes, and commanding softly, "Now strip."

Authors Note & Acknowledgements

In case you were wondering, the romance novel mentioned in the dedication is Goddess of the Sea, by P.C. Cast. A story about a modern woman who makes a deal with a goddess and switches places with a mermaid in medieval times. And y'all that book imprinted on my SOUL. I can trace a lot of my life choices back to that book—my teenage baby steps toward feminism, my college major (Classics), my love of the ocean, and ultimately a love of romance novels that has defined my reading and writing since the day I picked up that sparkly mass market paperback (RIP). Of course, I was still halfway through the second revision of Survival Guide before I realized Willa was my own version of that medieval mermaid (albeit a lot crankier).

This book, more than any of the others I've ever written, is me—my loves, my favorite stories, my experiences, my insecurities and hyper fixations—with every revision, this book, these characters, reflected how I was growing both as a person and as a writer. Writing is truly a weird, wonderful, magical and altogether terrible, sometimes painful hobby. But we fucking did it. All thanks to that weird little twelve-year old girl who wanted to be a marine biologist and who read about two mermaids having sex over and over until the pages fell out of her book (it should come as no surprise that I *still* love a monster romance).

Sadly, I didn't become a marine biologist (my brain does neither maths nor science particularly well) but I still LOVE the ocean and I hope that came through in this book. In the scene when Alex and Willa are playing the hand slapping game on the beach and Alex reveals why he became a marine biologist:

"He looked away from her out over the ocean, so dark and restless, dangerous—it had almost swallowed them whole—and yet still so beautiful and grand and unknown it made him ache with the same kind of wonder he imagined others had toward God."

I feel the same. I'm not a religious sort of person but I am constantly in awe or the beauty and miracle that is this planet. Consequently, I am also horrified and devastated and constantly grieve the impacts of climate change caused by the carelessness and recklessness of human beings largely via capitalism (and colonialism, imperialism, racism, etc.).

But that's why I write romance. Because I truly believe that any hope we have of saving the world, of building one that is equitable and just and sustainable, relies on believing whole-heartedly in happy endings.

To that end, here are some marine conservation organizations doing some incredible work. I hope you check them out and, if able, consider donating.

- Marine Conservation Society Seychelles
- WiseOceans
- Seychelles Conservation and Climate Adaptation Trust
- Ocean First Institute
- New England Aquarium
- Heal the Bay Aquarium

This is just a very, very small list and I hope you do your own research to find marine conservation works doing what they can to save our oceans and if you're fortunate enough to live near one, find an org and reach out to see how you can support!

To any real marine biologists who read this book—thank you for your work and I'm sorry for the liberties I took with your field—I know funding is hard to come by and the idea of a research boat in the Seychelles run by two professors and some grad students is probably more unbelievable than an uncharted haunted island. Sometimes Romance Reasons win out over Reality but I hope you enjoyed the book anyway.

Speaking of uncharted, haunted islands—I definitely took some liberties with my depiction of the Seychelles (sorry!) but I did ground many of my fun plot points in Real History. As Willa points out to Alex, saltwater crocodiles DID exist in the Seychelles until around the 1800's and the islands DO have a history of both ghosts and pirates. To this day, it's rumored the lost treasure of real actual French pirate, Olivier Levasseur, who was known as "La Buse" or "The Buzzard," is still hidden somewhere in the Seychelles. It's a fascinating story and I hope you look it up and enjoy the lore as much as I did.

Finally, publishing this book wouldn't be possible without the amazing friends and found family I am fortunate to be in community with every single day. Kati, Kaylie, Dana, Jess, Raven, Lex, Alicia—my incredible coven/cult/gay panics, you're everything good in the world and I love you. My fellow sisters of the Horizontal Writers Club, Hanna & Julie, thank you for being there for Willa and Alex from the very beginning and making sure the story went where it needed to go. And, of course, thank you Dash for making this INCREDIBLE, beautiful contemporary take on a clinch and using your amazing artistic talents to bring my vision for The Survival Guide to Alexander McBryde to life. You all are more magical and more precious than all the pirate treasure in the world. <3

About the Author

Ellie Devine has been writing for as long as she could hold a pencil. From childhood inventions about magical sisters living in the forest (inspired by playing pretend with her friends) to a 65,000-word Little Mermaid retelling on fictionpress.net completed her senior year of high school (no, she won't tell you what it's called), Ellie has always loved writing stories with a lot of heart and a little bit of magic.

She enjoys romance (obviously), K dramas (obsessively) and crying about how much she loves the ocean. She lives in Chicago with her cats, Ham and Hades (and yes, they DO have an Instagram @HamAndHades).